Jackal's Tango

Jackal's Tango

Michael Kennard

iUniverse LLC
Bloomington

JACKAL'S TANGO

This is a work of fiction. All of the characters, names, incidents, organizations, and dialogue
in this novel are either the products of the author's imagination or are used fictitiously.

iUniverse books may be ordered through booksellers or by contacting:

iUniverse LLC
1663 Liberty Drive
Bloomington, IN 47403
www.iuniverse.com
1-800-Authors (1-800-288-4677)

ISBN: 978-1-4917-2542-9 (sc)
ISBN: 978-1-4917-2543-6 (e)

Printed in the United States of America.

iUniverse rev. date: 02/19/2014

Dedication

To Peg

Acknowledgements

Bizarrely I'd like to thank 'Strictly Come Dancing' for highlighting the delights and erotic moves of the Argentine Tango, without which I would probably never have ventured into the world of Tango. On a trip to South America we chanced on El Viejo Almacen, an authentic old dance hall in Buenos Aires, where the inspiration for this novel was first born.

Thanks also go to Emma Sweetland for painstakingly proof reading, editing and generally correcting any mistakes.

Chapter 1

What the hell was he doing in Buenos Aires? It was a hellhole filled with the flotsam and jetsam of a world so recently released from the ravages of war. Here in this dirty back street cantina he rubbed shoulders with thieves, pickpockets, whores, heroin addicts, blackmailers, kidnappers, rapists and murderers. It was 1946, the war had been over for more than a year but these vermin were oblivious to such goings on. They didn't care that for half a decade the world had been tearing itself apart, no, they were too busy with their own sordid lives to care, and into this mix came Lucas Garrett; or to give him his rightful name Michael Burnett; ex cop, sometime fixer for the mob; a man totally at home with the dregs of humanity.

Lucas tossed back the last mouthful of bourbon, left a few pesos on the counter and unsteadily walked outside. To an outsider he'd have seemed an easy mark, although dishevelled and unkempt as his appearance suggested, Lucas Garrett was nobody's fool. The stiletto which he kept in a sheath strapped around his calf and the Colt 45 Army issue automatic tucked into the rear waistband of his trousers, attested to that fact. He was living on borrowed time, he'd lost the only woman that he ever really cared about, his finances were at rock bottom and he had to resort to pimping a two-bit hooker from the barrio.

It was three in the morning, and Lucas thought it was time to cash in on her earnings. He'd screw the fuck out of her; it was the least she'd expect. Somehow or other it comforted the poor bitch, being fucked by the man she loved, it was much more satisfying than the sweating heaving bodies that invaded her nightly.

Lucas was feeling mean, mean as fuck; he'd lost at cards, been spat at by a cheap whore, and for one heart stopping moment Felipe Salazar had looked in his direction. 'Fuck him,' he thought, 'in another world, another time; I'd have taken the son of a bitch out.'

'Yeah,' he thought as his drink sodden brain switched back to Lola Santos and his cock began to stir. He was feeling horny and even her sweat and the ever present stench of cum wouldn't stop him from fucking her up the ass. She liked it rough, the rougher the better, he thought excitedly, 'Well tonight my little Argentinean whore you ain't gonna be disappointed.'

As he climbed the concrete stairs to the hovel he shared with Lola his drink sodden mind momentarily flashed back to a time when he had everything. He began to smile as he recalled happier times, then he slipped on the stairs and fell heavily onto the jagged concrete, grazing his head and tearing a hole in the knee of his pants. "Fuck . . . . !" he exclaimed, as he picked himself up and surveyed the injury to his knee. All thoughts of happier times vanished as reality, self pity and self loathing set in.

Pushing the door open to the dwelling he shared with his whore, Lucas looked into the eyes of the woman he'd taken as his own. 'Fuck.' he thought. Lola was high; he could see it in her eyes. She attempted to kiss him the moment he walked into the room, but he turned his face away, as he held her tightly to him. With strong bronzed hands he twisted her body around. His hands clawed at the sides of her flimsy skirt as he pushed it upwards. Lola braced herself against the table, clearing it of used plates and utensils, she laughed and spread her legs wide and arched her buttocks towards him. She knew from past experience that the mere suggestive movement made him harder with desire. She reached behind and fingered the outside of her ass before wrapping her hand around Lucas's rigid cock. He gasped with anticipation as she guided it home. He pushed gently, she thrust backwards and then in seconds he was buried deep inside her. Lola groaned like the whore she was and pushed herself against his thrusting body. Their fucking was fast and furious, and in the humid confines of their room sweat poured from them in bucket loads. Lucas fought for a climax he knew from the copious amount of liquor he'd consumed would be long in coming. It took forty five minutes of intense sexual friction before they collapsed upon the floor, exhausted but mutually satisfied. Within seconds Lucas Garrett was sleeping soundly.

Lola released herself from Garrett's sexual embrace and staggered into the grimy bathroom to wash away the night's toil. Sexually relieved from her manual stimulation and coming down from an immense high always brought clarity to Lola.

She was a thirty three year old hooker, addicted to heroin and sex. She took what she could from any show of affection that Lucas was prepared to throw her way. She forced herself to believe he cared, but deep down she knew he was no different from the thousand and one men she'd bedded since the age of thirteen. They'd been together for almost six months, since the day he gave her former pimp a beating that he would never fully recover from.

Lucas had been in the bar drinking, when Fredo Rojo came in and demanded her takings for the night. She was short due to obtaining a fix half way though the evening. Rojo punched her hard, breaking her nose, it gushed crimson, but Rojo ignored the Technicolor floor show and began pounding on her. The bar looked on transfixed by the spectacle.

"She's had enough!" yelled Lucas.

Rojo stopped his beating and looked towards the man that had the temerity to speak up for the piece of garbage at his feet.

"What's that you say?" he questioned.

"You heard!"

The words were a challenge to his Latino pride, a challenge that he was prepared to answer. A switchblade appeared as if by magic and Rojo circled the small dance floor. Lucas calmly slid off his jacket and rolled it over his left arm as an improvised shield. Rojo laughed. The gringo had thought his brave words would have been enough, but would now have to be taught some manners.

The pair circled each other with Rojo slashing viciously at the American's face. Lucas unarmed parried with his jacket. Once, twice, three times the deadly blade missed its target, then suddenly a stiletto appeared in Lucas's right hand as if from nowhere and he plunged it deep into the man's thigh. Rojo screamed with pain and the big American without hesitation slashed at his hamstring. The man crashed to the floor, defeated.

But it wasn't enough, Lucas knew the law of the jungle, he turned the man over and pounded with his fists until the man's face was a bloody pulp. Then he kicked him several times before leaning down and whispering something into the man's ear. What he said was never known, the pimp spent weeks in the hospital. Not long after leaving the hospital he left the city.

Lola had taken Lucas's barbaric beating of her man as an act of chivalry. She invited him to share her lodgings and within a few days she was turning tricks for Lucas Garrett.

Lucas awoke around noon, and promptly wished he hadn't. His head throbbed like hell and his mouth tasted like shit. The night's events still locked away in the darkest corners of his mind. Picking himself up with his leg still trapped inside his discarded trousers he slipped back onto the hard floor.

"Fuck!" he exclaimed.

Shaking his pants off, he half walked, half staggered into the bathroom. Turning on the tap he filled the bowl with cold water and began to sluice his face and neck. Seconds later he caught a look at himself in the grimy mirror. There was an ugly graze on the side of his head, at the same time he felt the tightness of his knee. "Fuck," he muttered, he looked and felt like shit. Slowly the events of the previous day began to filter through. He called for Lola, 'where the fuck was she?' he thought, yet another irritant to the start of his day. Just then she came back through the door, a small bag of groceries and a bottle of milk clutched in her arms.

Lucas acknowledged her with a grunt and fished in his discarded pants for his cigarettes. Lighting one up he sat down on a high backed chair and took a long drag of his cigarette. He looked across at Lola, who was busily preparing him coffee and he guessed by the smell a concoction of bacon, potatoes and hot chilli peppers. He loved this strange recipe of Lola's, and complimented it with lashings of hot sauce; it kinda pepped him up for the day. He looked at the shape of Lola's ass beneath the loose fitting summer dress and felt his loins stirring. The events of last night now clearly in focus. She fucked like a crazy woman, she gave head like no other woman he'd known, she looked after him when he was sick, she kept him in the lap of luxury *he thought as he looked around the squalid room* and she cooked him his favourite breakfast. What more could a man want? Lucas knew the answer, but he wasn't going down that road.

"Fuck!" he shouted.

Lola carried on fixing his coffee, she didn't seem to notice or care about his outbursts, it was the same most mornings.

"Fuck, fuck, fuck . . . ." angrily he remembered losing at cards. It had been a pretty shitty night over all. Then his body turned icy cold as he remembered the look from Felipe Salazar. It was the look of a jackal as it eyed up its prey. For some reason Lucas had drawn the attention of one of the most vicious and dangerous criminals in Buenos Aires. With coffee in hand he weighed up his situation. If Felipe Salazar had taken a personal interest in him, then life in Buenos Aires could get a whole lot worse, as if that were possible, but if his interest was due to outside influence then that was an entirely different ball game.

Lucas had come to Buenos Aires to escape the attentions of those that wanted his hide. He could have just drifted into the fleshpots of Mexico or deeper still into Latin America but he'd chosen Argentina instead, and Buenos Aires in particular. The capital had seen a vast amount of immigrants fleeing from the persecutions of the old world, French, Dutch, Croats, British even, and a large number of Germans, all seeking a new life. Lucas reasoned that if Peron's government, knowingly or unknowingly could look the other way where certain war criminals were concerned, then an American, albeit one with a price on his head should be able to move about the city without raising a ripple.

Lucas soon realised that Buenos Aires wasn't like any place he'd ever lived, and considering he hadn't lived anywhere other than the environs of Los Angeles, the contrast was more than evident. To be fair, finances dictated just where he stood in Buenos Aires society. He hadn't expected the poverty, the filth, the degradation, the dog eat dog world that he had become a part of, but it was better than the world that awaited him back home. Chameleon-like he'd blended into the brutal under-world of South America's lowest class.

His rugged good looks, marred only by the slight crookedness of a broken nose and a zig-zag scar that started at the left hand corner of his mouth and splayed outwards towards his ear, had seemed to have been his passport to acceptance. His oily blue-black hair allowed him to remain almost invisible in the seedy back streets where tango was king.

Until now!

Lucas prided himself on his instincts.

Lola placed his food down in front of him, "Eat," she said quietly, breaking his mood and bringing him back to the more mundane tasks of the day. He forked a mouthful of potatoes and meat into his mouth. He chewed silently while Lola looked on.

'What was it with this woman, was she seeking approval for everything?' he thought angrily, then as a plan began to form he looked at Lola in a different light. She could be the key to finding out why Salazar had given him the evil eye.

"Get dressed," he said suddenly. She looked puzzled. "Clean yourself up, put some makeup on, wear that blue dress," he barked. Despite her heroin addiction, *he suspected she'd injected herself before he was awake,* she didn't look as bad as he felt. Washed, made up and dressed suitably, *apart from the permanent crook to the bridge of her nose* she wasn't such a bad piece of ass. Slightly big in that department, an occupational hazard, he'd told her one night.

He had it in mind for Lola to find out what interest Felipe Salazar had with him. On an occasion he'd caught Juan Aguilar, one of Felipe's trusted lieutenants showing an interest in her. She'd spurned his advances on several occasions, when asked by Lucas as to why, she'd looked at him with fear in her eyes, "He's a beast, he's a crazy man." Lucas hadn't thought much about it and had chosen to accept Lola's reasons.

Lucas finished up his breakfast and awaited Lola, who bounced into the room ten minutes later, washed and wearing the blue dress he'd asked her to put on. It was slinky, and tight, more suitably for evening than an afternoon in bright sunshine. It was a dress for seduction, for finding out what Felipe Salazar had in mind for the thirty two year old American.

"Where are we going Lucas?"

"We ain't going anywhere; you're going to pay someone a visit."

"Fuck you Lucas!" she shrieked across the room.

"Perhaps later," he countered. Her feelings as far as he was concerned were as nothing compared to his life.

"Who?" she cried with resignation.

"Juan Aguilar!" Lucas waited for Lola's protests.

"No way!" she screamed, "No fucking way."

"Yes way! Felipe Salazar has shown an interest in me. I need to know why."

"Why don't you go ask him yourself," she spat back at him.

"Because I need to be one step ahead of the game, you're doing it."

Chapter 2

Lucas knew that Aquilar was a creature of habit and liked to eat his evening meal just before the sun went down. He also knew that Felipe's lieutenant was an avid meat eater, as were most Argentineans worth their salt. Carlos Ramirez's bar and steak house was reputed to serve the best Argentinean steaks in the local area. It stood to reason that Juan Aquilar would dine there on an occasion. Lola now softened by an afternoon's love making and a syringe full of pleasure walked into the restaurant. Aquilar was halfway through the rarest of steaks, *his plate swimming in blood which he mopped up greedily with a chunk of bread,* spotted Lola the moment she stepped up to the bar.

It was early in the evening but a number of the bar's customers had taken a shine. As she sat down and ordered a drink, the man sitting next to her lit the cigarette she was holding between her fingers. She sucked suggestively on the cigarette and the man propositioned her. Lola was feeling good, the fix had kicked in and the cigarette smoke relaxed her. The alcohol burned as it went down, and Lola found herself feeling hot.

Aquilar watched the scene unfold and felt himself growing harder. Part of him wanted to muscle in and tell the fat business man to run home to his wife and kids, but part of him wanted to watch this most erotic of scenes as it unfolded before his eyes. He'd seen her around and recognised that she worked for the Americano that his boss was interested in. She'd spurned his advances on several occasions, partly he suspected because of his reputation with women.

He rubbed himself through his slacks as he saw her massage the front of the businessman's pants. Aquilar groaned as Lola and the fat businessman slipped off their stools and made for the exit. Quickly he threw money down on the table next to his empty plate and followed at a discreet distance.

Outside in the darkening night Lola took the nervous businessman by the hand and led him to a quiet spot behind a number of cars.

She held out her hand for payment.

"Just bl.. blow me off, right . . ." stammered the nervously excited businessman as he handed her the money.

"Relax," purred Lola, as she expertly undid the man's fly.

"Urrr," cried the man as he felt the coolness of her fingers whilst she grappled with his engorged cock and the maze of slacks and underpants.

Juan Aquilar watched the drama from a safe distance massaging his own cock as the excitement in him grew to a great intensity.

The fat business man felt her begin to masturbate him and fought desperately to think of other things. His wife would be preparing dinner right now, his kids would be listening to the new radio he'd so recently bought and they'd all be looking forward to the weekend.

"Oh my God!" he cried as he felt the warmth of her mouth close over the end of his cock. He forced himself to think again of his family, hoping to blunt the reality of the exquisite pleasure he was experiencing. It was his first time with a prostitute, it had happened by impulse, he hadn't meant to get himself so much involved, but it was so good. He wanted to fuck her, he wanted to take the next step, she was a whore, a dirty filth whore, a dirty filthy diseased whore. It was no use; he still wanted to fuck her.

Lola took him back into her mouth and ran her tongue around the head of his penis; it was a sport to her, a battle of wills. She knew he was fighting to save his climax, she knew he would be thinking about his wife at home, she knew he wanted to fuck her more than anything else in the world. At that precise moment she felt the first spasm, then the second and third as the salty fluid splashed into the roof of her mouth. He held her head in a vice like grip and thrust his cock into her face several more times before pushing her away like a discarded piece of rubbish.

Lola spat out the salty cum and cleared her throat several times, spitting the residue onto the ground. The fat businessman didn't even look at her as he tucked his now fast fading cock back inside his slacks. Then without looking back he turned and walked into the light. His thoughts now cleansed and a dinner waiting. Lola wiped her mouth with a handkerchief and began to tidy herself up when she heard a faint groan. She looked up in time to see Juan Aquilar doing up his pants.

"That was quite a show," he laughed as he advanced towards her. Lola stiffened, she looked towards the street lighting, judging the distance if she had to run for it.

"What the fuck do you want?" she snapped back defiantly. Why wasn't she surprised that he'd followed her outside.

Juan Aquilar smiled, "I'll pay you three times what that fat fuck did, but you'll earn it!" he said confidently.

"What makes you think I'm interested," she spat back at him defiantly. Suddenly pleasing Lucas wasn't foremost on her agenda.

"Because that pimp of yours will beat you if you don't bring home enough dinero."

"How do you know . . ." she let the words trail off.

"Your pimp," he finished. "I've seen him around, he's one mean hombre."

The man made her blood run cold, she couldn't put a finger on it, but there was something plainly evil about Juan Aquilar. But encouraged by his mention of Lucas she asked what he had in mind.

Lola came home in the early hours and found Lucas in bed asleep. She crept in beside him and snuggled up. She knew tomorrow he would be in a better mood. She had things to tell.

Lucas woke with a start; he'd slept deeply, too deeply. Reaching under his pillow he sought the comfort of the 45 calibre automatic. Lola stirred at his sudden movement but didn't wake. He slipped his feet out of the bed and sat there contemplating his next move. Glancing at Lola's sleeping form he wondered what news she had for him. He hoped the information would be worth letting Lola keep all of last night's earnings. It had been a calculated risk sending her off to find Aquilar. She'd been frightened, almost terrified, but the lure of keeping a night's earning to herself and the fix he'd administered prior to the night's events had lulled Lola into a confident and happy mood. He just hoped she'd not let him down and had found out if Salazar had an interest in him.

That he wasn't dead in his bed spoke volumes. That Lola had slid in beside him without waking her man also suggested that his life wasn't in any immediate danger. It was conjecture, nothing more. The whore might not have found Aquilar at all; they might even be coming for him as he sat there. He shook the sleeping Lola until she re-entered the land of the living.

"What the fuck!" she cried sleepily as she tried to return to her dreams. He shook her again, her dream faded. Reaching across she grabbed a smoke and lit up.

Lucas looked on angrily, as she drew on the cigarette causing her already emaciated face to look even more drawn than usual. She disgusted him, hell, she was a reminder of what he'd become. From what he'd been led to believe, she'd been a good looking woman once, but the effects of drugs and alcohol coupled with her profession had turned her into nothing more than a cheap whore, one teetering on the edge of self destruction. And he was no better, which was really the true cause behind his disgust. He'd sunk so low, and so quickly it was frightening. It was easy to blame Lola, but it was his own fall from grace that was behind his anger. After all said and done she'd been loyal, caring in her lucid moments even, and useful. He stopped himself from thinking on her virtues, life had taught Lucas not to get too involved. Lola was on a journey, a journey of her own making, she was a runaway train, nothing anyone could say or do would stop her as she hurtled towards the precipice; and in the world that she frequented, no one cared.

Lucas bit down hard on his lip as he waited for Lola to gather her thoughts. She took a deep pull on her cigarette and felt the smoke course down deep inside her lungs. She exhaled and re-entered the world.

"You owe me!" she declared. "You owe me big time."

"You saw Juan Aquilar?"

"I saw . . ." She let the words hang as she was forced to relive the night's events with Aquilar. "You're off the hook, Salazar has seen you operate. He likes your style. I think he's going to offer you work."

"What kind of work?"

"The work you do best," spat Lola contemptuously.

Lucas felt a wave of relief waft over him. He wasn't out of the woods, but Lola's information had been reassuring. Felipe Salazar might have been a face in the slums and barrios of Buenos Aires, but in a big city like Houston, New York or Los Angeles, he'd have been nothing but a cheap hood. Lucas tempered the thought, organised crime might be in its infancy here in Buenos Aires, but give it time. There was money to be earned in a thriving metropolis like his newly adopted city and Lucas Garret intended collecting his share. 'Perhaps,' he laughed inwardly, 'my luck is about to change.'

"How did Aquilar treat you?" he asked suddenly.

Surprised by Lucas's concern, Lola flinched at the perversions she'd had to endure, but smiled up at him, "It was okay, the man's an animal, but I can handle that." It was what he wanted to hear, Lola had spent her entire life studying men. She knew that if she was to survive she had to appease her man. Lucas was no different, no worse than any of the scum that she had known.

"Good," replied Lucas. "I want you to use your considerable charms to arrange a meeting with Salazar."

The thought of meeting up with Aquilar so soon caused her skin to grow cold and clammy. Lucas hadn't asked for any details of that night, she deduced he didn't care about what depraved acts she'd had to perform. If he'd have known would he have sent her back? It was a question that never entered Lola's head. That she'd been fucked by three men at the same time, that Juan Aquilar got his kicks from watching, that the men high on alcohol and amphetamines abused her physically and sexually while Aquilar masturbated over them, none of it mattered to her. It was part of the job. It wasn't what he did or the way he looked that unnerved her, it was the feeling, the gnawing feeling in her head that she and Juan Aquilar had unfinished business that scared the shit out of her. Would it have made any difference if she'd told Lucas her fears?

It wasn't hard to find Aquilar, he'd mentioned the night before that he could be found at Cesar's bar and grill during the late afternoon.

"You liked my company that much," cried Aquilar as Lola walked up to him. Ignoring his remark and the obvious pleasure he got from watching the fear in her eyes.

She gritted her teeth and spoke defiantly, "No way, not today or any other day." She was relying on the fact that his boss Salazar needed Lucas for something important. "Lucas wants to meet with Senor Salazar," she added, her revulsion still clearly audible.

"Tell the gringo, to come to Granero de Alvarado tonight at nine o'clock, Felipe might deem to talk with him. Come along yourself, I think I may have need of your talents." He laughed and turned his back. Lola sensed his words were an order not a request.

What was it about Juan Aquilar that instilled such fear, such loathing? She'd heard stories, nothing more. Most of the girls she knew stayed clear of him; they'd heard the stories too. Yet what was she afraid of, she'd spent the night with him and three fat fucks, she'd been abused, but that went with the territory. She'd had worse done to her. He'd paid her well over the odds, she should be looking to suck his dick at every opportunity, yet deep down she sensed there was something very different about Aquilar. She was letting her imagination run away with her. She consoled herself as she remembered that judging by last night's performance he was a voyeur, he couldn't get it up without extra stimulation, it cheered her slightly.

"Stay close to me tonight," she begged Lucas, after she'd told him of the evening's meeting. "I don't want that vile piece of shit Aquilar near me."

"Listen baby, tonight could be our way into the big time. Felipe Salazar needs my help. If Juan wants you, who the fuck am I to stand in his way."

"Please, please no," she cried vainly.

Lucas lifted her head up close to him and kissed her gently on the lips. He smiled down at her. "We need to keep Salazar sweet."

"There's something about him, he scares me!" cried Lola.

Lucas's face grew dark and angry. "You listen to me, that fuck's a pussycat, Salazar's important to me, and if that means you've got to screw his henchman's balls off, you'd better do it."

Lucas baulked at his own words. Since coming to this hell-hole he'd begun to lose his humanity, his compassion. He'd been living worse than a dog these past few months, every day was a fight for survival. He hadn't chosen Lola, she'd chosen him. Once he'd been a man of compassion, a man that cared about others, yet life had suddenly turned ugly and his life had spiralled out of control, he was fast sinking into the quagmire of hell itself.

"Lola honey, I'm sorry. If that fuck scares you so much, stay close. Forget what I said earlier."

"Oh Lucas!" she cried and sunk to her knees.

"No get up, there's no need."

Lola clung to Lucas's body until he gently prised himself from her clutches.

"Get some rest, then do you're hair and makeup, put on that red sleeveless number, we've a business meeting to go to."

Chapter 3

Lucas eased his way through the double doors, stopping momentarily to adjust his eyes to the dimly lit surrounding of Granero de Alvarado, *loosely translated meaning Alvarado's Barn*, a notorious tango dance hall. With Lola by his side he pushed his way through the early evening crowd and spied Felipe Salazar holding court some twenty feet above his head. The place was already jumping with several couples dancing seductively to the beat of the tango. For the briefest of moments his thoughts were of Erin, she'd loved the tango with a passion, but all that was gone, all that had ended one dark night on the seventeenth floor of the Mirabelle apartments. Quickly he erased his thoughts.

Lola gripped Lucas's strong right arm as they climbed the narrow stairs that led to the balcony and Salazar. Emerging at the top, the American stopped and got his breathing under control before casting his eyes casually at Salazar's table. There was the usual entourage of hookers, a couple of grease balls or two and judging by their appearance and demeanour some Europeans, *since the war Buenos Aires had seen more than its fair share.*

To Lola's relief Aquilar was nowhere to be seen. She squeezed Garrett's butt playfully as an air of foreboding lifted from her slender shoulders. Lucas hardly noticed, his attention focussed on Salazar. Lucas always sized up the opposition; he estimated Salazar was in his early forties, slightly overweight, but not unduly so. It was his appearance that he noticed more, the man dressed immaculately, his suit hung on his sizable frame perfectly. The man had an air about him. It wasn't just the cut of his suit, or the silk shirt and painted tie, he was well groomed; his jet black hair edged with a tinge of grey at the sides gave him a distinguished look. The man obviously took care of himself, which was confirmed when Lucas cast an eye over the man's hands, he'd recently had a manicure. All this Lucas noticed as he approached Salazar's table. He also noted there were no Americans amongst his party, a fact that made Lucas very grateful. Lola began to get with the Latin beat of the music as she seductively gyrated around the lone American.

"You are very lucky senor," cried Salazar, "So attentive, so sexy." His words carried a lack of conviction, which Lucas picked up on.

"I heard through the grapevine that you were looking for me," the words, though not a threat, carried with them a defiance, that cried out to be noticed.

"It is true, I do have some interest in you," said Salazar, as he gestured with his open hand to be seated. "I am; how you say in America, branching out. Since the war's end the opportunities to make money have become very plentiful for some, but not so for others. The strong survive, the weak go under," he cast a disdainful look in Lola's direction. "I need men around me that I can trust," he grinned wryly, "As much as anyone can these days," he added circumspectly. Felipe Salazar entwined the fingers of both manicured hands and cracked them. "Since the beating you gave to Rojo I have been keeping a discreet eye on you. You're wasting your talents!" He waited for the reaction. None came, he liked that. "You're running from something, I don't care. America is a far off place; it is of no consequence to me."

Salazar's eyes lit up; there was a slight reaction to his words. "I would like for you to come and work for me. I can make you rich, rich enough to maybe one day return to America to face whatever demons that are there awaiting your return, but on equal terms."

"What makes you think I'm running," replied Lucas. The big man had unsettled him slightly, catching him off guard, making him feel vulnerable.

"You did, by asking the question," said Felipe Salazar. He'd managed to unnerve the tall American. He liked that. "Ask around; ask anyone, they will all tell you I am an honourable man. If you are satisfied, then call me on this number." He held out a small piece of card. "Take it, ask your questions, if you're interested in my proposition call the number."

Lucas took the card and was about to say something when Salazar cut him off; "You will also hear that I am a very dangerous man, if you decide not to accept my offer I would suggest you leave Buenos Aires within the next twenty four hours."

Felipe Salazar's words were quietly spoken, yet the threat resonated within Lucas. He looked the big Argentinean in the eye, and quietly nodded, then turned and walked away. Lola scurried after him.

On the street Lucas lit up. Took a deep drag then exhaled slowly. Salazar had given him a lot to think about, but he had only twenty four hours to make up his mind. He walked three blocks before turning into a nearby cantina. Lola followed close on his heels.

"What the fuck are you hanging around for, get out there, get earning!"

Lola looked shocked, down hearted, then angry at Lucas's words. "Who the fuck do you think you're talking too!" she spat venomously.

One look was all it took before Lola Santo turned on her heels. She'd seen that look only once before, the day he took possession of her. Her anger at him simmered, then slowly it began to cool as she justified all Lucas's good points. He wasn't always that way; sometimes he was kind and gentle, almost loving in a sad pathetic way.

Lola hit on her first trick ten minutes after running out on Lucas. It was a quick fumble down a dark alley; the mark came in his pants before he could get it in her. Lola stepped clear, clutching his money tightly in her small delicate looking hand. Five minutes later she had the fix that she so desperately need.

17

Michael Kennard

Lucas had been impressed, Salazar spoke perfect English, a fact that he was still trying to get his head around. But it was more than that, the man had a sharpness about him that belied the fact he was a two-bit thug. He began to ask around, he knew Felipe Salazar by reputation but the more he found out about the man the more he realised that he'd underestimated him. He'd believed Salazar to be a cheap hood, bigger than most but a cheap hood all the same, what he found out later that night caused him to think again.

Salazar was connected, big time. It was said that he had a number of politicians in his pocket, the police he'd bought off, *that was a given,* but most importantly he had a brother who was a high ranking officer in the army. Felipe Salazar and his brother were staunch supporters of the newly elected President. Both men had invested heavily in the gravy train that was Juan Domingo Peron.

To the people of Argentina, Peron's stand on nationalising the railroads, telephones, gas and electric companies and to a great extent the banks was a godsend. His reforms included retirement benefits, higher wages, paid vacations, health care and the female vote; he was to the population almost a saint.

Felipe Salazar thought otherwise, these reforms coupled with mass immigration after the Second World War needed paying for, hence the government's ability to look the other way as Nazi money, transferred from Swiss bank accounts flooded into Argentina. Even during the latter days of the war in Europe many top ranking Nazi's had fled to the safety of the South American shores. Felipe learned through his brother Ruben, that the flood of Nazi money appeared endless. Both brothers although reasonably wealthy intended on getting their share. They realised that to hold onto what they had they needed to expand, to grow, to become ever more powerful.

Lucas Garret slept soundly that night, not even waking as Lola slid into bed with him at 3 a.m. His dreams that night were of patrolling the streets of the Sunset Strip, when he was a rare recruit just out of the academy. Back then the force was ripe with corruption and graft, but Lucas *'wet behind the ears'* Garrett was having none of it, partly due to his partner Tom Bannerman, a man that had seen thirty years of corruption and hadn't taken a cent. His sleep was that of the innocent, until reality reared its ugly head and he found himself back in the real world.

He washed and dressed, checked himself in the grimy mirror, ran his hand across his chin, decided a shave wasn't needed, then opened the door.

"Lucas . . ." cried Lola sleepily as she struggled against sleep. "Where . . . where are you going?"

Garret turned his head and looked back at the bedraggled form. "Out," then the door closed behind him.

Lucas shielded his eyes from the glare of the sun and ducked inside Chico's for a pick me up. Sinking his second cup of coffee he fished in his pants for change and walked towards the phone booth across the street. He pulled the card from his pocket and dialled the operator, gave her the number and waited to be connected.

Chapter 4

Lucas waited on the corner of Av, 9 de Julio and Av, Corrientes as instructed. Felipe Salazar was sending a car for him. 'Why didn't he arrange to meet in a public place? Why was he putting himself in harm's way?' Lucas knew the answer, 'Because Felipe Salazar deems it so.' In the course of one night he'd learned that whatever Salazar wanted he got, no matter how many questions were left unanswered. Despite a gut feeling that his luck was about to change Lucas couldn't stop the alarm bells ringing inside his head. His nerves told him to run, his whole being told him to flee. 'But where?' his mind countered.

He discreetly checked the automatic stuffed into his waistband, then bending down as if to tie a shoe lace he felt the comfort of the stiletto. If it was a trap, he was not going to be taken without a fight.

Before he had time to change his mind a black Packard pulled up to the kerb, the driver, a swarthy pockmarked native of Buenos Aires leaned across and without smiling ordered Lucas to get in.

Lucas surveyed the cut of the man, checked that the back seats were without surprise, then climbed in the front passenger seat, "Okay pal, where we heading?"

"Senor Felipe's Estancia."

"His what?"

"His ranch senor, it is an hour from here," replied the driver.

'Well I'll be,' thought Lucas. He'd not figured Salazar as the gaucho type.

As if anticipating Lucas's next question, the driver volunteered a potted history of the Salazar family. Felipe's grandfather had settled the Estancia in the 1870's wiping out the Mapuche that stubbornly refused to give up the land. Ruthlessly he carved a vast empire covering some 98,000 hectares. Then Luis as the driver was known, realising he might have said more than he should, clamed up. Lucas was left to speculate for the rest of the journey.

As they drove through the wrought iron gates of Estancia de Salazar Lucas got his first glimpse of the house. Built in an English colonial style it stood tall and imposing against a background of undulating green that seemed to stretch to the far horizon. It was his first peek at the habitat of the aristocratic Argentinean upper classes, a far cry from the slums and barrios of the city.

Dressed in a white suit and sporting a straw fedora, Felipe Salazar stepped down the three steps from the wide veranda that fronted the building and greeted his guest. Lucas took the offered hand and shook it firmly. It was clear from the look on Garrett's face that he was suitably impressed. Felipe Salazar noted the look and smiled inwardly.

"You may wonder why I have brought you out here to my home; all that in good time," he said, raising his hand to emphasize his point. "Firstly I'd like to show you around the grounds and explain to you my vision." He then proceeded to walk slightly ahead of Lucas, pointing out various works of art, his antique furniture and a magnificent art deco mural that spanned the entire left side of the imposing hallway. He stopped to admire the stain glass windows in the main room, looking back at Lucas for his reaction. Lucas nodded approvingly. Then Salazar walked out onto a large patio bordered by a stone balustrade with a view across the pampas.

"Magnificent, isn't it!"

"It's quite something," replied Lucas, wondering where all this was leading.

A man servant dressed in a green uniform highlighted by the whiteness of his shirt and matching tie approached the pair.

"Your table Senor Salazar," he said with a flourish of his hand.

Lucas followed the direction of the extended hand. A table was laid out for two. A waiter stood in attendance.

"Be seated Senor Garrett," said Salazar as he proceeded to sit down opposite Lucas.

This was a far cry from the dirty slum tenements that Lucas now called home. He wanted a piece of this opulent life style and he was prepared to sell his soul if that's what it took. This of course, thought Garrett, was the real reason why he was being wined and dined, and as Lucas sipped his wine and bit into the juiciest of steaks, he realised he was about to make a pact with the devil.

For what seemed an eternity both men concentrated on their meal. Lucas had many questions to ask, but knew the protocol was to wait for his host to speak. Finally Felipe Salazar put down his knife and fork, dabbed at his mouth with his napkin then pushed back his chair. He motioned for Lucas to continue eating.

"A little history lesson, my friend. This once great Estancia was created by my late grandfather. The land you see before you is vast. You agree?" Lucas nodded. "But once it was much larger, it stretched almost to the foothills of the Andes. My grandfather was a strong man, a powerful leader; a man of great vision. He knew that with land came power, he wanted to build a great cattle empire, but the Mapuche, the indigenous people of this land were in his way. He wanted their land so he took it; he destroyed their villages and killed many during the bloody battles he fought against them. Along the way he lost two brothers, a son and his third wife. He suffered many setbacks and heartbreak but eventually he created his dream. When he died he left all he owned to my father, his youngest surviving son." His demeanour changed slightly, "My father was weak, years of living well had softened him, he had become a philanderer, a chaser of women, and a degenerate gambler. His drinking and gambling grew worse as his wealth dwindled. He began selling off the land; his debts grew ever larger until he lost everything, he created nothing of consequence except two bastard sons by different mothers."

Lucas looked appropriately shocked.

"As a youth I watched him destroy what my grandfather had created. I was powerless to stop him, and the hatred grew. I vowed that one day I would restore Estancia de Salazar to its former greatness."

Felipe Salazar paused and sipped the fine Argentinean Merlot, "The wine, it is to your liking?"

"Perfect, it compliments the excellent beef."

"Salazar beef," replied Felipe proudly.

Both men fell silent and Lucas concentrated on finishing his meal. Felipe smiled as he watched Lucas wiping his plate clean with a chunk of freshly baked bread. The American couldn't think of when he'd had such an excellent meal.

"You were hungry," remarked Salazar. "I too have felt hunger; together with my younger brother Ruben we watched the disintegration of our father until we could stand it no more. Ruben was barely eleven; I was fourteen when we found him asleep in a filthy cantina. He was nothing to us, except as an embarrassment. We crept up on him, I wrenched his head back and Ruben calmly slit his throat. I remember his eyes growing wide with horror as he choked on his own blood, and the puzzled look he gave us as he stared at the only thing he'd ever done that was worth while."

Salazar motioned for the impeccably dressed waiter to top up Lucas's glass. The American put his hand over his glass to indicate he wasn't in need of the wine, after what Salazar had told him he believed he needed to keep a clear head.

"So what happened, how . . . ?" asked Lucas.

"How did I accomplish all this? Is that what you ask? A long story my friend. I will tell you one day; perhaps. Suffice to say my business interests have paid dividends, however I have a long way to go to surpass my grandfather's achievements."

"I'm impressed," said Lucas.

"To business!" exclaimed Felipe. "You came to my attention after you nearly killed Rojo. He was, until you messed with him, a man to be feared. Since then I've been keeping a close eye on you.

What are you doing in Buenos Aires I ask myself? An American alone in a foreign city, why? It is of no matter, you are here."

"No offence Senor Salazar, but why am I here?"

"I want you to deliver a package to a man in Montevideo, a very bad man, a very dangerous man. In return he will hand you a package. This package is very special to me. Lose it, and it could cost you your life."

"What if I don't care to meet this man, what then?" asked Lucas warily.

"Then I would say Vaya con dios. My driver would then take you back to the city." He paused to let his words sink in. "But if you do as I ask, I will reward you handsomely. You would then become part of my organisation. You would be safe here; you would be under my protection. You would have whatever your heart desires."

'If only that were so,' thought Lucas, as his mind drifted to a far off place.

"Well, your answer!" exclaimed Salazar, now showing a little impatience.

"Just how dangerous is this guy?" replied Lucas.

"Very!"

"Been here over six months and I've never been to Montevideo."

"You'll do it?"

"It wasn't what I was expecting, but hell yes, I'll do it."

Over the next hour the details were thrashed out. Lucas was given information of where to meet the man and how the transaction would take place, a recent photograph of the man and a thousand pesos. It wasn't as much as Lucas thought he'd get. It equated to a little over two hundred and fifty dollars, but then again this wasn't the United States. A thousand pesos could see him living it up in a fancy hotel for a few months.

Later that night as Felipe Salazar's driver took him back to Buenos Aires he reflected on the bizarre and chilling events that followed their discussion. Even if Lucas was having second thoughts, after what he witnessed they were quickly dismissed.

With their business finished Felipe Salazar proceeded to show Lucas around the estancia, stopping first at the stables. "These are the finest polo ponies in all Argentina," boasted Salazar. "Out there on the pampas I have twenty thousand head of cattle, a mixture of Argentine Criollo and Herefords, ten thousand sheep, some Argentine Merino, a few Cubana Rojo but mostly Chevoits from Scotland, and over there," he pointed to a fenced off paddock, "twenty British Landrace pigs." He swung around and pointed in the opposite direction to the hen house. "Over there is where we house our chickens. Quite a menagerie, don't you think!"

To Lucas the Argentinean overlord was a man of extremes, one minute he's all business, the next he's enthusing about his farm animals. What followed was an extreme that chilled him to the bone.

As they began to walk back to the main house Salazar stopped in his tracks, "I nearly forgot, come you must see . . ." He let the words trail off and walked towards a large barn. The double doors were both open. As they approached Lucas sensed this wasn't going to be 'more fun in the barnyard.'

Four men were gathered around what from a distance resembled a punch bag. He recognised Aquilar, the others he'd never seen before. One man stood out from the others, he had closely cropped blond hair and was without a shirt, exposing his muscular torso. It was he, Lucas presumed, that had been working out on the punch bag. It was only as they drew closer that Lucas recognised it as a man strung up by his arms. Punch bag wasn't such a bad description; the man had been battered beyond recognition.

"Allow me to introduce my loyal friends, Juan Aquilar, you already know, Clemente Ramos, my second in command and Tito Gomez, my protector."

"Bodyguard," volunteered Lucas as he inwardly struggled to come to terms with the situation.

"Si, bodyguard," said Salazar. And last but not least, this magnificent specimen of manhood is Franz Kauffman." Kauffman clicked his heels and nodded at the introduction. "Gentlemen, this is the man I've been talking to you about. He's agreed to do a little job for me. Then if everything works out, he's going to join us."

Lucas smiled a greeting he didn't feel. All he wanted to do was 'get the hell out of Dodge.'

"Pardon my manners; I forgot to introduce you to Humberto Vargas, a once loyal and faithful employee of mine, until he got greedy. Greed is such a terrible thing don't you think Mr Garrett. I gave Humberto everything he could possibly want and he betrayed me.

Lucas suspected what was coming, but he hadn't expected the means of execution. A bucket of cold water was thrown over the condemned man, waking him instantly. Felipe Salazar handed his jacket to Ramos and in turn was handed a butchers apron. The man's eyes bulged with terror at the sound of a chainsaw as it started up. Felipe Salazar revved the machine a few times before advancing upon the helpless screaming figure of Humberto Vargas. Lucas looked away. But it was no use; the scene was stamped into his mind as surely as if he'd watched it close up.

Fifteen seconds later the sound of the chainsaw ceased. Felipe Salazar untied the apron, stripped off his blood splattered shirt, sluiced his face in a bucket of cold water and then took a dry towel from Clemente. He towelled quickly before putting on a clean shirt that Aquilar handed to him.

"Well my friend, I think the tour is over. I think you've seen enough. That what you've just witnessed was unfortunate. Vargas bit the hand that fed him. As I stated yesterday I am an honourable man, those that do my bidding I protect. You work for me; anyone comes looking for you will receive the same fate as Vargas. I am loyal to those that are loyal to me. Remember that."

Minutes later Lucas was being seen to the car. Luis the driver stood with the passenger door open. "I'll expect you back with my package at your earliest convenience. Buenos noches; my friend."

Sitting in the back seat, Lucas realised the killing of Vargas, though inevitable, was put on for his benefit. Salazar was letting him know that he could murder quite openly, without fear of reprisals.

Chapter 5

Lucas slept little that night, what sleep he did get was punctuated by nightmarish visions of hell. The devil had never been so vivid. To say he'd misjudged Felipe Salazar was an understatement, immaculately dressed, cool, calm, confident, but the man was no respecter of human life. Lucas had seen people killed before, but not slaughtered like an animal. Had he bitten off more than he could chew? His first reaction was to get the hell out of Buenos Aires as quickly as possible, but to where and with what? Salazar had paid him a thousand pesos. Not enough to get him a new life and even if it was, where would he go? Back to the States, hell it was a big enough country to lose himself in, but Lucas knew that wasn't always the case. He didn't intend to be looking over his shoulder for the next thirty years. Europe maybe, but he'd need plenty of money for that. As he tossed and turned, he weighed up his options, turn down Salazar's offer, or deliver the package. The first wasn't an option.

It wasn't as if he was averse to danger, he'd been in tight spots on more than one occasion. 'Salazar hinted this man was dangerous, but how dangerous? Was this a test or was there a hidden agenda? Would I deliver Salazar's package and in return have my throat cut?' The thoughts kept coming. 'Was it a risk worth taking? A thousand pesos wasn't a great deal of money to risk one's life for, but on the other hand Salazar hinted that I could be part of his organisation?' Working for a brutal man wasn't something he took lightly. Lucas stared at the worn out ceiling fan, his mind in turmoil. 'A thousand pesos could be the tip of the iceberg. Salazar's words 'I'd have everything that my heart desired, resonated around his head' I could live like a king, and one day I could go back. LA had unfinished business with me, but I have unfinished business with it.'

He woke around nine, Lola had crept into bed beside him two hours earlier, he'd feigned sleep, the last thing he wanted was for her to start coming onto him.

By noon he was on a ferry crossing the Rio de la Plata to Montevideo, Uruguay.

Lucas checked into the Mirador hotel as instructed, under the name Nicolas Kincaid, it was the name on the passport he'd used to get out of L.A. almost a year ago. It was strange looking back, he hadn't intended taking the passport, it was an impulse. He'd been involved in an illegal gambling bust, with the Sheriff's Department when they came across a cache of counterfeit bank notes, a couple of kilos of cocaine and a number of passports. No one missed it when Lucas stuffed a passport into his inside pocket. Little did he know that three years later it would become a life saver?

In his room Lucas wedged a chair against the door lock, kicked off his shoes, took the Colt automatic from the rear of his waistband and tossed it onto the bed. Then he sat on the side of the divan and stared at the four walls before reaching across and retrieving the fifth of Scotch he'd brought for the journey. Taking a couple of swigs he felt its warming glow gradually creeping over him. Somehow or other the flaky emulsion walls slowly faded into insignificance. He checked his gun was in working order before placing it under his pillow with the package. He'd taken the package without question, was it drugs or something far more sinister? It wasn't his damn business he consoled himself before making himself comfortable as he reached again for the bottle. It had been a tiring and worrisome day, he'd checked and rechecked the details that Salazar had given him, memorised the photograph before tossed it into the Rio de la Plata. It would be difficult for him to sleep, knowing that if all didn't go as planned, this time tomorrow night he could be fighting for his life, hence the liquor.

Lucas awoke around nine, it had been a fitful night's sleep and he'd slept longer than usual because of it. He gave himself a stripped down wash, dressed and ventured out into the glare of the morning sunshine. He shielded his eyes from the sun as he made his way to the nearest café. After three cups of coffee and some food inside him, he walked back to the ferry terminal. He checked the last sailing, it was for 9pm.

It was still light outside at 7 pm, as Lucas entered the smoky atmosphere of Cantina Flores. His eyes furtively flitted from one side of the room to the other, then back again. Rodrigo Vasquez, the man he was to hand the package to was nowhere to be seen. To the left of him there were three burly looking individuals sitting at a table. Obvious to him from their clothes and the way they looked in his direction they had been expecting him. On the right side of the room, set further back than the table on the left, sat two more men both of similar stature to the others, the only difference was the sawn off double barrelled shotgun that lay in plain sight across the round table. Lucas was about to back out when he sensed a movement behind him. Instinctively his hand snaked to the automatic nestled snugly in his waistband. 'It was a trap,' his head told him, 'no chance to escape,' he reckoned to go down fighting and to take one or two with him.

"No senor!" came a cry from the back. A man who Lucas recognised from the photo he'd thrown into Rio de la Plata stepped forward. Rodrigo Vasquez, hands open in a gesture of calm, smiled crookedly showing off a line of perfectly white teeth. "It is only a precaution." Lucas lowered his weapon but didn't attempt to put it down. Rodrigo nodded to the man nearest to the door to shut it.

"A drink Senor?" he said looking directly at Lucas as he gestured to a table at the far end of the room. Glad to still be alive thirty seconds after he'd thought he was about to meet his maker Lucas accepted willingly, though the gun was still in his right hand. Rodrigo smiled at Lucas's precaution, "Keep the gun Senor if it makes you comfortable, but there is no need, I assure you. Felipe

Salazar and I have been doing business for sometime now. I would hate for something unfortunate to happen. It could spoil a very profitable business."

"If it's all the same, no offence, but I think I'll keep this baby handy." Lucas placed it on the table.

"As you wish," replied a smiling Vasquez. "The package, you have the package?" his face now sporting a slight frown.

Lucas began to relax; a grin appeared on his lips, "I've got the package, its safe. You didn't expect me to walk in here blind."

Rodrigo grinned, "I like your style, Senor?"

"Lucas, Lucas Garrett."

"A name I shall remember, it takes a lot of balls for a man to walk into Cantina Flores after dark, that or a crazy man. You have the look of a man going places, I think you have a future," he paused for a brief moment, "if you're careful."

"I kinda hope so."

"The package?"

"It's under a garbage can at the back of this cantina. I came around early."

Rodrigo's already dark eyes darkened with menace. "Esteban, quickly, find the package."

Esteban, lighter on his feet than his bulk suggested, rushed towards the back door.

"You had better hope that the package is still there Senor. Otherwise your future might not be forthcoming."

"Let's hope so," replied Lucas confidently, his hand no more than an inch from the butt of his 45.

Esteban returned, slightly out of breath, but with the bulky package in his meaty fingers. Rodrigo's frown disappeared and was replaced by a warm and generous smile. His eyes sparkled with mischief, as Esteban placed the package onto the table in front of him.

"You have a package for me?" said Lucas.

"I do, but all in good time. Firstly I have to open my package." Rodrigo was clearly enjoying this game of one-upmanship. "How much did Salazar pay you to bring this to me?"

"Is that relevant?"

"I'll let you be the judge, after I have opened my package."

"A thousand pesos," replied Lucas warily.

A toothy grin appeared upon Rodrigo's handsomely dark face. "What do you think is contained in this package?"

"Drugs maybe."

"He scared you pretty good, for you not to have taken a peek," laughed Rodrigo. He liked this American; he'd walked into the unknown knowing he might never walk back out again. Salazar must have scared the shit out of him to bring the package without being temped. It made Rodrigo shudder to think what he'd seen.

Rodrigo took out a sharp knife and carefully began to split open the package. Lucas stared in disbelief as the contents of the package spilled onto the table. Bundles of American 20 dollar bills, more money than Lucas had seen in his whole life, littered the table. "Forty thousand to be exact," said Rodrigo triumphantly.

Lucas continued to stare, his mind a gambit of emotions, he had it within his grasp, a new life, his future assured, his escape from the mob in L.A., from Salazar's clutches, it was with him the whole time. Back to the States, to Europe, to Australia even. All he had to do was cut open the bundle, but the little exhibition Salazar had laid on for him had scared him. It was something he hated to admit, but not for the first time Lucas realised how much he'd underestimated Felipe Salazar. He could have been the cat that got the cream, but he'd believed more strongly in the old saying that curiosity killed the cat.

Dragging himself back to reality he looked Rodrigo square in the eyes. "You have a package for me I believe?" Then Lucas's eyes caught what appeared to be an official document card hidden amongst the bundles of bank notes. His hand reached across the table, "May I?" he inquired.

"As you will," replied Rodrigo.

Lucas picked it up and realised it was an Argentine passport. He flipped it open and stared at the face staring back at him.

"I don't understand?"

Chapter 6

"Let me explain," said Rodrigo, clearly enjoying the puzzled look upon the American's face. "You have a package to collect, and without that," he indicated to the passport, "you won't get very far."

"What the fuck are you talking about?"

Rodrigo grinned, "Allow me to introduce Gretchen Kauffman, your er package!"

A willowy blonde of around twenty five stepped in front of him. She smiled nervously, then her eyes gave him a cursory once over. The smile became a distant memory replaced by a posture of superiority.

"How much does he know?" she asked; her voice, though edged with tension, carried with it an air of arrogance.

"Nothing as yet, but I'm sure Senor Garrett will be up to the task."

This wasn't what Garrett was expecting, 'Was it a trick, some kind of elaborate joke; and at Lucas's expense? Was this the double cross of all double crosses?'

"You've got to be kidding," snapped Lucas. His hand closed around the butt of the automatic.

Rodrigo's amused face altered slightly as he reached out to Lucas, "I'm not kidding, she is the package, now sit down and let me explain."

The tension in Lucas eased slowly as he loosened his grip on the Colt and sat back down.

"Kauffman, you've heard the name, yes?"

Images of the encounter in the barn at Salazar's Estancia flashed before him. The bare-chested man that had beat on the poor unfortunate Vargas.

"Yeah, Fritz, Franz, whatever, yeah, I remember him."

"Gretchen is his sister! You are to act as a couple returning to Buenos Aires from, how you say . . . . a dirty weekend." The crooked smile once more put in an appearance.

"Why all the subterfuge?"

"All you need know is that Gretchen has been living in Argentina since 1942, when she'd been granted citizenship. You met her through acquaintances and became attracted to each other. That's it; Gretchen will school you with anything else you need be aware of."

Lucas looked up at Gretchen, she smiled back condescendingly. If she lost that look of arrogance she would be quite sweet looking, thought Lucas. He guessed it was her sparkling blue eyes under a mop of natural blonde hair that made her stand out. Perhaps when they were away from Rodrigo and his men she'd loosen up.

He was wrong, Gretchen remained standoffish until they reached the ferry terminal, then she turned on the charm. She kissed him on the lips, smiled warmly and hugged him as they boarded. The moment they were seated she changed her demeanour back to what it had been when they were first introduced.

Lucas tried to engage her in conversation, asking her why she was entering Argentina in such a roundabout route. She answered, "I have my reasons; they are of no concern to the likes of you."

Lucas felt his hackles rise, "The likes of me, who do you think you're talking to, the hired help!"

Gretchen looked him straight in the eye and smiled smugly. The brush off rankled, possibly because there was an element of truth in what he'd said. He was the hired help. For the remainder of the crossing he kept his thoughts to himself.

As he gazed up into the starry sky he began remembering about when he was more than just the hired help.

Back then he'd been Mike Burnett, a man of principles, a young man fresh out of the academy, about to embark on an illustrious career as a policeman. Firstly as a rookie then as part of a two man team patrolling the streets of West Hollywood. During his time in uniform he'd seen others on the take; he'd resisted the temptation at first, choosing to follow the path of his mentor Deputy Sheriff Tom Bannerman, a veteran of the force. He'd seen some of his colleagues take the occasional bribe for looking the other way; good cops most of them, men that were prepared to put themselves on the line for the greater good of others.' What harm did it do to take an occasional handout?' thought Mike.

Tom Bannerman pointed out to Mike/Lucas what harm there was in crossing the line.

"Listen to me kid, it starts small, but somewhere along the way it gets bigger, until you're in over your head. Take my advice, stay clean."

It was good advice and Mike Burnett had adhered to it though all the temptations that he came across daily, until the day Tom Bannerman was shot and killed during a liquor store hold up, There had been the usual visits from the 'higher-ups' in the department, the sympathy for his wife and kids. There had been the ritual funeral, the peak cap placed on top of the flag that was draped across the coffin, yeah they treated Tom like the hero he was; then nothing, apart from a measly pension, then invisibility. It was after that, Mike began to question Tom Bannerman's wisdom.

It was while on patrol with his new partner Deputy Sheriff Ethan Kels that Mike got his first introduction to life on the take. Still resentful at how Tom's widow had been treated, he began to question Tom's code. Sitting next to Kels, daily he watched how the slightly older man operated. He took no shit from the public and was apt to use strong arm tactics at the drop of a hat. Kels was a cop with a huge rep. He'd been in three shoot-outs during his seven years on the force; each of them ended with a fatality.

"If those sons of bitches are carrying a piece, best put one in them before they put you in the ground," he advised all who served alongside him. "I expect you to watch my tail as closely as I'll be watching yours.

If there's a situation, pull your piece and let fly." Kels rode roughshod over any one that crossed him. In reality he was a good cop, a coppers, cop. But it didn't stop him taking hand-outs.

Lucas recalled one such conversation: *"This is yours, you earned it," Kels told Mike as he handed him a twenty dollar bill.*

"Nah! You keep it." replied Mike.

"What! You some kinda boy scout or somethin!" Kels exclaimed.

"Nope. Just don't want to feel indebted."

Ethan Kels looked puzzled, then he grinned to himself. "So if I was to say, hypothetically that is, that the man that slipped me fifty bucks could give you information about the death of Tom Bannerman, you wouldn't look the other way?"

"What!" exclaimed Mike.

"You wouldn't look the other way if he was to give up the man that killed your partner."

"Well yeah, of course I would," replied Mike.

"Then it amounts to the same thing."

"I guess," replied Mike.

"That's what I figured," said Kels.

"Look, don't get me wrong, I know how this thing works. I ain't about to rock the boat, but I ain't takin no goddamn money," Mike replied angrily.

"Your loss," laughed Kels.

Lucas was woken from his reminiscences as a hand sneaked around his waist. "Showtime, as you Americans like to call it. We're disembarking in fifteen minutes.

As they passed through customs Gretchen was all over him. She'd become the devoted lover that had nothing more on her mind than bedding her American lover. The customs official made a lewd remark in Spanish then waved them through.

It was 3.30 in the morning when they checked into a hotel close to the ferry terminal, too late to drive out to Estancia Salazar.

"Take the bed, I'll sleep in the chair," volunteered Lucas.

"Dankeschön," said Gretchen sleepily as she climbed into the bed and pulled the covers over her.

"You're welco . . . ." Lucas started to say, but it fell on deaf ears as the girl had fallen asleep the moment her head hit the pillow.

Lucas stretched out as best he could in the chair, he'd kicked off his shoes, hung his jacket on the door handle and loosened his belt, but sleep for him was nigh on impossible. It wasn't the uncomfortable sleeping arrangement so much as the young woman he was escorting. She was German, that part was obvious, what wasn't, was her clandestine entry into Argentina. It wasn't a secret that Peron had an open door policy; he welcomed immigrants from all over Europe. Hundreds, perhaps thousands of Nazis fleeing from persecution after the war had sought sanctuary in Argentina and other countries such as Uruguay, Brazil and Paraguay. What was it that made her entry so significant? She was just a slip of a girl, not that many years out of puberty. Was she someone of importance to the Allies or was it her relationship to Franz Kauffman that caused her to enter Argentina in the way that she had? The questions kept coming; the answer remained elusive, sometime during what little remained of the night Lucas dozed.

Chapter 7

Lucas awoke to find Gretchen had woken first and was nowhere to be seen. Panic stricken he jumped to his feet and pulled open the door, only to find her emerging from the bathroom across the hall cleaning her teeth. She smiled at the perplexed look upon his face then skipped past him humming a tune the American had never heard before. He watched as she retrieved fresh clothes from the small suitcase she'd brought with her. She looked up and smiled again; then motioned to Lucas that the bathroom was free and that he'd better get himself washed and dressed before someone else availed themselves with what washing facilities the hotel provided.

Her mood that morning was in complete contrast to the night before. She was bright and breezy, almost a totally different person. He guessed her manner was probably due to nerves and anxiety.

"War Sind Wir Kommissionierung Bis vorerst?" she inquired.

"Pardon!" exclaimed Lucas.

"Sorry, my English, what time are we being picked up?"

"I'm not sure; I've to ring Salazar."

"Go ahead, ring, I'm impatient to see my brother."

"I'll make the call in the coffee shop across the road. We'll grab a bite to eat while we're waiting."

In the taxi on the way to the estancia Gretchen opened up very slightly about the circumstances of her arrival.

"Franz was a very wealthy industrialist before and during the war, but by the end of 1944 he realised that Germany was on the brink of defeat. He knew that if the Russians got to him before the Americans or British then he would most likely be executed. Realising this he fled Germany and made his way to Argentina."

Gretchen paused wondering why she felt compelled to tell all to the tall American. That he was good looking in a rugged way sort of way might have had something to do with it, she thought secretly. He'd shown her nothing but kindness since they'd first met and she'd been mean to him. He deserved to know the reason behind the subterfuge.

"As his only surviving relative the American and Russian governing bodies thought that by holding me it would put leverage on Franz to give himself up. I went into hiding, awaiting my chance to follow my brother and that is why I had to arrive through the back door."

"You didn't need to tell me anything," said Lucas. "I was paid to do a job, and as it turned out, a very pleasant one."

Gretchen smiled coyly, then remained silent for the remainder of the trip.

The reunion between brother and sister was very Teutonic in manner, something the American found totally alien. He guessed that different cultures showed their feelings less openly. He didn't have much time to ponder, before Salazar motioned for Lucas to join him in his study.

"You did well my friend. A lesser man might have let curiosity get the better of him. Humberto Vargas was such a man."

A chill ran up Garrett's spine as he recalled the horrific scene in the large barn at the back of Estancia Salazar. That the same fate would have awaited Lucas if he'd strayed from his mission rang loud and clear, it appeared Felipe Salazar's tentacles were everywhere.

"Enough! I promised you that if you came to work for me I would reward you handsomely. My business interests are very varied. Over time you will become more aware, but in the meantime I want you to look after one of my establishments." He searched Lucas's face for a reaction. It was as he'd expected. "You know Granero de Alvarado, off course you do. Juan will fill you in with all the details tomorrow. In the meantime you'll excuse me as I have a number of guests arriving later this afternoon. You are most welcome to attend."

Lucas started to protest that he wasn't suitably dressed, but Salazar stopped his protestations with his hand. "I insist! Paulo will escort you to one of our guestrooms where you can freshen up. I'm sure he'll be able to sort you out some suitable attire."

"This is too much." cried Lucas.

"Nonsense! There are a number of important guests I'd like you to meet. Some of them may become very useful to you in the future."

"Can I ask, why me?"

"Why not!" replied Salazar with a twinkle in his eye. It would be weeks before Lucas learned the answer to his question.

Resigning himself to the situation, Lucas ran himself a bath in the most opulent bathroom he'd ever seen. Looking around at his surroundings he began to weigh up the pros and cons of his circumstances. He wasn't surprised to find the pros outweighed the cons big-time. Somehow or other he got the feeling that Salazar had taken a liking to him. He tempered that thought with the scene of the gruesome murder in the barn come abattoir.

He had three hours to while away until the party, so he decided a good long luxuriant soak in the bath was called for. Slipping into the foaming waters he let his mind drift back to a far different time.

Ethan Kels looked across at his partner and laughed, "I swear I can't figure you out, we've been partnered together for seven weeks and you ain't once given in to temptation."

"Like I said; I know how this works and just because I ain't on the take that doesn't mean you can't trust me." replied Mike.

"Hell, I know that, if it wasn't so, you and me would have parted company long since," laughed Kels. He couldn't believe his luck, a partner that was honest but knew the score.

Working out of West Hollywood, Ethan and Mike felt fortunate to patrol Sunset Boulevard. The Strip was glitzy, glamorous and lucrative, but more importantly, as far as Kels was concerned, it came under the jurisdiction of the County of Los Angeles and the area known as Sunset Strip fell under the authority of the Sheriff's Department, rather than the LAPD. Rather bizarrely it was illegal to gamble within the city, but legal in the county. During the twenties a number of casinos and nightclubs established themselves on the Strip. During the Prohibition years, life continued much as it had before the Volstead Act. Throughout the Thirties and Forties its restaurants and nightclubs became a virtual playground for the rich and famous. Movie stars, producers, directors, men of power and influence frequented the Strip. The rich mingled with the not so rich, all rubbing shoulders with professional gamblers, movie stars, gangsters, sports personalities and prostitutes. It was Mike Burnett and Ethan Kels job to keep the streets of West Hollywood safe.

Mike had held fast to his principles until one lonely night in February 1941. There was a nip in the air as they began their tour, which kind of indicated it would be a slow night. A night of low action, even the bad men didn't like the cold. Ethan and Mike chewed the fat some, then slowly cruised the streets. But it was that night, that night of low action that everything changed for Mike Burnett. They'd just taken possession of a scolding hot cup of coffee and a chilli dog each, when they received a call for a robbery in progress. They were reluctant to respond until they received the location. It was a liquor store not more than five blocks from where they were patrolling.

"Show us dealing," barked Kels.

Mike swung the wheel of the patrol-car and moved into the centre of the street, he was about to switch on the siren when Ethan stopped him.

"Ain't no point in giving these boys the heads up."

Coasting to a stop half a block over from the drug store, Ethan grabbed hold of the Ithaca 37 pump action shotgun. Mike looked at him.

"What, you think these sons of bitches would give us an even break, think Bannerman."

Mike pulled his service piece, adrenaline pumping through his body like a locomotive. It was like that every time they were called into action. Ethan being the more experienced man took charge as he scanned the immediate area. The street appeared deserted apart from a car parked in front of the open double doors to the store. Ethan motioned that he was going to approach the side window and assess the situation. Mike was to follow at a discreet distance. Kels stealthily reached the side of the building and peered through a side window. Inside he spied two men, one Hispanic, the other Caucasian, both men were armed, on the floor he saw two frightened shoppers and against the counter lying on his side appeared to be the store owner, blood pooling out from a wound. Ethan signalled there were two assailants inside the store, he motioned for Mike to take up a position. Deputy Kels was nearly at the open double doors when Mike glanced at the car; its engine was running, obviously for a quick getaway. He quietly stepped forward, his service revolver pointing slightly downward, when his eye caught a slight movement in the car. The barrel of a pump action shotgun silently sighted itself on Ethan's broad back. For a split second Mike froze, there was no chance to shout a warning. Instinctively he raised his pistol and fired four shots at the shadowy figure inside the car holding the shotgun. The bullets found their mark, puncturing the night with a cacophony of explosions and smashed glass.

Ethan now framed in the doorway spun around, "What the fuc . . ." Realising the dangerous position he was in he dived to the side, just as the Hispanic guy fired several shots at the open doorway. Sweat streamed down Ethan Kels furrowed brow as he realised he had missed death by milliseconds.

"Police," shouted Mike, come out with your hands in the air!"

"Fuck you copper," shouted the white guy as he snatched up one of the prone shoppers and used her as a shield. In that precise moment whether it was the adrenaline pumping through his veins or sheer bloody mindedness Ethan Kels made his move. Stepping into the framework of the doorway he fired twice at the Hispanic man catching him full in the stomach and sending him flying backwards into a store display. In almost the same moment Mike made his move and

appeared alongside his partner, his revolver now pointing steadily at the remaining robber's head. Ethan Kels held the shotgun still smoking and looked the robber in the eye.

"Give up your weapon!" shouted Mike, give it up or die! It's your only chance."

The woman hostage started to scream. "Easy ma'am, this man ain't gonna hurt you. Are you boy!" said Kels softly.

The boy couldn't have been more than seventeen, appeared to have peed his pants.

"Give it up!" cried Mike desperately.

The boy with resignation in his eyes, let go of the shrieking woman. Ethan Kels fired.

"Noooo . . . ." screamed Mike, but it was too late. The boy was dead before he hit the ground.

Ethan Kels had gunned the boy down, he'd given it up. In a court of law, it'd go down as justified homicide, but it was murder plain and simple, Mike had little choice but to back his partner. It left a bad taste in his mouth.

During the next few days the shooting was investigated. With both police officers telling the same story and the traumatised bystanders claiming the Sheriff's deputies were heroes it was recorded as a lawful shooting. Three young men had died in less than a minute and Kels had walked away scot free.

Mike took a week's sick leave and during his time off he decided that law enforcement wasn't for him. He reported back to the station house ready to hand in his resignation when the ballistics report on the bullets that had killed the liquor store owner came in. It showed that they had come from the same gun that had killed Tom Bannerman less than a year before. Ethan Kels had killed a cop killer, both he and Mike were heralded as heroes.

Chapter 8

When Lucas emerged from the bathroom, he found a dark blue double breasted suit, a white shirt and a hand painted tie laid out on the bed. A matching blue fedora was hanging on the hat stand and a pair of shoes was lying at the base. Amazed at every turn, Lucas checked the shoe size, it was a half size bigger than his own, but better that than a half size smaller. The suit jacket was a perfect fit, the trousers were the right length but the waist size was two inches too large. A pair of suspenders would fix that he thought, and then he spied a pair hanging on the hat stand. Salazar or his man servant had thought of everything. It beggared belief that such a man could be so brutal; but then he thought about his own situation. He'd killed, but not in such a grotesque way. He'd taken lives nonetheless, regardless of the method.

As he looked in the full length mirror to check his appearance he reflected on his decision to stay in the Sheriff's Department.

Ethan Kels had pulled him to one side as the news of the ballistics test filtered through the squad room. "I haven't had time to thank you properly since the shooting."

"You killed a man in cold blood," said Mike.

"I said to you at the start, if they're carrying a piece, put them in the ground. They wouldn't have thought twice about killing us."

Mike knew Kels was only telling it as it was. The boy was man enough to carry a gun, and to all intent he'd already killed Tom, what the hell was he getting too intense about. The kid would have been sent up to San Quentin and from there he'd have gone straight to the gas chamber. Mike screwed up his resignation and binned it. And in that symbolic moment things changed for Michael Burnett.

"The party is on the lawns sir," informed a smartly dressed waiter. Lucas walked out through the double doors and stepped onto the veranda with the stone balustrade. Accepting a glass of champagne from a waiter with a tray full, Lucas surveyed the scene that stretched out before him. There must have been at least a hundred people not counting the waiters that attentively kept everyone happy with their trays of canapés and glasses of champagne.

Lucas searched for a familiar face and after scrutinizing the crowd of partygoers twice he spied Gretchen on the far side of the lawn talking with her brother Franz. She spotted him and beckoned him over. Stepping down onto the lawns he began to weave his way through the sea of guests. As he grew closer he couldn't help noticing how well she looked. Her blonde hair shone brightly in the late glow of the afternoon sun, and the dress *an elegant low backed cocktail number* complimented her hourglass figure. Gone was the willowy blonde with the mean demeanour, in her place stood an angel, with Lucas hoped, a hint of the devil. She smiled warmly as he grew nearer and her eyes sparkled like blue ice.

Franz, although polite, seemed to look down his nose at the tall American with the charming smile.

"Franz," greeted Lucas.

"Herr Garrett, it is good to see you." Lucas noted that there was no warmth in his greeting. Turning slightly he looked down at the German's better half.

"Lucas, you look so.. so debonair."

"You look pretty good yourself," he responded.

"Franz, excuse us, we're going to take a walk, mingle with the local dignities," said Gretchen sweetly.

"As you wish," he replied. His eyes grew cold as he looked straight at Lucas.

Gretchen put her arm through his and began walking. "Remember, we have been seeing each other for the last few months. I have an apartment in Palermo Viejo. I've lived there for the past few months, before that I was living with my brother in Flores."

"How long do we keep this charade going?"

"Until I feel comfortable in my surroundings," she said thoughtfully.

Lucas decided to be bold, hell he was an American, it was kind of expected of him. "This relationship, any fringe benefits," he said with a warm smile.

Gretchen laughed, and any trace of the Teutonic seemed to evaporate. "That my dear Lucas depends on how well you please me." She giggled and then they moved into the main body of guests, but within five minutes of mingling Salazar's aide Juan Aquilar approached and begged Gretchen's forgiveness.

"Senor Salazar has some urgent business with Lucas. We won't keep him long."

Gretchen smiled sweetly and gave Lucas a knowing look that suggested far more.

"She's pretty, you think, yes?" stated Aquilar as he headed back into the house.

"You could say that," replied Lucas, doing his best to appear non-responsive to Gretchen's charms.

As they made their way through the vast hall with its array of large ceiling fans, Lucas couldn't help thinking about Lola and her irrational fear of Juan Aquilar. To be honest, the man was sinister looking. His dark greasy hair severely swept back from a high forehead and his cruel eyes set back in his head, gave him an air of menace. Some women would have found him attractive in a dangerous way, that much was plain to see, but for some reason Lola sensed an evil about him that made her shiver with fear at the mention of his name. Once the working relationship between them was established, Lucas intended to put Aquilar straight about leaving Lola alone. He was cutting Lola loose; there was no choice in the matter. Warning Aquilar off as far as he was concerned was part of his way of easing his conscience, that and the five hundred pesos he intended on giving her. He was moving into a different world, a world with no place for a drug addicted whore like Lola.

Juan Aquilar opened the door to Salazar's study and beckoned Lucas to enter. Four men were sat at a table; Salazar, Clemente Ramos, Franz Kauffman and a man in a military uniform bedecked with medals.

"Lucas, thank you for coming," said Salazar.

'As if I had a choice,' thought Lucas.'

"As you decided to accept my invitation I thought it prudent to personally run though the basis of your new duties." Lucas smiled awkwardly. Sensing the big American's discomfort, Salazar smiled, then said, "Pray be seated."

Lucas sat down on one of the two vacant chairs, Juan Aquilar took the other. They had no sooner made themselves comfortable when Salazar spoke again. "Allow me to introduce my brother Colonel Ruben Salazar."

Lucas took the hint and rose to his feet, his hand extended. The colonel reached across the table and shook it vigorously. With the pleasantries out of the way Felipe Salazar began to explain to Lucas what his duties would consist of. "Firstly you will be in sole charge of Granero de Alvarado, from the income you generate I will be taking fifty percent, understood. You will be responsible for retaining order; hiring and firing staff, entertainment, alcohol and wages. This will all come out of your end. What extras you earn are up to you. You will have free rein over the entire operation. As long as I receive fifty percent at the end of every week, then you will be left alone. Failure to comply is unacceptable. I have great faith in you. Don't fail me."

Minutes later Lucas returned to the garden party. His head whirling with uncertainty, he'd been given free rein, yet above all that, there was the veiled threat, it amounted to around a thousand pesos weekly and you will be left alone. Lucas was beginning to understand where Felipe Salazar was coming from. He'd shown him how he could be polite, cultured and charming, yet he'd also shown him the crudely violent side to his nature. The man wanted Lucas to fear him, to bend to his will, to become a loyal and trusted lieutenant.

Lucas wasn't buying any of it, in the space of that meeting he'd figured it out. Felipe Salazar ruled by fear, the men around him could snuff him out without a flicker of conscience or trepidation, the only thing that stopped them was Colonel Ruben Salazar, the real power behind the throne. In the moment before he caught sight of Gretchen Kauffman, he decided that he'd use the opportunity to his advantage. Felipe Salazar would get his thousand pesos weekly while Lucas would use Salazar's power and influence to make enough money to get out of this hell-hole. If it took six months, a year, ten years, Lucas Garrett was eventually going to answer to no man.

Gretchen saw him the moment he stepped back onto the lawn; she smiled and waved demurely even though she was in deep conversation with a couple of local dignitaries. Lucas walked casually through the throng of people until he was abreast of her. Gretchen took his arm and introduced him to the couple, "Darling, this is Senor Mendoza and his wife Isabella. I've been telling them about how we first met."

Lucas shook both of their hands, smiled politely and then put his arm around her trim waist. She smiled up at him lovingly and he found it hard to believe how practiced she'd become at spinning her cover story. So practiced he was beginning to believe it too.

The evening passed swiftly, too swiftly for Lucas. He was slowly getting to know Gretchen and strange as it seemed she was growing on him. Part of him said she was bad news, whilst another part had him believing every word she uttered. Was it all lies, was it part made up or was it the truth? What was so wrong living a life of privilege whilst others suffered? Was it because she was German? Didn't they, like the rest of Europe deserve a fresh start? How could anyone appear naïve as to what was happening during the war? Lucas could only surmise, he wasn't there, he hadn't seen the death and destruction inflicted on the vanquished. From what Gretchen told him she'd been ignorant to what was happening, she'd been cosseted from the truth; that was until she had to flee for her life. The Russians would surely have killed her or worse. The Americans, he suspected would have treated her more kindly, or would they? She was an innocent amongst thousands perhaps millions of innocents caught up in the maelstrom of war. Yet by her own admission she was a survivor, she'd done whatever it took to escape. Was part of her cover story a means to blot out the horrific realities of war? Lucas suspected that was so.

Later that evening as most of the guests had drifted off, Lucas suddenly realised he'd have to be going too. He made his excuses to Gretchen and asked if he could see her again.

"I'd like that very much, but as you'll appreciate I have to settle into my new surroundings. Give me a little time and I'll be in touch," she said sweetly.

In the taxi back to Buenos Aires Lucas reflected on all that Gretchen had told him. He'd missed the war but not for want of trying.

From before Christmas and through to New Years, the talk was of nothing else. The Japanese had bombed Pearl Harbour and every red-blooded American wanted to enlist, Mike probably more so. It was his chance to get away from the clutches of Ethan Kels and the mob. It was his ticket to freedom. Kels and local mob boss Jake Reis thought otherwise.

The mob's hold on Mike began a few months after the drug store shooting. Both men had been fast tracked to the detective division on account of the drug store shooting. Mike learned later Jake Reis had pulled a few strings.

It had started small just a few favours here, a few there. Nothing major, until a balmy summer's night up in the Hollywood Hills. Ethan Kels received the call at around 9.30 pm.

"We've a tricky situation that needs our attention." The look on his face told Mike this wasn't an ordinary call, this was something major. In the time he'd rode with Ethan Kels he'd never seen the man appear so nervous and twitchy.

"Shouldn't we call for back up," enquired Mike, although he already knew the answer.

"No!" exclaimed Kels, a little too quickly. "This is something only we can take care of." The look he gave Mike left no doubt, this was the big one. Ethan had been talking about nothing else since they both got their detective shields.

Leaving Cahuenga Boulevard behind, they negotiated the long and winding Mulholland Drive. Ten minutes later Ethan hung a left and drove at a slow pace until he came to a gated driveway. He flashed his headlights and the gates slowly opened.

"Oh sweet Jesus!" exclaimed Mike as he looked down on the body. She couldn't have been more than twenty, if that. He'd seen a few overdoses in his time but this one looked messed up pretty good. "Has someone called the corone . . . ."before the words had finished issuing from his lips, he knew the answer.

"We're the clean up squad," said Ethan in a matter of fact voice. This never happened; at least it didn't happen here."

Mike's face said it all. He'd turned white with the abnormality of what he was expected to do.

"This never happened," repeated Kels, "Now help me load her in the trunk."

"But . . ."

"No buts, no questions. We take the broad and dump her somewhere south of here. Dumb fuck died from an overdose, who cares where she's found."

Mike opened the trunk then took the young woman's feet while Ethan took her head and shoulders. Nothing more was said between the two Sheriff's deputies, as they closed the trunk and climbed back inside their patrol car. Ethan started the motor and followed the drive round *until he was on the long driveway to the front gate. It was only after they passed through the gate that Mike spoke again.*

"What the fuck are we gonna do now?"

"We keep cool, that's what we do. Then we're going to get rid of our cargo." Ethan Kels had ceased to think of the body in the trunk as human, in his eyes he was dumping trash.

"We can't just drop her at the side of the road!" exclaimed Mike.

Ethan laughed, "Under normal circumstances I'd disagree with you, but what we're being paid means we've to leave it in a rundown motel room in the downtown area."

"I don't like this one bit, it ain't dignified, the girl must have folks that care. Being found dead of an overdose in a seedy motel room, it just don't sit right."

"Maybe so, but being found dead in some producer's bedroom wouldn't look good either. And besides, most of these girls are either runaways or come from families that couldn't give a stuff. What we're doing is damage limitation."

An hour later the girl took up residence in a shady flophouse, where the comings and goings of it's many occupants caused little or no concern as the two men carefully arranged the girl's body by propping it up against the side of a well used and dishevelled bed. The offending used syringe was carefully placed beside her. Satisfied that everything looked as it appeared Ethan closed the door behind him. Mike Burnett was now officially on the payroll of Los Angeles mobster Jake Reis.

"He's Mister Fix It, for the rich and famous," laughed Ethan as he handed Mike his payoff from their chores of the previous evening.

"A thousand bucks!" exclaimed Mike. He'd never seen that kind of money in his entire lifetime.

"There's more where that came from, you just stick with me kid," said Kels.

In that moment Mike weighed up his options, follow the path of his mentor Tom Bannerman or embrace the life that Ethan Kels and Jake Reis had to offer. As he folded the green, and shoved it deep into his pants pocket he already knew the answer.

What Mike hadn't bargained for was the loss of his soul. In the company of Ethan Kels he'd do far worst than dispose of a body, he was in deep but he saw his chance when the Japs declared war. He hadn't banked on Jake Reis's influence. A great many younger policemen were preparing to join up, leaving the older men to deal with the ever growing crime wave. That was where Jake Reis came in, with all out war he saw profits to be made around every corner, there was no way he was going to allow Mike and Ethan to become cannon fodder, which was fine as far as Ethan was concerned, but Mike was showing signs of jumping ship until fate lent a helping hand.

It was 3.15 a.m. when Lucas stepped out of the taxi and began to climb up the stairs to Lola's apartment. Sobered by the journey and enriched by the lifestyle he'd only so recently been a part of, he surveyed his surrounding. The squalor and stench seemed to hit him in the face like never before. He'd been rich, well modestly so and he'd seen poverty on a scale that he'd never dreamed possible. As he drew closer to Lola's place he reflected again on his choice of lifestyle. He'd fucked it up last time, he'd drawn a line in the sand and where did it get him? He'd lost the only woman he had truly loved, he'd lost the respect of his former colleagues, and he was hunted and hounded out of his own country by lawmen and lawbreakers' alike. Felipe Salazar had offered him a way back, true his methods could be crude and brutal at times, but putting that aside, it was a chance to start over. This time there would be no line in the sand.

Chapter 9

Granero de Alvarado was heaving with people when Lucas pushed his way through to the back office. The place oozed with potential, and right from the off Lucas had plans. He was greeted by a surly Juan Aquilar who was sitting at a large desk that seemed to take up half the room. From the scowl that he gave Lucas, he wasn't happy.

"You're late! I was expecting you an hour ago," he snapped.

"Then you'd have been disappointed. I was under the impression I ran this place, not you!"

Lucas had learned early on to take shit from no one, he wasn't about to start with Aquilar. One thing he'd been taught by Ethan Kels was to set out his stall from the get go.

Surprised by Lucas's answer, Aquilar struggled to regain the advantage. "The club opened its doors two hours ago."

"Maybe so, but no one tells me what to do. Now before we get off on the wrong foot, Salazar has given me free rein, I'm to have full charge of Alvarado's. You I believe are to fill me in on the day to day operation." Lucas hadn't intended riling Aquilar, but he'd had a shit night with Lola, and wasn't prepared to take any more. He stared defiantly at Juan Aquilar, knowing it was the wrong move, he needed friends not enemies, but there was something about him, that Lucas didn't like. He could see the hatred building up behind the Argentinean's dark eyes. Lucas grinned inwardly, it was all a matter of timing, throw your adversary off guard, then counter with a vocal olive branch.

"Look, I get it, you're a main player. I didn't mean to disrespect you; all I'm trying to do is set my own ground rules."

Aquilar's eyes seemed to lose a little of their heat, but his pride allowed a little outburst, "I understand Gringo, but let me make it clear, step out of line, you're mine."

Lucas stifled a smirk, this wasn't getting them anywhere. He chose to ignore the veiled threat and decided to end the verbal swordplay, "As long as I kick back Salazar's share, we're good, right?"

Aquilar grinned; he had to have the final word. "We have an understanding."

Lucas nodded, "Agreed." Then his face came over serious, "Just one thing, Lola Santos, stay away from her."

Juan put his hands up in mock surrender, "No problem."

Within an hour Juan had filled Lucas in on the day to day running of Granero de Alvarado. Despite their short exchange of words the Argentinean had been very professional; he'd introduced Lucas to all members of staff and shown him the ropes. He also gave him a book with a list of names and premises. This was to be the other side of Lucas's operation. Extortion was the same in any language. The only difference was the methods. Lucas had seen at close hands the methods used by Jake Reis and Ethan Kels, you could say he'd had great teachers.

All along Lucas had the feeling Aquilar was holding something back. When it came Juan Aquilar was grinning.

"You are aware that Ramon Perez was heir apparent for Humberto's position, a natural step up from supplying the club."

"Who the fuck is Ramon Perez?" asked Lucas. "Supplying the club with what?" he added. Almost before the words came out, Lucas knew the answer.

Aquilar smiled, "Ramon Perez operates out of Granero de Alvarado. His clientele like his particular brand of China."

"The fuck they do! Not any more."

Juan was enjoying himself, "I'm afraid you have no say in the matter, Ramon Perez works for Felipe Salazar."

Lucas was beginning to see the predicament he was in. He'd been handed the reins ahead of Ramon Perez, a man that was next in line for Vargas's job. Salazar had thrown him in the deep end.

"He kicks back to Salazar?"

"You're learning, him and his brother Julio; they are how you say, very colourful characters."

He grinned as he noticed Lucas looked somewhat aggrieved,

"You didn't think this was gonna be easy? Well did yah, tough guy?" snarled Aquilar.

Lucas was in a bind, but he'd be damned if he'd let that low-life Aquilar think he was bothered. "Trouble with you Aquilar, you've seen too many Jimmy Cagney movies!"

Lucas closed the door to his office and sat down behind the desk. No one said this job was gonna be easy, he kept telling himself. In the quiet of the room he assessed his situation. He was alone in Buenos Aires, he was an American, hell he might as well paint a target across his chest. To add to that he had one mother fucker of an enemy in Juan Aquilar, two others in the wings, a business that had to remain successful and a boss that had a passion for chainsaws.

On the plus side, 'yes,' he told himself, 'there was a plus side.' Granero de Alvarado basically ran itself; but more important than that, Lucas could see the full potential of the club. True, the night club wasn't in the heart of the entertainment district, but the area had colour, drama and a hint of danger. In the right hands Granero de Alvarado could be turned into a goldmine. Salazar's key word had been legitimacy; it was something he craved as much as his beloved Estancia. If Lucas's hunch was right, given time and enough resources he could transform the 'Barn' into a real money making concern and in turn he could free himself from the shackles of Felipe Salazar.

But Lucas's first concern had to be the Perez brothers, two of the most vicious gangsters in all Buenos Aires. He had men at his command, *admittedly none of his choosing,* but would they support him? These men only respected the strongest and the most vicious. Lucas knew he'd have to prove himself first.

He made an unprecedented telephone call to Felipe Salazar. Praying on the man's pride and vanity Lucas asked which of his men would be the most able and loyal.

"You ask me, why not ask Juan?"

"Senor Salazar, from your own mouth you told me you were an honourable man. So whose advice should I take; yours or Aquilar's?"

Lucas detected a stifled laugh. "Cipriano Mercado," came the answer.

"Gracias."

It was a gamble, but life was a gamble. Hell he could have died last night, he thought reflectively. Lola hadn't taken kindly to him reappearing after five days. That was bad enough, but when he began packing his bags and telling her he was leaving for good, she flipped. At first she'd been angry, then after the initial rage she begged him to stay. She fell to her knees, she cried hysterically, but Lucas had hardened his heart, he didn't owe her a damn cent. She wasn't anything to him; she was an addict, a hooker of the lowest order. If he stayed with her she'd cause him grief, he couldn't allow his conscience to hold him back. Lola was a survivor, she'd make out; her looks would carry her forward for maybe a few more years.

As she sobbed at his feet, he reached into his billfold and counted out five hundred pesos, "Here," he said. "Take this; get yourself out of this dump."

Lola looked up and her eyes still wet with tears turned coal black with renewed anger. She dashed the money from his outstretched hand.

"You can't buy me off, I'll fucking kill you first!" Snatching up a knife from the kitchen table she slashed at his face. An inch closer, she'd have taken out an eye. Lucas retreated as she slashed at him again. Then her tactics changed as she lunged, she had murder in her heart.

"Fuck you bitch!"

Lucas angered by the near miss, moved quickly and stepped to the right. He slammed his fist as hard as he could into the side of her head. Lola fell like she'd been pole axed.

When she woke up, she was lying on their bed. Lucas was soothing her brow with a damp cloth. All the fight was gone as she slowly regained her senses.

"I'm sorry Lucas, I'm so sorry," she said weakly.

Her volatile temper only reinforced his resolve; she was a fucking liability, a liability that could sooner or later get him killed. True she was a great fuck, but that wasn't reason enough to stay around.

"Listen Lola, we both knew this arrangement was only temporary. I'm moving out, you should think about doing the same. Take the money. Start a new life someplace else. There's enough there to put you on your feet. At the very least, think about it."

Lola if nothing else was a realist, she looked at the money, and she even appeared to be listening to Lucas's advice, but both of them knew where the money was really going.

"Take care of yourself." he said as he was leaving.

Lola managed a feeble smile, "And you take care."

Lucas sought out Cipriano Mercado and was surprised by his appearance. The man was a year or two older than Lucas, a little under five eight in height, but what he lost in stature he made up for in bulk. He was dressed in an ill fitting tuxedo and standing at the entrance to Granero de Alvarado carefully scrutinizing the clientele. This was his official job but his dubious talents were used as hired muscle.

"I want a word, my office, five minutes," said Lucas.

Mercado simply looked at Lucas and grunted his understanding. He managed a slight smile, but Lucas couldn't read anything into it.

"You wanted to see me," he said with his hands clenched in front of him.

Lucas noted his square jaw and granite features and small dark penetrating eyes.

"Close the door," ordered Lucas.

The hulk of a doorman closed the door gently behind him.

"I'll come straight to the point; Salazar has given me a God given opportunity to make something of this place, which I can't do if I've got the Perez brothers breathing down my neck. I need someone I can trust, someone to watch my back, Salazar suggested you. If you're prepared to help me, the rewards will more than compensate. Without your help I'm stuck between a rock and a hard place." Cipriano looked quizzically at Lucas, "Basically I'm in the shit and I need your help."

The stocky Argentinean grinned at Lucas's turn of phrase.

"Whether you help me or not, is your choice. If you choose to help me and we're successful I will reward you big time." Lucas looked up from his desk and stared straight into Mercado's dark deep set eyes. "Well, what's it to be?"

"Felipe Salazar is my patron; if he wishes it so, then I will help you. You are a straight talker, and I have seen you fight. I was with Senor Salazar when you nearly killed Rojo. To go up against the Perez brothers you will need to be brutal, but are you prepared to kill?"

"If it's me or them, the hell I am."

"Good, because if you have to kill one of the Perez brothers you will have to kill the other, even in cold blood, you understand?"

"I understand."

"One other thing Senor Garrett, I have no love for Ramon Perez. We have history."

Lucas smiled, "Now tell me all there is to know about the Perez brothers, their strengths and their weaknesses."

Cipriano told him, there were no weaknesses. Ramon joined a street gang at eleven, ran errands; stole whatever was at hand; became very handy with a razor, slicing an ear off a rival gang member at the age of twelve. Even at that age Ramon Perez was making a name for himself. He killed his first man at fourteen as an initiation test. The guy was an ordinary Joe going about his business; Ramon walked up to him and asked him for a light. The guy obliged and got six inches of cold steel in his gut for his trouble. He rose steadily through the ranks and it wasn't long before he introduced his brother Julio into the gang. Julio was two years younger, but from the outset he proved to be just as ruthless as his older brother.

Then at sixteen Ramon fell in love, well more lust than love. Anica was from a good family and Ramon wanted her like nothing else. To Anica, Ramon was handsome, dashing and daring, a far cry from the boys at her school. She was an innocent playing at being in love like a great many young people, but she hadn't reckoned with Ramon's emotions. Unwittingly she was playing a dangerous game. They'd kissed, they'd fooled around some, but Anica wasn't prepared to give up her virginity just yet. Out of character Ramon accepted her decision and continued seeing her. The boy was in love, of course he'd wait. Then one night high on cocaine he tried to rape her. She fought him off and told him the relationship was over. Ramon fumed, his male pride was dented and he began to resent Anica. He'd wasted six weeks on the little prick teaser for nothing.

It was less than a week when Ramon, his brother Julio and six others burst into her parents' house at one in the morning. While his gang held her parents at bay he ripped of Anica's nightgown and proceeded to rape her. Her father tried to protect his daughter but was beaten to within an inch of his life. Anica's mother was screaming and yelling; a back hand from Julio sent her sprawling onto the floor. With a nod of his head two of his men took her into another room and began raping her. Anica fought as best she could but she was too weak to fight him off. He slapped her into submission, as his heavy body pounded on her small frame. When Ramon finished he picked himself up off the floor with a smile of elation.

"She is nothing to me now, she is yours!" Triumphantly he turned his back on her, leaving her to the mercy of his followers.

Some were busy with the mother while others took turns with Anica until three in the morning.

Ramon and Julio were arrested, but spent only a few weeks in custody, before being released for lack of evidence. Her parents fearing for the life of their daughter withdrew the complaint. Six weeks later Anica's father took his own life.

A year later Ramon and Julio both received three year jail terms for supplying cocaine. Julio got out two weeks before his brother, but Ramon had ordered him to keep his head down until he got out. Whilst they'd been away a new regime had taken control. He knew they'd expect him to demand his rightful place, but instead Ramon accepted a lower position. He'd prided himself on always being one jump ahead; his intention was to take back what was rightfully his in his own time. It took the brothers a little over three months to regain control. During that time four key members of the gang either left the city or disappeared. Ramon and Julio were back in business, harder, tougher than before. Now the brothers set their sights on moving up in the world. They were no longer punks; they needed to portray an image that they were going places. Sharp suits, handmade shoes, and silk shirts soon marked them out as snappy dressers. It was the first step on the ladder.

It took them a little longer than expected but several years honing their craft at street level inevitably brought them to the attention of Humberto Vargas.

A little over an hour later Lucas knew all he'd needed to know about the sick fucker Ramon Perez and his equally sick brother Julio. If he was going to compete in their world then he would have to be just as brutal. It was that or go under.

Lucas knew he had to stamp his authority on his territory. A day later he walked into Oliverio's bakery, "I'm here to collect," he said in Spanish. The proprietor looked shocked, but then believing it was a shakedown, told Lucas to get the hell out of his shop. Lucas smiled, then punched him hard in the stomach and banged his head against the counter top. Blood streamed from a broken nose. He waited until the baker had recovered slightly, then hit him twice more. The baker, who was pretty big but out of shape, slowly began to realise the man in front of him wasn't to be messed with. "Senor, please forgive me, but I already pay Ramon Perez."

"You did, you don't anymore!" 'So Perez was biting into my action,' thought Garrett. 'Not content with selling drugs in my establishment, the fucker was trying to take over.'

By the close of business the local shop keepers, café owners and several businessmen knew that life had suddenly gotten harder.

When Ramon Perez found out that an American had taking charge of Granero de Alvarado he was mad as all hell that he'd been passed over. Not content with the night club the gringo pig had lost no time in taking back another part of his business. Ramon was enraged, his first reaction was to kill the American, but then his rage turned to puzzlement. He'd expected Salazar to make him Humberto's successor, this American was something he hadn't expected.

"It shows a lack of respect!" snapped Ramon.

"A lack of respect that one day will be his downfall. He fears you Ramon," declared Julio. "We knew Salazar wouldn't be long in finding a successor, but this American confirms what we already knew." added Julio. Ramon's younger brother by two years wasn't afraid of Felipe Salazar, but he was a realist.

Ramon on the other hand was a thinker. "Ask around; find out all there is to know about the Americano." Since Vargas's demise, some people might have called it an absence; but not Ramon, he'd expected Salazar to name him as his replacement. He and his brother controlled around fifteen men, men that were as ruthless as them, but in an all out war with Salazar there would be casualties, mostly Perez men. Ramon suspected *like his brother Julio*, that Salazar was putting him to the test. He'd heard of the big American, he also knew though his sources that Salazar had given him the job with conditions. The American was virtually working alone; he was sure to fall flat on his face. Lucas Garrett would fail, he Ramon Perez would see to that. Then the order will be given and the American will be taken care of.

Ramon at thirty three had big plans, bigger even than Salazar's. It was his ambition to be the Al Capone of Buenos Aires. This promotion would have been the first step up the ladder, but Salazar had thwarted that, for the time being. In the meantime he needed to get the measure of Lucas Garrett.

Felipe Salazar wasn't a foolish man, he appreciated strength, ruthlessness and ambition, and Ramon Perez fitted the bill perfectly, maybe too perfectly. With the vacancy created by the death of Vargas, Salazar had watched as the Perez brothers started to make their move. Given the promotion, Ramon and his brother would bide their time, it might be years but one day they would strike and strike without mercy. This was something Felipe Salazar would not tolerate. His forte was in reading people, then using that knowledge to his best advantage.

Looking back he might even have granted Ramon the position made vacant by Vargas but for the slight distraction of Lucas Garrett. He'd been in the bar the night Garrett took out Rojo. *It was good to see that chivalry wasn't dead*, thought Salazar wryly. What impressed him was the cool way the American handled himself and the sheer brutality he inflicted on Rojo. Garrett understood the law of the jungle and in meting out the punishment that he gave Rojo he insured there would be no return match. Salazar saw a brutal but intelligent man, a man with the potential to become a member of his crew, a man that given time and nurturing could become a loyal and trusted ally, *well, as trusted as anyone could be in the business they were in.*

Lucas too was planning; Salazar had set him up big time. It didn't take much figuring; he was to act as a buffer between Ramon Perez and Salazar, keeping the larger threat at bay without the Argentine landowner getting his hands dirty. That he'd been wined and dined at Estancia Salazar spoke volumes as far as Lucas was concerned. Salazar was a gangster, but also a business man, he'd seen Lucas's potential and was prepared to use him. If the Perez brothers proved too much for Lucas, then so be it. He believed Salazar was putting his faith in him. If he failed, Felipe Salazar would have lost nothing, if he succeeded then both men would have the respect of their peers.

Ramon was not a stupid man, by now the American would know the score. He needed to set the American off balance, he would request a meeting with him, somewhere public, somewhere where both parties would feel safe.

It wasn't long before Lucas received a message from the Perez brothers asking for that meeting. Lucas told the messenger that he'd meet them in plain sight at Alvarado's that night around ten o'clock. The messenger looked wary and scared.

"Tell Ramon, it is good, we need to talk, I understand, we need to clear the air."

Cipriano looked at him as if he was mad, Juan who'd called on Lucas to collect the weeks takings shook his head in surprise, but no one spoke until Perez's messenger was gone.

"Senor Garrett, is it wise to face the problem head on? They do not understand fair play."

"Who said fair play?" said Lucas with a wry grin.

Chapter 10

"Felipe Salazar is a manipulator, he plays with peoples lives. He doesn't care who's in charge, us or the American," said Ramon. "What he really cares about is concluding this situation without an all out war. His brother although close to Peron, cannot afford to embarrass the new government, so Felipe Salazar will be held in check. Why else would he allow this charade?"

"But how will we conclude this problem?" said Julio.

"Firstly I will speak to Senor Salazar himself. I will explain that we are all businessmen and that the American and I wish to resolve the situation through talk."

"Will he believe you?"

"No! Would you? What it will show Felipe Salazar is that I am not the hot head he believes me to be

In the back room Lucas Garrett got his first look at Ramon and Julio Perez. They arrived punctually at 10 o'clock and were shown into Lucas's office. He stood up as the two entered. Lucas then motioned for them to sit down. Tension filled the air as Ramon nervously sat down. Julio remained standing. To de-fuse the situation, Lucas acknowledged Julio's choice; then sat down opposite Ramon.

"It is good that we should have this talk. I am here at Felipe Salazar's request, but I understand you must be a little disappointed."

"Disappointed ain't the half of it!" spat Ramon. He'd planned to be cool but the patronising way Lucas talked to him, made him seethe with anger.

Lucas knew only too well that to show any sign of weakness could get him killed. His eyes fixed on Ramon and his voice carried the authority required, "Sorry you feel that way. Make no mistake, I'm running this show from here on in. You don't like it, that's tough. Ain't a damn thing I can do about it! All I'll concede is, you'll continue to operate in Alvarado's as before, until I say otherwise."

"Then there's nothing more to be said." Ramon rose from his chair and hard eyed Lucas before turning and walking out the door.

Cipriano waited a few moment before saying, "Senor Garrett; Ramon, he means to kill you."

Lucas looked straight at his man and said, "I know."

For the next six days Lucas moved about continually, sleeping in different locations, a hotel one night, a boarding house another, even spending a night with one of Buenos Aires whores, not even Cipriano knew of his whereabouts. He knew the Perez brothers would be looking for him; they would want a quick solution to their problem; their frustration was to his advantage. He was hoping to force their hand. The only place they could be sure to find him was at Granero de Alvarado, the one place where they daren't make a move. Ironically it was the safest place for Lucas. The men at his disposal might not be loyal to him, but they worked for Salazar and as such would protect who ever he had put in charge. Any assault on Granero de Alvarado would be seen as a direct affront to Salazar's power. The hit, when it came, was a comedy of errors.

Lucas had one chink in his armour, his vanity. An ardent cinemagoer when in LA he never failed to miss a Humphrey Bogart film during the first week of its release. Lucas was a Bogart fan and even wore the same style raincoat and distinctive grey fedora when out on the streets of Buenos Aires. "Key Largo" was showing at the Teatro Premier around the corner to Granero de Alvarado during that week. It was due to close that weekend and Lucas was planning to see it if possible. As luck had it, it was raining; good cover for him to walk to the cinema unnoticed. He left a note on his desk for Cipriano, explaining he'd gone for a few hours.

Garrett put on his raincoat and grey fedora and nipped out the back entrance to the club. With head down he made his way briskly to the movie theatre. He paused at the entrance and admired the concave art-deco façade of the cinema, it was quite magnificent, a picture palace to rival those of Los Angeles. For Lucas it was a place where he could escape the worries of the world. He purchased his ticket, got shown to his seat by a delectable blonde usherette, took off his hat and coat and sat down to watch the movie. He'd only recently seen 'Dark Passage' and was hungry for more of the Bogart charm, or what passed for it.

As the credits rolled and the lights came on Lucas reached for his hat and coat. They were gone, replaced by a greasy trench coat and a battered homburg. Looking towards the exit he saw his hat and coat about to disappear amongst the crowd. Jumping up he ran towards the exit and the sneak thief, only to be boxed in by other cinemagoers. Breaking free he began to race down the ornate staircase to the brightly lit foyer when he stopped in his tracks. The thief, head down was making for the doors just as two men dressed in dark overcoats and matching hats approached him from different directions. Lucas knew even before the guns sprayed their cargo of lead that he was their intended target. He hung back as the drama unfolded. Both assassins emptied their revolvers into the unsuspecting thief. The man staggered backwards before crumbling into a heap near the ticket counter.

The cinema exploded into a blind panic as moviegoers ran this way and that in an attempt to escape the scene of carnage. As quickly as the killers appeared, they disappeared into the night, leaving Lucas slightly shaken at witnessing the sight of his own death. He walked through the hysterical crowd trying to keep an 'as' normal pace as possible until he reached Granero de Alvarado.

"Did you get my note?" demanded Lucas as casually as he could.

"What note?" asked Cipriano.

"It doesn't matter," said Lucas, not wanting to attract any more attention than was necessary. Realising there was a spy in his camp was a bonus he could well have done without. Was Cipriano the informer? Was he lying about the note? Or was it one of the numerous waiters, bar staff, doormen, dancers or musicians? Someone had tipped the Perez brothers as to what he was wearing and where he was heading. Lucas had to play it cool, act like nothing had happened, and think about who he'd spoken to, who would know of his passion for Bogart movies.

In the small hours before dawn Lucas lay on his hotel bed, chain smoking, with only the ceiling fan to keep him company. He'd left the club early if only to clear his head, but that wasn't working. He'd racked his brains for the one piece of information that eluded him. He'd confided most things to Cipriano, but nothing personal. In fact, he hadn't told anyone about his love of Bogart movies. Did someone stumble across the note directly after he left the club? Unlikely as he didn't go directly to the movie house? No one but himself knew what he was thinking. A coincidence, a chance sighting? Again unlikely, the hit was too well planned. Everything just kept going around and around inside his head.

Switching his focus he realised a second attempt wouldn't be long in coming. The instinct for survival kicked in. Lucas knew drastic action was called for, and fast. The Perez brothers wouldn't be expecting swift retaliation, but if Garrett was to survive *for more than a day at least* he needed to put his plan into action. It was a carefully thought out plan, simple, but one he'd hoped to avoid. The events earlier that evening had forced his hand.

Once he realised what he was up against with the Perez brothers he'd done his homework and learned all he could about them, their habits, their sexual preferences where they ate and in Julio's case, where he slept. Lucas chose his hotel accommodation accordingly.

His hotel was only five blocks from the apartment where Ramon's brother Julio lived. The plan; outrageous as it was, demanded immediate action. He glanced at his watch, it was four thirty in the morning; even a night owl like Julio would need to sleep sometime. Lucas donned a pair of work-mans dark pants, black sweater, cap and gloves, then picked up his Colt 45 1911 automatic from the bedside table and stuffed it into the waistband at the small of his back. Then working methodically he opened the small suitcase which he kept under the bed and took out a package wrapped in greaseproof paper. Lucas opened the package and carefully handled the Luger P08. He checked the mechanism and then loaded the weapon with 9mm cartridges. All the time he kept repeating the mantra, 'It's me or them' silently. When he was sure he'd got everything, including himself, under control he slipped out the back of the hotel and quietly began to climb down the fire escape. His heart thumped erratically, threatening to wake the dead as he descended the final ladder. Sweat poured from his forehead and trickled into his eyes as he finally reached the ground. He stood perfectly still against the rear of the hotel, almost frightened to breath in case his breath in the cold night air gave him away. He looked around furtively, if his plan was to work he had to remain as invisible as possible.

By the time Lucas negotiated the five blocks to his target his entire body had almost turned to mush. He was afraid, afraid that he couldn't go through with it. He was having second thoughts. "It's them or me," he kept saying over and over again. It wasn't as if he hadn't killed before, he'd been involved in several killings but under totally different circumstances. This time he was about to commit cold blooded murder.

Steeling himself Lucas crept around the back of the apartment building and forced open the rear entrance. It gave easily, courtesy of years of abuse and misuse. Sweat dripped onto the concrete stairs as Lucas made his way up three flights. He turned to the left and surveyed the dimly lit corridor. Walls of flaking cream and light green paint work greeted his eyes. "Jesus Christ!" he muttered under his breath, the place was a virtual dump. Taking an old rag from amongst the garbage that littered the floor Lucas unscrewed the light bulb in the hallway leading to Julio's front door. In almost darkness he struck a match and after a second or so of searching he found the wastepaper basket full of paper and cardboard cartons. Within seconds the bin was a blaze, black smoke billowed around the already darkened hallway. Bracing himself he rapped on six doors in quick succession, "Fuego! Fuego! Fuego!"

As the panic stricken occupants, dazed and shocked at being woken in the middle of the night began to understand the urgency of Lucas's cries they rushed for the exits of the building. In the melee Lucas rapped on Julio's door. "Fuego! Fuego! Fuego!" The smoke had nearly obscured his view when Julio, in nothing but a vest opened the door. Realisation came to him in less than a heart beat, but it was too late Lucas squeezed the trigger of the Luger three times. Julio spun backwards into the room; still alive as he tried making it to the bedroom. Lucas followed and fired twice more into the back of his head. Then he dropped the gun and raced out of the apartment block along with the frightened occupants. From lighting the fire to putting two slugs into the back of Julio's head had taken less than a minute.

"Chicago style shootings" The papers were full of the news of the two shootings. The police were all over it, but no heat was brought down on Granero de Alvarado. Lucas showed up at work as usual, to hear everyone talking about Julio Perez being shot to death in his apartment. There was no mention of the cinema shooting, it was of no consequence; the man was a small time hood, whereas Julio was connected.

"Someone did you a big favour boss," said Cipriano when they were alone together.

"Some favour. You can bet Ramon won't see it like that," said Lucas. "I want you to keep vigilant at all times. Understood."

"Yeah."

It was a day later when Cipriano walked into Lucas's office. "Boss, I've Ramon Perez outside. He wishes to speak with you."

"Who's with him?"

"Two of his crew, nothing to get excited about," replied Cipriano.

"Tell him I'll see him. But the goons and his weapons stay outside."

This was the moment of truth; Lucas pulled his Colt from his waistband and released the safety.

Ramon almost barged into his office, the grief and anger clearly etched across his face. Lucas braced himself. That Perez was unarmed meant nothing, a shiv in the right hands could be as deadly as any gun.

"We need to talk," he snapped.

Lucas motioned for him to be seated.

"Before you go mouthing off, here me out! Under the circumstances I should be grateful your brother's dead, but I'm not. It brings a shitload of grief down on me. Someone wants you to think it was me. Believe me or not, I had nothing to do with your brother's death!"

"I know you didn't, I'm not here to start a war, quite the opposite. I want to make it clear I don't think you're involved."

Slightly taken aback Lucas pursued the subject. "So, if I didn't do it who the fuck did?" The comment was designed to provoke a reaction. There was hardly a flicker.

"I've an idea who might be behind the murder of my brother and I'm gonna put things in place to see that the debt is paid."

"So why come to me?" asked Lucas.

"Who ever killed Julio will be coming for me. I don't need you against me."

Lucas nodded his acknowledgement.

"It's no secret that I wasn't happy about being passed over, that can wait. Someone, I don't know who yet, would like us at each others throats. We have a business arrangement; that stays in place."

Lucas nodded.

During their conversation there was no mention of the cinema shooting, it seemed to be of little consequence to the likes of Ramon. He was more interested in the weapon that had been used to kill Julio. Using the Luger had been a spot of genius. It had thrown a spanner in the works. Since the war, the German influence was everywhere.

When Ramon left, Lucas felt a little off balance, 'Perhaps he didn't order the cinema hit,' he asked himself, 'or is he just playing me?'

Now Lucas had a number of things to ponder, the Bogart connection and why no one had connected him to the cinema killing. There was one possibility; it chilled Lucas to the bone to even think about it, Ethan Kels and Jake Reis. They above all others would have known of the Bogart connection. But how did they track him to Buenos Aires? His mind was working overtime without any results.

Chapter 11

Steeling himself for the days ahead, Lucas took a leap of faith and made Cipriano his own personal bodyguard. He'd reasoned it out that there would have been no reason for Cipriano to lie about receiving the note. If it turned out to be Jake Reis and Ethan Kels then Cipriano Mercado would come in very handy. If he'd been telling the truth about his feelings for Ramon Perez then that too was covered. And then of course there was Salazar, there was always Salazar. He'd put Lucas in charge of business in and around Granero de Alvarado. Despite his problems he realised that if he didn't make a success of Salazar's lucrative businesses he'd have far more to worry about.

The first two or three week's business was slow but as Lucas began using his brain and muscle he gradually rebuilt *figuratively speaking* Granero de Alvarado. With his meagre profits from his various activities he began investing in top rate cabaret performers, musicians, dancers, the best chefs and kitchen staff, classy waiters, glamorous hostesses, new uniforms and the best quality food available. It was costing Lucas a small fortune but it was chicken feed if Alvarado's took off. Buenos Aires was an open city destined *Lucas hoped*, to be one of the greatest cities in the free world.

The only fly in the ointment that Lucas could see was the continuing presence of Ramon Perez and his men openly touting their business inside Alvarado's and several other night spots. It was an irritant but one he could live with for the time being. Fortunately the authorities presumably in the pay of Perez, cast a blind eye over the business, so it was of no consequence. The government was still very young and for the foreseeable future the big American could see visions of the 'Sunset Strip' of the twenties and thirties.

As the weeks turned into months without any repercussions, Lucas slowly began to understand why. Granero de Alvarado was fast becoming one of the top hot spot in Buenos Aires. As he'd predicted, Alvarado's though not in the best neighbourhood was soon attracting a higher class of person than ever before. He was making more money than he'd thought possible. Kicking back half of what he'd earned was a pain, but as he was to find out over dinner with Felipe Salazar and his entourage on the last day of 1947, it was a worthwhile investment.

"My compliments to the chef!" exclaimed Salazar. "That was a most exquisite meal, the best I've experienced in a very long time. You are to be congratulated."

"Thank you," replied Lucas.

There was more to come, "You've turned Granero de Alvarado around. What's more you haven't been tempted. My faith in you was justified."

"I can't say it's been easy," added Lucas.

"Ah yes! I am aware of your difficulties, but rest assured, your difficulties are my difficulties."

Lucas gave him a knowing look.

"I admire your entrepreneurial spirit, your sense of style and your ruthlessness."

"Senor Salazar, can I be frank with you?"

"Of course my boy, but call me Felipe."

"I've watched and observed your vision for the future; you are striving to become one hundred percent legitimate, correct."

Salazar looked at him quizzically, wondering were this was going to lead. "Go on."

You've acknowledged I've turned this club around, well I've plans to make it bigger and better, that's in the future."

"I'm pleased to hear it."

Lucas hesitated before continuing, what he was about to say could make all the difference. "Perhaps I presume too much, but over the next few years I've a vision of turning over all our business ventures to hand picked men, men like Cipriano Mercado. The reason; I'd like to become a legitimate business man, concentrating on Alvarado's and other future night spots. I believe we would both benefit."

"It's a tall order, but can you pull it off?" said Salazar.

"With your approval, yes I think I can."

Warily Salazar cast his eyes over the transformation that Lucas had achieved over a year, then tipped a glass of champagne to his mouth, "There is nothing more to be said. You have performed a miracle; to the future!"

"The future," concurred Lucas. It wasn't a yes, but then again it wasn't a no.

It was at that precise moment that Gretchen Kauffman accompanied by her brother Franz, entered the club. It had been months since he'd seen her last. It was small wonder that it had been months since their last meeting. Business, the small matter of an assassination attempt, the death of Julio Perez and the resurrection of Granero de Alvarado had kept him too busy to think about the willowy blond broad, but all that was about to change.

"You'll excuse me Senor Salazar," said Lucas.

"But of course," replied Salazar with an amused expression upon his face.

Before he could reach her, Gretchen stepped away from her brother and walked straight up to the tall American and kissed him gently on the lips.

"It's been a while," she said seductively.

"To long," replied Lucas, doing his best to appear unruffled by her surprise appearance at the club. She appeared to have put on a bit of weight, which if truth be told she needed, her blond hair was much longer than when they first met and she wore it much like the style of the actress Veronica Lake. He liked it, he liked it a lot.

"You've come a long way, since we last met," said Gretchen as a waiter handed her a glass of Krug. Her pale blue eyes, one partially hidden by her new hairstyle, seemed as always to sparkle with mischief as she flirted with him.

"I've been lucky," replied Lucas.

"Luck, maybe; but from what I've been told, a lot of forethought and attention to detail. I like a man who's successful."

Acknowledging the compliment, he smiled graciously. "Can I get you and Franz a table," he asked whilst snapping his fingers for the head waiter to arrange a booth close to the stage and dance floor.

"That would be so kind, provided you join us for a festive drink sometime during the evening."

"I'd love too, provided your uptight brother doesn't mind."

"Oh don't mind Franz, he's a pussy-cat."

Lucas smiled, pussy-cat wasn't quite the way he'd describe Franz Kauffman, remembering how he'd used the poor unfortunate Humberto Vargas as a punch bag.

What was unique about Granero de Alvarado was the space; Lucas had sacrificed several tables, allowing customers and waiters to move around with relative ease. During the early evening the musicians and singers played to the diners while a few professional dancers perfected their skills across the stage. As bellies were filled and alcohol steadied the nerves, couples young and old descended on to the dance floor to demonstrate the most daring of tangos.

Lucas joined Gretchen at ten minutes to midnight. Franz acknowledged Lucas with a begrudged smile, made his excuses and walked across the dance floor and ascended the stairs to where Felipe Salazar and his entourage were sitting.

"I'll say one thing for Franz, he knows when he ain't wanted," he said with half a smile.

"Oh, that's unfair; Franz knew I wanted to get you on your own."

"You know something, I'm beginning to warm towards him," joked Lucas.

"Its two minutes to midnight, help me toast the New Year," said Gretchen as she handed him a glass of champagne.

Lucas took the glass and stared into those beautiful blue eyes and was lost. "To new beginnings," he said as their glasses chinked and the countdown to 1948 began.

They stared into each others eyes oblivious to everything and everyone around them, as brightly coloured balloons began cascading from the ceiling. Music played in the background blending with the noise from the crowd of excited revellers, yet Gretchen and Lucas felt like they were the only ones in the room.

"Happy New Year," he said softly as he leaned across and kissed her gently upon her lips.

It was only a brief moment but for Lucas it seemed as if a lifetime had passed before Gretchen released herself from his embrace. "Ein gluckliches neues Jahr!," she replied. Seconds later Franz with some showgirl on his arm reappeared and the moment was gone.

As the evening was beginning to draw to a close, Lucas asked Gretchen to dance. She declined, he insisted, she replied sheepishly she couldn't dance tango.

"I'll teach you."

Within a minute Gretchen was being held in a passionate embrace and Lucas was whispering instructions in her ear.

Felipe Salazar looked on with approval, Franz's eyes narrowed with contempt and Juan Aguilar's face was a dark mask of concealed lust.

Lucas wanted the evening to last forever, but it soon became obvious that the evening was about over. He was sure Gretchen felt the same, but protocol called for Franz to escort his sister back to the hotel suite where they were staying. Lucas called for their hats and coats; then slipping a card with the telephone number of Granero de Alvarado and the words, *call me after six thirty tomorrow evening* written on it, into Gretchen's mink.

Salazar had said his goodbyes half an hour earlier. Franz gave a smart click of his heels and thanked Lucas for a wonderful evening, then led Gretchen to the exit and their ride back to the hotel.

Lucas poured himself a drink, lit up a cigarette and contemplated the events of the evening. It was strange how two such nights could have the same affect on him.

It was New Year's Eve 1941, Mike and Ethan arrived at Ciro's; the happening place on the Strip. They were there at the invitation of Jake Reis, it was Mike's first time inside Ciro's, Ethan on the other hand had been there several times. Often he'd regaled Mike about the many celebrities he'd bumped against. "I tell yah, it's the in place. Anyone that's anyone frequents Ciro's; why only a month ago I was on the next table to Randolph Scott."

Jake Reis had instructed Kels to talk Mike out of enlisting. "Do what ever it takes. He ain't enlisting, understand!"

"I'll do what I can, but he's a stubborn son of bitch!" replied Ethan.

"Just do it!" barked Jake Reis.

Jake Reis knew only too well how stubborn Mike Burnett could be, it had taken Kels at the drugstore shootout to get him on board, but it had taken the Jewish gangster a heap of green to change the Sheriff's Department's statement and ballistics reports to clinch the deal. His investment had paid dividends since. Garrett and Kels dealt very professionally with the unsavoury removal job up in the Hollywood Hills, for which Jake had been paid handsomely. Having two Sheriff's Department detectives on his payroll was to become very useful in his later dealings. Highlighted a month or so later when he had them run interference whilst a hit went down. Ethan Kels was a stone cold killer, who seemed to relish in whatever was handed to him, while Garrett was yet to make that break through. Given time and circumstance he was sure his man would come across; that was until Mike showed an interest in doing his patriotic duty.

They'd been at war for less than a month and already Jake Reis had lost some useful contacts at City Hall. He was damned if he was going to lose anyone else.

In the foyer Ethan took off his hat and coat, grabbed Mike's and handed them to the cloakroom attendant. "Jake has lined us up with a couple of swell looking broads, they're joining us for dinner."

Mike smiled, for swell looking broads read, well paid hookers off the Strip. He was in a rare old mood, ready to be wined and dined in the swankiest of places, possibly rub shoulders with his hero Humphrey Bogart or maybe Clark Gable. After the shock of Pearl Harbour and his initial urge to kick butt in the Pacific, he'd seen a way out of Jake Reis's clutches. He'd made the mistake of confiding in Ethan Kels; big mistake doesn't cover it, Jake Reis wasn't best pleased. Since then he'd thought about the alternatives and decided to see just where this war was heading. Neither Ethan Kels or the threats from Jake Reis would stop him when the time was right.

He'd appeased Ethan telling him that he wasn't going to do anything rash or foolhardy. And there feeble attempts at influencing him were just laughable. He even chuckled to himself as they approached the mobster's table. It was located in a prime position close to the dance floor. Tables like that in Ciro's were worth their weight in gold. He looked around the select tables and swore Dorothy Lamour was two tables back from where he was about to sit. He wasn't suckered in the slightest way into thinking that an evening with Jake Reis and his cronies, drinking the finest champagne, dining on lobster and screwing the night away with some sensational broad was the be all and end all. He'd decided earlier that evening that he'd give it until the middle of the year and if he felt the same then he was going to join Uncle Sam.

Jake Reis stood up to greet Ethan and Mike, and introduced them to the party of ten. Jake's squeeze was Katherine, a good looking dame, but nearing her sell by date, then take your pick, Susie the blonde or Paula the auburn haired beauty, next to them was Jake's enforcer Marco Rossi and his wife Leona, and at the other side of the table Angelo Morelli a business associate from New York, and his wife Cristina.

"*The Counties finest!*" added Jake as he patted both men on the back.

It was around eight thirty when they started to eat, and the place was already buzzing. The best tunes burst forth from the band and their singer; a wiry thin faced guy surprised everyone with his powerful renditions of favourites old and new. As far as Mike was concerned it was turning into a surprisingly good evening. Susie as already stated was blonde; slightly buxom and fun loving, with a great sense of humour. He grinned, it could have been a whole lot worse, Ethan had gone for the looker, Paula with her auburn hair, dark smouldering eyes and a body to die for, unfortunately she never stopped talking. Marco, despite his reputation wise cracked throughout dinner, busting Ethan's chops on an occasion. For some reason he left Mike alone. Both men knew him slightly from previous dealings with Reis. Angelo tired of talking business was ready to celebrate, "*It's New Year's Eve for Christsake, America's finally at war, life sure as hell is gonna get interesting, let's party!*" It was the extent of his conversation as he tucked into a giant porterhouse. Copious amounts of champagne, steaks and lobsters later, Mike and Susie ventured onto the dance floor.

Mike liked to dance and Susie turned out to be a great dancer. Despite everything he was having the time of his life. They danced the rumba the Lindy hop and the fox trot, Ethan in a vain attempt to shut Paula up dragged her onto the floor. In a brief exchange with Mike he remarked jokingly, that when he got this broad to bed he was going to bury her head into the pillow and keep it there.

Mike glanced at the clock at the side of the room as the large hand slowly inched towards midnight. Between them they'd drunk vast amounts of wine and champagne and it was taking its toll, he so desperately needed a pee.

"*Five minutes, don't worry I'll be back before you know it.*"

"*But, but . . .*" stammered Susie.

"*It's that or I piss my pants!*" he exclaimed with a smile.

"Don't be long."

Quickly he escorted Susie back to the table, before racing off to the restroom. As he hurried through the foyer he happened to glance across to the hat check counter.

That's when he saw her . . . .

Chapter 12

It was a strange feeling, one that Lucas never expected to feel again. But there it was, she was so completely different in appearance from Erin, 'Wow,' he thought, it was the first time since her death that he'd been able to even think her name without feeling true sadness. Gretchen had re-awakened his inner feelings like nobody else. That her brother was a thug and maybe much worse couldn't detract from these feelings. Happiness had been snatched from him in a cruel manner, would it, could it be possible that this time he wouldn't fuck it up? Then the inevitable self doubt crept over him, did she feel the same way?

Lucas arrived at the club a little after 5.00 pm, his nerves jangled as he stared at the telephone in his office, willing it to ring. The minutes agonisingly ticked by slowly. By seven o'clock he was barking orders at everyone that he came in contact with, until Cipriano entered the office. Lucas looked up sharply about to send a tirade of abuse in his 'second in command's' direction, but the knowing look on Cipriano's face caused him to hold back.

"Someone to see you boss," he said.

Gretchen entered with a flourish, while the stocky bodyguard discreetly closed the door behind him. "I so hate telephone calls, they're so impersonal," she said.

Lucas rose from his chair and invited her to sit, all the time fighting to control his emotions. "It's so nice to see you," he managed to say without giving away his feelings.

"What was it you wanted to see me about," she said with a Teutonic air. Aloof wasn't quite the word he was searching for, but it came pretty close.

Now with composure fully restored, his American flair for coming straight to the point took over.

"Last night was magical; I thought dinner might be on the cards?"

Gretchen smiled, showing off perfectly white teeth, a good smile, a strong smile. "After one dance, you presume a lot," she countered. Then her eyes sparkled with that same air of mischief that she'd demonstrated the night before, "I'm starving!"

Over dinner at a restaurant in San Telmo they spoke about their hopes for the future, the latest dance craze, music, movies, sports, they even spoke of Peron, his radical reforms and inevitably his new wife Eva, or Evita as she was affectionately known. Neither spoke of their pasts, "too painful," said Gretchen, 'too dangerous' thought Lucas. They had begun to form a bond; they were bother exiles living in a foreign country. "Too the future, too hell with the past!" proposed Lucas.

"Prost!" echoed Gretchen.

They were slightly intoxicated by the magic of the evening and the balmy night air as they climbed into a cab. Lucas settled in the seat beside Gretchen and leaned across and kissed her softly, their lips barely touching, brushing, tantalisingly, tempting. It was all too much as Gretchen seizing the initiative hungrily pressed her lips firmly upon his lips, her tongue seeking his. They were locked into a passionate embrace as the taxi pulled away from the San Telmo district.

"What about Franz?" said a breathless Lucas outside the door to her hotel room.

"What about him?"

"Yeah what about him," echoed the big American as Gretchen turned the key and they exploded into the room. Animal like in their behaviour, they tore at each others clothes as they inched towards the large bed. Within seconds he'd pulled her knickers aside and entered her amidst a chorus of pleasurable moans and groans. Their lovemaking was fast and furious and over far sooner than they'd wished. Exhausted by their efforts they lay in each others arms and slept until near dawn. What followed was the complete opposite of the night before as they made love tenderly.

Sitting up in bed, a cigarette shared between them, Lucas casually asked, "Where is Franz?"

Gretchen took a draw on the cigarette, savouring the flavour as it went down before answering. "He's in Lobos on some business venture for Senor Salazar."

"What kind of business," he asked.

"The legitimate kind," she sat up and looked at him, slightly angrily. "I told you before, Franz was an industrialist; he's using his skills to advance Senor Salazar's business prospects."

"Wow! Steady on. I didn't mean to pry."

"You weren't prying, it's me; I've always been protective of my brother. I'm sorry."

Lucas laughed, "There's nothing to be sorry about." He grabbed her arm and pulled her down next to his warm inviting body.

It was early days reflected Lucas as he took a cab back to the latest hotel room he was staying in, 'pathetic' he thought angrily. Everything going for me, yet I live like a fugitive. The urge to put down roots was becoming impossible to ignore. What was it that had drawn him to Gretchen? She was young, nice looking, trim figure, great personality, but under it all she had a vulnerability that cried out for him to protect her.

It was the same vulnerability that had attracted him to Erin.

An argument had broken out with a burly looking man and a young cloakroom attendant. Mike had noticed her earlier when Ethan handed her the hats and coats, well to be exact, he'd noticed her bouncy fire red hair, he hadn't noticed her looks until he was bearing down on the guy, who was obviously a little worse for wear. She was cute looking, with delicate features and a small button nose. Vulnerability radiated from every pore. Mike was to find out later that the man had been hitting on her most of the evening. She'd been polite and laughed it off at first, but he'd come back for more. The girl was new, she was trying to impress; she needed the job so she tried putting him off with a few kind words. He'd taken it as encouragement and came back to try his luck a third time. This time he wouldn't take no for an answer. He slipped his hand across her breast. The inevitable happened, she slapped his face.

"You like to play rough, do yah," he cried angrily, He slapped her back and then grabbed a hold of her.

"Put the girl down and back away," said Mike.

"Butt out Bub!"

Reaching into his jacket pocket Mike pulled out his badge and flashed it. The guy stopped, gave a cursory look at the badge, "Like I said, butt out before you get hurt sonny boy."

Without another word Mike grabbed the man by the shoulder and spun him around to meet a left and a right to the jaw. The man didn't know what had hit him as he crashed to the floor. His night was over.

It all became too much for the girl, frightened of losing her job, embarrassed by the scene and shaken by the rough handling she'd received, she burst into tears.

Mike immediately reached into his trouser pocket and handed her a handkerchief. She took it, dabbed at her eyes and thanked him. He stared into those vivid green eyes and was lost. From the dance floor he could hear a rendition of Auld Lang Syne. It was 1942.

Mike never went back to claim that dance from Susie. Everything changed for him that night. The girl was still clearly upset, more about losing her job than the drunk that had abused her. Along with the management he assured the girl that her job would be safe and then he acted on impulse and retrieved his hat and coat. He took the girl by the arm. "I'm taking you home," then he addressed the night manager, "That okay with you?"

No one was going to argue, they'd seen what company he kept. "Hey get her coat will yah," he ordered.

The girl started to protest, "I don't want to go home!" It was clear she was still distraught.

"Okay, there's a 24 hour coffee shop around the corner. It's New Years, hopefully it's open," replied Mike.

The girl only nodded.

Still holding her arm he turned left at the next block. They were in luck, it was still open. From the look of it the proprietor was looking to close up. Mike flashed his badge, an inaudible grunt followed, but they were led reluctantly to the seating area. Sliding into a booth Mike ordered two coffees, "Make mine black," he added.

As he sipped his coffee, he began to question his reasoning. He could so easily have put her in a cab, slipped the driver the fare and returned to the party. But as he gazed at that face he realised he'd chose this option for purely selfish reasons. In the foyer he couldn't put a name to it, but sitting opposite the girl he now understood. She was the most amazing looking woman he'd seen in his entire life, he was smitten by those eyes and that mop of red hair, she was a knockout, but what made it all seem so odd, she didn't appear to know what affect she was having on him.

"You okay now?"

"Yes, I'm so sorry to have put you out. I'm okay, I'll grab a cab; and then you can go back to your party."

"What if I don't want to go back?"

"Why wouldn't you?"

"Perhaps I was sick of the company I was with, seeing a damsel in distress I saw my opportunity to make myself scarce!"

The girl smiled and his heart rate went through the ceiling. "Well Sir Knight, we haven't been properly introduced; I'm Erin, Erin Albright." She extended her hand across the table.

Mike reached across and took her small hand in his and shook it gently. "It's a pleasure; Erin, Erin Albright," Mike felt a warm glow deep inside, "Mike, Michael Burnett."

Despite the lateness of the hour, Mike and Erin continued talking aided by the never ending coffee pot. Erin was twenty two, from a small town near Minneapolis, and like a great many young hopefuls she couldn't resist the lure of Hollywood. "That was two years ago, I've grown up a lot since."

Mike didn't push it, "So for the best part of two years you've been working part time jobs, hoping that one day the big break was coming your way."

Erin laughed, "That's about the size of it. Working part time jobs, that is. As for the big break, that ain't ever gonna happen."

"You can't say that, beautiful girl like you, you're bound to make it," he said, knowing that it was a cheesy line.

"Mister!" she said angrily, "Two things you need to know about me, one, I ain't dumb, two, I don't give it away."

"Sorry Erin I didn't mean to go all cliché. That was not my intention."

Erin dropped the defensive pose, "Sorry Michael, it's this town. Everyone seems to be on the make. If it isn't sleazy agents, it's the producers; in fact it seems that every-one I meet that's mixed up in the movie industry wants to get into my pants."

Mike laughed, "You know the first thing I noticed about you was your vulnerability, how wrong can one guy be?"

"This town makes you impervious to vulnerability. I might come from a small town, but I came with my eyes open. I knew of the pit falls, I didn't expect to fall so quickly." Then she started to sob.

Mike got up and made to comfort her, but Erin recovered enough to tell him to remain seated. "I don't know why I'm telling you this, but I feel you have a right to know what happened."

"You don't have to tell me anything," replied Mike.

"I want too. My parents were killed in an automobile accident when I was nine and I was brought up by elderly grandparents. All things considered I had a balanced and good childhood, doted on by my Grandma and Pappy."

Mike couldn't help noticing the warmth of her smile at the mention of her grandparents. Followed moments later with a frown etched with sorrow.

"At seventeen Pappy passed, it was the worse moment of my life even worse than the death of my parents, It seems the older you get the more hurt you get. At nineteen Gran had to go into a nursing home and I was left to cope on my own."

"I'm sorry to hear that."

"Thank you Michael,"

"Hey kid, you don't have to continue," said Mike getting all paternal.

Erin smiled, "You know I haven't told this to anyone before."

"And you don't have to now." Somehow or other he didn't want her to break the illusion.

She wiped a single tear with the handkerchief he'd given her earlier, "I know I don't, but I want too."

"If that's what you want," said Mike.

"Hollywood seemed to be the answer to my prayers. I'd acted in high school plays and believed I had a natural talent, I could act, I could dance and I could sing too. I'd heard stories about casting couches, but I didn't believe it would happen to me. I intended to make sure it didn't happen."

Mike nodded his understanding.

"Arriving in Hollywood I rented rooms just off Hollywood and Vine, you see Pappy had put money away for my education, it was enough to get me started. Then I waitressed at Schwab's for a time, met some famous movie stars, and finally got taken on by a young dynamic agent. We started dating but I wouldn't give out. We'd been together around six weeks when he informs me that he's arranged for me to have a screen test at Paramount the following day. I was over the moon. We went out for dinner to celebrate; well you can guess what happened."

Mike knew only too well.

"The next morning the screen test was cancelled. He told me that happened in Hollywood all the time; that my chance was just around the corner. Like a fool I believed him. It wasn't until three weeks later

when I met up with a girl that I waitressed with at Schwab's that I learned the truth. He'd been playing me along."

"Shit happens!" exclaimed Mike. It was an all too familiar story.

"I decided then and there that movie stardom wasn't for the likes of me. Since then I've moved into a smaller apartment not far from my old apartment, but less rent, took on three jobs and I'm saving enough money including tips to put myself though college."

"But you've got the looks, you could still make it," protested Mike.

"I'm not saying I wouldn't like to be rich and famous, of course I would, but I'm not prepared to sell myself short to some sleaze bag. I've too much integrity."

Mike smiled at that, the girl was a realist.

"That's enough talking about me, tell me about Michael Burnett."

Mike wasn't one for talking about himself, but Erin was somehow different from almost everyone he'd ever known. "Wow! There's not much I can tell, you already know I'm a policeman, actually I'm a detective for the Sheriff's Department. Been on the force three years, first as a deputy then a year ago I was promoted to detective. That's about it."

"You ain't getting away with that, there's more to tell, where you were born, parents, brothers, sisters, high school. I want the whole deal, Michael Burnett." Erin wasn't taking prisoners.

"You want the works, okay I'll tell you all there is to know about Mike Burnett, but not tonight, it's late, hell it's nearly morning." There was a faint light coming up over the hills. "How about having dinner with me this Saturday?"

No sooner had he asked her out, his heart stopped beating, at least it felt like that as he waited for her answer.

"I couldn't, I don't want you to get the idea I don't want too, its just . . ."

"Just you don't want to be making the same mistakes."

"Yeah, that's about it."

"What if I said I'd be on my best behaviour?"

Mike caught the hesitation in her eyes, he gave her his best puppy dog look.

"How could I refuse."

Chapter 13

Things were looking up for Lucas, Granero de Alvarado was booming, his insurance business, *as he liked to think of it,* as *extortion was such a dirty word,* was now in the hands of Cipriano and running smoothly. Salazar was getting his cut and a healthy bonus each month.

On the personal side he was seeing Gretchen openly, much *he suspected* to the chagrin of her brother Franz, *'hey you can't have everything'.* She'd taken an apartment in the Recoleta District of the city to be close to Lucas and her business commitments, working part of her time on the welfare reforms that the new government was implementing. Already a reasonably wealth woman, thanks in part to Franz's wise investments in the Argentinean economy, she told Lucas she wanted to give back a little to the country that had adopted her.

For appearance sake Lucas rented an apartment in the same city block. With his commitments to the club and other activates along with Gretchen's work load, it seemed the best utilisation of the time they could spend together.

Since New Year's Eve when he'd taught Gretchen the basic steps of the tango, she'd developed a passion for it. Late night romantic meals, a dance or two to get them well and truly in the mood, then the best sex he'd had in a long time. Lola was mind blowing but Gretchen was like reaching into his past. The difference between them was so palpable, with Lola it was pure unadulterated lust, nothing more, but with Gretchen there was something else. He would lie in her arms and feel at peace, much as he'd done with Erin in another life. He was blissfully happy for the first time in years, yet he remained unsettled, fearful for the future. He'd had everything once before, and he'd seen it snatched from his grasp.

Firstly there was the itch he couldn't scratch, it had been six months since the cinema shooting; but he was no closer to finding out who'd tried to kill him? Number one on his list was still Ramon Perez, the words of Cipriano echoed loudly, "You kill one brother you'd better be prepared to kill the other." The Los Angeles connection now seemed remotely doubtful; knowing Ethan Kels the way he did, he'd expected another attempt within the week. Of course there was the possibility that the shooting wasn't a case of mistaken identity, in which case he'd murdered Julio for nothing; it was just as well that Lucas didn't believe in coincidence. Which left only Perez, or did it? Something didn't add up.

A sudden thought zipped though his brain, and a trap door opened sending his heart plummeting into the depths of despair. Why had it taken so long for him to remember? Lola! It was pillow talk, nothing more, but he'd mentioned his obsession with Bogart movies to her.

The thought just wouldn't go away. How ever he tried reasoning it out, the thought just wouldn't go away. The best case scenario he could come up with was that Lola had used the money he'd given her to hire two hit men. A woman scorned and all that goes with it. If that was the case, he could no longer justify killing Julio in cold blood. It was even possible the Perez brothers, searching for a weakness in Lucas's armour, sought out Lola and paid her for any snippet of information she had about him. Lucas liked that scenario a whole lot better. It might be nothing to do with Lola, but until he'd confronted her face to face he couldn't be certain.

Lucas pounded on Lola's door, despite telling her to use the money wisely and move away he thought she'd just slip back into her old ways. The door opened and an angry unshaven man in a grubby vest and grey pants stood framed in the doorway.

"What the fuck!" he exclaimed but stopped from issuing anymore profanities as he weighed up the man stood in front of him.

"I need to see Lola?" said Garrett. The look on his face told the burly unshaven man not to mess with him.

"There's no one of that name living here senor."

Lucas pushed passed him and was confronted by a woman in her early thirties defiantly shielding four young children. He stopped in his tracks and looked straight into the woman's eyes. She reminded him of a lioness about to protect her cubs.

"Lola Santos, she lives here, right?"

"No, no one of that name has lived here in the past eight months. Ahora salir la mierda de mi casa!"

Lucas didn't argue. It appeared she'd left within a week of him leaving. Perhaps Lola had taken his advice after all, he reflected. As he turned away he was reminded of how far he'd sunk and how quickly he'd risen. The place looked even more squalid than when he'd used it as a base. There was no way he would ever admit to calling it home.

The pounding on the door and the ensuing raised voices had brought a few neighbours to their respective doors. Some nodded others turned and closed their doors but just as he had begun his descent of the concrete stairs, Enrique Suarez who lived opposite Lola's home called him over. "Lola Santo, you wish to find her no?"

Lucas hurried across.

"For this you are willing to pay?"

The big American grabbed him roughly and slammed him hard against the wall. "Yes, God damn you, but you'd better not be wasting my time!"

Suarez struggled to get his breath back, "A week after you left, two men came for her."

"What did they look like, did you know them?"

"No senor, they were both tall. That is all I know."

The Perez brothers, thought Lucas. He reached into his pocket and handed Suarez a few pesos.

"Thank you senor," cried Suarez, surprised by Lucas's generosity. "One more thing senor, it might be nothing, they were dressed like you."

"What!"

"Suits, senor, they were, how you say, dressed well."

Again Lucas thought about Ramon and Julio, they were both sharp dressers. "Thanks Enrique."

So he was right, The Perez brothers had done their homework, much as he'd done his, but why hadn't Ramon made his move after his brother's death? Lucas was tired of always looking over his shoulder. The move to the apartment in the Recoleta district prompted his decision, it was time to force Ramon's hand, it was long over due. Granero de Alvarado was now almost 100 percent legitimate all that remained was for Ramon Perez to be shown the door.

When Lucas killed Julio he'd crossed the line. He'd killed before but in the line of duty and only in self defence. Since the drug store shooting he'd sailed close to the wind but had always fought shy of actual killing. Three times he'd stood by while Ethan had taken lives. Sullied by Ethan's disregard for human life, Mike Burnett had always believed there was still a feint trace of passion left within him, but now in the guise of Lucas Garrett he was no better than Ethan Kels. He was Lucas Garrett; murderer.

Knowing in his heart the Perez brothers were behind the cinema shooting eased his conscience only slightly. He'd killed to save his own hide and mentally he was preparing to kill again for the very same reason. Hopefully the death of Ramon Perez would be the end to it. In his heart of hearts he could see that as a possibility.

His mentor, Felipe Salazar, brutal murderer of Humberto Vargas and God knows how many others, was close to complete legitimacy. His life's ambition had been to restore his grandfather's Estancia back to its former glory. Lucas had learned from Cipriano Mercado that Salazar was almost there. 'Why not me,' thought Lucas, in his dreams he was living with Gretchen, happily married with two kids and a future as a well respected owner of one of the premier night clubs in Buenos Aires, free from all criminality. But firstly there was Ramon Perez to deal with.

Happiness, contentment, a future, he'd come close, so very close . . . .

Dinner with Erin was a revelation; she was a bright articulate young woman. Gone was the timid cloakroom attendant, in her place was a vibrant fiery redhead with the most amazing green eyes he'd ever seen in his life. How she couldn't make it as an actress was beyond Mike Burnett. She had such a bubbling personality; Hollywood must be blind not to see her talents. Mike said as much over dinner at The Polo Lounge of the Beverley Hills Hotel.

Erin laughed, and made it quite clear that it was a road travelled only once.

"You see Mike; I believe this life is one great adventure. You start down one road and you meet a dead end. What do you do?"

Mike smiled, he'd thought much the same when he was her age, "What would I do, I'd look at that road block and I'd find a way to get around it."

"But suppose that was full of pitfalls and debris?"

"If I wanted something badly enough I'd find a way." he said triumphantly.

"Ah," Erin said, "That's my point, I wanted to be an actress, a film star to be precise, but did I want it badly enough? I looked at those pitfalls, those sleazy directors, actors, agents and producers and thought; I am not prepared to sell myself short for a dream, for a dream that I'm not sure I ever wanted."

'Wow,' thought Mike, this woman's attitude to life certainly takes some beating. "So what is it you want now that the road is blocked?" he asked.

"Easy, I take the next road and if that works out okay, if it doesn't there's a great big world out there."

By the end of their date, Mike Burnett Detective 1st class was completely smitten. With his heart in his mouth he asked her if she'd go out with him again. She smiled coyly, and Mike expected her to give him the brush off.

"I'd like that, I'd like that a lot," was her answer.

For the next month or so Mike Burnett and Erin Albright, whenever time and the Sheriff's Department permitted, did the rounds of all LA's top restaurants. On a night at the Melody Room Erin offered to go Dutch. Mike refused.

"I can afford it." He looked put out by the offer, and Erin thought she'd hurt his pride.

"I'm sorry I just thought it was about time I paid my share, I meant no offence by it." She looked at him with those wide open eyes and smiled.

"Until you came along, I hoarded my money, I didn't go out much" it wasn't a good lie, but it sufficed.

"I just thought on a policeman's salary . . . ." he stopped her there, leaned across the table and kissed her gently upon the lips.

Erin wasn't the only one to question his spending. "That dame must be costing you a fortune," remarked Ethan one night when they were on their way to investigate a possible homicide. "She must be quite something."

"She is, she's bright, she's funny, she has a great personality and she's the most gorgeous woman I've ever met."

Ethan slammed on the brakes of the sedan they were driving in, and brought it to the kerb side, his face a look of incredulity. "Hell, I knew it. I just knew it!" he exclaimed.

Mike looked slightly embarrassed by Ethan's outburst. Then it came out in a rush. "I tell you Ethan, she's everything I could wish for."

"This broad, she must be stacked in all the right places?"

Mike looked affronted, "Don't talk about her like that!" he cried.

The laughter faded from Ethan's face and realisation took its place. "You haven't, have you?" It was more a statement than a question.

Mike's silence spoke volumes.

Then Ethan's face exploded into a beaming smile. He reached across the front seat and grabbed his partner by the shoulder and gave it a squeeze. "*Well good on you buddy. If you've found someone in this town that commands that kind of respect, then good on you.*"

Mike was slightly taken aback by Ethan's show of affection. This man was his partner in crime, a man capable of cold blooded murder. A man with no scruples, yet here he was showing emotions Mike never thought he had.

"*You'll have to meet her; we're having dinner at Ciro's next Friday night. You're welcome to join us,*" then Mike added, "*with a date of course.*"

"*Sure thing, I'll bring Susie. You remember Susie?*"

How could he forget, he'd promised her a dance and he'd left her high and dry. "*Ain't that a little awkward,*" replied Mike, wishing he hadn't extended the invitation.

"*Nah, she'll be fine with it. Once I explain the circumstances,*" said Ethan.

From the moment Ethan saw Erin for the first time, he understood why Mike was head over heels in love with her. She was everything Mike had said she was and more. Susie, his escort, not shabby by half, made up the handsome party of four. True to his word, Susie smiled an acknowledgement in Mike's direction and began chatting happily with Erin.

"*You weren't kidding when you said how gorgeous she was, man I take my hat off to you.*"

"*Thanks, Susie looks the Cat's Meow. What she's doing with you?*"

Ethan laughed, 'Burnett's right, Susie does look the Cat's Meow, but this Erin's Ritzy.' "*With broads like these, champagne's the only tipple,*" said Ethan as he snapped his fingers.

Minutes later the band started up, it wasn't the resident musicians, it was a speciality band from South America, or as Ethan put it, a group of Latinos from East LA. They along with a troupe of dancers were touring the West Coast; their speciality was an exhibition of dancing the tango, Argentine style.

"*They look like cheap hoods,*" commented Ethan as the dancers strutted and twisted to the Latin beat. "*And the dames could be hookers off the Strip.*"

"Be quiet Ethan, they're supposed to look like that. Just watch, you might learn something," said Susie.

Mike and Erin were mesmerised by the music and the sultry moves of the dancers. Mike squeezed her hand under the table and smiled at her childlike enthusiasm. "We must learn how to do it," she said under her breath. The moves were sensual and erotic, like no other dance that they'd seen.

"I've seen the tango before, but not performed like this, it's like on another level."

After their meal, both couples got up to dance, along with several celebrities that had been seduced by the exhibition of dancing. Ethan gave it up after a few minutes much to Susie's disappointment. But Mike and Erin persevered. While no where near as polished as the professionals Erin seemed to pick it up real well. Mike, no slouch at dancing, fell a little short but with encouragement he was beginning to get the moves. Of course the darkened dance floor concealed most of their mistakes. As the sultry music reached its climax Mike kissed Erin far more passionately than he'd ever done before. He could only blame the sensuousness of the dance. Like a gentleman he apologised as they walked back to the table.

"Nonsense," replied Erin, "I liked it."

Ethan and Susie had retired to the bar so they were left alone at the table. No words were exchanged as they gazed into each others eyes. It was turning into the most romantic of nights. 'A night for couples, not a foursome', thought Mike as he cursed himself for inviting Ethan along. He and Susie were good company but the evening had progressed further than they'd both imagined.

With his heart in his mouth he just about managed, "Would you like to go somewhere else?"

Erin smiled and he was lost, "I'd like to go just about anywhere with you."

They stood up from the table as one; Mike threw a handful of banknotes on the table. "That should about cover it." Erin giggled as they stealthily made there way out of the club.

Chapter 14

During his time at Alvarado's, Lucas had gone from cannon fodder *as most of his crew believed him to be,* to an extremely tough overseer of Granero de Alvarado. It was a little over a year since he'd taken over, but the difference at the club was incredible. Alvarado's had been the home of many undesirables, fights broke out quite frequently and Lucas was forced to deal with them, which he did efficiently and with as least fuss as possible, thus earning himself the respect of those around him.

It was during those early days that Lucas, ever watchful for trouble, spotted a strangely familiar figure as he glanced down from the first floor balcony. The man judging by his demeanour was a little drunk but doing no harm. Lucas wracked his brain to recall, but before he could identify him, the man got drawn into an argument with some mean looking guys from the barrio. It looked to be a mismatch as the guy was clearly drunk and not in any condition to fight, which was evident when one burly looking guy pushed him backwards into the arms of his friends. They held him while the man began to pound on him. Lucas was about to swing into action, when suddenly the drunk miraculously fought back, breaking free and smashing a fist into the side of the jaw of his assailant. For a moment he managed to get the upper hand, spinning around and placing a kick to the right knee of another, sending him off balance. For the briefest of seconds it looked like the three men thought better of continuing, but then like a pack of wolves they moved in for the kill. Lucas rushed to the head of the stairs, but stopped when two of his doormen stepped in and separated the opposing parties. As was the club's policy, the three young guys were quickly thrown out. A wry smile on the drunk's face alerted Lucas to his identity. It was Rodrigo Vasquez the guy he met in Montevideo. Lucas quickly descended the stairs but by then his doormen had showed Vasquez the rear door.

Suspecting the three men would probably be waiting outside Lucas quickly raced after him. He was surprised to find the street empty, but then he heard a commotion coming from an alley at the corner of the narrow street. Vasquez was cornered by the three men. Lucas weighed up the situation; Vasquez was nothing to him, just another thug, but the ex policeman inside of him felt that he had to react. That they intended serious harm there was no doubt, knives had been drawn and this fight was going to end badly unless Lucas could put an end to it. He shouted at the men to stop, but to no avail, their blood was up. One turned towards him, his knife brandished menacingly. Without hesitation Lucas pulled out his automatic and shot the man in the hand sending the knife spinning into the air. The shot resonated loud and clear and the fight soon went out of the other men.

Within seconds the alley emptied and Lucas stood staring at the man from Montevideo. Rodrigo in that devil may care manner that Lucas recognised from the cantina, smiled, nodded to Lucas, "Gracias, nice to see you again amigo." Then he made to walk away.

"Hey wait up," said Lucas.

Vasquez smiled thinly, "I wasn't here."

"What do you mean, you wasn't here?"

"Senor Garrett, I've been here on a little business, personal business, I would appreciate your discretion." Then he was gone into the night.

Aside from the club, *which was the jewel in the crown,* he'd earned the respect of his men by being hands on when needed. The shooting never happened. Granero de Alvarado was under the protection of Felipe Salazar's brother Ruben which meant unless someone was killed outright the club and its employees had full immunity. Lucas had shown that he wasn't afraid to get his hands dirty, and if anyone opposed him or stepped out of line he was quick to deal with them. Lucas was earning Felipe Salazar's respect.

His meteoric rise had given Lucas ideas; big ideas. But Ramon Perez was the one fly in the ointment. Again, Cipriano's words came back to haunt him, "kill one brother, you'd better be prepared to kill the other." He needed advice, not just about Ramon, but his future ideas for the club, but who to ask? Despite his new found respect, there wasn't anyone he could share his fears and ideas with. Juan Aquilar was no friend, he'd made that clear, Cipriano, possible, but he was just the hired help. There was no one. Except . . . .

Why he thought of Rodrigo Vasquez he couldn't figure, it was just a feeling. But as Lucas knew, feelings aside, reading people wrongly could get you killed. The man owed him. And then there was the little matter of why Vasquez was in Buenos Aires on a little personal business. Still puzzled by Rodrigo's appearance at Alvarado's he decided a visit to Montevideo sometime in the very near future was on the cards.

Two days later he walked into Rodrigo Vasquez's lair.

"Gringo, you have some balls," was his welcoming greeting. "What brings you to my humble abode?"

"I think you owe me," said Lucas cautiously.

"You must be mistaken; I think I would know if I was in your debt."

"Okay," replied Lucas, doing his best to read something into the dark eyes that seemed to bore a hole straight through him. "Then it is I who owes you. I would like an audience with Rodrigo Vasquez. One to one; comprender!"

Vasquez looked at him darkly, then dismissed his men and invited Lucas to sit with him in a corner of the room. "What is it you want?"

Lucas stared back, thought about what he was about to say then calmly replied, "Don't take this the wrong way. I don't know why you were in Buenos Aires and I don't want to know, but I suspect you don't want Salazar to know either."

Rodrigo's features hardened as he recognised the veiled threat. "I could have you killed, you agree."

"But you wont, because you know I'm not daft enough to come here without good reason," replied Lucas. "Allow me to lay my cards on the table. You're aware of my position within Salazar's organisation."

"Si."

"I'm riding high, but I'm not a fool. My position could come crashing down on me quicker than shit! I don't trust anyone in Salazar's organisation; there my friend is the problem. I need a friend, to be precise an advisor I can trust."

"What makes you think you can trust me," said Vasquez cautiously.

"Firstly, I don't know if I can trust you, but I suspect you don't have any loyalties to Salazar. Secondly, my problem isn't with Salazar, so I'm not speaking out of turn. What I'm looking for is advice, and I can't get it from Salazar's crew."

"I think I understand, what is it you require of me?"

I've got two problems, firstly Ramon Perez. You've heard of him?"

"Who hasn't!"

"Can I negotiate with him?"

"Not a chance. He'll kill you first chance he gets. You said two problems?"

"Ah, the second one is a little more complex."

During the course of their conversation, Lucas outlined his plans for the future of Granero de Alvarado and subsequent other businesses. He confided in Vasquez his desire to be free of all criminal activity within five years, and his burning desire to be free of Salazar.

"It's a good plan, if it works, then yes I could see you free of criminal activities, if it doesn't, you won't have to worry about being free. As for Felipe Salazar I can't help you on that one."

"Oh but you can . . . ."

For an hour they talked, but not once did Rodrigo divulge the reason he was in Buenos Aires. Lucas let it lay.

"One piece of advice, if any of our conversation gets out; Ramon Perez will be the least of your worries." He fixed Lucas with a steely gaze, smiled crookedly then held out his hand. Lucas grasped in and shook it in mutual understanding.

"Goodbye my friend," said Rodrigo as they parted company at the ferry terminal.

Now secure in his exalted position Lucas called a meeting with Ramon Perez. It was more to assess Perez's reaction from being evicted from Granero de Alvarado than anything else.

"That's the deal. Granero de Alvarado is going places, celebrities home grown and otherwise are frequenting the place. Don't get me wrong I know that some of these types have a use for your merchandise; but not in my place."

Ramon's eyes grew darker as he listened to Lucas's words. Inside he was a raging inferno, but he knew it was prudent to keep his temper under control. The American had grown stronger over the past year, a year when he Ramon Perez had taken his eye off the ball. Garrett had bigger balls than he'd given him credit for. Someone had killed his brother but until now he hadn't known who.

"I understand where you're coming from Garrett, but this club is a big earner for me."

Lucas looked him straight in the eye, watching for any reaction as he delivered the sweetener.

"I appreciate that and I am going to give you control of protection, that should compensate for your loss of earnings."

Cipriano, who was also in the meeting flinched, then looked at Garrett incredulously, but kept his protestations to himself. Protection for him had been a good earner, he should have been consulted, but he'd learned over the last year that Lucas always had an angle. It rankled with him big time, but he would wait to hear Lucas's reasons after the meeting.

Ramon though taken aback by Lucas Garrett's generosity, caught the look in Cipriano's eyes, and stored it for future use. Then he nodded his approval.

Lucas added, "Senor Salazar has been apprised of my decision and has given me his backing." It was more to let Perez know this offer wasn't negotiable. "Of course you are free to dine at Granero de Alvarado whenever you wish; gratis of course."

"Agreed," replied a seething Ramon Perez.

Lucas rose to his feet, Ramon did likewise, and Garrett extended his hand. Perez ignored it.

"Then this meeting is at a close," said the American coldly. He'd sown the seeds, now all they needed was a little watering.

In his years as a cop, and his dealings with men like Jake Reis he'd learned to judge people's reactions and to always be at least two steps ahead. Living on his wits had kept him alive; so far. He didn't intend to slip up now. He motioned for Cipriano to join him. Then he offered him the seat that Ramon had been sitting on five minutes earlier, turning his back he reached into the drinks cabinet, brought out two glasses and a bottle of bourbon. As he poured the liquor into the glasses he began. "I owe you an explanation, and an apology of sorts."

Cipriano looked puzzled as he took the offered glass and took a small sip.

"Firstly I want to make it clear; you my friend will not suffer any loss of earnings. As you're aware I want this club to be run legitimately for a number of reasons; one, it's a goldmine and I don't want to rock the boat, now or in the future. I need, we need," he corrected himself, "a legitimate source of income. The club provides that. We're making enough money from our other sidelines, to make up for any shortfall."

Cipriano took another sip, nodded and was about to say something but Lucas wasn't finished. "You might wonder how we can afford to lose our insurance business. We don't!"

A glint appeared in Cipriano's eye.

"Which brings me to why I've been so generous to Perez, he sees it as a weakness. More importantly he sees me as a weakness in the organisation. That's why I never told you of my plans; he saw the shocked look you gave when I announced my intentions."

Cipriano started to protest.

"Its okay I wanted that reaction. I've studied Ramon since the day he came to me after his brother's death, he blames me, he believes I'm responsible."

"How can you know this?" questioned Mercado. "You had no reason."

"I know that, you know it too. Let's just say I have reliable information that leads me to believe he's about to put the hit on me . . . ." Lucas, let his words hang, there was no way he was going to divulge anymore of the facts.

'Why now?' thought Lucas, 'It didn't add up.'

Lucas shook off his self doubt. "Sooner rather than later he was going to have me killed, I've just given him the when, and hopefully the how."

Cipriano looked puzzled.

"You once told me there was no love lost between you and the Perez brothers."

"Si"

"So, if I've done my homework correctly, I've nothing to fear when Ramon Perez approaches you with a deal."

"What deal? What are you talkin' about?"

"Ramon Perez is going to contact you and offer you a deal. I saw it in his eyes. You see his nature won't allow him to ignore an opportunity, you're that opportunity."

The penny finally dropped. "Because I'm unhappy about the deal you'd cut with him."

"Exactly! When he does contact you, you're to act surprised and suspicious. You'll agree to meet him somewhere neutral and alone, except you won't be alone, I'll be with you."

"What then?"

"We take him out."

Lucas tried convincing himself that it was just a case of kill or be killed, but it wouldn't wash. He'd come a long way since he was Mike Burnett rookie cop. Looking back with the benefit of hindsight he'd have changed many things, but he'd deviated from the path. He'd convinced himself that he was a cut above Jake Reis and even Ethan Kels, sure he was a cop on the take, a cop that did favours, a cop that looked the other way, a dirty cop, yeah but not a low down murdering bastard. But that had all changed, since shooting Julio Perez dead in his home. Now he was planning the destruction of yet another life. He was becoming another Jake Reis.

He tried convinced himself that this would be the end of the killing, that one day in the not to distant future he'd be that legitimate nightclub owner, that husband, that father.

It had looked to be heading that way in the summer of 1942 until an unfortunate series of events nearly caused Mike to enlist: A Japanese submarine surfaced off of the coast of Santa Barbara, fired a number of shells at a refinery: the infamous Battle of Los Angeles ensued, whereby a false alarm possibly triggered by war nerves caused a barrage of anti-aircraft fire to darken the night skies of LA. It didn't amount to much but within weeks the distasteful executive orders given by Roosevelt resulting in the internment of people of Japanese origin took effect. It wasn't until the Battle of Midway that the people on the West Coast had anything to cheer about.

If it hadn't been for Erin, Mike would have enlisted despite any threats from Jake Reis. Erin understood his frustrations, but as the daily papers reported on the casualties of war she was fearful for his welfare.

"If you feel you must, I won't stand in your way." Tears began to form, "To be honest, I don't want you to go. I want you to stay here with me. I couldn't bear it if you were wounded or killed."

"I don't want to go either, but I feel it's my duty, I'll be letting my country down."

"To hell with the country, I don't want you to leave me. I love you so much."

It was the first time Erin had mentioned the word love. It hit Mike like a ton of bricks.

"What did you say?"

"I said, I love you," the words came out in a tremor.

"I love you too."

Mike convinced himself over the next few days that he was already serving his country. Being paid a retainer by Jake Reis didn't exclude him from keeping law and order, there were other low-life to harass, to throw in jail, to stop from robbing and killing. He was still there to protect and serve. Jake Reis even threw a few arrests his way. "Culling the competition," Jake Reis laughingly called it. All in all, the money was good, and since Erin had declared her love for him, he was looking to build for the future. But what kind of a future, the world was in turmoil. Any thoughts of a real or normal life seemed light-years away. Albeit their slice of life remained relatively untouched, they were young; life for everyone was becoming more uncertain as the war escalated. They lived the highlife, well to be honest Mike had become addicted to the highlife and it was he who wanted to share it with Erin. But he knew she wanted a settled home, she wanted a house by the sea. She once said. "I'd love to wake up every morning to hear the gentle pounding of the surf as it hits the shore."

Mike wanted to give her that, he wanted to give her the world, but even he knew that a house by the ocean was years away. In the meantime he rented a luxury apartment on the seventeenth floor of a swish apartment block, looking out towards the ocean, so what that it was five miles away.

With hindsight Mike Burnett realised that was the biggest mistake of his life. Foolishly he'd gone to Jake Reis cap in hand. The LA mobster said, "Leave it with me, I'll see what I can do."

Two weeks later Mike was handed the keys to the luxury apartment. His rent paid for the first six months, "Call it a house warming present," said Reis glibly.

Even Ethan raised his eyebrows when Mike told him of Jake Reis generosity. "You realise you owe him big time."

"Yeah I guess I do," replied Mike. "But believe me I've more important things on my mind."

"Such as?" asked Kels.

"Telling Erin that we're moving for one," he replied.

"She'll love it."

"That I don't doubt, but she'll want to know how I can afford it."

"Listen to me, Erin is a doll, but I'm sure there's a brain behind those pretty green eyes. You work for the Sheriff's Department, you're on a detective's salary, but you wine and dine in the swankiest places in town. Get real."

"So what you're saying is I should come clean?"

"Not exactly, embellish the truth a little."

Embellishing the truth nearly cost him his relationship with Erin. Sure she loved the apartment, why wouldn't she. It was to die for. Then halfway through looking over the apartment, the inevitable, "How can we afford it?"

What followed was a stand up row and Mike Burnett learned how fiery a redhead could be. "I thought you were an honest cop! I thought you had integrity, getting involved with gangsters. I don't know you at all Mike Burnett!"

Erin lashed out at him pounding her small hands against his chest. He grabbed hold of her slim wrists and desperately tried to calm her.

"Okay, I'll quit the department, we'll go back East, I'll get a job with another police force."

Erin wrenched herself from his grip, "You don't get it, do yah. I'm from Hicksville, you're from the big city, you'd think it was the other *way around." Anger made her nostrils flair and her red hair fell across her eyes, and Mike Burnett knew he was close to losing the only woman he would ever love.*

Then the fire slowly receded from those eyes as she continued, "Don't you see, this . . . this Reis guy, he's he's got his claws into you. He won't let you go so easily."

In that moment he loved her more than at any time in their relationship, he reached out for her and took her in his arms, "I don't want to lose you; I love you too much for that."

And it that moment all the fight went out of Erin, "I love you too, you dumb ox."

She looked up at Mike and her lips parted, he lowered his neck and gently brushed his lips against hers, moments later he swept her up into his arms and carried her into the master bedroom.

After their lovemaking they lay in each others arms, the fires of love and lust still simmering beneath the surface, and discussed the implications of Mike's predicament. "We look the other way on an occasion, we feed him information of a bust, we run interference for him, nothing more. We're cops for Christ-sake, there's a line that even Jake Reis wouldn't cross." Mike left out many of the unsavoury favours he and Kels did for Reis. "Things are no different now than they've ever been, its just fringe benefits."

Erin slightly reluctant at first slowly began to accept the situation. A night out three weeks later at the Los Angeles premier of Casablanca with all the glitz and glamour, a meal mingling with top celebrities and a fabulous cabaret that followed, smoothed out any remaining wrinkles.

"You know what Erin; I'd love to be like Bogart, lording it at Rick's Place. Be the owner of a night club, mixing on an even keel with celebrities, politicians, and the like. It's just a dream, but one day when this war is over, I'd love to open a bar, something exclusive, with a touch of class. Top singers, great bands, a dance floor full of patrons dancing to the latest tunes. And each night we'd take to the floor, we'd dance the Lindy Hop, the Fox Trot, the Rumba and of course the Tango."

"Argentine style," added Erin, joining in with his pipe dream.

Lucas was going over the stock with his bar manager when Cipriano Mercado walked in. "I need a word." He didn't have to say anything else. Lucas quickly finished with his bar manager and walked past Cipriano. "My office."

Shutting the door behind him Mercado looked across the desk at Lucas, a look of awe spread across his ample face. "I wouldn't have believed it if I hadn't heard it with my own ears. I received a call from Ramon Perez offering me a job in his organisation. He said as I knew the business we should talk. I didn't have to act shocked, I was shocked. I couldn't believe it."

"You arranged a meet?"

"Just as you said boss."

"When?" enquired Lucas.

"Tonight, nine o'clock."

Chapter 15

At eight o'clock Lucas and Cipriano made their way into the back office of Granero de Alvarado, both men making a point of being noticed. Once inside the office Lucas locked the door. He pulled out the 45 automatic from the back of his waistband and checked it was in working order. Neither man spoke. Lucas glanced at the clock on the wall, it was five minutes after eight; it was time they were going. They took the back exit, which Lucas locked after them. In the darkness they walked ten yards down the road and climbed into a four door sedan.

Lucas could smell his own sweat as Cipriano gunned the car into life. It was the second time he'd gone out with the intention of killing a man, it wasn't a good feeling. he wished there was another way. It was a cool moonlit night yet both men were sweating profusely. Lucas wondered whether Cipriano had the same feelings. Steeling himself for the ordeal he went over the plan in his head. The plan was simple, Ramon had phoned and suggested one meeting place, Cipriano responded with another.

"Cipriano my friend, don't you trust me?"

"As much as you trust me," replied Cipriano.

"It's in both our interests," insisted Ramon.

"You asked me to meet you, why can't you tell me what it's about over the damn phone," continued Cipriano.

"It's delicate," was all Ramon would say, "You win, I'll meet you at the place of your choice."

"No, I'll meet you where you said."

Ramon laughed, "I thought you didn't trust me?"

"I don't, but as you said, we don't hold any grudges, but let me assure you, I'll be coming armed."

"I wouldn't expect it any other way," responded Ramon, "I'll also be packing heat. But I assure you this meeting is in both our interests."

"I'm intrigued," said Cipriano dryly.

"We'll meet a couple of miles out of the city on the road to Salazar's Estancia. You know that flat area of ground just a hundred yards from the old derelict gas station."

"I know it," replied Cipriano.

It was originally cleared to build a rival gas station and truck stop but planning was abandoned. It was a perfect meeting point, just off the road. No trees, no bushes, no buildings, just a flat area that stretched as far as the eye could see.

On the drive Cipriano asked Lucas why he'd ordered him to agree to Ramon's meeting place.

"He doesn't trust anyone, nor should you, by agreeing to meet at his chosen place, you've throw him off guard. And besides, it's me he wants dead. You're tight with Salazar, Ramon would not risk any upset."

It was a logic that Cipriano didn't quite understand, but the gringo had been right about most things.

A mile from the rendezvous, Lucas ordered Cipriano to stop the car. Then the big American wound down all the windows of the vehicle before climbing into the rear and crouched down. Just as they were reaching their destination, Lucas cracked open the rear passenger side door very slightly. Seconds later Cipriano drove in, telling Lucas that Ramon's car was already there. Beads of sweat were forming on Cipriano's brow as he pulled to a halt parallel to Ramon's car with thirty feet between them.

Lucas was now stretched out on the back seat of the sedan, his 45 Colt automatic, cocked and ready, his feet now edging towards the open rear door. He wanted to hear Ramon, even now on the eleventh hour he wasn't sure; something didn't sit right. He wanted confirmation that he'd been right all along. Cipriano switched off the engine and slowly climbed out of the sedan. Perez did the same. The eerie silence added to the tension between them, you could hear a pin drop

Ramon was the first to break that silence, "Let's take this nice and easy," he said nervously. Then he began to walk slowly towards Mercado.

"Tha . . . that's far enough!" cried Cipriano. There was a little more than fifteen feet between them. "Say what you've got to say."

"Alright, I'll lay my cards on the table. The gringo pig has stolen what should be mine! He treats you no better than a peasant. You deserve better, I deserve better. Who does he think he is, offering me the protection business, without even consulting you? The man has no respect. I saw the way he treated you, he treated you like a dog! I'm prepared to offer you respect and much more." The speech was designed to get at Cipriano's masculine pride.

Cipriano looked suitably angry, as he spat upon the ground. "You brought me out here to offer me a job, you could have come up to me in the club and done that," he replied, cool as you like. Lucas had to admire his second in command's acting ability.

Ramon laughed nervously, "You have a sense of humour, I like that."

"Enough of the preamble, spill."

"It's simple. I plan to kill Lucas Garrett; I need you to set him up for me."

"I suspected as much," replied Cipriano.

"That club's mine by rights. Help me rid the world of the gringo and I'll give you back the protection business. Granero de Alvarado and the American's other assets are mine, understood."

Sweat stung at Lucas's eyes, he'd heard almost all he needed to hear. He edged himself further through the rear door, praying their voices would conceal any movement.

"How do I know you'll keep you word?" asked Cipriano, warming to the conversation.

"You don't, but you have one thing going for you that my men don't possess. You're sanctioned by Senor Felipe Salazar."

"That is true," cried Cipriano. "Ah ha, I see where you're coming from," he added.

Lucas continued to inch his way further out the door. Crouching low he moved to the rear of the sedan. Risking a look, Lucas saw that both men had moved closer to each other. Cipriano was six or seven feet from Ramon but Lucas was all of thirty feet from the kill zone. He couldn't risk a shot until he was much closer He gauged that he could get ten feet, maybe fifteen before the man would react.

"If I agree, how do you propose we do it?

Lucas steeled himself, his hand gripped the automatic tightly, he hoped Cipriano was ready. His plan was to move once Ramon started to outline his plan, hoping to catch him off guard.

"You won't regret it," said Ramon.

Taking a deep breath, Lucas spun around the car and advanced quickly towards Ramon and Cipriano.

Everything happened so fast.

"What the fuck . . ." Ramon twisted in his direction and froze as he stared down the barrel of Lucas's automatic, his 38 still in his waistband. His eyes flashed defiantly as he looked back at Cipriano. "You fuc . . ."

His words were unintelligible as Cipriano moved at lightning speed. All Lucas could see was a glint of a blade as it sliced at Ramon's exposed throat. For a millisecond there was nothing until a thin dark line appeared on his neck followed immediately by violent arterial spray from his open throat. He staggered towards Lucas choking on his own blood.

Lucas shocked by the turn of events stepped back as the man clutched at his throat. It wasn't as he'd imagined, it was pitiful to watch as Ramon desperately tried to stem the tide. Then he fell to his knees and within minutes he was dead.

Cipriano wiped his blade on the dead man's jacket. Then Lucas watched mesmerised as he systematically undid the man's belt and trousers. He then pulled Ramon's briefs and trousers down below his knees. "What the fuck . . . ." Lucas let his words trail off.

Even in death there was to be no dignity, thought Lucas as he stared at the man that had threatened to do much worse.

"Let's go," he said.

Both men got back in the sedan and drove in silence back to Buenos Aires. Parking the car in the same place they unlocked the back door to Granero de Alvarado and stepped inside the office. Immediately Lucas grabbed a bottle of scotch and two glasses he sloshed more than a generous amount of liquor into both glasses and handed one to Cipriano.

It was over, thought Lucas. A feeling of relief wafted over him, he was free of his nemesis. His only regret was he hadn't been able to ask Ramon why he'd waited so long for a second attempt. It didn't matter; it was over. It was midnight, another day had begun. In a few short hours someone would find Ramon's body. There would be a brief investigation. Questions would be asked, but realistically no one in the police department would give a rat's ass about a lowlife like Ramon Perez. Fancy clothes, handmade shoes and silk shirts couldn't conceal that Perez was a cheap thug that got caught with his pants down.

Lucas was reminded of an incident back in early December 1942, where he so very nearly ended up like Ramon Perez.

He and Ethan were almost coming off shift when a call came in of shots being fired, in one of the local projects. Ethan was for ignoring it, but Mike still had a sense of duty. "Best we handle it than some one else coming at it cold."

Ethan didn't follow his logic, just shrugged his shoulders, "Oh brother, step on it."

When they arrived there was an all night party still going on. "Let me handle it," said Mike.

"Your call," replied Kels.

Both men climbed out of their car, Mike walked up the short concrete path and rapped on the door.

Ethan in the meantime walked to the rear of the car and opened the trunk. He was no risk taker when it came to gang bangers; he reached inside and took out an Ithaca 10 gauge, which he held nonchalantly at his side.

From where Ethan was he could see clearly the front door slowly opening.

"Sorry to break up the party guys," cried Mike showing his badge. "We've a report of shots being fired."

The dude was Hispanic, slightly worse for wear from all night partying, shook his head innocently and tried shutting the door.

"Oh shit!" cried Ethan, he knew what his partner would do next. The door flew open and Mike stepped inside. The moment he did he wished he hadn't. He was confronted by four men and three women all high on drink and drugs. Strewn across the room were empty bottles of booze, the inevitable syringe and traces of cocaine littered a table. One man had a 38 calibre Smith and Wesson stuffed in his waistband; another was reaching behind him for a 45 Colt.

Mike started to back out, about now wishing he'd left the call to the early shift. Too late he was caught from behind and a stiletto held to his throat. It was as quick as that. For one heart stopping moment he thought he was a goner. The man was strong, some 260 pounds of pure muscle and he held Mike in a vice like neck lock.

"He's a cop!" exclaimed one of the men.

"Shoot the fucker!" cried another.

"Pluck his fucking eye out!" said the third.

"There's another pig outside!" cried one of the women. "Where the fuck's he gone," she shouted.

Mike acted instinctively. He slammed his foot down hard on the man's instep and at the same time slammed his elbow into the man's side. The Ithaca boomed once and the man with the 38 in his waistband slammed against the wall. The second shotgun blast nearly took the leg off the guy holding the knife. The room was filled with smoke and body-parts.

"Freeze, or join your friend!"

Mike clearly shaken by events pulled his revolver and suddenly the fight went out of the party.

"Do that a-fucking-gain you're on your own!" spat Ethan as he eyed Mike angrily.

It was then that Mike realised he'd been cut. The man holding the stiletto had sliced open his cheek.

Erin raced to the hospital to find Mike sitting in ER with a bandage around the lower part of his face. "I came as quick as I could," your face, your poor face," she cried.

"He won't be that handsome son-of-a-bitch any more," laughed Ethan. "Best you swap him for someone like me," he added.

"Handsome or not handsome, he's my man, I don't need anyone else," she said defensively.

Mike took hold of one of her tiny hands and through the bandages managed to say, "Leave off Ethan. If it wasn't for him, you'd be visiting me in the morgue."

A week later and he was back on duty. Most of the bandages had been remove, though the stitches were still in place. It was nearing Christmas when the stitches were finally removed. Mike looked at himself in the mirror and admired the gang-banger's artistry; he was left with a reddish zig-zag scar that stretched from his left ear to the corner of his mouth.

"The redness will fade over time," said Erin reassuringly.

It was coming up to New Year's when Erin said, "I've been thinking, we should hold a party in Ethan's honour. If it hadn't have been for him you wouldn't be with me now."

Erin had thought long and hard over it, she hadn't taken to Ethan from the word go, and to make matters worse she'd laid into him at the hospital. Despite everything he was Mike's partner and the man had clearly saved his life. She was slowly beginning to think she'd misjudged him after all. This could be her way of thanking him.

"Listen doll, Ethan might have saved my life, but we ain't what you'd call life long buddies."

"That's pretty mean of you, but don't get me wrong, I understand where you're coming from."

"You think you do," replied Mike.

"Well, we're having a party, Ethan's honour or not," said Erin forcefully.

"Putting it that way, how can I refuse," said Mike with a wry smile upon his face.

The New Years Eve party was a mishmash made up of a couple of Mike's high school friends, several colleagues and their wives from the Sheriff's Department, the guest of honour, his date Susie and some friends from the bar across the street. Erin had left nothing to chance she hired caterers who set out a selection of hor's d'oeuvres, canapés, cheese puffs, and a magnificent centre spread sea food buffet. Mike, the genial host poured the Martini's, the Manhattan's, the whiskey sours, the champagne cocktails and the inevitable gin fizz. The background music of Billie Holiday, Glen Miller and Sinatra issued forth from Erin's new gramophone.

The guest of honour was toasted; Mike rather reluctantly did a speech; John one of Mike's high school buddies recited anecdotes about school days; another continuously cracked jokes. Susie ever the party girl got everyone up to dance. She did a great Lindy Hop with Mike and Ethan's immediate superior, Homer. Erin oblivious to the cacophony was content to smooch the night away with Mike.

Ethan went through the motions but deep down, deep within him a monster stirred. Had he misread the signs? Why else would Erin throw a party in his honour? Yet she'd virtually ignored him, content to drape her arms around his partner. He'd saved Mike's life, hell he'd brought him into the fold. Without his help the two of them would have been scratching out a living and would probably be housed in some rundown housing project. He told himself he wasn't jealous, he had Susie; he had a partner that he could rely on; a friend that would back him whatever way the chips might fall; hell we make a great team. But it was no use, *the more he drank the more he was convinced that Erin was too good for his partner, she needed a real man.*

As the countdown began Ethan edged closer to Erin. In his drunken state he intended being the first person she was going to kiss as the clock struck twelve. 'I'll show her what a real kiss feels like.'

"Five, four, three, two, one . . . Happy New Year!"

Ethan made his move, "Happy New Year Erin," and then he grabbed hold of her and kissed her fully upon the lips.

Erin shocked by this turn of events excepted gracefully, "Happy New Year to you too," then quickly almost too quickly she swept into Mike's arms, "Happy New Year, sweetheart," she whispered as her tongue went in search of his.

Ethan turned and found himself in Susie's arms, "Easy tiger, she's already taken. Happy New Year!" Ethan looked into Susie's eyes, his own now slightly glazed, "It was nothing doll, just thanking her for a swell party."

"Yeah, sure you were," replied Susie dryly.

By two o'clock Mike and Erin finally closed the door. "That went well," stated Mike.

"Yes it did," she agreed, but that kiss from Ethan troubled her. She'd been shocked at first, expecting Mike to have claimed the first kiss, but the more she thought about it, the more she was convinced that Ethan had a thing for her. It wasn't something she'd encouraged or wanted; she hoped it had been just a drunken miscalculation.

A week later she realised it was a little more than a drunken outburst. Mike was at the automobile shop getting their car fixed when Erin received a knock at the door.

Opening the door she was surprised to see the smiling face of Ethan Kels. "Mike's not here at the moment," she said nervously.

"I know. That's why I called. We need to talk."

It was the little boy lost look that caused her to drop her guard, she let him in the apartment.

"It's about that kiss," he began. "I've thought about nothing else since that moment."

"Ethan, it was nothing, it meant nothing more than a celebration of the new year."

"No, I know it meant more than that. You feel the same way I do," there was desperation in his voice.

"Stop it!" said Erin," stop it right there. I love Mike, you mean nothing to me! You're a sweet guy, but that's where it ends." Ethan's face twisted in anguish, he wanted to grab hold of her and show her how he felt, but his instincts kicked in. 'She doesn't want me now, but one day she will. It was enough to console him for the time being. One day it won't be like this. His thoughts were in turmoil.

"Please forgive me; it's just that you're the most beautiful woman I've ever seen. I thought . . . Hell I don't know what I thought!"

"We'll say no more about it. No harm done."

"This stays with us Mike doesn't need to know?"

"It didn't happen," replied Erin to reassure him. "You're a good looking man Ethan, a great catch for someone. Susie's a lovely lady."

"She's a broad, she ain't like you! You got class lady, real class."

Chapter 16

Though badly shaken by the events of the last few days, Lucas realised that with Ramon out of the picture he could be more creative and adventurous. Granero de Alvarado was reaching heights he'd only dreamed of. To think only a couple of years ago he'd arrived in Buenos Aires with little more than the shirt on his back.

Peron was riding high, his wife now fast becoming a national icon and for Senor Felipe Salazar there was the completion of his dream. It was the perfect time to seek an audience with the Argentine mobster. Dress it up any other way from Lucas Garrett's perspective, Salazar was still nothing but a cheap hood.

Lucas, now driving a two year old Oldsmobile, took Gretchen with him when he received the invitation for tea on the lawns of Estancia Salazar. To others it might have appeared that Felipe Salazar had gone soft but Lucas knew otherwise, the scene in the barn was as vivid today as it was back then. Salazar had completed a lifetime's ambition; with the restoration of the Estancia Salazar to its former glory. He'd, with help from his brother, severed all ties with the criminal underworld, on the surface that is. He was a well respected Argentine landowner, a pillar of the community, a major donor to the many charities that Eva Peron had become patron of. It was to him that Lucas came, cap in hand.

They were shown onto the magnificent manicured lawns where Felipe Salazar *dressed in an off white linen suit; pale blue shirt and silk tie,* sat with his wife of twenty years. He stood up to greet Lucas and Gretchen as they were escorted to the table. A cursory shaking of hands was followed by formal greetings before they sat down and waited while tea was served.

"Such a civilised way to do business, don't you think?" said Salazar. "One of the few English traditions I find appealing." He sipped at his tea. "Well Lucas what is it that has brought you here?"

"Granero de Alvarado, Senor Salazar." Lucas always remembered the protocol. Life had taught him manners opened many doors. "You've shown faith in what I've accomplished, and now I come to you with another request."

Felipe Salazar shifted his seated position. "Go on," he said warily.

Lucas smiled, "I want to expand."

"Surely the place is big enough."

"You misunderstand me. We have a brand, Granero de Alvarado. I wish to open another Granero de Alvarado near Casa Rosada, 'The Pink House.' The world has gone through a devastating period in its history, people are tired of war, they want, no crave entertainment, and cities like ours should lead. I'm proposing opening another venue."

"Wouldn't that take business away; wouldn't they be in direct competition?"

"True, that's a possibility in the short term, but if we don't someone else will."

Salazar mulled it over, "I think I see where you're coming from."

"Buenos Aires is big enough to accommodate more than just us. But if we expand now, rather than wait for others, we'll take the prime locations."

Felipe was warming to Lucas's idea, "I can guess what you want from me."

"Pardon my assumption, but you'd be wrong. A little capital perhaps, but what I want is someone to go guarantor on a bank loan; someone to short cut planning applications; in essence your influence with your brother and the current government."

Salazar laughed, "You don't want much!"

"You once told me, that you had a dream of one day bringing Estancia Salazar back to its former glory. Well you did it." Lucas then made a show of admiring the house and grounds. "I want the same, but in a modest way, you see I want to own Granero de Alvarado outright. By going guarantor on the new club and possible subsequent clubs, I'll have enough money to buy the Barn from you."

"Supposing I agree, why would I sell you it?"

"We would have a contract drawn up, whereas you would sell me Granero de Alvarado at market price, once the second and who knows; successive clubs have shown a profit equal to Granero de Alvarado. I in turn will sell you the new clubs."

Salazar looked amused, then slightly puzzled, "Why would you sell out, when you can make more money with these future clubs."

Lucas smiled and squeezed Gretchen's hand. "Because I'm not greedy and I value your goodwill."

Salazar nodded at the compliment.

"Owning more than one club would interfere with my other plans. You see I never thought to feel this way." He looked into Gretchen's eyes and smiled, "I've asked Gretchen to be my wife. And she's done me the honour and said yes."

Felipe Salazar sat back in his chair, his eyes lit up and a grin formed upon his face. He motioned for the table to be cleared, "Champagne, this announcement calls for champagne." As the waiter began clearing the table, the Argentine landowner turned serious. "If I agree to these terms I'm risking a large part of my wealth and reputation."

"Senor Salazar, with all due respect, business is always a risk, but I fear I would be risking far more than money."

Felipe laughed, "Of that you can be certain."

The champagne arrived at a most timely part of the proceedings. "Do we have a deal?" asked Lucas.

"I'll put it in the hands of my lawyers; leave your plans with me. They'll need to go over everything. If they say it's a sound investment, we have a deal in principal.

Lucas had proposed to Gretchen three days after the murder of Ramon Perez. He'd never expected to feel so wretched, he'd sunk far lower than he'd have ever believed possible, but the threat from the Perez brothers was now gone. It was over, he could look for new beginnings, he wanted out of the murky and dark world of organised crime.

In those three days before he'd proposed he began thinking about the expansion plans he'd kept at the back of his mind. It made sense if he could get Felipe Salazar's backing. He was sure he'd be able to turn at least one of the numerous rundown nineteenth century brick warehouses of the old port of Buenos Aires into another Granero de Alvarado. A bonus he hadn't foreseen suddenly became crystal clear. With Salazar's backing, he would no longer need to watch his back, for everything to succeed Salazar needed to keep him healthy.

That night he and Gretchen dined at Huerto's. It was a candlelit dinner with moonlight shining thought the small window adjacent to their table. It was the most romantic of settings for what he had in mind. As they ate he discussed his plans with Gretchen, she listened intently as he explained with great enthusiasm his ideas for a Garrett/Salazar empire. Then to conclude his plans, he got down on one knee, *something he'd failed to do with Erin* and proposed.

"If I accept, when will you have time for us to make babies?"

She hadn't said no, his heart raced. He smiled, "I've thought of that, within two years, three at the latest, I intend off loading them in exchange for complete ownership of the original Granero de Alvarado. We'll have plenty of time to make babies."

"Then my answer is yes."

More good news was to follow, Salazar's lawyers turned up with a contract and Lucas gave it to his lawyers to peruse. A few days later Salazar and Lucas signed the contracts. An old warehouse large enough to accommodate all Lucas's needs miraculously became available two streets from Casa Rosada. Lucas applied for a mortgage and took out secured loans, all were approved without fuss. The brick warehouse was purchased and building work began. Gretchen was busy preparing for the wedding. The date had been provisionally booked for late May, the autumn leaves against a backdrop of blue skies, a fitting accompaniment to the radiance of his bride. Life for Lucas was as close to perfect as was humanly possible.

Life for Lucas was perfect once before, the only difference was that this time he'd crossed the line and reaped the rewards.

Erin and Mike were blissfully happy, the D-Day landings had taken place and the allies expected an end to the war in the not too distant future. Since the party he and Erin had grown even closer together and Erin now shared Mike's reservations about Ethan Kels. They still went out as a foursome now and again, but since Susie had dumped Ethan their meetings had been less frequent. She hadn't told Mike of Ethan's visit, nor the fact he'd hit on her on at least three occasions in the past year. Each time he'd been rebuffed, and each time he'd taken the rebuff like a gentleman, showering her with compliments. Erin accepted the compliments at first but as time went on they became a little wearing. She threatened to tell Mike after the last time and he hadn't tried it on since. He'd made it quite clear it wasn't a quick fumble or a roll in the hay that he wanted, he needed her in the best possible way. 'Quite cute really, in a slightly unsettling way' thought Erin. In the end she decided to leave sleeping dogs lie. There was no harm done.

Mike was saving hard to get the money for a deposit on a house and enjoyed the increase in kick backs that Ethan had negotiated on their behalf.

"The increase is welcome; I've almost enough to put down a deposit on that house I've seen," Mike said gratefully.

"You've had it easy so far. One day Jake's gonna make you earn every penny you've took," spat Ethan.

"He's earned plenty out of us. I've looked the other way more times than I can remember."

"One day you'll get your hands real dirty," said Ethan.

"I've done most things, but I draw the line at killing. I ain't going to the gas chamber for Jake Reis."

"You're as dirty as me, you might not have done the killings but you've been there. If Jake says jump, you'll jump."

It was a conversation they had at least once a month, usually after they'd performed some service or other for the LA mobster.

1944 slowly merged into 1945. With the news that the allies were advancing on Germany, Mike began thinking about what would happen after the war was over. The men that were lucky enough to survive would be looking to come back. Things would change, they had too. With luck he'd be able to free himself from Kels and Jake Reis.

It was nine thirty in the evening; Mike was at home with Erin drinking Martini's, whilst snuggling up on the sofa listening to Bing Crosby on the radio. They were relaxed, and in the mood for love, when the phone rang.

"Leave it," purred Erin.

Mike smiled, leaned up and kissed her martini tasting lips, what the hell he thought, Erin's right.

The phone continued to ring, somehow breaking the mood. "I'd better answer it," Mike said reluctantly. "Don't change that pose," he joked, "I'll be right back."

"Hello," he said into the telephone.

"It's me, Ethan. Don't hang up!" There was urgency in his voice. "Listen to me, this is the big one, you want that deposit, I can practically guarantee the whole fucking house."

"Forget it! I ain't doing it," whispered Mike.

"Nah, it ain't that, it's a clearance job. A big one!" he insisted.

"Still ain't interested, see you in the morning."

"Don't' hang up! Don't you fucking hang up on me!" There was panic in Ethan's voice that stopped him from hanging up. "We're it, there's no one else. It's a two man job, Jake needs it done and pronto.

He's paying top dollar, enough my friend to buy that pad and leave you with change."

He looked across to Erin and the sofa and could see the moment was gone. He shrugged his shoulders, "Just go," said Erin.

"Give me five minutes, I'll meet you downstairs," replied Mike Burnett.

They drove in silence up into the Hollywood Hills, turning onto Cahuenga Boulevard then they turned towards Mulholland and Mike had a déjà' vu moment. When they turned left ten minutes later, he shook his head in dismay.

"If this is what I think it is, I want no part." In Mike's book once was an accident, twice was murder.

"You don't understand, this guy is head of the studios, he's a fucking bigwig producer. He's that important to the industry the fucking governor of the state would look the other way."

"I don't give a fuck who he is, I ain't doing it."

"Mike, you don't go ahead with this, Jake Reis will have your cojones! You'll be a dead man by tomorrow night."

"Stop the car, I need time to think!"

"We ain't got time!"

"Stop the fucking car!"

Ethan brought the car to a grinding halt. "You've got a minute."

Mike's life rushed before him. If he ran his life wouldn't be worth a plugged nickel. All his plans, the house by the beach, the wedding proposal, and Erin, always Erin, they'd all go up in smoke. If he came clean, he'd spend time in the slammer, and Jake Reis would find a way to get at him. On the other hand, if he went through with it he'd have the leverage with Reis, he'd have the house, he'd have Erin. This could be his swansong.

"Okay, you win."

They drove slowly until they reached the gated drive. Mike couldn't help noticing that nothing had changed since he'd been there last. The gates opened at a flash of the car's headlights. Ethan drove around the circular drive and parked adjacent to the two large oak doors. He turned the engine off and the lights out. They both stepped into the vast hallway. "Best you wait here until I call," instructed Kels.

Mike Burnett nodded and watched as Ethan walked confidently up the great oak staircase. He lit a cigarette and waited. Staring about him he could only find contempt and disgust at the opulent surroundings. 'These people, these scum thought they were above the law; they suck the life blood out of some innocent then dispose of them like yesterdays trash'. He felt dirty; then he felt the presence of someone staring down at him from the staircase. His eyes were drawn to the oak balustrade that circled the great hallway. It was then that he saw him, he was there one second and gone the next, but there was no mistaking who he'd just seen. It was Tristan Pierce better known as Rex Blaze, one time matinee idol and now cowboy superstar.

'What the fuck was he doing here,' thought Mike. Before he could answer his own thoughts, Ethan appeared at the top of the staircase, carrying a bundle in his arms. Mike strained to hear the conversation but it was too muffled for him to make head or tail of it. The words, disappear; never; traced; were about the only words he could make out.

"Open the trunk," ordered Ethan as he descended the stairs, "Then start the car." Mike now on auto pilot walked out through those huge double doors and climbed inside the car. He turned the ignition. "Open the fucking trunk," shouted Ethan angrily. Mike jumped out and did as he was bid. Seconds later both men climbed back into the car. "Drive!" screeched Ethan.

Neither man spoke until they'd driven through the wrought iron gates, "Make a left and keep driving," said Ethan aggressively.

Mike said nothing until they came to a stop sign. "Which way," he growled.

"Head towards Glendale," said a subdued Ethan.

"Glendale!"

"You heard," replied his partner.

Once they reached Glendale, Mike asked, "Where now?"

"Keep driving."

Mike looked at his watch, it was fast approaching one in the morning. Ten minutes later they were the only traffic left on the road.

The road ahead was pitch black as they headed for the San Gabriel Mountains. They drove for another twenty miles, then Ethan ordered Mike to pull off the road. The car tyres crunched and bumped as they drove across the desert floor. They had driven off the road and continued in a straight line for about three hundred yards when Ethan called a halt.

"*This should be far enough.*"

Both men got out, sweat streaming from every pore.

"*Jesus, fuck Ethan! What the fuck have you got us into?*"

Ethan Kels ignored the question and walked to the rear of the car and opened the trunk. He reached in and brought out two shovels. "We dig!"

Twenty minutes later they'd managed a three foot deep hole. "That should do it." stated Kels. Grim faced he turned and walked back to the car and reached into the trunk. Without saying a word, he carried the bundle and gently laid the body of a young girl into the makeshift grave.

"*Holy fuck!*" *exclaimed Mike, as he shone his torch into the grave.* "*She can't be more than twelve years old.*" *Without thinking he climbed into the grave, and shone the torch up and down both arms. Finding no needle tracks he did the same with her legs and feet. He then gave her face and neck a cursory look, and was certain there were ligature marks around her neck.*

"*Fuck, fuck, fuck.*" *He looked up at Ethan,* "*This ain't the usual drug overdose; this kid's been murdered.*"

"*Overdose, murdered, what's the difference, she's dead ain't she!*"

Mike stopped himself from hitting Ethan with the shovel, instead he shone the torch over her undergarments, the blood and traces of semen confirmed what he already suspected.

"*Those bastards raped and killed her!*"

"*Look Mike, I feel as bad as you, I didn't sign up for anything like this, but the facts are the facts. She's dead, and we're burying the evidence. We get caught; those bastards have enough money and power to bury us both.*"

"*It ain't right, those bastards need to pay.*"

"That maybe so, but in the meantime, we'd best cover her over, then get the hell outta here."

Ten minutes later they were back on the highway heading for Los Angeles. Neither man spoke, Mike was feeling wretched, his life up until that night had been pretty much all he'd ever wanted it to be, with the exception of a few distasteful jobs he and Ethan had handled for Jake Reis, but this changed everything. How could he look Erin in the eye after what he'd just covered up? He was truly ashamed.

Ethan had similar thoughts, it was the worst night of his life. Sure he'd killed people; he'd covered up for prominent members of society, he'd gone against every code in the book, but he shared his partner's outrage, they'd been used in the worst possible way. Yet there was one fundamental difference between him and Mike Burnett. He was a survivor, he'd been put in a horrific situation and he only saw one way of getting out of it. Unlike Mike Burnett, ashamed took back seat to surviving.

Chapter 17

Lucas was well on his way to being a wealthy businessman, something he'd never contemplated when he first arrived. Back then he was a man with vengeance eating away at his soul. He couldn't go back; he'd wanted so much to avenge the death of Erin, to right the wrongs that people with power wielded on others less fortunate. It was impossible and Lucas turned all the hatred, the hurt, the vengeance in on himself. Mike Burnett re-invented himself as Lucas Garrett, he was like them, cold, hard, cruel and without remorse.

Yet in becoming like them, he'd risen to dizzy heights, heights that in his wildest dreams he'd never have imagined. And from those heights he'd seen a way out. Senor Felipe Salazar, despite his proclivities for violence had against all odds become a pillar of the community. More importantly he'd seen in Lucas the same entrepreneurial spirit and nurtured it. He'd given him the chance of a new life. Salazar had opened doors that would, under normal circumstances, have remained closed.

His rage, his brutality in dealing with Lola's pimp, had brought him to the attention of Felipe Salazar. But it had taken the botched attempt on his life to push him over the line. Killing Julio in cold blood; less than twenty four hours after the cinema shooting, was when he finally crossed over. Subconsciously the act of murder had given him a confidence he'd never fully attained before. He was one of them, as ruthless and as dangerous as anyone. His confidence grew with every decision he made. After that it had been relatively simple to plan the murder of Ramon. 'Was that all it took,' he asked himself, he'd taken charge and two men were dead because of him and now he'd reaped the rewards. There was a time when the deaths of two men would have caused him more than a little anguish. Was it written in the stars, was he always destined for this kind of life? He couldn't help thinking that if only he'd reached this moment in time sooner, perhaps the tragic events *just a few days prior to the overall victory in Europe*, might never have happened.

Mike Burnett called in sick the morning following the trip to the desert, claiming a stomach bug. Erin knew there was something up. Mike had climbed into bed around four, she'd woken and asked him where he'd been. It was the only time he'd ever snapped at her. He apologized almost instantly, but when she asked him what was wrong he said he didn't want to talk about it. That it was something to do with Jake Reis, she was sure. He'd done favours before, but he'd never reacted like this.

Throughout the next couple of days he could hardly look at her, he was frightened she'd be able to read his thoughts. She was everything he'd ever wanted, if she knew what he and Ethan had done she'd leave him, of that he was pretty sure. But the guilt kept gnawing at him.

Two days later Mike returned to duty, he'd explained his moodiness as fatigue, but he wasn't sure Erin was buying it. The problem was he couldn't get over that night, but Ethan was right, Hunter Northrup and Rex Blaze would bury them, and if they didn't, Jake Reis would.

"I've thought of nothing else since that night, exposing them would only get us locked up or worse," he told Ethan when they were driving down Sunset Boulevard.

"You got that right!" replied his relieved partner.

"I tell you Ethan, this don't sit right with me, those mother fuckers have to pay. They need rubbing out, that fat fuck Northrup and that son of a bitch Rex Blaze!"

"You're joking of course," said Ethan.

"Who said I was joking," replied Mike.

Ethan brought the car to a halt. "Are you crazy? If you're thinking what I think you're thinking; forget about it! Do you know the kind of heat you'd bring down on us?"

"I can't think about that, those fuckers don't deserve to breathe the same air as decent people. You don't have to be a part of it; I'm doing this for me."

"Oh sweet Jesus! We've got a good thing going, don't fuck it up. At least sleep on it."

"I've done nothing but sleep upon it."

Ethan had never seen Mike Burnett so worked up and determined, "Look, don't do anything half-cocked. Let me think on it awhile."

"You got until the weekend."

It was Friday night in Malone's Bar. The talk was all about the imminent defeat of Germany. The papers were full of it. Everyone could talk of nothing else except the two off duty cops in the far booth.

"I can't look at Erin without feeling dirty, that's why it has to happen."

"Okay, I can't talk you out of it, but we've got to make it look like an accident or something," said Ethan.

It was six o'clock and to anyone concerned both men were having a couple of drinks in Malone's bar and shooting the breeze, which wasn't unusual, Mike and Ethan often stopped by after work. The problem, as far as Ethan could tell was the large bourbons Mike had been drinking. Since that fateful night he'd stopped off and sunk more than his share. It was early days but already a couple of guys from the squad had taken an interest. "Nothing to worry about," assured Ethan, "slight friction on the home front. Leave him be, it'll sort itself out in time."

That time was soon, Mike had already consumed three shots of bourbon and was going for his fourth as they spoke.

"Mike cool it will yah. I'm here to hear you out. If I don't like what I hear I'm out."

"I understand, but I think you'll like what I have to say. Rex Blaze since breaking up with his second wife, lives alone in a small mansion just off Laurel Canyon, he's working on a new western for Northrup

Studios, his work schedule puts him home around nine o'clock. His housekeeper leaves around eight. There are no elaborate security systems to take care of, why would there be, the man is loved and idolized by millions," added Mike sarcastically.

"Wow! You've really done your homework."

Mike gulped down his bourbon and called for another. "We leave the car a couple of blocks from his house. Then around nine thirty we walk up to his door and knock. We flash our badges, and use some pretext, there's a prowler in the area, something like that. Once we've gained entry we overpower him.

"What if he fights back, he's a big fella," said Ethan.

"I've thought of that, we use a blackjack. One of us distracts him, while the other hits him across the back of the head."

"Then what, I thought you said we'd make it look like an accident."

"Suicide, not accident," replied Mike. He's an avid gun collector. While he's unconscious we put him in a chair, take out one of his favourite guns, preferable a large calibre, stick it in his left hand.

"Why left hand?" asked Ethan.

"Ain't you seen his movies, he's left handed. Then we cock the hammer open his mouth, bingo!. No trace of him being sapped, with half his fucking head blown off!"

"You've really thought this thing through," said Ethan, "But aren't you forgetting something. The sound of a gunshot will most probably alert the neighbours."

"A series of shots maybe, but a single shot, could be a car backfiring. It's unlikely anyone will take notice, but two men hurrying away from the scene would certainly draw attention. That's where we keep our nerve. We stay inside the house and wait for any reaction; I doubt there will be any. An hour later one of us leaves, twenty minutes later the other follows."

"What about Hunter Northrup?" asked Ethan.

"A month, maybe two, he's gonna be a little put out without his leading man."

For the next ten minutes they mulled over the plan. Ethan asked question after question. "If we're doing this, we're doing it right."

Eventually the finer points were worked out and both men were satisfied Mike finished up his drink then stood up and looked at his watch; it was close to seven o'clock. He reached for his wallet.

"I'll get that," said Ethan, "You get home to Erin. Once this weekend's over, you'll find everything will come good."

"Let's hope so," said Mike, "but as soon as it is, I'm out."

"We'll talk about it," said Ethan.

"See you tomorrow."

"Can't wait," replied Ethan.

Ethan Kels watched from the bar's window as Mike Burnett climbed into his car and drove away. Seconds later he was out of the booth and heading for the pay phone near the restrooms. Nervously he fed the machine and dialled.

"He's just left me, seven o three. He should be at his apartment by seven thirty on the nail."

Mike Burnett fortified by booze pulled into the underground garage. He knew he'd been a heel, Erin deserved better. Well after tomorrow things are going to change. According to Ethan he had a fat bundle heading his way from Jake Reis. He grinned to himself as he thought about telling Jake Reis that he'd need to find another boy to graft for him.

He entered the lobby and waited for the elevator. It was then that he realised he was reeling; he'd already attracted the attention of a couple of people. It was time to sober up; Erin deserved better. He fumbled in his pocket for his keys and promptly dropped them.

Another disapproving glance, this time from the elevator operator.

'Fuck em,' thought Burnett 'another two weeks and we'll be outta here.'

Mike stepped inside and directed the operator to the seventeenth floor.

'Shit, I should have brought Erin flowers.'

Too late, the elevator stopped at his floor. He stepped out just as two men walked past the elevator heading towards the fire escape.

"Evening," said Mike.

The men ignored his greeting and just kept on walking.

"Suit yourself," said a disgruntled Mike Burnett.

It wasn't something he could pinpoint but a strange feeling took hold of him as he drew closer to his apartment door. Those men had looked out of place. Something wasn't right. He quickened his step.

"Holy fuck," he cried. His apartment door was wide open. He raced inside; the place looked like it had been in a train wreck.

"Erin," he cried panic stricken. Then he caught sight of the balcony curtains wafting in the breeze, he ran towards the balcony. The sound of sirens hit him fully in the face. "Erin! Oh God no!" he cried. Steeling himself he edged towards the balcony and looked down to the pavement seventeen floors below, just as a patrolman shone his torch across a broken body. The scream stuck in his throat, "Oh no, oh no! Please God, it's someone else," he sobbed, and at that precise moment the light from the torch exposed her vibrant fire red hair. His heart sank. Even from that distance he was staring at the unmistakable body of Erin. He screamed her name over and over again.

His first reaction was to race downstairs, but as he looked around their apartment, he realised it was a set up. Everything seemed to come at once. The open balcony windows, the train wreck of the apartment, the looks he'd received from members of his squad room, the extra drinks he'd consumed, the raised voices in the apartment, the looks from the lobby. The timing was perfect, too perfect. It wasn't a coincidence his path crossed with those two guys. They'd wrecked the apartment and thrown Erin over the balcony as he entered the elevator. Jake Reis was behind it, then his mind exploded. Ethan Kels had blabbed to Reis.

It was over, his life was over. Without Erin he was nothing. He wanted to grieve, he wanted to hold her in his arms one last time, but he knew that was impossible. That's what Jake Reis would figure he'd do. In his head he worked out the scenario. He'd be arrested for killing Erin. They'd question him about their relationship, they knock him about some. No one would listen to his story; they'd see a tough cop that beat up his girlfriend, then thrown her off the balcony to make it appear like suicide. Two days in the county jail, if that. Jake Reis would have him on a slab before Monday morning.

He had nothing but his grief, he wanted to throw himself off that same balcony, but Jake Reis would win. Mike Burnett would be ~~history~~, and Jake Reis, Hunter Northrup, Rex Blaze and Ethan Kels would walk away scot free. Mike Burnett wasn't about to let that happen, he had to run. It would be a sure sign of his guilt, but he was dead anyway.

There was to be no panic, panic could get him arrested or killed sooner rather than later. Thinking on his feet Mike went into their bedroom and pulled out the second drawer of the dressing table. He turned the draw over and unstuck a brown envelope from the bottom. He placed it in his inside jacket pocket. Then he reached up and felt along the top of the wardrobe. There was three thousand dollars in ten's and twenties, neatly stacked and tied with rubber bands. He stashed them in his pockets, then closed the balcony doors and exited the apartment, closing the door behind him. Hopefully it would buy him a few minutes.

Using the back stairs he made his escape. An hour later he was in a cheap motel room ten blocks from his apartment. Sitting on the bed with a bottle of bourbon he'd purchased two blocks over, he tried blotting out the events of the last couple of hours. But the drink was no use, in the darkness of the room he began to cry. Erin was dead, and indirectly he was to blame. In those dark hours he prayed for death, there were no thoughts for his safety, all he wanted to do was crawl into a ball and die. Eventually the booze took effect and he fell into a fitful slumber, accompanied by the low hum from the radio.

When he awoke the following morning the radio was full of it. "Sheriff's Deputy being sought in connection with the death of live in lover Erin Albright," began the headlines. "The fact that Deputy Sheriff Mike Burnett has flown the coop seems to suggest his guilt," stated Sheriff Homer Jones in a statement late last night. "We expect an arrest imminently." It was as Mike figured.

He looked at the near empty bottle and was tempted to drain the contents, but thought better of it. Last night he'd been in his cups, he wanted it over, but in the cold light of day he realised he had to live, if he was ever going to get the chance to avenge Erin's death. He was a fugitive; he was running for his life. He had to put distance between him and L.A. He thought Mexico, too obvious; they'd be looking for him at every border crossing. He considered heading for Canada, but that was fraught with danger also. In the end he decided to head for Chicago, but first he had to get away from the motel without attracting attention. Gathering up his meagre possessions he walked out into the California sunshine. The sun felt good on his face as he mingled with the crowd. Something he'd always taken for granted, he thought it funny how the small things suddenly take on such importance. He hailed a cab, and headed to Union station. It was a calculated risk, they'd be looking for him at airports, train and bus depots, but he had to try.

Then his luck changed. Firstly because of the imminent end to the war in Europe, the papers had his story on page five. His second stroke of luck, the police had posted men at Union Station but they were only checking the trains heading south towards Tijuana.

Several days later he arrived in Chicago. Mike's next port of call was to check into a mid-town hotel and begin figuring out his options. Fortunately the war in Europe had finally ended and the people of Chicago were in high spirits. No one was paying him the slightest bit of attention. Mike knew the euphoria wouldn't last, and even if the cops in LA lost interest in finding him, he knew that Jake Reis's tentacles stretched all the way from Los Angeles to Chicago and New York. Over the next few days Mike sadly realised that his life in the States was over. He looked at the passport he'd retrieved from the underside of the drawer. Nicholas Kincaid; read the legend. A week later he checked in at Chicago's main airport and booked a flight to Buenos Aires.

Chapter 18

'Granero de Alvarado' and in smaller neon lettering 'en la Casa Rosada' read the sign. 'The Barn' was opening to the public on New Years Eve, 1948. It had been touch and go as to whether it would be finished in time, but Lucas cajoled, bribed and bullied the contractors into bringing the night club in on schedule. Then he was confronted with the mammoth task of interviewing bar and catering staff. Lucas was a perfectionist and wanted only the best, which was why he'd taken on all the interviewing himself. That was until Gretchen stepped up.

"Do you trust my judgement?" she said in Teutonic style. "I've taken a leave of absence from my charity work so I will lessen your workload."

How could he refuse, it allowed him to concentrate on the job he loved best, hiring class acts, a resident band and star names to attract the attention of the larger world. He was nervous, there was so much riding on it; opening night had to be a success. They'd already triumphed with the dress rehearsal. A week before Christmas, Granero de Alvarado en la Casa Rosado opened to a select clientele of a hundred. The venue could cater for four times that amount but Lucas wanted it to go perfectly. He needn't have worried, it was a resounding success. Felipe Salazar, his brother Colonel Ruben Salazar and their wives, a couple of very high ranking officials from Peron's government, and a select group of Argentine celebrities from the worlds of show business, movies and sport attended. Some were that impressed they booked dinner for the New Year's Eve opening night. Lucas was leaving nothing to chance, he had standards to maintain; Cipriano Mercado had become indispensable and had taken on the assistant manager's job at the original Granero de Alvarado. What one venue did the other duplicated, there was to be no lowering of standards. Lucas was extremely grateful to Gretchen as she'd agreed to play hostess at the new venue while Lucas flitted between the two.

"I think you'd like to take over," he said jokingly.

Gretchen laughed, "Just make sure you're back here before midnight," she playfully warned him. He laughed and for the first time since Erin's death he started to believe his life had turned a corner. Gretchen had been a tower of strength throughout the building work and beyond, nothing was too much for her, and Lucas loved her all the more for it.

Tango, 'Argentine style' was the dance of preference for the red blooded male and his equally red blooded partner. The theme of Alvarado's was the tango. Lucas knew his clientele, and while tango was king, other dances like the fox trot, the quick step, the rumba, the samba and the swing dances of the big band era were becoming more popular. He'd modelled the original Granero de Alvarado on the style of the night clubs of Los Angeles, places like Ciro's, the Melody Room and the Trocadero. Fashions changed and Lucas was keeping his finger on the pulse, nothing was being left to chance. He'd be prepared to change when the time came, but he wasn't prepared to sacrifice quality. Lucas looked over the books and smiled, judging by the advanced bookings Granero de Alvarado en la Casa Rosada was going to be big, even bigger than the original.

Lucas and Gretchen waited nervously as the doors were finally flung open. At first the clientele arrived in a rush, taking whatever tables were unreserved. A bigger smile spread across his face as the new arrivals surveyed their surroundings. From the expressions upon their faces he could see they were suitably impressed.

Lucas put his arm around Gretchen as the stage lit up. The opening floor show was a dazzling display of Argentinean Tango. He'd seen the dance troup perform before and knew just what to expect. They didn't disappoint as they wowed an audience that danced to this music week in week out. Satisfied that the evening had got off to a promising start he left Gretchen to supervise while he drove across town to look in on Cipriano.

The stocky Argentine greeted his boss with reference, something Lucas would never have expected a year or so back. Within minutes Cipriano had brought Lucas up to speed. Relaxed that things were running much the same as always, he grabbed himself a drink at the bar and felt himself getting in the mood. He watched from the bar area, studying peoples faces at the entertainment, it was as expected; top drawer, then he began to mingle. He knew a great many of his patrons by first names and walked between tables shaking hands with a number of them. This was truly his kingdom; it was where he held court. Granero de Alvarado was within his grasp. All he had to do was turn the new venue into the success it so richly deserved.

Satisfied Cipriano had his fingers on the pulse Lucas glanced at his watch; it was a few minutes after eleven o'clock.

"I'll bid you goodnight, and a happy new year to you and your family."

"And to you Senor Garrett, and the Senorita Gretchen, compliments of the season," replied Cipriano, as he shook Garrett's hand vigorously.

The traffic was light as he sped across the wide streets of Buenos Aires, making good time he arrived back at the new Barn at Casa Rosada with twenty five minutes to spare. He smiled to himself; there was enough time to check everything was running smoothly, before joining Gretchen on the dance floor for the traditional celebrations. It was turning into the most perfect of opening nights.

He finished his checks then cast an eye over the party crowd as he searched out Gretchen. There were bodies everywhere; it seemed everyone wanted to be on the dance floor at once. He stifled a smile, this was better than good, this was an amazing night. He studied the faces of the crowd, they were happy, excited, jubilant, inebriated, and as one with Granero de Alvarado en la Casa Rosada as he could ever wish for, this was a night to savour.

Then his world turned upside down. He gave out a startled gasp, and his eyes widened with alarm. In the centre of the dance floor, dancing, smiling, having the time of his life was Ethan Kels.

Lucas retreated to the back of the hall yet keeping the dancing crowd still in focus. What the fuck was Kels doing in Buenos Aires, more importantly what the hell was he doing in Granero de Alvarado. It couldn't be coincidence, Lucas didn't believe in it. He retreated to his office and opened the desk drawer. He reached in and took out his Colt 1911 automatic. He checked the clip, before sticking it in the rear of his waistband. 'Ethan Kels, here in my club, what the fuck was that all about?' The questions kept coming. He glanced at the clock and realised there were three minutes to midnight. Gretchen would be fretting; he had to get her away from the dance floor. If it meant unburdening himself about his past, so be it. A thought suddenly sprang to mind, perhaps he was seeing things; for Christ-sake it was New Years Eve and he had been under considerable stress. Yeah, that would be it, he kept telling himself. He decided to risk taking another look, while searching out Gretchen.

As Lucas pushed his way through the crowded dance floor he spied Gretchen at the far side of the room. He was right; she looked worried and a little agitated as she kept glancing in the direction of the back office. Everything looked normal; it was his imagination after all. Then his world came to a screeching halt as his eyes focused in on the one person he never expected to see again. He recognised the unruly mop of fire red hair. He was staring straight into the eyes of Erin and she was staring right back at him. What unnerved him the most, she didn't look surprised. She smiled at the man she was dancing with, and from where Lucas was standing she appeared to be making some kind of an excuse. The man was Ethan; he looked disappointed, as he pointed to the watch on his wrist. She made a gesture, back in two, he surmised, before hurrying from the dance floor towards the restrooms. Lucas followed with his eyes, making sure his ex partner didn't follow, then moving swiftly through the crowd he grabbed Erin by the arm. She looked startled, yet not shocked as he led her towards the back office. She didn't struggle or make a scene, she came willingly. He opened the door to the office and bundled her inside, then he locked the door behind him.

All thoughts of Gretchen went out the window as he stared into the face of the woman he thought he'd spent the rest of his life with, "I thought you were dead!"

"Oh Mike, you don't know how many times I've dreamt of this moment."

Lucas didn't know whether to kiss her or slug her. All he knew, she was here in his club with Ethan Kels.

"What gives?" he asked.

"There's no time to explain, if you still have feelings for me, you'll meet me tomorrow at noon. I'll be in Franco's coffee house on Avenida Santa Fe at the Plaza San Martin. I'll explain everything."

"Does Ethan know I'm here?"

"No! And he won't know. Look I've got to go, open the door." Lucas could feel her trembling, as he let go of her arms and unlocked the door. "If you still love me, be there tomorrow at noon." She reached up and kissed him gently upon the lips. Seconds later she was hot footing it across the dance floor. Stunned by the turn of events Lucas watched from a distance as Erin walked up to the table where Kels and another couple were sitting. It appeared from Kels reaction that he wasn't too happy; Erin was feigning a headache or something and asking to leave. Seconds later Ethan got up from the table made his excuses to the other couple and escorted Erin from the club.

Butterflies churned his stomach as he followed Erin and Ethan out through the foyer and saw them get into a taxi. 'Erin was alive! How was that possible? The papers and the radio were full of it.' He was shocked, confused, angry, elated, and fearful, as a whole gambit of emotions streamed through his body. 'Erin and Ethan, what the fuck was that all about?' He had to pull himself together; he had too, for Gretchen's sake at least. He was in love with her, of that there was no doubt, but seeing Erin had thrown a monkey wrench of epic proportions into the works.

Lucas walked into the restroom and splashed water over his face. He needed a clear head. Wiping himself dry with a towel, he steeled himself for confronting Gretchen. He was late; it was now twenty five minutes into 1949. She was going to be sore, but he promised himself he'd make up for it big time.

When he found her she gave him an icy look, and turned her back on him. He pulled her around, kissed her softly upon the lips, mouthed an apology then blustered away his excuses. Pretty soon the ice was melting as they took to the floor and danced their way into the New Year.

On the surface Lucas showed a great deal of restraint as his inner demons struggled with the presence of his dead girlfriend and his arch enemy Ethan Kels. The back slapping and hand wringing went on long after the last of the guests had left. The opening night had been a resounding success and Lucas dedicated it to the hard work his staff had put in. "Rest assured there will be a bonus for tonight!" To a crescendo of applause he made his excuses then he and Gretchen left them to finish up.

They fell into bed around three. Lucas lay there staring up at the ceiling fan, mulling over events that had turned his world on its head. He prayed for sleep, but Gretchen had other plans, the adrenaline that had seen them through a very stressful day and night was still buzzing. She straddled him and reached between his legs, only to find his cock was limp. "Oh baby, I need some loving," she purred as she worked on him, but his cock remained in a semi flaccid state. Tiring of using her hands Gretchen slid down the bed kissing his chest and stomach as she moved ever closer to his cock. She took him into her mouth and gently caressed him until she felt a response. His erection was now hers, to do with as she wished. Her tongue snaked around the purple orb, her teeth gently nibbled playfully, and then she took him deep into her mouth, sucking him into a world of ecstasy he hadn't dreamed possible. He groaned with pleasure, his hands forcing her head further between his legs, his male instincts rising to the fore. Then slowly she withdrew her mouth from his penis and climbed back upon him. She was wet as hell and needed to be released from this exquisite torment. Gretchen guided his cock inside then lowered herself onto his shaft and slowly began to move herself up and down. She sensed he wouldn't be able to last for much longer and began working on her clitoris to bring herself off as soon as she felt the first hard thrust of his orgasm.

Lucas had remained aloof until Gretchen worked her tongue over his penis, then all thoughts of Erin, Ethan and whatever tomorrow would bring, flew out the window. He thrust his cock hard into her and felt himself on the abyss of sexual pleasure, and then almost without warning, he came. Gretchen screamed with excitement as she too reached her climax, one that seemed to go on and on.

Sated by their joint efforts, Gretchen collapsed to the side of him and fell asleep almost immediately. He in turn closed his eyes and drifted, but sleep evaded him, as Erin's face leapt into focus. There were many questioned that needed answers, but the one question he was afraid to ask himself was, 'did he still have feelings for Erin?' The answer was obvious.

Chapter 19

Lucas woke the following morning, and the facts of the night before knocked him sideways. Everything had happened so fast; flitting between both venues under normal circumstances would have been bad enough, but add New Years Eve, opening night at Casa Rosada and the not so small matter of a visitation from the dead, his head was all over the place.

Gretchen was still asleep when he glanced at the clock at the side of their bed. Could his day get any worse, he asked himself, it was eleven fifteen, he'd promised to meet with Erin at noon. Tiptoeing from the bedroom he gave himself a quick sluice, looked at the reflection in the mirror and nearly climbed back into bed, he looked like shit.

There was no time to shave and his hair had taken on a life of its own. Grabbing the nearest pair of pants, he threw a tee-shirt on, stuck his feet in the nearest pair of loafers, grabbed his keys and threw on a jacket. He was almost out the door when he stopped. Ethan Kels, he'd almost forgotten what a dangerous son of a bitch the man was. He walked back into the bedroom and retrieved his automatic from under the suit he'd been wearing the night before. He kept telling himself it was Erin he was meeting, but after the events of last night nothing would surprise him.

On the drive across town he tried second guessing what Erin had to say, but nothing made any sense. What the hell was she doing in Buenos Aires, what the fuck was she doing with Ethan Kels? Had Jake Reis sent them? But the biggest question mark of all was Erin Albright, the woman he'd pinned his dreams on, was alive. By the time he arrived at Franco's he was ten minutes late. His heart was filled with mixed emotions; it was racing faster than a locomotive. Part of him wanted it to be a bad dream, while the rest of him prayed she'd still be there. Supposing she'd grown tired of waiting, maybe having second thoughts. He knew he wouldn't rest until he'd discovered the truth. He had to find answers; he'd go insane without them.

He took one brief look at himself in the coffee house window before entering; he took a deep breath then pushed the door open. Erin looked up as a tiny bell announced his entry. She smiled nervously. His heart turned to mush. Those eyes, that flame red hair and that 'oh so cute button nose,' she was as gorgeous as the last time he'd seen her. He walked the length of the coffee house floor without taking his eyes off her and then took a seat opposite.

"Erin, I.. I don't know what to say? Except maybe, I look like shit!"

His outburst brought a warm smile to her lips. "Oh Michael, you don't have to say anything. It's me that owes you an explanation. And for the record you look good."

Lucas snapped his fingers and a waiter took his order for black coffee, he pointed to Erin's half empty cup, but she shook her head. He took a pack of cigarettes from his pocket stuck one in his mouth and offered Erin one.

"No thanks, I gave up about a year ago."

Lucas lit up, took a long cool drag, savouring the taste as it went down. His coffee appeared almost simultaneously. "Gracias," he said in way of dismissal.

Somehow or other Lucas brought his feelings under control. This wasn't a romantic tryst; this could possibly be a matter of life or death.

"Okay sweetheart, begin." He hated himself for being off hand, but he had to find out the truth.

"I don't know everything, but I'll tell you all I do know."

"That'll do for starters."

"It was around lunchtime; I'd gone across to the diner and had just given my order when Ethan walked in. He looked worried, my heart went to my mouth, I thought something had happened to you."

"Nothing to worry your pretty little head about, Mike's fine. It's you that ain't. Something bad is going down and you need to be as far away from your apartment as possible."

"I knew then this had something to do with the way you'd been acting throughout the week."

Lucas reflected on his guilty secret.

"He said I needed to go with him for my own protection. I protested, I asked why you hadn't come in person. Ethan replied you were in a meeting with the Chief and that when you were done you'd be joining me later that evening. I was scared Mike, I knew just what Jake Reis was capable of."

Lucas stopped her there, "What do you mean, you knew just what Reis was capable of? You knew we did favours for him from time to time, but I never told you what kind of man he was."

"He's a mobster, everyone knows what kind of a man he is," she said unconvincingly.

"My life has been fucked with and you're telling me half a story, I ain't dumb Erin. I came here for answers; at least have the decency to come clean. And while you're at it, why are you with Ethan Kels?"

Tears welled up in Erin's eyes, she stifled a sob. "You're right Michael, you need to know it all, at least everything I know."

"Now we're getting too it." His words belied the feelings his heart was giving out.

Erin took a deep breath, she reached across the table; "I think I'll have that cigarette now."

She took it from the packet and Lucas lit her up. He watched as she took a long hard pull on the cigarette.

Erin was stalling; she had things to say, things that would destroy any hope of a future together.

Lucas could see the pain behind her eyes, he wanted to tell her everything would be okay, but deep down he feared things would never be the same. He felt for her, but he needed the truth.

Erin fought for composure; she knew the next few minutes could be the end of everything.

"I want you to hear me out; then I'll tell you what you want to know."

Lucas nodded.

"Like I said, I knew what Jake Reis was capable of."

"Ethan took me to a small hotel in Santa Monica. There were two guys waiting in the room, I assumed they were Sheriff's deputies, but they weren't they were Jake Reis's goons. Around about eight o'clock that evening Ethan paid me a visit. What he told me scared me half to death. He said you were about to do something very stupid and Jake Reis had put a stop to it. I thought he was going to tell me you were dead. Instead he told me, "Killing a cop, although not impossible, brings down a lot of heat. Throwing his long time girlfriend over a balcony and making it look like a lovers quarrel, now that's easier to deal with, Mike gets put in the frame, he either resists arrest or gets a shiv in his stomach courtesy of the County Jail. End of problem." It was the matter of fact way he told it that chilled me to the bone.

Lucas took a sip from his cold coffee.

"I was horrified; I said," "Surely we should go to the police?"

"Too late for that," replied Ethan coldly. "Your five foot three frame hit the pavement thirty minutes ago."

"What!" I screamed. "No, no, this can't be happening!"

"Believe me doll, its happened." He then coldly told me that you were as good as dead the moment you decided to do something stupid, that he had intervened on my behalf and called in a favour from Jake Reis. He said Jake knew a hooker off the strip, about my height and size, had long red hair, same shade as mine. They took her off the streets, fed her enough drugs and alcohol to keep her compliant, gave her a make over in the hair department. Cut it to my length, took her to our apartment late Friday afternoon, and told her she was going to take part in a scam on some well heeled dude. Dressed her from my wardrobe and threw her over our balcony around the time you got home."

"Jesus H Christ, those callous bastards!" exclaimed Lucas. He remained quiet as he digested all Erin had told him. 'It made sense; Ethan had taken time out at lunch to visit a sick aunt in the hospital. He'd obviously got cold feet; he'd been as shook up as me after our trip to the desert. He must have gone to Reis the following day and told him I was shaky. Reis being a conniving son of a bitch always had a get out of jail card. He'd helped us with the apartment; he'd probably had this as a contingency plan all the while. The only thing that didn't make sense was Ethan intervening on Erin's behalf.' "Why did Ethan stick his neck on the line for you?"

"Ethan had a thing for me." It was out; there was no way of putting the Genie back in the bottle.

"You were having an affair?" said Lucas angrily. His life with Erin was nothing but a web of lies.

"No! I wouldn't do that to you. I love you; I've never stopped loving you."

Relief, fought against anger and doubt, Lucas was beside himself. "You'd better explain."

"It all started when we threw that New Year's party in Ethan's honour. If you remember he stole the first kiss from me."

"Yeah, I remember, the son of a bitch."

"I was shocked; I didn't expect it or want it. I put in down to him being drunk and thought no more about it. Then he showed up at our apartment a week later."

"He did what!"

"He came with the pretext that he wanted to apologise for that kiss. I told him it was nothing, to forget about it. "That's the point," he said, "I can't forget it," Then he poured out his heart. He wanted me, not for a quickie, but for real. He envied you and me. He wanted what we had. I told him in no uncertain terms, that wasn't likely to happen. Once he got the message he accepted it with good grace. I thought that would be the last of it, but he came on to me three more times that year. In the end I threatened to tell you. Then he backed off."

"Okay, I get that," said Lucas unconvincingly. "You're here in Buenos Aires; you're at the opening night of my new night club, that ain't a coincidence!"

"You're right, it's no coincidence. I stayed in that motel for the best part of a week, during which time Ethan came around and questioned me about where you might be. I was scared to death. According to Ethan, I didn't exist and Jake Reis could have me killed on a whim. He was all that stood between me becoming another statistic. Jake Reis was hopping mad, things weren't going to plan, and you'd disappeared off the face of the earth. Within a few weeks you were old news, just a domestic that went tragically wrong. Victory in Europe was across every page, and even Jake Reis was beginning to relax. The news quickly turned to the war in the Pacific, by that time Ethan had found me an apartment on Redondo Beach, and I was given a new identity."

Lucas twisted uncomfortably on his seat.

"And no, before you ask, I wasn't sleeping with him. You have to remember, I had no one, I was alone. Ethan was my only real contact. Of course he tried it on, I'd be lying if I said he hadn't, but I resisted mainly because I believed you were still alive." Erin paused and collected her thoughts, "Sure Ethan took me to dinner a couple of times a month, and strange as it seems we became attached to each other. You see he was trapped like you, but unlike you he hadn't the courage to get from under Jake Reis."

"Yeah I think I know where this is heading."

"But you'd be wrong!" cried Erin. "There wasn't a day that went by that I didn't think about you. I didn't know where you were, but I had an idea. It was an idea I clung on to for three and a half years."

She reached across the table and squeezed his hand. "Do you remember our dreams, our hopes for the future? You wanted to open a bar, a night spot, not I'll grant you on the scale of Granero de Alvarado, but a place where people would be able to dance to the latest dance crazes. I remembered the tango was your favourite, mine too. We often dreamed over a candle lit dinner in that tiny restaurant off the Strip, of one day visiting the home of the Argentine Tango. You told me once that you should always follow your dreams."

Lucas smiled as he remembered those nights; they were some of the happiest moments in his life. "That was a long shot to actually pinpointing my whereabouts," he said suspiciously.

"True, and if truth be known, it was a pipe dream nothing more. A hunch if you like, until a couple of months back when I picked up a copy of 'Moviegoer' one Sunday morning. Maybe you remember, I was an avid cinemagoer and I devoured movie magazines, like 'Photoplay' and 'Moviegoer' reading them from cover to cover." From the faraway look he gave she saw that he remembered. "I came across a two page article about the influx of American films in Latin and South America and how the importation of such films was damaging the movie industry in places like Argentina, and Brazil. There were brief interviews with various Latin actors and actresses, but one in particular caught my eye, it was with Sabina Olmos, tango singer, dancer and actress. She'd recently starred in 'Albeniz' alongside Pedro Lopez Lagar and when asked about the influx of American movies she said, "It's not just the movies you Americans are infiltrating; you're bringing your influence to bear on our traditional night life. In fact I've been invited to the opening of a brand new dinner and dance venue, close to Casa Rosada. Judging reviews from his first venue Lucas Garrett seems to have the Midas touch." I couldn't believe what I was reading. I read it over and over again. I remember you telling me once that your grandmother on your mother's side was somehow distantly related to Pat Garrett, the man that killed Billy the Kid; I also remembered that your father's given name was Lucas. I knew I'd found you."

"Does Ethan know any of this?"

"No, I haven't told him anything and I won't, despite . . . ."

"Despite what?" asked Lucas

Erin felt a deepening hue of shame drift over her, "Despite we're married!"

Lucas's face grew ashen with shock, his heart hit rock bottom; he'd heard enough. He snatched his hand away. For the longest time there was silence between them. Lucas was dying inside, he looked into Erin's green eyes, "I've heard all I need."

He stood up and Erin reached across and grabbed his hand, "Don't go, please hear me out!" she pleaded

Lucas pulled his hand free a second time, "There's nothing more to be said. I wish you well," but his words held little conviction. He turned his back and walked away, leaving Erin sobbing behind him.

Chapter 20

Erin was devastated when she got up from her chair; she paid the check then quickly walked outside into the Argentine sunshine. She had to catch him, she had too, but she was too late, Lucas had disappeared from view.

"Oh why oh why did I have to tell him I'd married Ethan," she said out aloud. Erin knew the reason, the burden had been too much for her, she'd felt she had to tell him everything. "Why wouldn't he let me explain," she sobbed quietly, "if only he'd let me explain."

She stood on the sidewalk for a few minutes, then turned right and began walking back to her hotel. On the way there she cursed herself for being a fool. Ethan wasn't Mike, how could he be, but despite everything he had been a good friend; he'd been kind, generous and attentive, more importantly he was the buffer between her and Jake Reis.

For years she'd spurned Ethan's advances, making one excuse after another. 'Would he be so keen if he knew the truth?' Erin shuddered at the thought; her whole life had been a lie. 'I was one of Jake Reis cast offs?' It made her feel dirty inside. It had been a one off thing, before Michael's time, before she played the role of her life. Erin had been a starlet; she'd been through the Hollywood system and back again. She'd met Jake Reis after yet another audition had fallen through. Down on her luck she was easy pickings for the mobster. He'd taken her to dinner that night and it wasn't long before she found out Jake Reis liked his dessert hot.

She'd written if off to just another Hollyweird experience. When he phoned her two days later she was about to give him the brush off, but it wasn't a date he was after. It was a job of sorts; he offered her a starring role in a Jake Reis production. He had a young cop on his payroll that wanted to do his patriotic duty.

"He needs a little persuasion to stay Stateside. I think you're it doll."

Down on her luck with three weeks rent to pay, she agreed. What harm was there in that? Depending on how long the job lasted she might make enough money to pay her bills and get out of the cesspit they called Hollywood. Things didn't quite work out the way she had planned. Mike Burnett was a gentleman from the word go. He'd respected her; he hadn't taken advantage of her superficially vulnerable position. She didn't think she was doing wrong, most everything she told him about herself was the truth, she just left out some of her past. Then the unexpected happened, she found herself falling in love with the guy. When he told her he felt the same, she felt elated, happy, excited at the prospects of spending the rest of her life with him, but most of all she felt dirty. She had to free herself from Jake Reis, a phone-conversation later, it was done.

"If that's what you want doll, I won't argue, saves me a bundle."

Seeking assurance Erin asked, "This is between me and you, no comebacks."

Jake laughed, "Listen doll, I'm many things, but if I give my word, I keep it."

It was the words she'd desperately wanted to here. She knew Mike was a little crooked, that he did favours, that he looked the other way on an occasion but then half the force was bent, in fact most everyone from movie directors, producers, agents, all the way down the food chain to politicians and cops had their noses in the trough. She knew 'her' Mike was different from the rest; there was a line he wouldn't cross. And it nearly cost him his life.

As she grew closer to the hotel entrance she reflected on the last three years. She'd been living a lie, and was still living it. Jake Reis could have pulled the plug at anytime. Erin lived in fear ever since the hooker was thrown from her balcony. What if he told Ethan Kels that the woman he had placed on a pedestal was nothing but an out of work actress that screwed around. Would Ethan still feel the same? The hell he would. Her life wouldn't be worth a plugged nickel. She should have got out; she should have taken the train back to Minneapolis, but she'd stayed. She often wondered why, but deep down she knew the reason. If she'd gone home, Mike would have been lost to her forever. Then one Sunday morning she found the article in Moviegoer, it changed everything. It vindicated her three year long ordeal.

If her hunch was right, then Mike was alive and living in Buenos Aires. Her immediate reaction was to hop on a plane, but Jake Reis always had his finger on the pulse, he was the most suspicious person she'd ever known, it was the sole reason he was still alive after almost a decade in power. He would know something was up. It might only be a whim but the last thing she wanted was to lead the mob to Mike Burnett's doorstep. Then the idea came to her, it was off the wall, it was unreal, but it was her only chance. Ethan had proposed to her several times over the last couple of years, what if he proposed again? She wasn't in love with him, but would it be so bad? It was a means to an end, but what if her hunch was wrong, what then? Trapped in a loveless marriage, it was something Erin didn't want to contemplate. At the very least it would award her some kind of protection.

Watching from a distance as Erin emerged from the coffee house; Lucas could see she was clearly upset. He wanted to go across the road, put his arm around her, tell her it was okay, but it wasn't his place, she was Mrs Erin Kels, the wife of the man that had sold him out. He felt choked, sick to the pit of his stomach, nauseas beyond anything else he'd felt in his life, yet he knew he had to harden his heart. Erin was lost to him now, even more than when he'd thought her dead. It was the future that counted, he told himself, he had to know whether his life with Gretchen was compromised.

Erin clearly upset stood at the side of the road for a couple of minutes before turning right, Lucas acting on instinct followed her at a distance. As he walked along the busy avenue he reflected on why he was going to such great lengths. He'd been a fool not to hear Erin out, he'd let his heart rule his head. The worse part of it; he'd begun to question how much he loved Gretchen; that hurt the most. He consoled himself with the knowledge Gretchen had breathed new life into him, without her the success of Granero de Alvarado and the new club would be nothing but wishful thinking. Gretchen had given him a reason to get up each morning. He owed it to her to find out whether he could trust Erin to keep his identity from being exposed.

Erin paused before entering the Plaza Hotel. Lucas still a discreet distance behind watched as she entered the hotel. He quickened his pace, his overwhelming urge to hear her out rose to the fore. He froze as he was about to enter the lobby, Erin had just taken receipt of her key when Ethan emerged from the elevator. For a split second he held his breath, he detected a brief moment of panic from Erin, then she smiled and Ethan took her in his arms and hugged her. Unable to hear the conversation Lucas reluctantly turned around and headed back to his apartment. He'd seen with his own eyes Erin and Ethan embrace, he'd heard from her that they were married, it surprised him how much it hurt.

Erin had just picked up her key and was returning to her room when Ethan emerged from the elevator. The instinct for survival took over from sheer panic and she smiled excitedly as a puzzled Ethan walked towards her. Living on her nerves and wits the last three years had taught Erin to always think ahead. As they embraced she took the initiative and looked him square in the face and frowned.

"Oh Ethan, you've spoiled it now!"

"Spoilt what!" he asked.

"After last night, you were sleeping like a baby; it was a pity to wake you. I've been shopping, I've bought you these."

She handed Ethan a small package. He looked at her with incredulity, "What is it?"

"Open it and you'll see," she replied with a smile of expectation upon her face.

Ethan ripped open the package, and found it contained a small leather embossed case. He opened it and stared at a pair of silver cufflinks.

"They're beautiful," he exclaimed, "Why, what reason?"

"Okay, it's not your birthday, I didn't miss Christmas, so what other reason? Husband . . . ." She left him to fill in the blanks.

It had been a close shave, she'd hoped to get back before he'd woke. "I know how much you hate shopping and I had this irresistible urge to check out the shops."

She wasn't aware of whether he heard the rest of her explanation he was too busy admiring the surprise gift. "You're a doll," he said as he kissed her on the cheek, let's go eat. I'm starving."

Erin looked at him coyly, "You go, I've already eaten. I'm going up to our room to freshen up."

"You look fine to me," he replied.

"That might be as far as you're concerned." She smiled, "I'll see you in the hotel dining room in half an hour."

Reluctantly Ethan shrugged his shoulders, "Okay doll, see you in thirty minutes."

Within a few seconds the elevator doors closed and Erin was alone apart from the operator as it sped up to the tenth floor. That's where she broke down. The tears came in a rush, followed by an involuntary howl. She'd kept it together just, but now her emotions were taking over. Three and a half years of hoping, of living on the edge, all for nothing. Mike, Lucas what ever he called himself now, had changed. He was still the Mike Burnett she'd fallen in love with all those years ago, but there was a hard exterior she couldn't hope to crack. It was over; she was trapped in a marriage without love, with a man that had done terrible things, a man that wouldn't think twice about putting a bullet in Mike Burnett's head.

Leaving the bathroom, her make up intact she thought about what the future held. Then a thought crossed her mind, maybe Mike regretted leaving so quickly, it was a possibility. Their stay in Buenos Aires had five more days to run. She'd get Ethan to take her to Granero de Alvarado once more. It was a risk, but she knew Mike would be on his guard. If she could just explain, it would be worth that risk. Looking in the mirror she noticed a feeble smile begin to radiate.

During the next few days Lucas made discreet enquiries about the couple in suite 1021. He panicked when he learned they were due to fly back to the States the day after next. If he was to find out Erin's intentions he needed to speak to her, but time was running out. Then he remembered Ethan was an avid tennis player, he use to play at least three times a week when they were together at the Sheriff's Department. A quick check at the concierge desk and he learned Kels was playing a match that afternoon.

With a newspaper as shield Lucas watched as Kels dressed in tennis whites shook hands with a blonde haired man. They joked with each other before heading towards the hotel's tennis courts. Looking at the time he judged a five minute knock up, twenty five to thirty a set, at the very earliest Ethan Kels wouldn't be back to the suite for at least an hour and a half. Enough time to hear Erin's explanation and judge her intentions. He took a brief look at the courts and saw Ethan spin his racket to decide who would serve first. A minute later Lucas stepped into the elevator and asked for the tenth floor.

His heart was pounding as he stood outside suite 1021. He knocked on the door. "What have you forg . . . ." The words died on her lips as she looked into the eyes of Mike Burnett.

"Hello Erin," he said.

"You'd better come in," she said nervously as her heart skipped a beat. "What is it you want, Ethan might come back any minute."

"Last I saw of him he was knocking up on the tennis court. I think we're good for an hour."

It was the way he said it, that sent her heart plummeting into the pit of her stomach. "Oh Michael!" she cried.

Hearing his name fully, sent his brain racing back in time. Erin had almost always called him Michael, and with the name had come floods of affection. It was a moment in time that for the briefest second threw him.

"In the coffee house you asked me to hear you out, now I'm giving you that chance," he said in a matter of fact manner.

Erin tried to ignore his coldness, she had things to say, Michael deserved the truth.

"What I'm about to tell you will cause me more pain than you could truly imagine. You see, I'm still so deeply in love with you." She thought she caught a flicker in his eye.

"Okay cut to the chase!" he said cruelly.

"Before I continue, I married Ethan because of necessity, nothing more. On my part it's a loveless marriage, it was the only way I could fly down to Buenos Aires without attracting suspicion from Jake Reis."

"You're on your honeymoon!" cried Lucas incredulously.

"Here goes," said Erin, only by telling Mike the sordid facts could she hope for him to understand why she'd married Ethan Kels.

"If you ever cared for me you'll listen to what I have to say, I've always loved you and I guess I'll love you until my dying day. Our life in the beginning was a sham. Everything I'd told you about my life before I came to Hollywood was true, you must believe me. The story I told you about the agent was also true, but I'd left out the other agents, and a couple of producers. Then I met Jake Reis, he wined and dined me, while listening to my sob story, one I don't doubt he'd heard many times before. We slept together that night."

"You fucking slept with Jake Reis!" It was Lucas's turn for his heart to hit rock bottom.

"Only the once," sobbed Erin.

0

'It gets better and better,' he thought ironically, 'This is a fucking nightmare, I don't know her at all.'

"You must listen to me," she pleaded.

"There's more!" he spat viciously at her.

Tears streamed from her eyes, her face twisted in anguish, her body wracked with convulsions, but it was nothing compared to the look of disgust that she saw in his eyes.

"He needed someone to persuade you from enlisting. Our meeting was a setup."

"I don't fucking believe this, it was a lie from start to finish. What kind of patsy am I?"

If Ethan walked in at that moment he'd have put a bullet between his eyes. His mind was in turmoil, he felt like hopping on a plane and walking up to Jake Reis and blowing his fucking face off. He almost felt like throwing Erin out through the balcony window; almost.

"I thought what harm could it do. Then I met you, you were so kind, so caring, so decent. I got caught up in the romance of it all."

"You got caught up in what money Jake Reis was paying you, you mean!"

Erin wiped her eyes with the back of her hand, she knew she'd lost, she knew he was lost forever, but he needed to know it wasn't a lie, that she loved him, that she'd never stopped loving him.

"That's where you're wrong, I admit I deceived you, but even from our first date I knew you were someone special. When I realised you felt the same I phoned Jake and told him I didn't want any of his filthy money."

"You expect me to believe you?"

From somewhere Erin found enough spirit to fight back, "Yes! Frankly I do!" she countered. "We shared a life together for more than three years. That was real, fake never came into it. Do you think I'd be here telling you this if I didn't care. I love you Michael Burnett, I always have."

Lucas fought for control, he was raging inside, he so wanted to believe her, but after the revelations of the last few days he didn't know what to think. He'd come here to listen, to hear her out, this wasn't what he expected. Time was against him, he had to let her finish.

"Go on with your story," he said coldly.

"I knew you were dirty, I knew you did favours for Reis, but I knew in your heart you were a decent human being. I knew it was petty, I knew that when the time came you'd get out. What I didn't know, and didn't until after you'd disappeared was just how dirty you'd become."

Lucas felt the colour rising to his cheeks, the guilt, the fear, the disgust all flooded back. 'He who is without sin cast the first stone,' the words had never felt so appropriate. Erin, like him had been trapped in the spider web created by Jake Reis.

"You know?"

"I don't know the details, suffice to say Ethan told me you and him were involved in something that turned both your stomachs. He didn't elaborate."

Lucas felt a tinge of relief.

"Ethan told me after, that because of the consequences of your immediate reaction you'd put not only your life in danger but also mine and his."

"He knew about your little arrangement with Jake?" What other secrets was she keeping from him?

"No, he knew nothing and still knows nothing. He's a bad man, I know that, but he's not as bad as you might think."

"You've got to be kidding. Ethan Kels is a stone cold killer despite what he may say to the contrary."

Erin ignored his accusation. "For three years I lived with this dream, then I saw the article in 'Moviegoer' it was the answer to my prayers. You'd think it would be easy to just board a plane and fly here. If you believe that you don't know Jake Reis as well as you think. He has a file on everyone that has ever been on his payroll, from politicians, certain law enforcement, business men, movie producers, directors, movie stars, entertainers, all the way down to cocktail waitresses and beyond. Nothing moves in LA without Jake

Reis knowing about it. If my hunch was right I'd be putting your life in mortal danger."

He was listening, the anger, the anguish, the sadness all of it was laying subdued while she completed her story. At the very least she wanted him to believe her.

"Ethan had been in love with me since we met. He'd saved my life, risking his own when he called in that favour."

Lucas interrupted her, "Called in a favour maybe, but a young woman died all the same."

"I know, and I'm sorry it happened. You don't know how sorry, but what choice did Ethan have? He told me he knew nothing of Jake's plans until it was too late."

Lucas held his tongue, time was ticking away.

"During the first few weeks it was a living hell. Once I'd gotten over the shock of my apparent death and your disappearance I thought about getting out of L.A, but I believed I knew where you'd gone. It might sound dumb, foolish even but it was all I could cling onto. The last three years have been an eye opener. Ethan was my lifeline, he was all that stood between me and Jake Reis. He told me once that as far as Jake Reis was concerned I was already dead, for me to disappear would be easy. It was Ethan standing in the way that kept me from being killed."

"Ethan told you that?"

"Why would he lie? I saw the way Jake Reis looked at me whenever he saw me."

"When was that?"

"Not often, maybe a couple of times a year. Ethan would invite me to a function and there he'd be, eating dinner with a crowd at Ciro's. He'd come over, exchange a few pleasantries then he'd re-join his latest woman. Ethan said it was his way of checking everything was okay."

"Did you ever think Ethan was playing you? That Jake might not be in the slightest interested in who you were. You've only Ethan's word for it."

"Ethan wouldn't, he's better than that, he could have forced himself on me but he didn't."

"Nonetheless, he never stopped trying. He got you in the end."

"Only because it was my way of finding you, I would never have married him if it wasn't for that."

"So what did you hope to achieve if you found me? Did it ever occur to you that I might have a new life? I thought you were dead, if I'd have known, don't you think I'd have come back for you?"

Erin felt her heart beat a little faster.

"Its funny, I'd have done anything for you, but you're dead to me."

"Don't say that Michael, I love you. It's not too late."

"I've changed Erin; I'm not the man I use to be. You wouldn't like what I've become. Life kicked me in the teeth once, now I do the kicking. I run a couple of very successful night spots here in Buenos Aires. With luck I'll own one outright pretty soon. I've a fiancée . . . ."

"A fiancée . . . ."

"Yeah, I never expected to get over you, but along came Gretchen. I won't go into any details of how we met only to say she's as different; yet strangely as close to you as I could possibly get. She's German; she fled Germany along with her brother in 1942."

"Why Argentina, why not the US?" asked Erin.

"Perhaps, he didn't want to go to the States. Not everyone does."

"What's she like?"

"Gretchen's waif like and vulnerable, a bit like someone else I once thought I knew," he said cruelly. "We didn't hit it off at first, but as time went by we clicked. She's been my rock ever since."

"I meant what does she look like?"

"She's blonde, petite, and has the most amazing blue eyes."

"Was she working at the club on New Years Eve?"

"Yes, she was."

"I met her, only passing, she seems nice."

"She is, and we're getting married in May. You won't be the only newly weds this year," he added sarcastically.

Erin knew she'd been beaten. It was over. Even if she hadn't taken the drastic step of marrying Ethan Kels, the outcome would have amounted to the same.

Lucas looked at the time, he'd pushed it farther than he'd expected, but as much as he was tempted to put a couple of slugs into his old partner he realised his whole future was at stake.

"Just one more thing, I've been given another chance, have I your word you won't spoil that chance."

"Oh Michael, I didn't spend the best part of three days travelling to betray you! I thought you knew me better than that. I love you with all my heart; I'll never stop loving you." It was her last throw of the dice. "I've wronged you, and for that I'll never forgive myself." She paused for the briefest of seconds, "I wish you all the happiness in the world. And yes, you have my word."

He didn't know why he did it; he just reached across, brushed a tear from her cheek and kissed her gently. "I'm glad you're alive."

He turned to go and had the door half open, when Erin cried out, "Michael, I'm sorry, I've just remembered, I was hoping to have a chance to see you one last time and I persuaded Ethan that we should go to Granero de Alvarado en la Casa Rosada tonight. I can't get out of it."

"Thanks for the tip; I'll make sure I'm at the other club. Gretchen can cover Casa Rosada." A smile appeared on his lips, "One last thing, can Ethan dance the tango better than me."

Erin smiled back, "Not in a million years."

Chapter 21

The moment Mike closed the door behind him, Erin died inside. It was over, there was no coming back. She was beside herself with grief. She'd told him everything; there wasn't anything more she could do. Looking in the mirror she realised she looked a sight. Her eyes were bloodshot from crying. If Ethan arrived back in the suite at that moment he'd want to know what was wrong. Stifling her misery she went into the bathroom and washed her face. She still looked a mess; her face was still scarlet and swollen from crying. Thinking on her feet she gave herself a quick once over with her makeup, added a pair of sunglasses to conceal her eyes then quickly she raced to the elevator. With luck Ethan would still be playing. Her plan was to meet him as he came off court.

He was coming back in as she reached the lobby.

"Hi doll, you missed some match, Henry took me to the limit, I beat him 6-4 in the third."

Henry gave a half-hearted smile, "It was a good workout."

"You nearly had me buddy," added Ethan as Henry made his way to the elevator. Then he looked at Erin, concern etched across his face. "Are you okay?"

"Sure, I'm fine, just a little sleepy," replied Erin.

"You get some sun; you look a bit washed out, I'm going to take a shower. I'll join you in half an hour." He leaned across and kissed her cheek. Then he rushed towards the fast closing elevator.

Erin went outside and felt the sun's rays warm her chilled bones. She didn't realise she was so cold. She grabbed a lounger by the pool and sank down into it. Until that moment she hadn't been aware of how weary she'd become. She felt all used up. Her emotions had taken a severe pounding.

As the sun began to warm her, she reflected on her meeting with Michael. She'd told him everything, there was nothing more to fear. She'd lost him, but she'd lost him anyway. He had a new life, he was successful, a great future ahead of him and a soon to be beautiful wife at his side. It suddenly dawned on her that life could have been so much worse. Michael Burnett could have so easily ended up dead in a police cell. She consoled herself that he was alive, that he was happy. Surprisingly the warm afternoon sunshine and these thoughts caused her to smile. She still had her life, being married to Ethan wasn't all bad, the man worshipped the ground that she walked on. He'd risen rapidly in the Sheriff's Department over the last three years, and was now an Area Commander. One day he would get out from under Jake Reis, then who knows what the future might bring.

The thought of returning to Granero de Alvarado en la Casa Rosada wasn't high on Erin's priorities. She'd much rather have found a low key restaurant and spent their last night in Buenos Aires quietly, but surprisingly Ethan was looking forward to it.

"It'll be fun; it's a fitting end to our honeymoon, our last tango in Buenos Aires. It'll be great."

Erin smiled, 'fun,' she thought, 'for you maybe.'

"We've got to go; I've invited Henry and his wife." As was his charm and charisma Ethan had invited Henry his tennis playing opponent, his wife Gloria and the couple they'd dined with on New Year's Eve, Charlie and Lucy Morrison from Ohio.

He'd phoned Charlie and said, "I'd like you both to join me and my beautiful wife Erin for one last night together. The evening is on me, I insist!"

Despite everything Ethan was charismatic; everyone that met him seemed to fall under his spell. Erin guessed it was his easy going ways and partly the whiff of danger his persona gave off. He had the charm of the devil, yet beneath this rugged charm he could be warm and gentle. She didn't doubt there was another side to him, a dangerous side; one that he kept carefully locked away. He was a good catch, but for Erin, sadly she knew she was accepting second best.

Erin caught sight of Gretchen the moment they entered the club, she was busily overseeing the staff in a discreet and professional manner, whilst greeting as many guests as was possible without over doing things. Thankfully, thought Erin, she was occupied when they were shown to their table. An attentive waiter appeared almost immediately. Ethan took charge and ordered three bottles of their best champagne.

"To start the evening off right," he'd joked.

Within a few minutes it was brought to their table while they perused the menu. Ethan insisted on the best Argentine steaks that Alvarado's had to offer, *courtesy of Estancia Salazar.*

"Good choice, senor" volunteered the waiter.

Then as they sipped at their champagne and waited for dinner they turned their attention towards the stage. The lights dimmed and a spotlight lit up a sultry couple, the woman was dressed in vivid colours of reds, purples and midnight blues, while her partner was dressed in a dark blue pin stripped suit, matching fedora and black and white patent shoes. To the accompaniment of piano, violins and accordion they re-enacted the dance of passion, performing the most erotic Argentine Tango Erin and Ethan had ever seen. Erin was mesmerised, then a solitary tear trickled from her eye. Self consciously she wiped it away. Tonight was a night for remembering past times, tonight was to be the finale to her past life. As the female dancer crumbled to a heap at the foot of her lover, seamlessly a tango singer took centre stage. Although she couldn't understand the language, the meaning she believed was the same. To her it was the most beautiful, haunting and poignant song she'd ever heard in her life. No sooner had he finished, three men in dark fedoras, pinstriped suits and traditional Spanish heeled shoes strutted upon the stage accompanied by three gaudily dressed women and began to perform another sultry dance. She loved their costumes, the extravagance of their slit skirts as they swished and swayed as the couples flicked their legs around each other in the most suggestive of moves. Erin sipped at her champagne, intoxicated by the movements and music of Argentina. Oh how she wished she had been able to make a new life for herself here in Buenos Aires with the only man she'd ever love.

Ethan called for another bottle of champagne, which his guests accepted gratefully. Their meals arrived as the dancers moved off stage and the band took up a moody and melancholy compilation of songs. Erin secretly enjoyed the eye for detail Mike/Lucas had put into the night spot. Everywhere she could see his professional signature.

After dinner they watched as couples took to the floor. The vast majority of them embraced the tango like a second skin. Ethan and the others were as captivated as Erin, each wanting to be the first to get up and dance. The dance floor was big enough for a reasonably large number of dancers to strut to the music without bumping into each other. While they were watching the music switched to the quick step, which was followed by a fox trot before returning to the tango. By this time all three couples were on the floor.

Gretchen oversaw the running and noticed the three American couples as they enjoyed themselves. The reason, *apart from the fact they were spending big and seemed to be having a great time*, was she'd seen two of these couples on New Year's Eve. She took it as a good sign and made a note to introduce herself sometime during the evening.

Another bottle of champagne arrived and by then Charlie and Lucy had retired to their table, "We're bushed," said Charlie. "We're sitting this one out."

"Yeah, think we'll join you," said Ethan.

They were half way through the bottle of champagne when another landed on their table. "Compliments of the house," said the waiter, looking back towards Gretchen.

Gretchen nodded and smiled. Ethan looked in her direction and beckoned her over. She gestured that she'd be over when she could. It was the last thing Erin wanted. She'd hoped to avoid this confrontation, but Ethan's natural exuberance had caused her to deal with her demons up close.

Five minutes later Gretchen joined them. Ethan stood up and gave her a chair next to Erin.

"Is this your first time at Alvarado's," asked Gretchen, then she smiled, "Of course it isn't, you were here on opening night. A return visit, I hope it won't be your last?"

"Sadly," said Ethan, "it is. We're flying home tomorrow. We've got the best part of three days travelling. But who knows, maybe one day." He looked across to Erin and smiled. "We're on our honeymoon," he added gesturing warmly towards Erin.

Gretchen looked at Erin and smiled, "You have a beautiful bride."

Erin smiled politely, but said nothing.

"Well thank you, senorita . . . . ?"

"Gretchen, Gretchen Kauffman, very soon to be Gretchen Garrett."

"You're getting married too, well congratulations. I take it you're not a native of these parts."

"German, but don't hold that against me," she said coyly.

"Garrett, an American?"

"Ja!" she said in her native tongue.

"Good choice doll, we hope you'll be as happy as us." Quickly Ethan snapped his fingers and a fresh glass appeared. "We must have a toast, a toast to us, and to your forthcoming nuptials."

Gretchen tried to decline, but propriety prevented it. She took the offered glass, just as the requisite night club photographer came into view.

"Hold that pose!" said the photographer as Gretchen, Ethan and Erin had raised their glasses.

Before they could move, they were dazzled by the light from the flash bulb.

"Sorry buddy, we're leaving tomorrow. Here's five bucks anyway."

"That is too much. Senor, tell me what hotel you're staying at and I'll see you get the photo before noon."

"Don't worry about it," replied Ethan.

"But I insist," said the photographer forcefully.

"Well alright then. The Plaza Hotel at San Martin, we leave around two in the afternoon, suite 1021," replied Ethan.

'Just what I don't need,' thought Erin. Gretchen seemed nice enough but having a constant reminder wasn't what she had in mind.

Gretchen was politely making her excuses, when suddenly Erin grabbed her by the hand. Why she did it she couldn't say, except maybe it was a subliminal message to Michael. "I hope you'll both be very happy." She smiled sweetly, just as a small tear formed in her eye.

The following morning came around too soon and Erin felt sad and slightly reluctant to be going home. This was it; this was the final chapter in her life with Michael Burnett. She was leaving Buenos Aires and she knew she was never coming back.

She sat on the bed, going over the fleeting time she'd spent with Michael, reliving those precious moments over and over again.

The moment was broken when Ethan burst into the room having been down in the lobby checking out. "These people are really something, that photographer was as good as his word. Not only did he develop the photo on time, he put it in a damn frame. Here look at it; it's a great one of you."

"I'll look at it another time; we've a plane to catch."

Chapter 22

Lucas heard about the good looking American couple the following day from Gretchen. "She was nice Lucas, a little subdued, but nice all the same."

"What made you single them out?" he asked; curiosity getting the better of him.

"The man was a big spender. It only seemed courteous to send over a bottle of champagne. Don't you agree?"

"Yeah sure, you did the right thing."

"The guy called me over, asked me to have a drink with them. Said they were celebrating. They were on their honeymoon."

"What did you say to that?"

"I told them I too was getting married."

"How did the woman react to your news?"

"She was kind of strange, subdued, a little sad maybe; I couldn't quite make her out. She didn't react really. But then just as I was leaving she grabbed me by the hand, smiled sweetly and said she hoped we'd be very happy. I think all is not well in their relationship."

Lucas felt his heart breaking, and wished he'd been a little kinder. She'd flown down to Argentina on a hunch in a bone shaking DC4, suffering though three days of takeoffs and landings, and for what. He'd thrown her love back in her face. About now she'd be boarding her plane for the long journey home, her life like his, a little in turmoil. Shaking himself out of his melancholy mood, he smiled at Gretchen, "Enough about other peoples problems; it's our first day off since before Christmas, where do you fancy eating tonight."

During the next few days, Lucas threw himself back into work; it helped take his mind off Erin. She was gone; she was from a past life, a life of betrayal and heartache. He shrugged it off and looked to the future. The days merged into weeks and slowly things started getting back to normal. Gretchen went back to her job working on more welfare reforms while Lucas worked on rotas for the running of the two night clubs. It was proving more hectic than he'd imagined, so for the time being he'd put Cipriano Mercado in sole charge of Granero de Alvarado and approved two under managers. Likewise he'd put himself in charge at Granero de Alvarado en la Casa Rosada and had been lucky to recruit two very capable under managers. With their wedding just a few months away, he wanted to make sure of his investment before concentrating on wedding arrangements.

Senor Salazar had generously offered his Estancia for the wedding reception and had also suggested the nearby chapel for the wedding itself. Lucas had to pinch himself, he was afraid it was all a dream. He was in charge of two of the most popular and profitable night spots in all Buenos Aires and was soon to marry the most beautiful and seductive women he'd ever known. Who would have believed that in such a short space of time he'd be mixing with the cream of Buenos Aires society? He owed it all to his association with Salazar. It was getting harder and harder for him to identify the chainsaw wielding murderer with the new benevolent landowner Senor Felipe Salazar. It seemed the more legitimate Salazar's holdings became the more wealthy he'd become. Salazar's work with Gretchen's brother Franz *whatever that concerned* was showing dividends and his nefarious business association with Juan Aquilar and Clemente Ramos was raking in vast amounts of money.

On the surface Felipe Salazar was a very powerful and respected member of that Buenos Aires society, but beneath the surface he was a master at manipulation, a man that dealt in murder, extortion, political corruption, drug dealing, prostitution, sex trafficking, gambling, loan sharking, insurance fraud, pornography and blackmail.

Felipe Salazar, was a man to be feared and respected, all the more so because of his arrangement with his brother Colonel Ruben Salazar, who when asked could muster a small army at a moments notice. Add to the mix the ever present Tito Gomez who was either at Salazar's side or lurking in the background and Felipe Salazar was a formidable foe. Lucas counted himself fortunate to be on his right side.

Since formulating the plan of re-creating Granero de Alvarado, Lucas and Gretchen had been invited once a month to Estancia Salazar, either for dinner, a garden party or just drinks. "I think he likes you," said Gretchen on more than one occasion.

"Likes the money more like." replied Lucas. He was under no illusions where Felipe Salazar was concerned. "I'm useful to him, turning Granero de Alvarado around, changed everything. That's why it's important that we make a success of Granero de Alvarado en la Casa Rosada. Soon as it starts to show a profit, I can off load it and take full ownership of Granero de Alvarado."

"Do you think Salazar will relinquish his ownership of Alvarado's?" asked Gretchen as they drove through the gates of Estancia Salazar on their first visit since the new venue had opened. "You did promise him two nightclubs."

Lucas laughed, "I promised one, perhaps two. It was a tall order. I think he'll be satisfied once he see's the money rolling in."

"Let's hope so," replied Gretchen as they drove into Estancia Salazar's extensive driveway.

They pulled up to the front of the Estancia and stepped onto the paved walk way. Lucas handed his keys to the valet and glanced across at his beautiful fiancée.

"Ready to celebrate Enrico's eighth birthday," asked Gretchen with a wry smile.

They soon found themselves walking onto the well manicured lawns of Estancia Salazar and being greeted by their host. "Welcome to my humble abode," he took Gretchen's hand and kissed it, then turned toward Lucas, shook his hand and said, "It is always good to see you my friend."

"Likewise," said Lucas in his mock Bogart accent, "If this is humble, bring on the riches."

"Always with the jokes," replied Salazar.

Lucas smiled, "A little something for Enrico," he said as he handed Senor Felipe Salazar an envelope.

Salazar took it gracefully and put it inside his jacket pocket, his eyes looked greedily back towards the big American. Lucas grinned inwardly, it couldn't have been more than a millisecond but the facial tic was there as always. Lucas read it every time, then he reached into his own inside pocket and handed over a larger package. The smile was instantaneous, warm and full of affection.

Armed with a glass of champagne each, the couple began to mingle. It was a smorgasbord of Buenos Aires society. Politicians high up in Peron's government were there mixing with eminent doctors, lawyers, the military, industrialists, landowners and business men. Lucas spotted a few familiar faces, patrons of Alvarado's. Then someone waved to him from one of the many tables that had been erected on the lawns. At first Lucas thought it was another client of Alvarado's as he waved back, but there was an air of familiarity about him that couldn't be mistaken. The man beckoned Lucas over, those dark sparkling eyes and crooked smile belonged to none other than Rodrigo Vasquez, the man from Montevideo, a man that wasn't easy to forget.

"Senor Garrett, it is good to see you again!"

Lucas took his extended hand and shook it. "Montevideo," said Lucas with a warm smile. "I hardly recognised you in all your finery."

"I look good, don't I," he replied and flashed that crooked smile of his.

Lucas didn't know what it was about the man but he always felt comfortable in his presence. Vasquez had an aura about him that was hard to explain. Lucas supposed it was his easy going manner, the way he treated everything as just one big game.

"Different, I'll grant you, but it's good to see you too."

"I see you've still got the package!" laughed Rodrigo.

Gretchen looked at him disapprovingly, but managed a weak smile.

"Best investment I ever made, we're getting married in a few months."

"So I've been hearing. Why not sit awhile," said Rodrigo as he gestured to the empty seats.

Gretchen started to decline but Lucas had accepted and was already offering her a seat.

"We can't stay long we've friends we have to meet up with," she protested.

"I understand," said Vasquez, "I just want to congratulate you both on your engagement." He turned back to Lucas his infectious smile beaming. "I once told you that you'd make something of yourself!"

"You did at that. How long are you here for?"

"Just the weekend, I head back to Montevideo Monday morning."

"I owe you dinner, and a floor show," said Lucas. "The place is much changed since your last visit."

"Aha, I remember it well. Shouldn't it be me that buys you dinner?"

Lucas laughed, "Without your help I wouldn't be marrying such a beautiful woman."

Gretchen looked approvingly in Lucas's direction and smiled, "I'm sorry, you know I can't wait, Franz has been so mysterious about the new woman in his life, I just have to meet her."

Rodrigo stood up and kissed her hand, "It's me that should apologise, I didn't mean to keep you."

"Nonsense, I'm sure Lucas would enjoy your company rather than listen to us women with our idle chatter. It was nice meeting you again."

When Gretchen had moved a safe distance, Rodrigo stifled a laugh. "She's certainly changed since our last meeting. I'd got the impression she disapproved of me. I'm not refined like these Argentine gentlemen; I think I'm a little too rough around the edges."

"Gretchen's fine when you get to know her. Break down that Teutonic exterior and she's a fun loving wonderful person."

"Said a man, who's very much in love!" replied Rodrigo.

Lucas laughed and before long they were deep in conversation about the difference between Uruguay and Argentina, but then Rodrigo touched on a nerve. He asked whereabouts in the states Lucas came from.

"Let's leave the past buried," said Lucas.

Rodrigo accepted the snub with good grace and changed the subject, "I see you took my advice."

Lucas hadn't thought about Ramon Perez for months. "It was necessary."

"But not to your liking I fear?"

"Lets just say it left a bad taste in my mouth," replied Lucas.

Rodrigo seeking to justify Lucas's actions said, "Let me tell you the difference between Rodrigo Vasquez and Felipe Salazar. I'm a thief, a smuggler, a trader in stolen goods and a good many other things that aren't wise to be spoken of, but I know what I am, whereas Salazar masquerades as a true pillar of society, which we both know he is not."

"I thought you were friends?"

"Business associates, it isn't quite the same. I'm here under Salazar's protection because of the business I provide. You're mixing in bad company. Why I'm telling you this is beyond me. I guess I liked your style when you entered a cantina full of dangerous bandidos, not once but twice."

Lucas took a sip from his champagne flute, his face clouding over suspiciously. "What is it you ain't telling me?"

Rodrigo laughed, "You think you're a bad man, but take a look around you, look past the lawyers, doctors, society dames and what do you see. Over there, Clemente Ramos, he's killed fifteen men to my knowledge, and from what I've heard none of them were quick deaths. Talking to him is Juan Aquilar, drug dealer, sex trafficker, murderer of at least five people, amongst them two women, his buddy Cipriano isn't much better. Over by the house, looking slightly bored with the proceeding is Tito Gomez, bodyguard to Felipe Salazar; he's responsible for numerous disappearances and at least three decapitations. At the centre table Colonel Ruben Salazar, apart from Salazar, the worst of the lot. His hit squads are responsible for a number of murders, sometimes killing entire families."

Lucas's face grew serious, "Yeah I knew they weren't boy scouts. Why are you telling me this?"

"Despite what you've done, you aren't like them?" Rodrigo flashed a smile, laughed and then took a sip of his champagne. "Laugh, laugh at one of my jokes, I'm renown for them."

Lucas took the cue, and laughed back at Vasquez. "Again I ask the question, why are you telling me this?"

"From what I've heard you're making serious money for Salazar, which on the surface is good, but your dream, the one you outlined for me, it's a dream!"

"I'm getting married, Franz Kauffman is soon to be my brother in law, Salazar wouldn't rock that particular boat."

"Maybe; maybe not! Come see me sometime, we might be able to do each other some good."

It was a warning of sorts, but nothing specific. A few minutes more of small talk then Lucas stood up, shook Rodrigo's hand and went in search of Gretchen. He grabbed a glass of champagne from one of the waitresses. Meeting Rodrigo should have been light and of no consequence but his visit had left Lucas disturbed. By the time he found Gretchen he'd managed to recover his happy demeanour.

"Sorry I was so long," he said as he located Gretchen and kissed her on the cheek.

"It's not your fault, he might be a charmer, a joker, whatever. I just find him uncouth, rude even."

"Yeah, I guess he comes over that way, but he doesn't mean anything by it. It's just his way."

Gretchen smiled, then spontaneously kissed him gently upon the lips, "You know, it's funny but I hated being by myself. I nearly came back for you." She laughed, "I think you're growing on me."

"I should hope so," he said and kissed her more suggestively than the garden party warranted. Gretchen gave him their secret look. All thoughts of Rodrigo's cryptic warning went straight out the window.

Chapter 23

With their lust for each other sated they fell back exhausted upon the bed. Lucas glanced at the clock it was 2.33 a.m. They'd been at each other for close on two hours, a fitting climax to an eventful day. He'd at last had Franz's approval of their forthcoming marriage, not that Lucas cared otherwise, but even he reflected that it was better with his approval than without. It came after Gretchen and he had left the other dancers standing in their wake as they danced them off the floor with their version of the Argentine Tango.

"Bravo, bravo," cried Franz as the couple eventually left the improvised dance floor that Felipe Salazar had erected for the evening's events.

A while later Franz walked over to Lucas and motioned for him to follow him away from the cacophony of conversation. In pure Germanic style, *rather stuffed shirt,* thought Lucas, he smiled and put out his hand. "I wasn't sure of you when we first met, but I am happy to give you my blessings for this marriage," he said.

Lucas took the offered hand, shook it and said thank you in German. 'Yes', thought Lucas, 'it had been very eventful, especially Franz's begrudging approval, but it was what Rodrigo said, or to be precise what he didn't say that disturbed Lucas. 'It was as if he was marking my card, warning me of something or was there more in it.' That they were jackals, he already knew, after all he was one too. Eventually he drifted into a troubled sleep.

Lucas put aside Rodrigo's warning, wasn't he as much of a jackal as the rest of them. Jackals were as a rule solitary animals; hunting alone or as a pair, but like their human counterpart their prey was always smaller and weaker. He shrugged the warning off as just a friendly piece of advice, nothing very sinister in it.

He'd almost forgotten Rodrigo's warning when a week later he received a knock on his office door.

"Lucas, there's a guy here says he's got information for you."

Lucas looked at his relief manager and was about to tell him to deal with it when a familiar face came into view.

"Senor Garrett, it is I, Enrique Suarez."

Keeping his emotions in check he quickly dismissed the relief manager as a sense of foreboding descended upon him.

"What the fuck do you want?" snapped Lucas. His ex neighbour had caused him unexpected panic.

"Senor Garrett, I have something of interest for you."

"I'll be the judge of that," said Lucas, now full recovered.

Enrique hesitated, his eyes betraying his greed. "Those men, those men that were with Lola Santo . . . ." He stopped himself from continuing, as he judged the interest in Lucas's face.

"What about those men?"

"You pay Enrique?"

"It depends what you have to sell," replied Lucas cautiously.

"I've seen those two men again."

Lucas felt his blood turn to ice, a feeling of pending doom wafted over him. "What men!" He jumped up from his chair and lifted Enrique off his feet, "What men?" he demanded, even though he knew what men he was referring too.

"Don't hurt me, I'll tell you." said the frightened Enrique.

Lucas loosened his grip whilst holding himself together. "What men, you mean the men with Lola?"

"Si. I saw one of them only yesterday, I thought you might want to know."

Running on adrenaline Lucas questioned Enrique further. "Where did you see him?"

"I was walking passed Adriano's steak house and I saw him through the window."

"Are you sure? Could you be mistaken?"

"I thought you'd pay many pesos, so I waited until the man left, I saw him leave; it was the same man."

"It couldn't have been," uttered Lucas, 'they're both dead,' he thought silently.

Enrique suddenly became brave, "It was him I tell you. I waited until he was gone, and then went inside. The waiter I know, he's my cousin, he gave me the man's name."

Lucas was about to throw Enrique from his office, but stopped in his tracks. "His name, he gave you his name!"

"Si senor, you pay Enrique?"

"I'll pay."

"His name is Aquilar, Juan Aquilar."

Lucas slumped down into his chair, his breath catching in his throat. Any other name and he'd have kicked his ex neighbour out. On auto pilot he reached into his desk and handed Enrique a handful of notes. "You did good," said Lucas as he dismissed the man with a flick of his hand.

Within a minute he was seated alone staring into space. He was in shock, more than that, he was consumed with guilt. He'd killed the wrong men. He'd executed innocent men. 'Innocent' *maybe not*, of that crime at least, his conscience added.

He had to think, he had to reason out who had the most to gain by having him killed. He ruled out Ethan and Jake Reis immediately, the Perez brothers might still have ordered the hit. He couldn't rule them out entirely. But Aquilar, that was a different ball game. Yet it fit, he felt it in his gut. Why would the tall Argentine not heed his warning? Juan Aquilar wasn't afraid of Lucas but he wouldn't rock that particular boat, not without feeling the wrath of Salazar. And then like clockwork it all began to click into place, Salazar was at the heart of it!

Lucas was the new kid on the block, he'd shown Salazar what he was capable of, he'd been given Alvarado's over Ramon; causing resentment that Salazar couldn't afford and didn't want, but why? What madness! What madness indeed, until he remembered that above all else Salazar was the master at manipulation. His own arrogance had blinded him to the truth. When he'd learned what he was up against he thought he was being so clever. He'd sought out Senor Felipe Salazar and asked his advice as to who he could trust, who would be the most loyal. "Cipriano Mercado," was Salazar's answer.

"You kill one brother you'd better be prepared to kill the other," those were almost the first words that came from Cipriano's mouth. Good advice Lucas had thought at the time, not knowing that his second in command was sowing the first seeds of deception. 'What didn't fit was the botched assassination attempt, Aquilar must have learned from Lola that I was a Bogart fan, and sent those killers to rub me out. It didn't make sense; unless there was more than one patsy. The man that stole my raincoat and hat had been too slick. The man was nobody; his death didn't register with the police, but it did with me. I killed Julio a few hours later.' Lucas shuddered at the enormity of his actions. He could hazard a guess as to how Aquilar had got his information, but he wouldn't have had the guts to approach Lola without it being sanctioned by Salazar himself. It was all speculation, but it was beginning to make perfect sense.

Anger coupled with rage seethed through his body, he was the ultimate patsy and he'd been manipulated into getting rid of Julio. 'Why didn't Ramon come after me? I was the logical choice, unless Ramon had also been manipulated.' And then it all began to come together. The one question that remained unanswered was why Ramon hadn't taken swift retaliation. Before he could ask Cipriano had sliced the man's throat. Then the final piece of the jigsaw slotted into place, his second in command had stated there was no love lost between him and Ramon Perez. Lucas had missed it! 'Why would Perez have placed himself in such jeopardy if there was bad blood between him and Cipriano?' As the cogs began to turn Lucas remembered the note he'd left Mercado *stating where he would be on the night of the movie house shooting*, it needed no further explanation. This in a roundabout way was what Rodrigo was eluding too. Like 'the man from Montevideo', he was safe while he was of use to Salazar.

It was becoming abundantly clear Salazar would not relinquish Granero de Alvarado or Lucas from his vice like clutches. Lucas's plans for the future were all but in tatters, although not quite. Disappointment coupled with anger caused him to rethink his position. He was now aware of Felipe Salazar's manipulations and would use this knowledge to circumvent these plans.

His first thoughts were not of self preservation, but of Gretchen. Firstly he would continue as if he was none the wiser, which meant keeping Gretchen in the dark for the time being. The wedding, the two clubs, he might even show Salazar that he was thinking about yet another project. At the least it would keep the jackal off his back. He hated keeping anything from Gretchen but, he was dealing with very dangerous people. His thoughts now turned to Lola.

It seemed most likely that Juan Aquilar had got to her. Without shoving a gun in Aquilar's mouth and threatening to blow the roof of his head clean off Lucas didn't have anything to go on. There was only one place to start: street level.

During the next few days Lucas questioned the girls, the pimps and even some of Lola's old clients, but came up with nothing. He asked if she had places where she could go, family maybe, but the answer always came back the same, "No". She'd literally dropped off the map. Lucas knew in his heart that she was probably dead, but he didn't want to believe it.

He'd given it his best shot, he'd exhausted all avenues and was returning to Alvarado's when a shady figure appeared from a side alley. Lucas recognised him at once; it was Lucio Oliverio a notorious sleaze bag drug pusher.

"Lola Santos. How much you willing to pay amigo?" said Lucio.

"I ain't your amigo, now get the fuck outta here!" spat Lucas. He was sick and tired of the freeloaders, telling him what they thought he wanted to here.

Oliverio realised this ploy was likely to land him in hospital, but the lure of hard cash was too much for him, he took a deep breath. "It might be something, it might be nothing."

Without warning Lucas grabbed him with both hands and threw him against the wall with such force it knocked the air from his lungs, "You scum sucking pig; if you know anything spill!"

The blood drained from Lucio Oliverio's face, as he struggled for breath. Lucas raised his fist, his eyes darkened like a crazy man.

"Hold it man! I don't know what happened to the bitch, but I might have a lead that could take you straight to her."

Lucas let go of him, "This better be good!"

"There is a place, a very expensive place, where for the right price you can create your wildest fantasies, nothing is forbidden."

"You're talking about a whore house."

"No senor, nothing could be farther from the truth. These are young women, girls, virgins, if you're to believe what we hear on the street."

"There's nothing new in that," snapped Lucas, his irritability clearly showing.

"An endless supply . . ." Oliverio let his words sink.

"What do you mean an endless supply?"

Oliverio looked wary.

"You mean . . . ."

"Like I said, your wildest fantasies, nothing's forbidden," then he added, "for the right price."

"How's this connected to Lola Santos?"

"It was her that told me about this place and what goes on there. She was scared to death."

"Where is this place?"

"That I don't know, if I did I would tell you."

"If I find out you're lying, I'll hunt you down and kill you like the dog you are!" Lucas reached into his pocket and counted out some notes. "If you find out anything, and I mean anything, you let me know; understand!"

Inside Alvarado's, Lucas mulled over what he had, it wasn't much to go on, but if Lucio was to be believed something really bad was happening. Lola had disappeared; she was last seen getting into a car with Juan Aquilar and another man. That in itself was strange, she was frightened of Aquilar, but then he realised she'd risk anything for a quick fix. That she'd told Lucio Oliverio about the brothel and that she feared for her life, would on the surface suggest she'd been taken there. The question was why? If they only had use for young women what value was she to Aquilar? And then it hit him; 'Perhaps she was acting as a mother figure, someone to keep the younger girls in line?' He found that hard to swallow, Lola was tough as leather, but cruelty wasn't in her nature.

The key was Juan Aquilar, he was in control of the sex trade since Felipe Salazar had handed him the reins, no doubt taking his cut once a month as usual. Lucas needed to find out more about this whorehouse, Lucio had said it was more than just a whorehouse, but until Lucas knew better he couldn't call it anything other. If there was any truth in what the drug pusher had told him then this was much too big for him to handle, it was best to cool it, in case he attracted the wrong attention.

Switching his thoughts to his own problems, he mulled over his options. He and Gretchen were safe for the time being. Both businesses that he controlled were performing better than the competition. What Lucas needed to do was to attract more international entertainers, which in the short term would cost. He'd run this pass Felipe Salazar when they visited Estancia Salazar at the end of the month. One thing that could be said for Salazar was his ability to understand forward thinking; he wouldn't be happy investing more money into Lucas's night clubs, but his concerns would be outweighed by the projected income in the long term.

Life settled into its usual routine and Lucas found himself being drawn reluctantly into the planning of the wedding. Gretchen was trying to involve him in everything.

"My brother is going to escort me," said Gretchen one morning, "Who have you nominated to stand for you?"

"You know, I haven't given it much thought."

"Well, I suggest you start looking," said Gretchen in a mocking but not unfriendly tone.

In an instant Lucas realised that here in Buenos Aires he had almost everything he could ever wish for, except a good and faithful friend. Sure he had acquaintances, colleagues, people who worked for him, but Cipriano was the closest to someone he could call a friend, *his partner in the murder of Ramon Perez.* Then it came to him.

"I can choose who I want as best man, what if that person was slightly uncouth, you might say rude in fact."

Gretchen was becoming more American in her choice of words, "You've got to be kidding! You don't know him that well; you've probably seen him no more than six or seven times." She wasn't mad, but he could clearly see Rodrigo Vasquez wasn't her ideal. "Cipriano at least you know him," she suggested.

"I think I'll hold out for Rodrigo. He might not accept," he said firmly.

"Your choice," she said smiling. Gretchen liked a man that was decisive.

Lucas had more than one reason why he wanted Rodrigo Vasquez to stand for him, firstly he would hate to start off his married life to Gretchen with Cipriano at his shoulder, and secondly it would give him a chance to talk to Rodrigo. Nothing seemed to get past the man without him latching on to some information. Lucas needed to know more about his cryptic warning and thirdly he could ask him if he knew anything about the mysterious whorehouse.

Lucas paid his monthly visit to Salazar, handed over his cut of the month's taking and then broached the subject of bringing in international stars to perform at Granero de Alvarado and the new venue. Lucas laid out his plans as they sat drinking tea on a sunny Sunday afternoon. Gretchen had taken her cue and allowed Pilar Salazar to show her around their expansive gardens.

"It'll give you men time to talk," Gretchen said as she took Salazar's wife's arm.

Lucas laid out his plans.

"So how much is this going to cost?" asked Salazar.

"A lot more than you'll want to pay," said Lucas glibly. "We go for single artists, not bands; the cost of them would be prohibitive. I'm suggesting singers like Crosby, Lena Horne, and Sinatra, that calibre of artist."

"Always with the jokes," said Salazar.

"Who said I was joking?" replied Lucas. A dark frown appeared across Felipe Salazar's face. "Just here me out, we sell the idea to their agents. Buenos Aires will in the future be rivalling New York, London, Paris and Rome. I've got to convince their agents that a few international dates in Buenos Aires will enhance the artists' careers."

"They'll want to be put up in the best hotels, wined and dined in the best restaurants and that's without paying their airfares, oh and the entourage they'll bring with them," stated Salazar.

Lucas sensed that although Salazar, an astute businessman was putting up barriers he hadn't dismissed it out of hand; it was an encouraging sign. "I never said it would be cheap, but with your connections a few nights accommodation at a top Buenos Aires hotel wouldn't be prohibitive. We sell the idea to the hotel as cheap publicity. Food and drink would be covered at Granero de Alvarado. That leaves the airline; Aeroposta is soon to merge with A.L.F.A and two other carriers to become the international airline of Argentina. I'm sure a deal could be worked out with the airline's management much the same as the hotels."

Salazar sat back in his chair, a look somewhere between incredulous and admiration spread across his face. "You've done your homework, I can see that, but it better not be hot air," he warned.

"On paper it's sound, but until we put it to the test I can't be a hundred percent sure. I'm not saying we can do this overnight, it's just a projection of where we could go in the near future."

"Lucas, I like it in principle, do whatever you need to, find out if it'll work in practice."

"Thank you Senor Salazar, that it is more than I could have hoped for," replied Lucas. In truth, Lucas didn't know whether he could make it work, a few minor stars maybe, but the concept was good. At the least it would buy him time while he worked on a get out clause for him and Gretchen.

"Enough of business," said Salazar, "How are plans coming for your wedding?"

"They're coming along just fine," Lucas replied, sounding as casual as he could, "I'm thinking of asking Rodrigo Vasquez to stand for me."

"I didn't think you knew him that well," said Salazar as he motioned for his man servant to bring over two brandies.

"That's true, but I've made his acquaintance, a few times, here and in Montevideo, and besides he makes me laugh. We seemed to hit it off."

"Your choice, my friend, but I feel I have to warn you, the man isn't to be trusted."

'And you are,' thought Lucas. "It just seemed appropriate since it was through him that I first met Gretchen."

Two days later Lucas took the ferry across the River Platte and arrived in Montevideo a little after two in the afternoon.

Chapter 24

Rodrigo was there at the ferry terminal to greet him. "It is good to see you again my friend, and so soon."

"It is good to see you also," replied Lucas.

He had a plan; a variation on an earlier plan, a very dangerous plan, what he gleaned from Rodrigo would determine whether he put it into operation.

The man from Montevideo suggested a little cantina along the banks of the Rio de Platte. On the way they exchanged pleasantries, but neither spoke about what they were really there to discuss.

Rodrigo drove them along the banks of the river and pulled into a riverside cantina. Both men climbed out and made their way to an outside table close to the river's edge. As they waited for their drinks they watched as the sun slowly began to drop, casting its rays across the river and basking them in a golden glow.

"What is it you want of me?" asked Rodrigo, his tone clearly changed from the pleasantries of earlier.

Lucas smiled, "Firstly, will you stand with me when I wed Gretchen?"

Rodrigo was taken aback, "Wha . . . . !"

"Will you be my best man?" repeated Lucas.

A grin spread across the darkly handsome face of Rodrigo Vasquez, "You're serious!"

Lucas nodded.

"Then yes my friend, if it is your wish, I'd be honoured." He laughed, "Why me?"

"Why not, wasn't it you that pointed out the behavioural habits of my closest acquaintances."

Rodrigo laughed, "That is true senor, so very true."

"Now to my second reason for visiting you personally, "I already knew what my fellow men were capable of, why did you feel the need to elaborate?"

Rodrigo's dark eyes became black diamonds as he digested Lucas's question. He paused for a moment while he gathered his thoughts. "You saved me from a vicious beating or worse, I owed you."

"That's not what you said when I was last in Montevideo," replied Lucas.

"Time moves on." The smile had vanished from Rodrigo's lips, leaving a hard line in their place. "Felipe Salazar is a shark, and you my friend are swimming in dangerous waters. At the moment you're riding high, I just wanted you to be aware of the consequences of failure; make one mistake and Salazar will cut his losses, and you will find yourself just another piece of meat in the abattoir at Estancia Salazar."

It was a warm balmy afternoon but Lucas felt an icy chill run down his spine.

By Lucas's silence Rodrigo detected his warning was registering. "Your animosity towards Juan Aquilar is dangerous, very dangerous, but it has been tolerated because Salazar believed you could be useful. He saw in you a man capable of solving a number of his problems without him getting his hands dirty."

"You mean the Perez brothers," said Lucas, breaking his silence. If he was right about his suspicions, those few words would unlock and confirm what he'd begun to suspect.

"Indeed, the Perez brothers. It is good that you are aware." replied Rodrigo. "They had been a thorn in Felipe's side for far too long. You my friend removed that thorn."

"Why did he need me? Why all the subterfuge? Surely he's powerful enough to have snuffed them out without my help."

"That is true, he perceived a threat to his leadership in the not to distant future. In an all out war against the Perez brothers Salazar would have emerged the victor, but at a cost. A cost he wanted to avoid. If it appeared to be a minor power play between you and the Perez brothers and you overcame the odds, then so much the better, if you didn't, the blame wouldn't have been left at Salazar's door. You my friend got lucky; hitting Julio so swiftly shocked even Salazar and those closest to him."

"They've known all along?" cried Lucas. "How did they know?"

"From what I've managed to learn, Aquilar arranged a little show and you my friend passed with flying colours. Suddenly Salazar realised your full potential and usefulness. I would suspect that he pointed Ramon in another direction. But make no mistake, if Perez had discovered his brother's death was by your hand, Salazar would have thrown you to the wolves."

"How do you know all this?"

Rodrigo smiled, "I have my ways. I've learnt that knowledge is a powerful weapon, without it I could be half-way to the grave."

Lucas nodded his understanding. It was all becoming much clearer; he'd been taken for a fool, a rookie dealing with the big boys. "The respect I received from Salazar's men, was it all a charade?"

Rodrigo grinned, showing off his perfectly white but uneven teeth, "No, that was no charade. You earned the respect of Felipe Salazar's crew, all except Juan Aquilar, but then you knew that already."

"Yeah we kinda have a love hate relationship." said Lucas showing a little bravado.

Rodrigo sought to dispel it, "Don't underestimate Aquilar, he's one bad hombre."

It didn't go unnoticed, but he was here to gain as much information about the people he might be up against. "Cipriano, where does he stand?"

"If Tito Gomez is Salazar's right hand, Cipriano's his left."

"So what you're telling me is I'm fucked six ways to Sunday!"

"Elegantly put," said Rodrigo dryly.

"What would you suggest?"

"As they say in your country, Get the hell outta Dodge," replied Rodrigo smiling, "But in the meantime enjoy your wedding, enjoy the fruits of your labours and make sure you're putting enough dinero by, for when the time comes."

"When in your opinion is that likely to be?"

"As long as you keep your mouth shut and Salazar's kept sweet you'll be okay, it could be two years, five, maybe never. It depends how successful you become and whether he perceives you as a threat. One word of warning, when it comes it'll be when you least expect it

Lucas had suspected as much, but now he'd had it spelled out. After his strange conversation with Vasquez at Enrico's birthday party he'd been a little disturbed, coupled with what Gretchen had said about Felipe Salazar giving up Alvarado's he'd begun to revise his future plans. Everyone should have a plan B. He'd already started putting plan B into operation. It would take a few weeks maybe a month or two, but the day after his and Gretchen's wedding, they were indeed getting the hell outta Dodge. Rodrigo had all but confirmed his decision.

It was an off the cuff remark, and Lucas wasn't expecting an answer, but what the hell, "One last thing, what do you know about a whorehouse where all your fantasies come true?"

Rodrigo laughed, "I thought all whorehouses were where all your fantasies came true."

Lucas couldn't help noticing a tell-tale facial tic at the corner of Rodrigo's mouth. His curiosity was aroused; he decided to push it further. "You know exactly what I'm talking about!"

Rodrigo sought to extricate himself from Lucas's question but knew it was useless. "Lucas, my friend, you don't want to go there. We need to do lunch."

"Rodrigo, I need to know."

"You already know how dangerous Salazar can be, please don't ask me!"

"I have to know," insisted Lucas.

"On your head be it!" said Rodrigo. "Firstly I'd like to say; I've never been there, nor wished to go there, what I've heard is mostly rumour. I call the place 'Fabrica de Muerte,' the death factory. It's a farmhouse; off the road some forty miles from the city. It looks innocuous enough, but from the little I've heard it's the gateway to hell itself. The place houses twenty or so girls; aged between twelve and seventeen, it's policed by six of Juan Aquilar's men and four older women, hookers, women hardened by the streets, who look after the girls' needs."

'Lola,' thought Lucas. "Go on."

"This is only rumour, hearsay. I can't vouch for the validity. Top people from business, law, military, bankers, in fact anyone that can afford to stump up a hundred American dollars a time can use these girls as they see fit. Nothing is forbidden, torture, rape, sodomy, anything goes." Rodrigo's face grew ashen as he relayed the stories he'd heard about the place.

"What if there's an accident?" Lucas couldn't bring himself to say the words.

"If they die, you mean! It costs the client a further five hundred dollars for the problem to go away."

"Jesus! Fuck! It's worse than I thought."

"Have you heard enough?"

"There's more!"

"That ain't the half of it."

"What do you mean!" cried a concerned Lucas.

"Keep your voice down!" said Rodrigo. "They have a fresh intake of girls every three to four months."

"What happens to the ones they get rid of?" He was expecting Rodrigo to tell him the women were left to fend for themselves, discarded like yesterday's newspapers, thrown back onto the streets of Buenos Aires to hawk their trade until they die from disease, malnutrition or a drugs overdose

Rodrigo looked down, he felt ashamed, ashamed to be a member of the human race. "These women just disappear."

"You mean!"

"What do you think I mean!" cried Rodrigo angrily.

"And Juan Aquilar's the man behind it," asked Lucas with murder in his heart.

"Aquilar's only second in command."

"Who's behind it?" Lucas was raging inside. He'd left L.A. because of sick fucks like Rex Blaze and Northrup. He thought he'd been given a second chance but this; this was as bad as it gets. "Who's behind it," he repeated.

"The man behind it, the man that created this hell on earth is soon to be your brother-in-law Franz Kauffman!"

"That can't be, he's an industrialist; he works for Salazar."

"He works for Salazar, you got that part right, the rest is fiction."

Lucas could feel the bile rising up into his throat, but then his thoughts turned to Gretchen. He hated himself for even thinking it; he had to ask, "Does Gretchen know?"

"Rodrigo managed a slight smile, "From what I've been able to find out, she's as in the dark as you were."

Relief hit him like a flash flood. The relief turned to concern; he needed to get her away before it was too late. "I have to get back, we have to get away."

"Easy man, you ain't thinking straight. Stay the night like you planned, go back on the first ferry in the morning if you like, but sleep on it."

Lucas saw the wisdom in Rodrigo's words and nodded.

"Going off half cocked will get you and that girl of yours killed before you can look round. A word of warning, don't even breathe a word of this conversation not even to your future wife, one wrong word, no matter how innocently said to her brother and your cards are marked. More importantly mine too."

"Why have you told me all this, it can't be because I intervened that time? Or even our business arrangements?"

Rodrigo laughed, "Ha, it is true, but the answer is even less likely, but true all the same. When you walked into the cantina on the Quayside, you showed no fear. I saw it in your eyes; the odds were against you. Death could have come at any moment, and you were figuring out how many of my men you could take with you. I liked you instantly. That's it my friend."

Lucas knew why he'd walked into Rodrigo's lair without showing fear. It was because he had nothing to lose. But now things were different, now he lived with fear daily. "I'm glad I did something right," said Lucas trying to sound a little more up beat.

"Lets order," said Rodrigo, "all this talk has left me with an appetite."

Lucas caught the mid-morning ferry and arrived back in Buenos Aires in the middle of the afternoon. Rodrigo's advice about sleeping on it had calmed him down immensely. Nothing had changed, except his determination to leave Buenos Aires the morning after the wedding. A simple enough escape plan was to go on honeymoon and never come back. Rodrigo was right, he had to keep his plans to himself, one slip from Gretchen and Salazar would have them killed, or worse. The images of Humberto Vargas were still very much alive inside Lucas's head.

Rodrigo's warning and advice had given Lucas plenty to think on. By the time he arrived back in Buenos Aires he'd re-formulated his plan of action. It was a little under three months to the wedding, three months and one day before he and Gretchen left Buenos Aires forever. They'd settled on honeymooning in Monte Hermosa, a beach resort just sixty two miles east of the city of Bahia Blanca; a week's relaxation in a fancy hotel, courtesy of Felipe Salazar, who crudely put it, "The perfect place for you to make babies." What Gretchen didn't know, and wouldn't know until they were on the way to the airport, was his change of plan; he'd bought two tickets to Rio.

He'd already begun siphoning off money from both Alvarado night clubs, disguising the transactions as future business expenses. He'd been clever enough to run the idea of bringing in international entertainers to Salazar, who'd been a little sceptical at first, but when Lucas ran the future profits by him, the Argentine landowner's greed took over. Lucas had even pushed it further by suggesting, for tax reasons, a separate banking account for the transactions. Seeing it as a legitimate way for him to launder money Felipe Salazar contributed moderately towards the fund. To all intent and purpose everything was transparent and above board. What Salazar didn't realise was this particular account could be accessed from several branches in one or two other South American countries, namely Brazil.

Everything was in place, but there was one thing Lucas had to ask himself; how much was he prepared to gamble? Just how greedy and courageous did he feel? One final transaction on the day before the wedding would see both Alvarado's Barns being taken over by the main Argentine banks. The downside of course was the possibility of having his head served up on a platter at the wedding feast. He estimated that without that last transaction he'd have amassed around the equivalent sum of one hundred and sixty thousand dollars, enough to start afresh in a country of their choosing. The upside to the gamble could add a cool three quarters of a million, more money than he could spend in a handful of life times. What might add reason to making the gamble was the extra bonus, the loss inflicted on Felipe Salazar's empire would ensure the Argentine mobster would be reduced to the cheap crook he'd always been.

He'd already thought about how he'd stay one step ahead of Salazar. Lucas intended on paying a couple to take the flight to Monte Hermosa, and for them to check into the hotel. What they did after that was their business. It would buy him enough time to get to the bank in Rio and make his prearranged withdrawal. After that he and Gretchen would be home free.

Telling Gretchen that Rodrigo had agreed to be best man and that he was planning on arriving a couple of days before the wedding was the easy part, but keeping his change of plans from her hurt like hell. She was the woman that he intended to spend the rest of his life with, yet the stakes were too high to risk a chance remark. Keeping secrets had been the undoing of his relationship with Erin; he hoped Gretchen would understand when he told her the full story.

The next few weeks flew by as Lucas poured most of his efforts into both his clubs. It had been hard to find the same enthusiasm he'd had when he believed he was going to become sole owner of Granero de Alvarado but he had too; his future and his life were at stake.

At the end of the month he and Gretchen paid their once a month visit to Estancia Salazar, where Lucas handed over Felipe's share of profits. Cleverly when he sat down with Salazar to discuss business, he brought all his banking transactions with him, partly to judge the Argentine's reaction as to where the money was going and partly to allay any suspicion of wrong doing. The only time Lucas would feel vulnerable was if or when he chose to make that final transaction. Even allowing for making that transaction at the close of business it still left *at the very least* thirty six hours where his and Gretchen's lives would be in grave danger. The upside, *if he pulled it off*, was with that kind of money he could guarantee staying out of the reach of Salazar indefinitely.

Chapter 25

Erin stared at the ocean from the window of their home and reflecting on what might have been. Since returning from honeymoon she was finding it difficult to make love to Ethan. She tried, but her heart wasn't in it. Over the course of a couple of months their love making had drained to a trickle. Despite the fact that Michael didn't want her, the very fact that he was alive made it almost impossible. At first she'd feigned sickness, blaming the long plane trips and foreign food. Ethan had understood, but there was only so much he would take before he'd demand his marital rights on a more permanent arrangement. She knew sooner or later she'd have to agree to his demands, but those words of Michael's kept ringing in her ears. If they were true, if it was all a pack of lies, then it was over. But how could she learn the truth, she couldn't just walk up to Jake Reis and ask him.

Her recent conversation with Michael had made her think again. He'd said, "Did you ever consider Ethan was playing you? That Jake might not be in the slightest interested in who you are. You've only Ethan's word for it." Until that day in her hotel room in Buenos Aires it had never crossed her mind. 'If it were true,' she thought, 'then every day since Ethan whisked me away from our apartment has been a lie, a lie that ruined our lives.'

Life for Erin since Michael's departure *at the end of the war* had lost all meaning. Where once she'd thrilled to the whirlwind tour of nightclubs and fantastic restaurants mixing with the rich and famous, now every day was just an existence; a fight for survival. Crime had escalated; Los Angeles was awash with East Coast gangsters. Jake Reis wasn't the only fish in town. Mob hits continued unabated, the most high profile of these was that of Ben 'Bugsy' Siegel, gunned down in the living room of his home in Los Angeles in July of 47. It was another mob hit that would go down in the files as 'No prosecution to date.' Then there was Mickey Cohen; a flamboyant character, a man that craved the lime light. Once Bugsy Siegel's muscle, now the East Coast's mob representative; he was to all intent and purpose the king of the Los Angeles underworld. His squabbles with Jack Dragna *another hood with East Coast connections* had become known locally as "The Sunset Wars," after an attempt on Cohen's life in '48, which left him shaken and a member of his crew lying dead on the floor of Cohen's haberdashery store. This only caused a tense situation to become a virtual powder keg.

Erin had met Cohen only once and Dragna at a couple of charity dinners. Both men had been polite and addressed her with respect mainly because she was on the arm of Ethan. She feared the men that Ethan did business with, but it was Jake Reis that scared her, although on the few occasions she'd been in his company he'd always treated her kindly. It was that kindness that unnerved her. Even after all these years she couldn't stop thinking about how he'd ordered her to be thrown from the balcony, a thought that left her cold. If it hadn't had been for Ethan intervening . . . .

The surf continued to crash against the shoreline.

Jake Reis neither craved the limelight nor wanted the aggravation that an all out gang war entailed. L.A. was a big city and he couldn't figure out why anyone would want the whole cake when a slice was enough for anyone's appetite.

Jake had always kept his finger on the pulse of the city and knew good times don't go on forever. Times were changing. Fed up with a corrupt police force, a squad had been formed to fight fire with fire. Illegal wire taps, beatings, illegal searches, fit-ups, were just some of the methods used in the fight against organised crime.

Although they didn't know it at the time the days of mobsters like, the larger than life Mickey Cohen and Jack Dragna were numbered. It might take years, but even Capone in Chicago had toppled in the end. Jake was ready, the first sign they were coming for him and he'd find himself on a plane to another country without any extradition. He'd amassed a small fortune, cash, bearer bonds and a couple of accounts in the Caymans. He'd been married once, but that hadn't worked out, and to be honest Jake didn't feel the need. He had all the broads he wanted, he wasn't good looking but he wasn't ugly either. His dark complexion, the permanent five o'clock shadow and a broken nose all added to the allure of Jake Reis. He had it all and he intended keeping it. He was forty nine, fifty before the year was out. But judging by the papers and the news on the street, retirement was beckoning.

Then fate took a hand.

Ethan realised the wedding, the honeymoon, the quick change in their arrangements had taken its toll on Erin. Since their honeymoon the marital bed had started to go cold on him which caused him great pain. He'd listened to her excuses, taking what little she offered, even understanding to a degree, but there was so much a man could take. He loved her like no other; why else would he be so patient.

"I thought we had something, but once we got back from Argentina our love making began to dry up. We haven't done it more than a couple of times in months. It was too quick, the wedding, the honeymoon, Argentina for Christ-sake." said Ethan to his latest squeeze.

"I know honey, but you've always got me," said Penny.

"That ain't the point doll, she's my wife, I could demand what's rightfully mine. I could take it!"

"But you won't," replied Penny sympathetically, "You love her too much to do that."

"You're right; you don't worship someone from afar for as many years as I did, without being in love."

"Buy her flowers."

"Buy her flowers!" erupted Ethan, "I bought her a house overlooking the fucking ocean! What more can I do?"

"Buy her flowers, Buy her flowers every day of the week, it's the small things that make a difference," persisted Penny. "Make a grand gesture, buy her an expensive piece of jewellery; something personal." added Penny. "Throw a damn party in her honour. Prove to her that she means the world to you."

Ethan thought about it for a moment, then he smiled, "You are a real doll, if I wasn't married," he left the rest unfinished. 'Penny had struck gold, yeah he'd adorn the house with flowers, he'd buy her that expensive necklace she'd looked at just before Christmas and he'd throw a party, a party in her honour.'

It was the middle Saturday of April and the weather had been unusually kind when he sprung his surprise. He'd hired outside caterers from Mocambo's, flowers from Daphne's and that certain piece of jewellery from Tiffany's. The sun hung over the Pacific for the longest period of time, basking the open sided marquee erected on the manicured lawn that stood between the ocean and their open lounge area in a gentle golden sunlight. It surprised Ethan how quickly and efficiently the marquee company and caterers had set out their wares the minute a friend of Erin's, *a fellow conspirator* whisked her out of the way on the pretence of helping her choose a new dress for a party she was co hosting.

Ethan was corrupt and would stop at nothing *including cold blooded murder* to get what he wanted, but what he wanted most in the world was for Erin to truly love him. He reflected on his new status, he had a great career, a beautiful wife, a lovely home, but these were just trimmings. In his heart he knew that Erin still yearned for Mike Burnett. 'If only the mother fucker had been killed whilst resisting arrest. Life would have been much simpler,' thought Ethan. 'Burnett was out there somewhere but if he ever dared to show his face, it would be the last thing he'd ever do.

With his anger suppressed Ethan began greeted his guests, they included a bunch of cops and their wives, friends from the tennis club, a couple of minor celebrities and Jake Reis, with a couple of broads adorning each arm. He'd extended the invitation half expecting Jake to have a previous engagement, but he'd shown up much to Ethan's agitation. He'd put this party together to show Erin just how much she meant to him, he just hoped seeing Jake Reis wouldn't undo the work he'd put in.

Erin's first reaction was one of surprise; her new husband had pulled out all the stops. Overwhelmed by Ethan's efforts she reached up and kissed him. A roar of approval from the guests was followed moments later by wows of excitement when Ethan presented her with the diamond necklace. She turned around for him to fix the clasp before turning back, "It's beautiful," then she kissed him tenderly upon the lips. She was suddenly feeling guilty about the way she'd treated him since they'd got back from Buenos Aires. In all the years she'd known him, apart from the times when he'd come on to her, he'd always been a gentleman. 'Perhaps,' she thought, 'it was time to extinguish that torch,' then she noticed out of the corner of her eye someone that chilled her to the bone. Jake Reis chatting with some of her guests outside on the lawns looking out towards the ocean.

Her first reaction was one of fear, followed by anger, "What's he doing here," she said quietly under her breath.

"Sorry honey, I had to invite him, I just didn't think this would be his scene," said Ethan in way of an apology.

This was a time for new beginnings, thought Erin. The realisation that 'now' was the perfect opportunity to confront Jake Reis sprang into her mind, to put to bed the niggling doubt she'd carried with her since her conversation with Michael.

"Guess we all have to face our demons once in a while," she said with a conviction she'd never felt before. This was her life now; she'd stayed hoping Michael would come back to her, but that dream was over. Ethan was her life now. Her newly promoted husband was in a position of power; even Jake Reis would find it hard to cross him now. She smiled up at him warmly, "The necklace is very beautiful." She kissed him again. "It's a wonderful party."

It wasn't until the late afternoon just before it gave way to dusk that Erin found the perfect opportunity to speak to Jake Reis alone. Throughout the afternoon he'd spent most of his time chatting to this person or that, his female escorts never far from his side, but he'd sneaked outside alone and was gazing at a glorious sunset.

"How are you Jake?" asked Erin in a newly found confidence that she'd never felt before.

Jake smiled, "You know, you and Ethan are very lucky to have this fantastic sight every night."

Was this Jake's way of reminding her of how things could have turned out? His remark made her mad; it brought out a courage she never believed she possessed. "So should I be grateful to you for the rest of my life!"

Jake looked shocked, "What brought that on?" he asked.

"You've dangled my life in front of me for the last time."

"What the fuck are you talking about?" he demanded angrily.

"If you'd had your way it'd have been me your goons threw over my balcony!" she replied. Her legs turned to jello, yet somehow she felt elated. She'd said it; she'd stood up to him.

Reis looked shocked and slightly taken aback. "That was nothing to do with me. Is that what he told you? Believe me sister, if I'd have wanted you dead, Ethan Kels or God couldn't have stopped me."

Something in the way he spoke made her believe him. Her heart sunk like a stone. "You never ordered that hit?"

"No lady, not in a million years; that ain't my style. You need to talk to that man of yours."

The truth hit Erin like a thunderbolt. She struggled to keep it together."What about Michael Burnett?"

"What about him?"

"You have a contract on him!"

"I what! Are you for real? Mike Burnett got fit up, but not by me. I liked the kid."

Confused, disorientated, out of her depth, Erin realised that she needed to keep her head. Fortunately no one had seen their altercation. 'This changed everything, was Michael right, or was Jake Reis spinning me a line.' She was bewildered; she didn't know what to think.

"If that's the case then I'm sorry to have accused you Mr Reis," said Erin as she regained her composure, "I'd appreciate if you'll keep this to yourself."

Jake nodded and then said, "It's your husband you need to be talking too!"

Erin gave him a half smile, drew a deep breath, then using her acting skills she rejoined the party. She still wasn't sure; Jake Reis was an extremely cagey guy, but if it were true it changed everything. She needed a glass or two of champagne to steady her nerves. After the way Ethan had treated her and the way she'd acted when he'd presented her with that necklace anything less than sleeping with him would appear suspicious. She felt the need to be fortified for when they were alone. Erin took another glass, drank it down fast, before starting on another. Ethan watching from across the room walked over and grabbed her hand gently. "Careful with that stuff, you'll be tipsy if you're not careful."

"It's my party, I can drink as much as I like, my darling husband," her voice though not unfriendly, contained just the right tone of inebriation.

Ethan laughed; the party was going with a swing, so why shouldn't his new wife let her hair down; as long as she didn't over do it.

As it happened Erin did over do it, but not before she'd said goodbye to all her guests. She had a certain decorum about her, collapsing in a heap through drunkenness wasn't something she did in public. However Ethan had to help her up the stairs. With a little help from him, Erin managed to get her clothes off before collapsing onto the bed. Within seconds she was asleep. Ethan though disappointed, felt the party had been a great success and Erin's reserve was melting quicker than a slab of ice in the centre of Death Valley. With his wife lying on her side facing the curtains and blinds, Ethan climbed into bed beside her and turned out the light. Only then did Erin dare open her eyes.

Erin's problem was who to believe, Jake Reis or Ethan. One was a notorious mobster, the other an Area Commander of the Los Angeles County Sheriffs Department. All the next day feigning a headache, she realised she'd have to come to a decision before nightfall. Luckily Ethan had been called in to work; although a Sunday if anything of importance went down he had to respond. This gave Erin time to ponder her next move.

It was mid afternoon and Erin expected Ethan home within the hour, when out of nowhere the front door bell chimed. She wasn't expecting anyone. Cautiously she peered out through the small window in the oak door.

"Jake!" she exclaimed. Panic set in, should she open the door, should she call Ethan or should she pretend she hadn't heard him. A sickening wave of terror wafted over her, replaced moments later with a strange feeling of calm. If he'd meant her harm he wouldn't be parked outside the house in broad daylight, she reasoned as she hesitantly opened the door.

"Jake," she said, feigning surprise, "Did you leave something behind?"

"No." was his abrupt reply. "Can I come in?"

"Yes of course," she replied with a confidence she didn't feel. "What is it you want?"

"Our conversation yesterday, It bothered me!"

Erin was nervous, but managed to offer Jake a seat and asked if he'd like a glass of lemonade or iced tea. He sat down but declined both.

"I watched you after our conversation; you were no drunker than me. I suspect there's trouble in paradise," was his opening gambit. "We haven't been close, once maybe, but I've always thought we weren't enemies. From the little you mentioned yesterday I think you have a very wrong opinion of me."

Erin felt sick, all morning she'd been convincing herself that Ethan was on the level, this man it would appear, was about to shatter that illusion.

"Go on Mr Reis," said Erin in a resigned manner.

"As you know, Ethan does work for me. He and your Mike did the odd favour, but Ethan got greedy. They did a clean up job for me up in the Hollywood Hills a few years back, a good job they made of it too. But Ethan was ambitious and saw a way to cut out the middle man, that's me by the way." He sought to lessen the tension between them. "Hey doll, guess I will have that iced tea."

Erin stood up and went out into the kitchen. She reappeared a minute late with two glasses of iced tea. Her manner and demeanour now considerably more relaxed.

"Thank you," said Jake politely. "Where was I, oh yeah, Ethan offered his services to this producer fuck, saying to call him anytime if he was ever in a similar situation. No need to go into details, but a few years later this producer calls him up and offers him a larger than life bundle if he'd do a similar clean up operation."

"Did Michael know he'd made this arrangement?" asked Erin.

"Doubtful. Anyway to cut a long story short, this clean up operation was a little different. It left Kels and Burnett in a dangerous position, if they'd been caught they would both probably have ended up in a gas pellet ceremony at San Quentin."

"Did they kill someone?" asked Erin, anxiety clearly showing in her voice.

"No, like I said, they were the clean up crew," answered Jake. "On the way back from the desert both men thought about the implications. Your Mike had a harebrained idea to extract retribution on the producer and a well known actor. Ethan, though outraged about the position they'd been put in saw it differently.

There was no money in retribution, but the producer and actor would pay plenty for his silence."

"You mean blackmail!"

"Indeed I do, and in your husband's defence I have to say, the smart thing to do," replied Jake humorously. "He knew Mike would be dead set against his idea, which set his mind thinking. He wanted Mike's silence, he also wanted the money he'd get from the Hollywood Hills duo, but he also wanted you."

"You mean . . ."

"Yes, I mean . . . . He couldn't just kill his partner; it would have been too risky, but to fit him up for a domestic that went tragically wrong was more like it, the only problem was you."

"You're saying he planned everything to do with my apparent death and Mike's framing?"

"That's it in a nutshell doll. What you don't know about Ethan Kels and what I didn't know until a few months ago was that he does work for Mickey Cohen and Jack Dragna, he's also tight with a crew down San Diego way."

Erin's face had grown paler the more he spoke.

"How do you think he could afford a pad like this, he has at least four pay checks coming in."

"So you're saying everything about Ethan is a lie. And you've known this since . . . ."

"Since way back," continued Reis. "For his plan to work he needed a lookalike, and Ethan knew the very broad. He'd busted her a few times. She worked the Strip, high dependency on drink and drugs, same height, same colour hair. I must say one of your striking features. He then paid a couple of goons to do the dirty work and the rest is history."

For the briefest of moments the room was silent. Erin, still suspicious of Reis motive asked a poignant question. "I know I approached you, but why are you filling me in with all the gory details?"

"Like I said until a few months ago, I didn't know he was working for the opposition. You asked. I delivered."

Erin was in a state of shock, she knew he was corrupt, that both he and Michael were corrupt but she'd never realised how deeply Ethan was involved with the criminal underworld. "What should I do?"

"You've three choices, you can pack a bag and get on the first train outta here or you can go upstairs, open the dresser or wherever you keep that snub nosed 38 and blast him the moment he comes in the front door; of course then you'd be looking at 99 years to life. The only other choice is ride the storm. You've a good life style, why spoil it. One day, he'll overstep the mark and either get himself killed or end up in San Quentin."

At that precise moment Ethan's car pulled into their driveway. "Oh my God, how do I explain your visit?" Erin was clearly panicking.

"Relax Red, sip your iced tea."

They heard the front door open.

"Hey Erin ain't that Jake Reis car parked out front?"

"You're very observant, you should have been a detective," said Jake glibly.

"What brings you here?" asked Ethan warily.

Jake smiled, "Left this behind yesterday," he said brandishing a lighter.

"Would you like a drink honey," asked Erin as she rose to greet him, kissing his cheek.

"Scotch rocks," he said as he planted himself down on the couch opposite Jake Reis.

"I was just saying to Erin, what a wonderful home you have here. That view outside is just extraordinary."

"It is, isn't it," replied Ethan, surprised that someone like Jake Reis should take an interest. "Has Erin shown you the rest of the house?"

"No, I only arrived a short time ago."

Erin reappeared with Ethan's drink, along with a large glass of wine. "Can't I tempt you," she said to Reis, hoping he'd decline and make himself scarce.

"No I'm fine. But I think I'll take your husband up on his offer of a guided tour. I must admit I was quite in awe of this place when I saw it yesterday."

Ethan took the offered drink, stood up and proceeded to show the mobster his new home. He had bought the home two days after Erin accepted his proposal. He'd got interior designers to create the kind of ambience he knew Erin would fall in love with. Open and spacious, with tasteful furnishings, plain walls with an occasional painting, a couple of wedding photographs tastefully presented on a polished coffee table more for show than purpose. A new television stood in the corner. Ethan had gone to great lengths in his efforts to please. 'Until now,' he reflected, 'Erin had done little to turn it truly into a home.'

Jake followed Ethan upstairs, admiring the three bedrooms and two bathrooms, nodding his approval after entering each room. Then back down the stairs to the open plan kitchen.

"Out of this world," he remarked.

Ethan smiled smugly.

Erin nervously hoped Jake Reis would cease from this charade and depart soon. Ethan led the mobster though to the lounge, with Erin's eyes burning into Jake Reis until he caught that look. He put his now warm iced tea onto a place mat on the coffee table and casually picked up one of the photographs of their wedding. "You do indeed look a handsome co . . . ." the words caught in his throat.

Chapter 26

Lucas sought out his old passport in the name of Kincaid and checked that it was still in date. Satisfied that his documents were in order he could now concentrate on Gretchen's passport. He knew of someone that could falsify documents, and had been quietly assured by the forger that given any passport he could easily change the name. But there was some risk, he couldn't go to Gretchen and ask for her passport, Monte Hermosa was in Argentina so it wasn't needed. The last thing he needed was for her to start asking questions. His only course of action would be to sneak into her apartment when she was at work and find her passport.

Lucas didn't have a clue where Gretchen would have stashed it. Mainly because the only time he was ever in her apartment was when they both had other things on their minds. As he worked the lock, he felt guilt ridden like a thief in the night, and questioned why he hadn't told Gretchen. His reasoning was obvious, how do you tell the woman that you love, her brother runs a whorehouse where even murder is on the menu. She'd flip; she'd say he was mad; she'd want to confront Franz. Convinced this was the only way, he set about the lock and within a couple of minutes the door opened with an audible click, which Lucas swore could have been heard three blocks over. He entered Gretchen's apartment and closed and locked the door behind him. Standing perfectly still he scanned the apartment looking for the obvious places where she'd keep important documents.

Taking the bedroom first he stealthily checked her wardrobes, making sure nothing was out of place, then he started on the chests of drawers, carefully removing them one at a time, searching more by feel than sight. He checked under each drawer in case she'd taped her passport there for safe keeping. But as each drawer turned up nothing he began to panic. 'Supposing Franz kept all their documents for safe keeping,' it was a possibility he'd not thought of until that very moment, it unsettled him. Next he checked the bathroom, and the medicine cabinet, and drew another blank. The kitchen was next, then the spacious living area, again nothing. He took another look around Gretchen's bedroom before turning and making for the door. He'd resigned himself to the fact she left everything to Franz. It was then that he looked at the small innocuous painting on the far wall, it was slightly askew. His heart began to race. He reached it in three giant strides and swung it to the side. It wasn't much of a safe, just a small nine inches by five, with a key lock, fitted flush against the wall.

Beads of sweat began forming on Lucas's brow; he'd been in Gretchen's apartment much longer than expected. His hands were shaking as he inserted his pick into the small lock. Agonising seconds ticked by as he fumbled and dropped the small lock pick. He took a deep breath and composed himself, as he re-inserted the pick. This time the safe opened. Lucas reached inside and took out the contents, making a mental note of their placement inside the safe.

He let out an audible sigh of relief when he found Gretchen's passport, but couldn't help noticing a few family photos of Gretchen and Franz as children playing happily in a garden, then another slightly older one of Franz in the uniform of the Hitler Youth. 'It figured,' thought Lucas, 'he had to get his training from somewhere.' Intrigued Lucas sifted through the documents and photographs hoping to learn a little of Gretchen's background before the war. She'd said precious little about her past and Lucas hoped to get a better understanding of the woman he was going to marry in less than three weeks. He knew she'd come from a privilege background, the photos of them at play testified as much, but there was very little else. Gretchen never spoke about the war; he guessed she'd seen sights that were best forgotten. Quickly he replaced the contents of the safe, locked it and slid the small painting back in place. He gave a cursory look to make sure everything looked as before; then froze in horror as he gazed down at a document that in his haste to leave had fallen to the floor. He picked it up gave it a brief look before returning it to the safe. Minutes later he was back inside his own apartment.

Chapter 27

The realisation that Ethan had played her was too much for Erin. Jake was on the point of leaving and having to face Ethan alone caused her to panic. "You'll excuse me; I don't feel well; I need a lie down."

"Is there something I can do," asked a concerned Ethan.

"It's just a headache; I'll take a couple of aspirins, rest my eyes for a while."

Ethan looked concerned, "I'd better see what's bugging her," he said, "You can see yourself out."

"Yeah, sure," said the equally rattled mobster.

Erin had thrown herself upon their bed, desperately trying to buy herself time. She couldn't live with Ethan after everything he'd done. But Jake Reis was right about one thing, she had to ride the storm. She had to bide her time, but she had no intention of ever sleeping with Ethan again. Then the idea came to her, it was cruel, but it was what that lying cheating scumbag deserved.

Ethan entered their bedroom and knelt at the side of the bed. "Honey, what's wrong? Did Reis unsettle you?" Then he added, "One day I'll fix him for good."

Through tear stained eyes Erin pushed herself up into a semi sitting position and smiled, "It's not Jake, it's not even you, it's me."

"I don't understand!"

"I should have told you, before you went to such lengths, before the party, you've been so good to me and I've given you nothing but grief." She paused as only a good actress knows how, "We're having a baby!"

"Wha . . ."

"We're having a baby, I wanted to tell you, but I was frightened I might lose it. That's why I haven't let you near me. There's a history of miscarriages in my family."

"It, it's okay, you're not . . ." he left his sentence unfinished.

"No, everything is fine, but I'd rather we left it until I'm sure."

Ethan was putty in her hands, she almost felt sorry for him, until she remembered he'd destroyed everything she'd ever loved. He was worse than Jake Reis; he'd had an innocent young woman murdered for his own carnal lust. Just one of so many crimes that she now believed he was capable of committing.

"Whatever you want, it's yours for the asking," his face betraying a trace of a smile.

Erin had bought herself time, but in a couple of months that time would be up. She had no one to turn too, except Jake Reis. They'd been friends once, *correction acquaintances*, but would it count much when the time came. She waited until Ethan had gone to work, then waited some more. She was having misgivings, what would she say to him? Would it make matters worse, should she empty their bank account and leave before Ethan got home? Her thoughts weren't rational. She nearly jumped out of her skin when the phone rang. Nervously she picked up the receiver.

It was Jake.

"You're still alive I see, and there ain't cops crawling all over your house, so I guess the 38 wasn't necessary," he joked.

"I told him I was pregnant!" blurted Erin, her voice giving way to panic.

"You did what!"

"I told him he was going to be a daddy!" She let out a nervous giggle.

"And is he?"

"Get real," replied Erin, her nervousness giving way to anger. "It was the only way I could get him to leave me alone."

"I bet it worked too. Now listen carefully," said Jake, his tone altered considerably. "I might be able to do you some good. Maybe able to get you out of the fix you're in. But for that I'm going to need your help and cooperation. I need some information. It's ten fifteen, if you take a cab you should be able to meet me at my place around eleven thirty."

"What information?"

"It would take too long to explain on the telephone, I'll tell you when I see you; just bring that photograph from your coffee table."

"Why?"

"Don't ask, just do it!" he replied.

Thirty five minutes later Erin with he heart in her mouth, climbed into a cab, clutching the framed photo of her and Ethan. 'Had Jake Reis inadvertently stumbled onto Michael's whereabouts? How could that be? Did Jake lie? Was Ethan innocent?' the questions inside her head were relentless.

As the cab pulled up outside Jake's bungalow up in the hills of Los Feliz, Erin felt an uneasy feeling waft over her. She paid the cabbie and walked up the short drive to the oak door, which opened almost before she'd got there.

"Come in," he greeted her, "Good, you brought the picture." Jake seized it and turned and walked back into his living room. Erin followed closely behind.

He stood in the middle of the room unmoving, just studying the framed photograph. For a good couple of minutes silence reigned, until Erin broke that silence.

"Are you going to tell me what this is all about or are you just going to look at that photo?"

Jake Reis slowly put the photograph down on a small table. "Sorry," he said. "I forgot my manners, would you like a drink or something?"

"No Jake, just tell me what you want."

"I think you'd better sit down and have a drink; the only way I can make you understand is to tell you everything."

Erin begrudgingly sat down and accepted the offered scotch; the ice crackling as it settled.

Jake sat in the chair opposite her and began, "I came to America in 1921, from Dusseldorf, Germany. After the First World War, life was hard in Germany, the economy was in tatters, work was scarce and my parents fearing I would get myself thrown in prison before too long shipped me off to an uncle in New York City. New York, I ask you, what kind of madness possessed my father to send me to New York?"

He stretched out his arms and turned his palms uppermost in a typical Jewish expression.

"The Volstead Act had been in place a little over a year when I hit these shores. I was nineteen, green behind the ears, but not that green. It wasn't long before I became a member of one of many street gangs; Italians, Irish and of course us Jews, each out to claim their own piece of the American dream. Over the years I met them all, the Rothstein's, the Masseria's, the Luchese's. I did what I was told and I kept my trap shut, pretty soon I rose amongst their ranks. Though only one of their soldiers I was on nodding terms with Lansky, Siegel, Luciano and Dutch Schulz to name but a few. Then, what a bummer, they repeal the Volstead Act."

Erin couldn't help interrupting, "Interesting as your life history is; what's this got to do with me?"

"Patience doll, when I get there, you'll understand. Needless to say we channelled our knowledge in other directions, namely drugs, prostitution and gambling. What can I say, I'm a bad boy!"

Again; the gestures.

"Anyway, the long and the short of it is I had a good life, whereas my parents in Germany didn't. My father was a hard working baker, rising well before dawn and home well after dark. One day with the police looking on, a mob descended on my father's shop. A man had started to paint the Star of David on the windows. My father outraged by this, rushed out to stop him. He

214

was immediately grabbed by the mob, some of them neighbours and customers. All hell broke loose; they smashed the windows and threw burning torches inside the shop. As it burned the mob kicked my father to death. My mother and sisters living in the flat above barely escaped with their lives. The writing was now clearly on the wall, my mother had warned my father time and time again but he hadn't seen it. Although half mad with grief she managed to write me a letter asking for money to get my two sisters out of Germany."

Erin was shocked to see tears in Jake Reis's eyes.

"I sent the money, whether it got there I never knew. I lost contact after Hitler invaded Poland. I kept my ear to the ground, hoping for news, then a year and a half later I received word they were living in hiding at a small farmhouse close to the Polish/German border. I prayed constantly that they'd remain hidden until after the war ended, but my prayers were in vain."

Erin saw the pain and anguish in Jake's face as he relayed the story.

"It was in late September 1943 when they were betrayed to the Gestapo. The poor family that had been hiding them for the last two years were marched into the farmyard and shot in front of my mother and two younger sisters."

Erin let out a gasp of horror.

"My mother would have been sixty seven, Bettina was thirty one and Anna was twenty nine when they arrived in Auschwitz. From the sketchy details I've managed to obtain over the years, my mother was sent to the gas chambers at Birkenau within half an hour of stepping off the train."

Jake Reis paused, reliving the details that he'd paid dearly for. Clearing his throat he took a sip of scotch. "Both Bettina and Anna were strong and fit, their muscles honed from working around the farm. They were put to work with other prisoners under inhuman conditions and then because of their fitness they were singled out and put to work sorting out the clothing and personal affects of other unfortunate prisoners; a brief respite from the horrors that were to come. It must have been around October of 1944 when they were sent to a satellite camp a few kilometres from the main camp, a place called Monowitz."

Erin noticed Reis clearly shudder as he said the name.

"It was a slave labour camp where an arrangement between the SS and officials of an industrial company would pay between three to four Reich marks daily for a never ending supply of labour. In charge of these men, women and children were SS guards and some trustees, other prisoners, usually vicious unfeeling rejects of humanity. The SS methods for productivity included beatings, torture and executions for anyone that didn't fulfil their daily quota. The life expectancy of these prisoners was three to four months after which they'd either died from disease, beatings or had been sent back to Birkenau for resettlement, which was a euphemism for the gas chambers."

Jake took another sip of his scotch and glanced again at the photograph.

"My sisters, and I have this from a reliable source, lasted almost to the liberation. According to an eye witness, it would have been late March; they remembered the snow was thawing; when they witnessed the horrific deaths of my two sisters. Bettina had been severely beaten the day before and was too weak to rise from her bed, but Anna realising this would be a death sentence somehow managed to haul Bettina to her feet. With encouraging words and the help of others Anna managed to disguise the fact that her sister was too ill to work until the shift change of the SS guards, then their luck ran out."

Jake's eyes had grown darker as he told his tale.

"One of the most vicious sadistic bitches at Monowitz, was about to start her shift. She was nicknamed "The Jackal of Monowitz," on account she took a sadistic delight in searching out the weak and vulnerable. Most she sent for resettlement at Birkenau, with a smile upon her lips. Until that afternoon it was claimed she'd drawn her Luger and shot at least two prisoners in the head and on two separate occasions kicked other helpless prisoners to death. She was feared and hated by everyone that came in contact with her.

She spotted Bettina almost immediately as she came on shift. Her eyes lit up at the prospect of sending another one back to Birkenau."

"Take her to the resettlement area," she barked. Another eyewitness recalled how my younger sister begged the guard to spare Bettina stating that a day's rest and she'd be fit to work. "Quiet! Or you go too!" she barked. Whether the thought of the imminent death of Bettina or whether she just snapped we'll never know but Anna summoned the little strength she still possessed and lunged at the 'Jackal of Monowitz' grabbing her around the throat with both hands. For a moment it looked like a revolt was about to take place. Anna was five nine, big boned and even with the little strength she had left, over powered the five foot two inch guard and was choking the life out of her when two guards raced over and dragged my poor sister off. Struggling to her feet the Jackal knew her position had been undermined, sought to reclaim it.

"Bind her hands and feet," she snapped. With her composure in place she drew her pistol and shot Bettina in the head, then turned towards my helpless sister, "Your fate won't be so quick," an evil smile emanated from her lips. Held upright by two heavy set guards Anna was helpless to resist. The Jackal slowly took a short piece of thin rope with handles attached at both ends from a box, and looped it around my sister's neck and began twisting. Sixty prisoners watched in horror and resignation as that bitch choked the life out of Anna."

Jake Reis looked physically and emotionally drained. He took a minute to compose himself before adding, "That woman is Oberaufseherin Astrid Buchler, the woman, in this picture!"

"You must be mistaken!" cried Erin.

Calmly Jake Reis agreed, "That's a possibility. That's why I asked you to visit me. I need to know everything you can tell me about her."

Alarm bells began ringing inside Erin's head. If it wasn't this Astrid creature then she could be putting Michael's life in danger. "Have you got anything that can maybe verify her identity?"

"Come with me," said Jake as he led her towards his study. On the far wall were documents, notes and photographs of several people in Nazi uniform.

"Where the hell did you get all this?" asked Erin, but before Jake could answer she was drawn to a photograph that stared out at her in defiance. Erin stepped in close and scrutinised the face. "Oh my God!" she exclaimed.

"It's her, isn't it!" said Jake excitedly.

Both of them looked at the smiling face on the framed photograph and matched it against the stern military identity card. "I only met this woman once and that was for a brief while in a night club."

"But you think it could be her."

"Oh my God," she repeated. The similarities were striking, but what if it wasn't her; she'd be leading Jake Reis straight to Michael. She looked at the two photos, then she looked at the description, five feet two inches in height, natural blonde, blue eyes, circular scar on left knee. It wasn't much to go on, but apart from the circular scar it fit the description of the woman in their photograph. Knowing Ethan would be only too willing to add the little he knew, Erin decided to level with Jake Reis, but leaving out any connection to Michael. "Yes I think they're one and the same, but you need more confirmation than that. For the record she is of German origin."

"Holy fuck, it's her!" exclaimed Jake.

"You need more proof than that," warned Erin, "You can't just waltz into Argentina and announce she's a war criminal, you need proof!"

"Who said anything about announcing she's a war criminal. This is all I'll need," said Jake, opening his jacket to emphasis the Colt in his hand tooled shoulder holster.

"What if you gun down the wrong woman, have you thought of that!"

"What do you suggest; that I go up and ask her?"

"No, of course not, but what are you planning to do?"

"That's no business of yours, other than to tell me everything you know about this woman."

"Then you'll fly down to Argentina and execute her."

"Got it in one sister!" replied Jake.

"You think it'll be that easy. If she's who you think she is, don't you think she'll be connected? I'm telling you it won't be a cake walk."

An air of suspicion crept into Jake's voice, "You know more than you're letting on. Spill, Red, or I'll make you!"

Erin held her ground, "You don't frighten me, once maybe, but not anymore! Yes I know more than I'm letting on, not enough to say she's Astrid Buchler, but I know how to find out for sure."

"How?" cried Reis.

"Firstly you show me everything you've got on this woman, then you take me with you!"

"No fucking way," spat Jake.

"Then you'll never know the truth." Erin knew it was a dangerous game she was playing, but she needed to protect Michael whatever the cost. She studied Jake's face, she could almost see him weighing up whether to do as she asked or find out what Ethan knew. "I can tell you that Ethan knows where she works, that she's German, but nothing else. I can get you positive proof she's either Astrid Buchler or she isn't. I can virtually vouch for it. Now do we have a deal?"

Jake thought on it for a moment, surprised by the urgency in her voice.

"You drive a hard bargain Red, but you win."

"Good, I'm glad that's settled. Now show me all you have on this Astrid Buchler."

"Monowitz was the third camp at Auschwitz after Auschwitz 1 and Birkenau; its sole purpose was to supply slave labour to the factory. A deal had been struck with officials of the company and the SS Commandant of Auschwitz to use the prisoners as slave labour. Basically they worked them until they dropped, then they were disposed of like garbage. In charge of one particular sub section of this labour camp was SS-Unterscharführer Klaus Buchler. He came from a wealthy aristocratic background, joined the Hitler Youth in 36, then graduated to the Waffen SS in 39 and quickly rose through the ranks, vicious, sadistic, and anti-Semitic, a perfect choice for Himmler's death camps. He flew the coop six months before the Russians liberated the camps, leaving his sister Oberaufseherin Astrid Buchler *who came to Auschwitz from Ravensbruck concentration camp where she'd earned an infamous reputation as senior camp guard,* to fend for herself. It's believed he escaped from Europe and made his way to Argentina, but this is unconfirmed. What is known is that brother and sister had an unhealthy relationship."

"They hated each other!" exclaimed Erin.

"Quite the opposite," replied Jake. "Klaus Buchler escaped with a vast fortune and from the little we know about their relationship he'd pay what ever it took to get his sister out of Russian hands."

Erin realised that if Gretchen Kauffman was really Astrid Buchler then Michael was in grave danger. Methodically she noted down the questions she'd ask Michael if she had the chance, number one on her list was the circular scar on Gretchen's left knee, number two and number three were connected, she already knew that she had a brother, but she only had Michael's word that they both arrived in 1942, she could so easily be lying. If the answer to number one was yes and Michael couldn't honestly say when Gretchen entered Argentina, then he was in mortal danger. Part of her hoped she was wrong, he'd seemed so happy when he'd mentioned Gretchen. But if she was right, would she be able to turn back time? And then there was Ethan, there was always Ethan!

"You said we might be able to do each other some good. What did you mean by that?" asked Erin.

Jake laughed, "If this pans out, I'll make sure you're free."

Chapter 28

Jake Reis wasn't dumb, he knew Erin was holding something back and he had a shrewd idea what that something was. It could wait, there were more important things to take care of first. He could feel it in his gut that the woman in the photograph was Astrid Buchler, more importantly Erin believed it too. Being a cautious man Jake kept things close to his chest. If what he suspected was true, she would want the same outcome that he desired, there was no sense in distracting Ethan.

"Okay Red, this is how we're going to play it, we'll fly to New York, then take the Clipper down to Buenos Aires. We leave next Tuesday, which means we should arrive and be fit for purpose by Friday. You kiddo have until Sunday afternoon to get the goods. You do or you don't, it's all the same we're going in guns blazing!" Jake loved a metaphor; basically his true intentions were to kill the bitch and get a flight home by Tuesday. But Erin had been right about one thing, Jake Reis wanted to be sure this woman was Astrid Buchler, and if she was he wanted to know the strength of the opposition.

"Supposing this woman is Astrid Buchler, won't she have some protection? You mentioned a brother."

"That would be a bonus. We're breaking the bank on this one, it might be a straightforward hit, or it might be all out warfare," which told Erin all she needed to know. Jake Reis wasn't leaving Argentina with the job half done.

"Once I find out the truth, I'm out of there, right. I want no part in what follows."

"Listen Red, you get me a positive identification, I'll do the rest."

It was the best she could squeeze from him, it had to be enough. "How do you intend selling the idea to Ethan?"

"I'm paying top dollar, which means, you and that husband of yours are taking a second vacation whether he likes it or not!"

"What if he kicks off about me being pregnant?"

"You ain't, so stop worrying."

"But . . . ."

"Leave him to me," replied Jake.

Jake broke the news to Ethan later that night. He showed up at Erin and Ethan's house around 8 o'clock along with Aaron Chudzik and Lorenzo Calabria, two of Jake Reis trusted henchmen.

"You my friend are going to take a leave of absence; I don't care how you spin it."

"I can't . . . ."

"It's in your interest, just do it!"

Erin looked at Jake suspiciously, but said nothing.

Ethan dwelled on his answer, it wasn't insurmountable to take a leave of absence, all it took was the folding stuff. Reis was paying a small fortune, how hard could it be to off some broad. "Okay, I'll fix it, but why's Erin tagging along? She's pregnant for Christ-sake!"

"You both met that bitch, am I right? Yeah of course I'm right. What's her name?"

Ethan looked dumbfounded.

"Exactly my point, Red knows her name, which makes her more observant than you. Plus, I need to be sure this woman we're going to ice, is the real deal. That's when Erin earns the dough. As a woman she can get close. Understand!"

Jake Reis arranged for extra luggage to be stowed in the hold of the DC4 now waiting on the tarmac at Idlewild Airport in New

York, courtesy of Meyer Lansky. He was given assurance that said luggage would arrive in good working order when they did. Jake hoped it wouldn't be needed, it was just a precaution, but two Thompson submachine guns, complete with three fully loaded drum magazines apiece would certainly gain peoples attention.

The night before they arrived in Buenos Aires, Jake Reis knocked on the hotel door of Erin's room.

"Open up Red, it's me Jake."

Through the door Erin shouted, "Ethan, ain't here, he's in the bar drinking with Chudzik and Calabria."

"Yeah, I know. It's you I need to speak too."

Cautiously Erin poked her head out, "What do you want?"

"To come in would be nice. We need to talk."

Erin opened the door wide and Jake stepped in.

"Let's cut the crap, I ain't sure of your motives but I've a pretty good idea."

"What are you talking about!" snapped Erin.

"I said cut the crap," barked Jake. "You know, I wondered about you, when you agreed to marry Kels, I wondered some more at your choice of honeymoon destination. Buenos Aires might be a great place to visit, but spending almost as much time getting there and getting back as you do holidaying, that didn't make any sense, unless . . . ." He left the sentence unfinished as he studied Erin's reaction. "I'll tell you what I think; you fill in the blanks if I'm wrong. Somehow or other a certain ex Los Angeles County Sheriff's deputy got in touch with you."

"You're wrong," she protested.

"Right or wrong, it means nothing to me. Like I told you a week back, I liked the kid. It was Ethan's doing, not mine. All I'm interested in is finding that Nazi scum and ridding the world of it. I don't know where Michael Burnett figures in this story, but I know he's in there somewhere. You got a choice, tell me what you know or I'll tell Ethan my suspicions."

"Don't try threatening me," she spat back. "Ethan loves me."

"Maybe when I tell him the pregnancy is just a sham he'll think otherwise."

"You wouldn't, you promised!"

"I promise a lot of things Red. Look I ain't an unreasonable man. I need to know just what I'm dealing with. Not knowing could get us all killed, you understand!"

She'd suspected all along that he knew, or thought he knew, it amounted to the same thing.

"Okay, I'll tell you!" cried Erin dejectedly. "I found him, he's involved with this woman, and from what I can tell they're due to marry soon."

Jake Reis, let out a howl of laughter, "He sure knows how to pick 'em."

Erin ignored his outburst, "She has a brother."

This took the smile from Jake's face. "You've been holding out on me!"

"A girl needs insurance. Where he is I don't know, but if they're who you think they are, I'll find out."

"I like your style Red, but don't hold out on me again," replied Reis.

Erin ignored his veiled threat, "According to Michael, they both arrived in Argentina in 1942, which if true means she isn't Astrid."

"That could all be a lie; Argentina is renowned for being a safe harbour for Nazi war criminals."

"I appreciate what you're saying, that's why I have to confront Michael and tell him of my suspicions."

"Tip him off you mean," snapped Reis.

"No that's not what I meant. I listened to that harrowing story of yours, I saw the photo identity card, I matched it against the photograph. Believe me that woman's face has been etched in my mind from day one. Like you, I'm convinced, but we've got to be sure. The scar, Michael must have seen the scar."

"What are you actually proposing to do?"

"Confront him, tell him of my suspicions, find out if she has a circular scar on her left knee, find out the truth of when she really came to Argentina, and find out as much as I can about her brother. You have your reasons why you're here; mine are to warn Michael about the jackal in his midst."

"How do I know you won't tell him we're here?"

"You don't, you have to trust me. If I told Michael about you, he'd not believe me and he'd warn Astrid, which wouldn't be in mine or your best interests."

"Then we both have to trust each other."

A day later they landed in Buenos Aires.

Chapter 29

Lucas waited across the road in a bar three blocks from the forger. The guy had assured him that altering Gretchen's passport wouldn't take more than an hour. With time to kill the big American downed his second cold one of the early afternoon and mulled over the last few hours. Everything had going smoothly until a document dropped to the floor when he was closing Gretchen's safe. He bent down and picked it up but couldn't help noticing that it was a title deed to a property in the country. As he returned it to the safe, curiosity got the better of him and he looked at the name on the deed; it was Gretchen's. None of my business he quietly told himself, but once he was home free and on the way to the forger, it began to trouble him. It was nothing, just his paranoia at work, mainly he reasoned because of the clandestine way he'd come across it. Sinking the last of his beer, he nonchalantly gazed out the window at the sun baked streets, then looking at his watch; he realised it was time to retrieve the passport.

With Gretchen's passport safely in his grasp he headed back towards the apartments. He was almost there when his paranoia took over as Rodrigo's warning began ringing in his ears. "Trust no one, not even those closest to you."

'What if the deeds were to a certain farmhouse some forty miles from the city? Why would they be?' his mind countered. The though filled him with dread. That Franz could quite easily have put the farmhouse in Gretchen's name so as to keep his involvement secret; crossed his mind. Lucas wouldn't put anything past Franz

Kauffman. But he was getting ahead of himself; the deeds could be entirely innocent and not connected to Fabrica de Muerte. His doubts were growing to monstrous proportions.

His only course of action was to find Lucio Oliverio, the man obviously knew more than he was letting on. Lucas did a u-turn and headed for La Boca. It was still afternoon and the chance of finding Oliverio at this hour was pretty slim. Parking the car Lucas asked a couple of hookers where Lucio lived. As usual they were closed mouthed, even the sight of the folding stuff couldn't shift them. He asked several others, but the law of the street prevailed. In the end Lucas had to settle for the uncertainty of one of the hookers getting a message to him. Checking his watch he realised he was cutting it fine if he wanted to put Gretchen's passport back in the safe without her knowing. Driving back to the apartments he considered his options, he could wait for Gretchen and come clean about what he was planning or he could just forget about it. After all in a few days they'd both be out of Salazar's clutches forever.

Everything changed when he replaced the passport. He hesitated, willing himself to close the safe, but an irresistible urge found him taking the property deed from the safe and studying it. An icy feeling ran down his spine as he realised the property in question was a farmhouse flanked by acres of land. As he studied the document, the lay out, the distance from the city he gave out an audible sigh of relief. This farmhouse was close to the town of Lujan and less than sixteen miles from the city, a far cry from forty miles. Noting certain details to memory he returned the deeds to the safe and re-locked it, before carefully rearranging the painting.

Buoyant from his findings he passed Gretchen in the hallway as she headed into her apartment, "Got to run, I'll catch up with you at dinner, say around ten," he said, quickly giving her a swift kiss upon her lips.

"Where shall I meet you?" she cried.

"I'll pick you up here," he replied as he hurried into the elevator.

Just one more week and it'll all be over, he thought as he drove to Granero de Alvarado. There was so much at stake, marrying Gretchen and getting her away from her scheming brother and Salazar was his top priority. The uncertainty of the day had refocused Lucas's aims. Much as he wanted to screw Salazar by taking him to the cleaners, he realised he would be gambling not only with his own life but that of Gretchen's. Settling for the lesser amount was the safest option. At least he'd sleep sounder now that he'd come to a decision.

In his office at Granero de Alvarado Lucas phoned Alvarado's at Casa Rosada and made a reservation for dinner at ten thirty. They were leaving in a week so Lucas wanted to take one last look around the night club that he'd created.

He was working on some figures when a member of his staff poked his head around the door.

"Senor Garrett, I have a gentleman here that wishes to speak with you."

Judging from the tone his staff member used he didn't actually mean gentleman. Lucas glanced at the clock on the wall, it was already eight o'clock.

"Show him in," he said impatiently.

Lucio Oliverio stuck his head around the door.

"Senor Garrett," he said as he advanced into the room, "I understand you were looking for me."

"What the fuck." cried Lucas, realising why Oliverio was there. After seeing the deeds he'd lost all urgency in the matter. His relief that Gretchen's property wasn't anything to do with her brother was all that mattered.

"Senor Garrett, you wished to see me."

Lucas was about to shove the little creep against the wall and tell him to stay the fuck away, but stopped himself, he had in fact asked for Lucio to contact him.

"It's nothing, a little misunderstanding," Lucas reached into his wallet. Lucio's greedy eyes followed every movement.

"I am here senor, what is it you ask of me?"

Lucas was about to tell him to forget it, but said, "You lied about not knowing the whereabouts of a certain whorehouse. I was going to ask you to take me there, but it's a little late, we wouldn't get back in time."

Lucas's wallet was still open and Oliverio suddenly developed a backbone, his greed being his biggest vice. "Senor Garrett we can be back within an hour.

"What!" stammered Lucas, "you said it was around forty miles from the city, we couldn't possibly get there and back in an hour."

"You must be mistaken," replied Lucio, "Talking about that place makes me nervous. It's around ten, maybe fifteen miles, no more."

Lucas's world took a nose dive. It wasn't Lucio it was Rodrigo that had told him it was forty miles. Running on adrenaline he made a snap decision, "Meet me at the back entrance, I'll pick you up in five minutes."

"Senor, the money," said Lucio as his eyes focused on Lucas's open wallet.

Minutes later they were speeding out of the city along the Lujan road. It was getting dark as the street lights gave way to open countryside. A few miles further and they passed the old gas station and open space, the scene of Ramon Perez's murder. Lucas felt a deepening degree of shame, mostly because he'd been played. He'd been manipulated into arranging the death of Ramon by the puppet master.

Lucas switched his attention to the left side of the road and watched as they passed endless fields dotted with the occasion tree, then as the odometer reached the fifteen mile mark they spotted lights of what appeared to be an old farmhouse.

"Don't slow down senor, keep driving," warned Lucio. The American kept the car at a steady forty as they passed the entrance, spotting a lone figure standing at the side of the road. In the crook of his arms Lucas could just make out what appeared to be the shape of a pump action shotgun. They continued towards Lujan,

Lucas willing another farmhouse to come into view, anything but the certainty that the farmhouse was the one on Gretchen's deeds. Just before Lujan they turned around and headed back to the city.

As the lights of the city came into view, Lucio turned towards Lucas, "Senor, there is something else you need to know. It concerns Lola."

At the mention of Lola's name Lucas stopped the car bringing it to a halt at the side of the kerb.

"Don't fuck with me Oliverio, I ain't in the mood!"

"I'm not fucking with you," replied Oliverio defiantly. "Believe it or not, Lola was my friend."

"This better be good," spat the American.

"No senor, this isn't good, and I don't want your money!"

Lucas was taken aback by the venom in Oliverio's voice. "Spit it out man!"

"When last we met I told you what you wanted to hear, but didn't tell you everything. Aquilar enticed Lola to come and work for him at the whorehouse on the Lujan road. He needed her to keep the young ones in order and in return paid her in heroin."

"I don't believe you, Lola was into most things but she'd fight shy of murder."

"You're right about Lola. It was only after she'd been there sometime that she realised she'd made a big mistake."

Lucio sighed.

"Go on!" snapped Lucas.

"She saw what went on in that place and knew that she'd end up with the same fate as those unfortunate girls. They kept most of the girls doped up, but Lola was so into the heroin that they allowed her to shoot up herself. Feigning a fix she managed to slip away into the night. She came to me scared to death asking for money."

"Why didn't she come to me," asked Lucas.

"Maybe because you're one of them," replied Lucio.

Lucas felt deeply ashamed, "If only . . . ." His words trailed off. She was dead, of that he was certain.

"They caught up with her a day later. From the little I've been able to find out; she was tortured savagely before Aquilar slit her throat. Then she was thrown in a truck and taken to the abattoir at Salazar's Estancia." There was genuine fear in Lucio Oliverio's eyes, "Aquilar is a mucho bad hombre, he kills for the pleasure it gives him."

Lucas could feel the bile rising up inside him.

He dropped Lucio off at La Boca and looked at the time, it was nine fifteen, enough time to make his dinner date with Gretchen, but suddenly he didn't feel hungry. He was in the depths of despair; Juan Aquilar had killed Lola. He needed to die! But his main thoughts were about Gretchen. Had he been fooling himself all along, was she as evil as Salazar and her brother or was she just an innocent caught up in this maelstrom of evil. He didn't know what he believed; everything was closing in on him. He'd been led down the garden path, so many times; he didn't have anyone he could trust. For the first time since he'd been in Buenos Aires he felt truly alone. His brain cried out for vengeance, Aquilar, Franz, Salazar.

Yet he was only one man, the only way he could wreak havoc with Salazar and company was to take the biggest gamble of his life, but did he have the courage to go through with it? The abattoir at Estancia Salazar loomed clearly in his mind. He figured that instead of waiting until after the wedding his best bet would be to take the first plane to Rio after he'd made that transaction. If Gretchen was on the level, there was still time to snatch victory from the jaws of defeat; it was just a matter of timing. Knowing if his plans were to work he had to make that dinner date.

Lucas phoned Gretchen and told her he was tied up and for her to take a cab to Casa Rosada, he'd meet her there. She didn't seem put out by his change of plan and was in good humour when he joined her.

"Once we're married, I'm going to see you work less."

At Granero de Alvarado en la Casa Rosada they dined in style, watching as the floor filled up with customers and strange as the goings on inside his head were he took a pride it what he'd created. Allowing the fact it was financed with mob money, the design, the entertainment and the forward thinking was all his and his alone. It grieved him that to create his dream he'd committed every crime known to man including murder. Lucas disguised his torment by drinking far more than usual. It wasn't long before he had Gretchen on the dance floor. Of late he'd seen little of her, but the smell of her perfume, the fragrance of her hair and the exotic moves of the tango caused his blood to run hot. He embraced the dance, the sense of danger, the intrigue; the utter sensuousness, it was the tango of all tangos; it was the Jackal's Tango. He wanted her like he'd never wanted her before. When he whispered in her ear that it was time to go, she responded with a sultry look. It was enough for him to forget what might or might not happen.

They were of the same mind as they crashed through Gretchen's apartment door, their lips hungrily devouring each other. There was no finesse, no gentle persuasion, just animal instinct as they tore off each others clothing. Lucas pushed her roughly onto her bed and quickly mounted her. He wanted to fuck her hard and savage. His mouth nibbled at her neck sending shock waves of exquisite pleasure through her body. She was hungry for him as her hips thrust upwards burying his rigid cock deep inside. He roughly caressed her breasts; sucking at her nipples, which grew harder at the sensuous touch of his tongue.

"Fuck me, fuck me, make me cum, fuck me harder!"

At her command he thrust himself harder and deeper; while she tore at his back racking her crimson talons deep into his flesh. He cried out in ecstasy and thrust even harder, so hard he felt that he would rip her in two, but she cried out for more.

"Keep going, keep going," screamed Gretchen as she felt her climax nearing. Sensing the moment, Lucas thrust even harder and faster, until the tell tale sound of Gretchen's orgasm became audible. "Ja, ja, ja . . . ." she cried as she felt herself coming in multiple waves of frenzied pleasure.

"Ahhhhhhhhhhh," cried Lucas as his cock exploded inside her. Nothing in his entire life had ever come close to that exquisite moment in time. With their bodies still entwined they lay together helplessly savouring the final throes of sheer gratification before it quickly began to evaporate. Relaxed and comfortable, their ardour spent, they drifted into a deep sleep, and Lucas sensed it would be for the last time.

Chapter 30

Ethan was troubled, he'd been troubled from the start of the trip, but on their final descent into Buenos Aires he sensed things were different between Erin and Jake. It was an itch he couldn't scratch, but the moment he got Erin alone in their hotel room he intended to find out.

"It doesn't make any sense! All you had to do was tell Jake everything, you didn't need to come, especially in your condition," said Ethan, the second the hotel door closed behind them.

It was the moment she'd been dreading, how Ethan reacted would be key to how things turned out. "You're right, I could have told Jake, but there are reasons why I haven't told him everything, the same reasons why I haven't told you. This woman Jake's after, might or might not be a Nazi war criminal, I can find out for sure."

"How?" asked Ethan.

"By asking someone a few personal questions about her," replied Erin, knowing that at any moment the nickel would drop.

"What someone?"

As Ethan asked the question the answer slowly dawned on him. The sudden urge to marry, the honeymoon in South America, the interest in tango, it could only be one someone. "You mean Burnett, Mike Burnett!" Ethan's eyes turned ebony. His world began to crumble as it dawned on him that life with Erin had been one almighty charade.

But Erin had one last card to play, "Yes, Michael, but things are a whole lot different, I'm carrying your child."

This stopped Ethan in his tracks.

Lying to Ethan had got a whole lot easier, "Because Michael is still alive, nothing's changed between us. He wasn't there when all that stood between me and Jake Reis was you. If you hadn't stepped in I'd be dead." The words just seemed to flow from her lips; they were that convincing. Erin knew come hell or high water she had to get Ethan on side or Michael was a dead man.

Ethan wasn't convinced. "You must still have feelings for him; why else would you have suggested Buenos Aires?"

"You're right, but you're so wrong," she stammered, as she searched for a reason that would pacify him. "I came on a hunch, nothing more. You have to understand, before I could really start a life with you I had to at least try to find him. I had to say a final goodbye." Erin was now relying on Ethan's vanity; it was her only hope of getting him on side. "I know I should have told you, but you wouldn't have worn it. You'd have gone off half cocked and gone looking for him."

"You're damn right I would!"

"I needed to put things right."

"You had a life with me!" snapped Ethan.

"Half a life," she uttered. "What good's that? Don't you understand, I had to find him, how could I start a new life without putting an end to the old one!"

Ethan swallowed hard; he so wanted to believe her. She hadn't stayed; she hadn't gone off with Burnett. She'd come back to L.A. She was having his baby. Or was she? His dark thoughts returned with a vengeance.

"It's his child you're carrying!" he shouted.

Erin looked hurt and shocked, but saw her advantage, "How dare you accuse me! Look at me, do I look four months pregnant, look damn you, feel if you don't believe, I'm three at best."

235

It stopped Ethan in his tracks; his dark thoughts slowly began to lift. "I'm sorry, but you must understand where I'm coming from."

"Why should I; it was a cruel thing to say," she responded, pushing her advantage.

Ethan looked sheepish, "I'm sorry I shouldn't have said it."

Erin gave him a semblance of a smile.

"You must still have feelings for him?"

"I'll not lie; yes of course I've feelings for him. But things have changed, he's not the Michael of old, but more importantly I'm not the same person that I was back then. You've been kind, no more than kind, you've been patient; we've everything we'll ever need; more than that, you've been my rock over the past three years."

The anger disappeared from his eyes; this was more than he could have hoped for. 'I'm her rock!' those few short words meant everything. A new found confidence emerged. "How did he take it, when he realised you weren't dead?"

"It was a shock." She replied, relieved that Ethan's outburst hadn't escalated into something far worse.

"I bet it was. Does he know you're Mrs Ethan Kels?"

Erin nodded; momentarily she relived those brief few moments when she'd told him; it was the worst moment of her life. She felt saddened, knowing that in a few hours time she could be breaking his heart for the second time if her suspicions about Gretchen were true.

"Who is this woman to Burnett?"

Erin knew she had to tread carefully. "I think he may have been seeing her." Hopefully Ethan didn't recall the conversation Gretchen had with them about getting married soon.

"Then you aren't so important to him after all," declared Ethan joyfully.

"It looks like it," replied Erin, "I'm here to learn the truth about this woman, what ever way it goes, I want assurances that you and Jake will leave Michael alone."

"That might not be easy to do," declared Ethan, knowing if he came within a few yards of Mike Burnett he'd put a bullet between his eyes.

"Easy or not, that's my sole condition. Leave Michael alone, he means nothing to me anymore. Do that and we go back to LA as husband and wife," she said forcefully.

"What if something happens to him that I'm not responsible for?"

"You make sure it doesn't."

There were questions Ethan wanted answers too, but now wasn't the time. Jake had made it quite clear that finding out this woman's true identity was top priority, and fired up as he was, Ethan wasn't about to cross him.

Mike Burnett was a different proposition, once Erin had the information Jake required, then Burnett was going to be dead meat. Calabria or Chudzik, would take care of Burnett, it didn't matter who, then when it was over he'd put a bullet in which ever one had done the killing. It would be easy to lay Burnett's death at Jake's door. Burnett would be dead, his killing avenged, even Erin knew that in this line of business nothing was certain.

Jake Reis could feel it in the air, the balmy breeze blowing in from the Atlantic; the sweet smell of spices emanating from the kitchens of the numerous bars and restaurants, and the renewed energy of a city coming to life, this was his kind of town. When it was over, when the bitch was rotting on a garbage dump, he'd return to L.A. and put his affairs in order. He was getting out before the big crunch came. Siegel was gone, Cohen was using up his nine lives faster than he could blink and Dragna wasn't up to taking on the big boys from back east. But inevitably before that happens there would be all out war between the mob and the forces of law and order. And when it was over, when both sides were weakened physically and emotionally, another crop of hard men would move in.

As Jake contemplated his future he even gave a brief thought for Ethan Kels, Area Commander of the Los Angeles Sheriff's Department and wondered whether he would be part of the new regime or whether he'd be collateral damage. It mattered little to Jake; he wanted no part in it; he'd worked for his retirement and he damn well intended on collecting it. He reflected on why they were here, in this most cosmopolitan of cities, planning the death of a woman he'd never met. His reason was clear, he wanted retribution for the deaths of his sisters and maybe to absolve himself from a little guilt.

His thoughts were interrupted as Ethan and Erin joined him at the outside dining area of the hotel. Jake stood up and greeted them, "Red, you look a million dollars."

Erin smiled, Ethan scowled, the plan for the early evening was for Erin to locate Burnett, find out what she could about this woman, then return. That was when Jake would take over. It was a half baked plan at best, but with one minor flaw as far as Erin was concerned. Once she'd confronted and warned Michael of her fears about Gretchen, she was leaving Buenos Aires and taking a flight to the nearest US destination. No way regardless of the outcome could she go back to L.A with the monster that was Ethan Kels.

Jake stood up as Lorenzo and Calabria joined their table. "Right gentlemen, enjoy the rest of your evening," announced Jake, "me and Red have a date with destiny."

"What the fuck!" exclaimed Ethan.

"But . . ." cried Erin open mouthed.

Jake laughed, "Hey Red, you didn't think I was letting you go on your lonesome!"

"She's my wife, if anyone's going with her it should be me."

"Relax kid; I'll bring her back safe and sound. Do you really think I'd trust you with Burnett?"

Erin felt foolish, she knew Jake Reis, she should have realised he wouldn't let her go on her own. Reluctantly she smiled at Ethan as Jake lead her to a vacant cab parked at the nearside curb.

"That went easier than planned," sighed Jake as he climbed in beside the bemused Erin.

"Don't bet on it," replied Erin.

"Listen Red, I've kept my side of the bargain. I could have played this different. I could have left you at home and gone with Ethan and the boys, and did my version of the O K Corral. But it ain't my style."

"What do you intend doing?"

"I don't intend getting myself killed, that's what!"

Erin looked confused.

"If this woman is who we think she is, then I'd be a fool to think she ain't connected. The reason I've stayed alive for so long isn't just down to luck. Now where are we heading?"

Erin stared ahead, then after contemplating her options, ordered the cab driver to head towards La Boca district.

"Hey, this ain't anywhere near Casa Rosada, what kinda stunt you pulling," cried Jake.

Erin turned towards him, "Trust me. Now tell me what you've got planned."

"Okay, I'll tell you Red. We're gonna find Burnett, then he's gonna tell us what we want to hear, then I'm gonna off the bitch!"

"You've already made that quite clear, what I meant was what have you got planned for Michael?"

"If he cooperates; nothing! As for that husband of yours that's a different story."

Erin shuddered at the implication.

"Firstly I don't take kindly being blamed for something I didn't do, namely throwing that broad off your balcony, secondly using my name to keep you in line. And thirdly, probably the most important reason, I have no more use for that worthless piece of shit you're married too."

Erin looked shocked at Jake's outburst.

"This might shock you, after listening to what you told me at your home I contemplated putting a hit on Ethan, until I saw that photograph."

It was the cold matter of fact way he'd spoken about taking a life that chilled her to the bone. "How do I know you're not just saying things I might want to hear?"

"You don't, that's why I'm going to let you have a few minutes alone with Mike. Don't make the mistake of running out on me, I'll find you."

"Granero de Alvarado!" said Erin as they turned into La Boca.

In the dimly lit night club, Erin and Jake were shown to a table, their drink orders taken and menu's presented.

"Michael owns or manages both clubs, don't ask me anymore, I don't know."

Jake was enthralled by the music, the seductive atmosphere and the familiar feel the place had. "You know, this place could be a Latin version of Ciro's."

"It's got Michael written all over it," replied Erin proudly.

"You still love him."

"I've never stopped." The tears spilled from her eyes, as Jake reached for a handy napkin.

"See here Red, if this pans out, well who knows," his words were interrupted by the drinks waiter. He swiftly put down their Martini's, and was about to disappear, when Erin grabbed his arm.

"Is Senor Lucas Garrett here tonight?" Her heart was in her mouth, if he wasn't here she didn't know what she'd do.

The drinks waiter looked oddly at her, until Erin made him understand.

Senor Lucas Garrett," she repeated.

"Si."

"Could you please say a friend would like a moment of his time."

As the waiter moved away, Jake manoeuvred his chair so his facial features were in shadow. "Don't want to freak him out," he said, clearly enjoying the subterfuge.

Ten minutes, ten agonising minutes went by and Erin was about to get up and find him herself. "Hold it Red, our man's heading this way."

Erin's heart started to pound, she was excited, nervous, terrified all rolled into one.

"You wante . . . . Erin," he stuttered.

"Hello Michael," she replied with a confidence she didn't feel.

` "What are you doing here?" Then he noticed the man sitting to her left. His face partly shaded by the darkness of the room.

Jake leaned into the light, "Hello Mike," he said, a trace of the melodrama in his voice.

"Jake Reis, what the fuck . . . ." His words were directed towards Erin. A look of betrayal etched across his face.

"It's not what you think . . ." protested Erin, "I can explain!"

Mike had started to back away, until Jake broke the silence.

"Much as I'm enjoying this reunion of old friends, we should cut to the chase. I'll give you fifteen minutes, after that all bets are off," said Jake as he stood up and offered Michael/Lucas his seat. "I'll be waiting over by the bar."

Erin mouthed a silent thank you, while Lucas looked bemused as he took the offered chair. Were all his dreams and nightmares coming together? Was he dead? Was he alive? He didn't rightly know. One of the deadliest killers on the West Coast had given up his chair and allowed him fifteen minutes, was this what they called purgatory?

"Erin," he started to say.

"Listen to me carefully, it's very important."

"Where's Ethan," cried Lucas, ignoring her words. "If this is a trap?" he warned.

"I didn't betray you, you know I wouldn't."

"I don't know what to believe any more," he replied.

"It's a long story, and I hope I'm wrong, for your sake." For the briefest of moments Erin was lost, she'd rehearsed what she was going to say but her mind had gone blank. Quickly she gathered her thoughts. "When Ethan and I were here three and a half months

241

ago, we had a photograph taken with a woman. That woman has a striking resemblance to a Nazi concentration camp guard. The woman in the photograph is . . . ."

"Gretchen," finished Lucas. "That's what you want me to believe isn't it," his tone angry and defensive. Over the last twenty four hours everything pointed towards Gretchen.

Momentarily Erin was taken aback that he should mention Gretchen, she could see the hurt in his eyes. "We're not one hundred percent sure; we need you to answer a couple of questions. When did Gretchen arrive in Argentina?"

"1942, I told you that already."

"Are you sure?" insisted Erin.

"Of course I'm sure," said Lucas, remembering the clandestine entry into Argentina in 1946. The cloak and dagger subterfuge, the money he received, the play acting that had eventually turned to love. The people he was mixed up with, her whoremaster of a brother, the deeds to Fabrica de Muerte, why was he denying what was as plain as the nose on his face?

"Has she a circular scar on her left knee?" persisted Erin.

Lucas slumped back in the chair. Even now on the eleventh hour he'd still tried convincing himself that he was wrong. Then he looked up at Erin, at her sweet vulnerable face, the woman that had meant everything to him and like Gretchen had betrayed him; no, not like Gretchen, not like her at all. He'd so wanted Gretchen to be innocent. Erin had delivered the final piece of the jigsaw.

"I brought her into Argentina from Uruguay in the fall of 1946, and yes she has a circular scar on her left knee."

Erin's face turned pale as she saw the tortured look in Michael's eyes, she wanted to caress him, tell him everything would be all right, but she knew that wasn't going to happen. The man leaning at the bar, the man who hadn't taken his eyes off them since Lucas sat down, was going to see to that. That man was judge, jury and executioner and their fifteen minutes were up as he put down his drink and walked back to their table.

Chapter 31

"We're to sit around waiting like a bunch of palookas!" snapped Ethan. "Jake thinks he's smart, well I'm telling you he ain't. L.A. is changing; pretty soon there won't be room for the likes of Jake Reis. It'll be the likes of me that'll be calling the shots."

"You better not let the boss hear you saying that," warned Chudzik.

"I ain't talkin' behind Jake's back, he's smart enough to know his time's nearly over. Enough about Jake, what say we swing by this Alvarado's and snatch the broad."

"I don't know about that," said Chudzik. "Jake will be pretty mad us pissing on his parade."

"That's the point, we won't be. We'll either get there first, in which case we hand the broad over to Jake, or if we're late, it'll be the cavalry coming to the rescue."

"If you put it like that," said Calabria.

Ethan made a mental note. "What about you Chudzik?"

"What you say makes sense, but what if we're walking into something bigger than we expect?"

"It's a broad; she might or she might not be this psycho bitch. How dangerous can she be?"

"Okay, but we don't go steaming on in there, kapeesh!" stated Calabria.

Ethan reluctantly nodded, "Okay, we'll do it your way."

Still smarting because of Erin's ultimatum, and the fact he'd allowed Jake to call the shots, Ethan was looking for some action.

He wasn't daft by any stretch of the imagination; Jake was a dangerous man to cross but he couldn't sit still. While Reis's was hell bent on getting proof, he intended snatching the woman. If she had that tell-tale scar that was all the proof that was needed.

They arrived at Granero de Alvarado un la Casa Rosada around nine that evening. A little negotiation got them a table on the second floor overlooking the stage and dance floor. Ethan ordered drinks and began to peruse the menu. "It's a good thing I like steak," he jested, all the time looking around for his genial hostess.

When the drinks were served Ethan casually asked where the lady that ran the place was hiding.

"No senor, there is no lady running the place, Senor Mercado runs it in the absence of Senor Garrett."

The name struck a chord. 'So that's what he goes by,' thought Ethan angrily. He'd been played, Erin had lied to him. The conversation they'd had with the woman became crystal clear.

"You have a beautiful bride."
Erin had smiled politely, but said nothing.
"Well thank you, senorita . . . ?"
"Gretchen, Gretchen Kauffman, very soon to be Gretchen Garrett."
"You're getting married too, well congratulations. I take it you're not a native of these parts."
"German, but don't hold that against me," she said coyly.
"Garrett! An American?"
"Ja!" she said in her native tongue.
"Good choice doll, we hope you'll be as happy as us."

How could he have missed it, the reason why Erin had returned with him was because Burnett had found someone else. 'What a fool I've been, right now she could be filling him in on his murdering scumbag fiancée.' Suddenly Ethan had lost his appetite. "This Senor Merca . . . whatever, is he around. I'd like a word with him." His tone left the waiter little choice.

Minutes later Cipriano appeared. Ethan recognised him for what he was, struggling for control he somehow managed to use good grace to extract information. "I'm here on business with my associates," indicating Calabria and Chudzik, "but I was here before, around New Year's with my wife. We met a lady who I naturally assumed was in charge. I wondered was she around, I'd like to buy her a drink."

"No senor," said a wary Cipriano. The lady you speak of doesn't work here. She was helping us with the grand opening."

"She doesn't work here?" snapped Ethan a little too quickly.

"No senor, I already said," Mercado's tone was becoming agitated and menacing.

Ethan ignored the change of tone, "Garrett, wasn't that the name of the guy she was marrying?"

"Senor Garrett runs this and another night spot in La Boca."

"There are two?" said Ethan, more curious by the minute. "La Boca, you say."

"Enough Senor, enjoy your meals, and the show."

Without another word Cipriano turned on his heels and walked away.

Ethan looked at his two companions, his eyes ablaze with excitement. "Well, what do you make of that?" said Ethan, "Two night spots, any guesses where Jake is right now."

"I'd suggest we get outta here while the goings good," said Aaron Chudzik. "That Mercado feller weren't what you'd call friendly."

"I think Aaron's right said Calabria. "Let's eat our meal and get gone."

"For once I agree with you guys, that son of a bitch was a mite more unfriendly than he had a right to be. And right now that goon's talking to some hired muscle."

By the time they left they'd attracted more attention than necessary. Cipriano being Salazar's right hand man was always suspicious when people *especially Americans* started asking questions about certain people. He couldn't make out whether the guy asking the questions was interested in Gretchen or Garrett. But the fact they had asked, meant something.

Ethan wasn't thinking about what attention he was causing, all he wanted was to get to La Boca as fast as he could. As the cab sped through the wide streets of Buenos Aires, Ethan checked and double checked his automatic. Eaten up by jealousy he was determined to have at it the moment he saw Mike Burnett.

Shaken by Erin's revelations and Jake's assurance that he had nothing to do with the frame up, Lucas quickly and as discreetly as possible guided them to his back office. He'd thought he was through with being shocked, but once Jake had filled him in on the deaths of his sisters and Gretchen's part in it he became numb with shock. This woman, this woman that he'd loved for almost three years was a sadistic vicious killer. It was hard to believe, but as he cast his mind back to the first time he'd met Gretchen he could just about picture her as that concentration camp guard. Her demeanour, her Germanic attitude to him, her air of superiority, he should have seen it. But then he realised he was seeing only what he wanted to see. Gretchen was his second chance, a chance he'd never expected after the tragedy of Erin's death. And then things just fell into place, he'd been taken under the wing of one of the most dangerous men alive. He should have cut and run after witnessing the horrific murder of Humberto Vargas, but instead his greed, his vanity, his love for a woman he hardly knew blotted out that blood splattered day in the back of Felipe Salazar's abattoir.

His mind was all over the place, in the space of a few weeks, his world had started to crumble. It had begun when Rodrigo had spelled out the company he was keeping, followed by the discovery that the gates of hell were only a few miles from the city, aptly named Fabrica de Muerte, and the revelation that it was being run, not by Juan Aquilar as he'd suspected, but by the man that was soon to be his brother-in-law. And yet he'd closed his mind even when he'd found the deeds to the 'Death Factory' in Gretchen's name. The cloak of denial had finally begun to slip after their frenzied lovemaking, but it was Erin's words that really stripped away that cloak.

Jake broke the silence, "I might as well get this out in the open, I aim to kill that woman and if anyone else tries to stop me I'll kill them too."

Erin looked to Michael for a reaction, but there was none. "Surely we can go to the authorities, have her put on trial. If what we know is true the chances are they'll hang her. It's got to be the only way," stated Erin.

"No way, I can't take the chance that some overpaid lawyer gets her off with a short prison sentence," declared Jake.

"This country has laws for pity sake," cried Erin. "Do you really want this woman's death on your conscience? Do you want to be like Ethan!"

The door crashed open and Ethan stood framed in the doorway. His automatic held steady in both hands, the barrel pointed in Lucas's direction. "You thought you'd fooled me," he spat as his hate filled eyes stared at Erin, "and it nearly came off, now you're going to watch him die."

"You shoot him, you're dead half a second later!" roared Jake Reis, his gun pointing straight at Ethan's head. Then two more audible clicks broke the momentary silence as Calabria and Chudzik pointed their weapons at Ethan's back.

"You want to kill each other, you won't find an argument from me, but not until after we've finished what we came here to do!" said Jake firmly.

Ethan's instinct for survival outweighed his blood lust. His jealousy subsided as he lowered his automatic, "This isn't over."

"We're drawing a small crowd," stated Chudzik suddenly. "We need to get out of here."

Lucas realising the situation his ex-partner was putting them in, swung into action. While Ethan looked back over his shoulder at a couple of heavy looking guys as they approached the office door

Lucas saw his chance and knocked the gun from Kels' hand while aiming a right hook to the jaw, and a left to the side of the head followed by a swift punch to Ethan's solar plexus which sent him sprawling.

"Just a misunderstanding guys, throw the son of a bitch out, no heavy stuff, remember we run a respectable joint, his friends too."

Chudzik looked towards his boss for direction. Jake nodded; he understood what Lucas had just done.

"We're going, no trouble," said Chudzik as he shrugged off the man's hand from his shoulder.

Once the commotion had died down Lucas casually bent down and was about to pick up Ethan's automatic.

"Leave it be," snapped Jake, his pistol pointing at Lucas's stomach. "We ain't finished. I said before we were interrupted that I was going to smoke the bitch."

"Tell him he can't do that!" cried Erin.

"I wish I could, but I'm afraid he's right." Then he switched his attention toward Jake Reis, the sudden expenditure of energy when he floored Ethan had renewed Lucas Garrett. "If you intend going ahead with your plans, you need to know just what you're up against."

"I didn't spend the best part of three days getting here without getting what I came for."

"You could get yourself very dead, but the flip side, you could find yourself very rich."

"Enough of the conundrums, you got something to say, spit it out!" snapped Reis.

"Gretchen has a brother Franz, Franz Kauffman," continued Lucas.

"For the record she's Astrid Buchler, her brother was a high ranking Waffen SS officer called Klaus Buchler. They are both wanted for war crimes committed at Auschwitz and Ravensbruck," replied Reis

"It's good to know the real name of the woman I'm to marry in a little under a week's time," replied Lucas, injecting a little humour into his voice. "Franz is bad news; I've known it since the first time we met. He works with or for a wealthy landowner called Felipe Salazar."

"So the man has influence," said Jake.

"You could say that. Salazar is behind most of the major crime in certain districts of Buenos Aires. On the surface he's now a legitimate business man, but don't let that fool you. I've seen him slice a man in two with a chainsaw."

Erin let out an involuntary cry, "Oh my God!"

Lucas ignored her cry, "He did it for my benefit. He rules by fear. This club and the one near Casa Rosada are his; I'm his business partner in both of them, which means I have access to certain funds, basically I could almost bankrupt him."

"Why haven't you," asked Jake, his interest peaked.

"Because, I'd be dead, before I could spend it," replied Lucas. "It's funny but only the other day I was contemplating doing just that."

"What stopped you?" asked Jake.

"I don't believe in suicide," Lucas replied glibly. "Do I take it you intend to kill Gretchen and her brother Franz?"

"Got it in one," replied the L.A. mobster.

"To do that, you'd need to start a small war."

"That can be arranged," replied Jake confidently.

"You wouldn't get out of Buenos Aires alive!" replied Lucas.

"Nonetheless I didn't come here to chicken out at the last minute."

You'd need plenty of fire power," replied Lucas.

"How does two Thompsons and six hundred rounds sound, plus our respective pieces of hardware."

"I'd say you were fucking mad! No one's gonna take that kind of a risk. Unless there's a bonus in it," said Lucas.

"You're crazy, both of you!" yelled Erin.

"What kind of bonus?"

"One hundred grand a piece, more if some don't make it," there was a hard edge to Lucas's voice. He knew Jake Reis wouldn't leave until he'd accomplished what he'd started out to do. Aaron Chudzik had been with Jake since the late thirties and a hundred grand would be a good incentive. Lorenzo Calabria was a stone cold killer, but he'd never seen a hundred grand in his life and Ethan, he'd stand fast if only to put a bullet in Lucas's back. Counting himself they'd be five against possibly a small army. But if they could coordinate their strikes, catching them off guard there was a chance they could all get out alive. But then he thought about Erin, he needed her out of the country. He needed her as far away from the bloodshed as possible.

"Keep talking!"

"I've a plan, it'll take a couple of days to arrange, but by Wednesday, Thursday at the latest we could all be that little bit richer."

"I wanted to be flying home Tuesday," said Jake.

"Not possible, but Erin should make that flight."

"No way, I'm not leaving you!"

"You can't be around when the shit hits the fan!" snapped Lucas. "These are seriously bad people. Being a woman won't save you."

Chapter 32

After Jake and Erin had left, he sat in his office chair staring up at the ceiling fan. Things had moved on at a lightning pace since his fuck fest with Gretchen. It was after their passionate night of lovemaking that Lucas finally accepted that Gretchen, he couldn't think of her as Astrid, was involved with Fabrica de Muerte, how much involved he didn't want to think about. As he lay in Gretchen's arms he considered taking the biggest gamble of his life by ripping off Salazar and skipping the country, he had everything in place, but with his passion spent he'd thought better of it and decided to just cut and run. With the money he'd amassed and the weekend's takings he reckoned to have the equivalent of around one hundred and fifteen thousand dollars. It was the coward's way out, but he knew he couldn't face being with Gretchen again.

But then Erin had come back into his life, not as he'd have dreamed, but there as the messenger of bad tidings. Her revelations hadn't come so much as a shock but as a lifeline. He'd dismissed his original plan to rip off Salazar as fool hardy, but Jake's obsession with Astrid and Klaus Buchler might be the smokescreen he needed. Jake Reis had bought with him three dangerous men, men that could and would wreak havoc on other equally deadly opponents, suicidal possibly, achievable not so likely, but in with a chance, a chance to pay back Salazar for all his manipulations and for the simple pleasure he'd get at wiping Juan Aquilar off the face of the earth. There was one fatal flaw in his plans; Erin. He wished he'd thought it through before outlining it to Jake.

If only he'd been thinking straight, if he hadn't mentioned the money, if he'd just given Jake the locations of Franz and Fabrica de Muerte and Gretchen's apartment and left him to get on with it, but he hadn't, he'd let his own personal feeling towards Salazar and Aquilar cloud his judgement. He could so easily have left them to kill each other while he spirited Erin to safety. Jake Reis was a clever and resourceful man, once Lucas had mentioned the money, there was no way he was going to let Lucas be alone with Erin.

No one was an innocent, he acknowledged that, but she was the closest he'd ever come to a decent human being in his entire life. She didn't deserve the fate that might await her. He had to find a way to keep her safe.

Sunday morning Lucas found himself with a big problem. Salazar and Tito Gomez paid him a visit. He was a little groggy having not arrived home until three in the morning. "What th . . . ." He exclaimed before adding, "You should have phoned, I'd have got dressed." He tried to sound casual as he stood aside as Salazar and the hulking frame of Gomez entered the room. "Orange juice anyone," he said cheerily.

Salazar declined, "We were in the neighbourhood, thought we'd give you a call."

"You're after an extra couple of places at the wedding, right," laughed Lucas, doing his best to appear casual.

"Not exactly, last night three men were asking questions about Gretchen at Casa Rosada."

This was news to Lucas, he hadn't realised Ethan had caused a scene at both clubs. His wits suddenly clicked into gear. "You're mistaken, it was at Granero de Alvarado, I fixed it. The boys threw them out."

Unperturbed, Salazar looked straight at Lucas. "Yes I heard about that also."

Lucas feigned puzzlement, "You mean, okay got it. The guy I beat on was some drunken American. He was asking me about

Gretchen. He was agitated, angry, said he had a yearning for European pussy, that's when I hit him."

"He was trying to hit on Gretchen and all you did was slap him around. Incredulous!" stated Salazar, suspicion etched across his face.

Lucas realised the best way out of the situation was to attack. "Senor Salazar, I did what I deemed necessary. Granero de Alvarado isn't a back street dive anymore; it's a respectable night club. No, it's more than that it has a chance of being one of the world's top night spots. I did what I thought was right for my club!" Lucas searched Salazar's face, before adding, "If Gretchen had been there, that would have been an entirely different ball game."

Salazar's expression became genial, pleasant almost. "I think I'll have that drink after all," he said as he sat down opposite Lucas.

"Is that it?" asked Lucas as he walked towards the kitchenette to retrieve the orange juice, his demeanour showing a natural annoyance. "You want one," addressing himself to Gomez. The hood shook his head.

"I have a question, why the third degree?" He said as he handed the orange juice to Salazar. "And why ask me, why not Gretchen?"

"We'll do that right after we leave," replied Salazar. "As you know only to well, you can't be too careful in our line of business."

"I was hoping those days were gone," volunteered Lucas.

"I also, we have done each other some good; yes."

"More than good Felipe, you've given me the chance I could only have dreamed of. I must confess, because of the wedding I have taken my eye off the ball somewhat. But once we're back from honeymoon I intend to put body and soul into both clubs. If Alvarado's at Casa Rosada continues with its initial success I was thinking we should get together and work out a plan to expand even further."

"Always with the jokes," responded Salazar.

"I'm serious; we need to put our heads together."

"Come Tito, before this man spends more of my money," laughed Salazar. "I thank you for the drink, we'll see ourselves out."

Half an hour later Lucas watched from his window as Tito Gomez and Salazar drove off. Dressing quickly he knocked on Gretchen's door.

"What the fuck's with him!" he demanded as she opened the door. "Some drunk you met a few months ago comes looking for you, what's that all about?"

Gretchen looked unsettled, frightened, "It's probably nothing, my brother is too protective. I told you once that he was an industrialist during the war and was being looked for by the Russians and Americans, it might be nothing, but we have to be sure."

"I understand," he said and cradled her in his arms, his mind slipping into overdrive. 'That crazy fuck Ethan Kels has put all our lives in jeopardy.'

An hour later, he returned to his apartment, Gretchen had been really shaken by the news that someone was looking for her and it had taken him all that time to convince her everything was fine. And for the very first time since he'd known her she really did appear vulnerable. Despite the terrible things that had been said about her, he just couldn't get his head around the fact that she'd been a guard at Auschwitz. He offered to stay with her, but she said she was okay and she had things to do concerning the wedding.

"Things that you're not suppose to see until after."

She'd bucked up when he told her his version of events. "From what I could make out he was just another drunken American. And if the clubs take off like I hope, I dare say we'll see more of the same."

In the safety of his apartment he knew he had to warn Jake and Erin, but which hotel were they staying in. He'd failed to ask, but assumed it was the same one Erin had stayed in at New Year. He could hardly drive across town and warn them, someone could be watching and all the phone-lines of the apartment block went through a switchboard. If Franz was as thorough as he appeared to be, Lucas couldn't take any chances. His only chance was the pay phone at the corner of Av Alvear and Av Callao inside Antonio's coffee house. It was tucked away discreetly towards the back.

He took a stroll down the street, lit a cigarette and bought a paper at the corner newsstand. Then after browsing the front page, he nonchalantly walked into the coffee house. He sat down and ordered, lit up a cigarette and pretended to read his paper. He drank his coffee, all the while checking new patrons as they walked through the door. Once he was satisfied he laid his paper next to his coffee cup, ordered another then casually walked towards the back of the building. He dialled the operator and asked for the Plaza Hotel. What seemed like an eternity followed before he heard the desk clerk pick up the phone.

He took a chance, "Could you put me through to Mr and Mrs Ethan Kels room."

"One moment," she replied, then silence. He prayed they'd booked into the same hotel. "Who shall I say is calling?"

"Mr Burnett."

Another agonising wait."

"Putting you through now."

"What do you want!" snapped Ethan.

"I need to speak to Erin, it's urgent."

"What if she ain't available," came the reply.

"Listen, you dumb fuck, put Erin or Jake on the line now!"

"Who are you calli.."

"Just do it! It might just save your life."

Lucas heard the phone being laid down. "Come on, come on," he cried into the phone.

"Michael!"

"Erin, listen very carefully to what I have to say, then get Jake on the phone."

Five minutes later Jake picked up the receiver. "What is it?

"They know someone's looking for Gretchen. That dumb fuck made a scene at both Alvarado joints. I smoothed it over, saying he was a drunk looking for some action. I think they bought it, but they're very thorough. They don't leave anything to chance."

"What are you saying, I should abandon my mission?"

"It would be for the best, but I ain't going to waste time trying to dissuade you. You need to get out now! But don't check out, leave some of your clothes in the rooms, go down the fire escape and get yourselves over to El Presidente Hotel on Lavalle. Do me one favour, don't let that fuck near her. In fact it would be safer for Ethan and the guys to check into another hotel. They're not looking for a couple; they're looking for three men. I'll be in touch later tonight."

What followed was pandemonium; Ethan screaming that Erin was his wife and no one was telling him what to do.

"You'll do what I say or I'll let you have it right here!" shouted Jake.

"No one tells me what to do!" screamed Ethan.

Guns were drawn, insults passed back and forth, the mission was going to hell in a handcart.

"This is madness, Ethan even if you don't care about me, think of the baby! You have to do as Jake says."

This stopped Ethan in his tracks, that and the fact that he was in a Mexican standoff with three guns pointed at him. Jake shot Erin a look; he couldn't help admiring her guile.

"This ain't right, you're my wife!"

"I don't know where this is going, but I do know us arguing about it is likely to get us all killed. Do you want that!"

"You know I don't," said Ethan reluctantly. "When this is over . . ."

"Then we talk," finished Erin.

Minutes later they were ready to go. Ethan agreed to go with Chudzik and Calabria, but insisted on taking the two Thompson's with him. "Insurance," he said as Chudzik locked the door behind him.

Jake and Erin hung back for a few minutes before making their exit. "Got to hand it to you Red, you got some moxie."

"I said what I had too," replied Erin unsmiling.

Lucas called in on Gretchen just before he left for the club. She still appeared nervous and judging by the cigarette butts in the ash tray, that visit had really shaken her up.

"It's probably nothing," reassured Lucas. "Didn't you say you thought his new bride looked unhappy?"

"Ja, I did say that didn't I."

"There you go, his marriage turns sour, he hops on a plane with a couple of his buddies. Wants to show them a good time, wants to impress, then remembers that really hot chick at Granero de Alvarado."

Gretchen gave him a coy smile. "Ja you're probably right Lucas, it's just me being silly." 'It was Franz being over protective;' she thought, 'like the day after the photograph was taken when a terrible fire consumed a certain photograph shop. As Franz had said many times, you can't be too careful, but it probably was as Lucas had said, just a coincidence, but nonetheless her brother was at that moment on the hunt for these three men. If anything, it's them that should be living in fear.' The thought comforted her.

On the way to the club, Lucas started having misgivings about Jake's information about Gretchen. He knew the woman, he slept with her, he'd intended marrying her, up until he'd found the deeds to Fabrica de Muerte. But that wasn't reason enough to believe Jake's version of Gretchen. His head was all over the place, he was getting out, but could he really let Jake Reis kill Gretchen in cold blood?

Despite his misgivings he was going ahead with his plan, hoping that in the next day or two, things would resolve themselves in a more civilised manner. He was five minutes from the club when he pulled up at the kerbside and contacted Jake from a pay phone. According to Jake nothing out of the ordinary was happening, but the strain of inactivity was beginning to show. "I'll be there around nine o'clock tonight," he said before putting down the receiver.

Tensions were riding high when Lucas knocked on Jake's hotel door, Jake wasn't kidding; everyone appeared on edge.

"Right I'll get straight to the point," said Lucas. "The stakes are high, higher than you can possible imagine. But I'd say it's too late to turn back now. Ethan saw to that!"

"You fuck.."

"Easy, I said that to illustrate the predicament you're in. Franz has men out looking. If he finds you, you're dead men. He wouldn't care if you were just regular guys. Which leaves us with only one course of action; tomorrow before close of business I'm going to make a large bank transaction from Salazar's account. Within less than twenty four hours Salazar will know about this transaction unless he's preoccupied, which is where you come in."

"Okay, I get that, but there's one thing that's bothering me; by all accounts you've a pretty good set up here, why rock the boat? Why risk your ass when there's no need?"

It was a loaded question. Lucas knew he'd have to tread very carefully with his answer. Ethan wasn't a fool, so anything less than the truth could set him off.

"For fuck sake Ethan, I've just learned that the woman I thought I was marrying is a Nazi war criminal. I want out and fast, but I'd like to give a little pay back.

"I don't follow you?" said Ethan, barely keeping his temper under control.

"I want to take them all down, which means hitting them where it hurts, in Salazar's case it's his bank account. His money goes into the business account of Granero de Alvarado, ordinarily that wouldn't raise eyebrows, except for the large amount I'm transferring. Only I, Salazar or someone I nominate can withdraw that money from another branch of that bank."

"It can't be that easy," interrupted Ethan.

"You're right, it isn't that easy, but when you've been in talks with the nominated bank, when you've formulated a business plan to expand, then it does become that much easier."

"So retrieving this money depends on you getting out alive."

"That's pretty much it," replied Lucas.

"Except we're going to earn it," added Jake, who was itching to put in his dimes worth. "We're going to hit a farmhouse a few miles from the city. It isn't your run of the mill farm, the livestock is young women, some as young as fourteen, possibly younger. These women are used and abused in the worst possible way and when they're used up they get rid of them, literally."

"You've got to be kidding," said Lorenzo.

"I wish he was," replied Lucas, taking up the slack. "Franz Kauffman runs this establishment. He has at least six hoods working with him at all times, one at the entrance, possibly two at the door, where the others and Franz are I don't have a clue, but they're there and they aren't a pushover. On top of that he has four older women that look after these girls."

Jake interrupted, he didn't think Lucas had the stomach to say what needed saying, "We hit them hard; we do what it takes to secure the farmhouse."

"Back to the money side of things, how much do we get assuming we survive," asked Lorenzo.

"As I said yesterday, at the least one hundred and fifty thousand apiece, more if some of us don't make it."

"So we've got to keep you alive," sneered Ethan.

"It would be preferable, but I've thought of a contingence plan." 'Here it comes,' thought Lucas, 'it's make or break time.' "I'm nominating Erin to do the withdrawal, which means she leaves before the shit hits the fan."

Erin gasped, "I'm not leaving!"

"Erin, you must, if you don't the deals off. That's my condition."

Surprisingly Ethan didn't kick off. "Okay, I follow where you're heading, but if you ain't amongst the living where will we meet up with Erin?" he said.

"Good question. Once it begins I'll tell Jake where he can contact Erin if I don't make it."

Chapter 33

Lucas's heart was pounding as he left the bank. He'd reached the point of no return; there was no going back from here. He quickly made a phone call to Jake confirming the bank transaction, then asked if Erin was ready.

"She is, and as soon as you join us she can take the cab to the airport."

So there would be no chance of a double cross Jake had insisted that Erin stayed until Lucas joined them. Her plane wasn't taking off until noon the following day, but Lucas had insisted that she should be as far away from them as was possible. It wasn't ideal, but a small hotel close to the airport was the best he could hope for.

The scene that greeted Lucas when Jake opened the door to the small hotel room was one of strained cordiality; even Ethan forced a smile as he checked the mechanism of the Thompson. Erin looked fretful, knowing that in a few short minutes she would be saying goodbye to the only man she'd ever truly loved. Lorenzo Calabria sat nervously, his leg pumping up and down like a piston. His haunted look was infectious, even Aaron Chudzik *usually so cool under fire*, fidgeted in his chair as he cleaned and checked his own personal arsenal of weapons. Apart from himself, only Jake Reis seemed together. Lucas cast Jake a worried look.

"Don't worry about them, they're wired at the moment, but once we get to it, they'll settle down."

Lucas hoped he was right, because in a little under an hour if everything went according to plan Franz Kauffman aka Klaus

Buchler would be lying dead in a farmhouse. The full enormity of what they were about to do was beginning to hit home, but he held it together until Erin had left for the airport. It had been a tense parting and only a few sharp words from Jake had kept it together.

Lucas and Ethan watched from a hotel window as Erin climbed into the cab and drove away.

"Jesus; fuck, are you two out of your minds. We're about to create our own St Valentines' Day Massacre. Arguing amongst ourselves will get us killed for sure! We have to stay focused."

Lucas realising the implications of what they were about to do, took Jake aside. "It's madness, even if we pull it off, do you realise the kind of heat we'll attract. Salazar will have his own private army out looking and if that ain't bad enough he'll get his brother Ruben to have the whole fucking Argentine army out as well."

"It's a bit late now!" spat Jake.

"I've an idea!" said Lucas. "It came to me last night. Instead of hitting the farmhouse, we lure Franz away from it. We hit him on the road between the city and the farmhouse."

"How do you propose to do that!" snapped Jake.

"He's looking for Ethan, so why not use him as bait."

"Get the fuck outta here," shouted Ethan.

"Here me out!" cried Lucas, "There's an open space just past an old derelict gas station on the way to the farmhouse. We lure Franz there."

"He's gonna come on your say so, yeah right!" sneered Ethan.

"Not on my say so, but on the say so of Cipriano Mercardo, my night manager," said Lucas excitedly. "I don't know why I didn't think of it before. I phone him and tell him I have the guy Franz is looking for."

"How's that going to lure Franz?" asked Jake.

"All along, Franz has believed Ethan was looking for Gretchen. I tell Cipriano it was me he was after. Basically I tell him the truth. Ethan flew down to Buenos Aires with the express intent on killing me; that my past was catching up on me."

"Ain't that the truth," cried Ethan.

"I tell Cipriano I'm at the old Perez place and that I need a ride home."

"The old Perez place, I don't understand, I thought you said this place was deserted."

"It is. Cipriano will understand, but more importantly I'm betting he'll be on the phone to Franz the minute we stop talking."

"What if he ain't, some poor sap drives out here, only to end up dead," said Ethan.

"What, you're developing a conscience all of a sudden?"

Lucas's remark brought out nervous laughter from Chudzik and Calabria.

"Believe me, I know these people. Cipriano will phone Franz. And I'm betting Franz won't be convinced and will feel the need to interrogate Ethan."

"Wait a minute, you're proposing they come at us from two directions!" said Chudzik.

"That's right. Allowing for traffic Cipriano should arrive first."

"Sheer madness," said Ethan.

"Maybe, but it's a better option!" declared Jake. "How sure are you that the Kraut will buy it?"

"I've seen the way he operates. Until he's beaten the truth out of Ethan he won't rest. He'll come."

"Then we're down to numbers," declare Jake. "How many do you figure we have to deal with?"

"That I can't say, if we're lucky it could just be Cipriano and Franz, but on the other hand, I'd expect Franz to arrive with two, possibly three men. He can't leave the farmhouse un-manned. Cipriano will arrive either by himself or with one other, hiding on the back seat of the car."

"At best two, at worst six, let's get it done," cried Jake.

Ten minutes later Lucas using a call box on the edge of the city called Cipriano. "Listen carefully, I screwed up, that guy that Franz is looking for, was looking for me, not Gretchen!" he said breathlessly.

"Take it easy, what's that you're saying?" answered Cipriano.

"That guy was looking for me, not Gretchen. I found him and I'm taking him to the old Perez place. I'll need a ride back."

"Is he alive?"

"At the moment, but he won't be. I just need a ride back to the city."

"Keep him alive! At least until I get there!"

"Make it quick!" Lucas hung up, waited a minute, then redialled the number, before handing the ear piece to Jake. The L.A. mobster put the earpiece to his ear and listened to the busy signal.

"He bought it!"

Franz listened as Cipriano relayed the garbled call from Lucas. "He said he'd got the guy you're looking for. That it was someone from his past, nothing to do with Gretchen. Lucas wants me to pick him up where Perez's body was found."

"Is the American alive?"

"I think so, but I can't be sure. I told Lucas to keep him alive until I got there."

"That fuck better not have killed him, I want the other two that were with him. I have to know my sister is safe."

"I'm on my way," said Cipriano.

"Keep him alive until I get there!"

"I'll do what I can," replied Cipriano speaking to a dead phone.

Twenty minutes later Cipriano drove by the derelict gas station and scanned the open space. It was a good thirty seconds before he made out the rusting remains of Perez's car, the one he personally torched almost two years earlier. As he turned off the highway his headlights revealed a second car. In front of it was Lucas, shielding his eyes from the glare of headlights. Cipriano pulled to a stop twenty feet from where Garrett was standing. He switched off the engine but kept the lights on. Checking his watch he guessed that Franz would be there within five or six minutes. Acting on instinct he took his revolver from his shoulder holster and checked his rounds. Cautiously he slid across the driver's side and emerged from the passenger door. His headlights obscured Lucas's view. He hadn't reached forty nine years of age from being reckless. From the darkness he called to Lucas.

"Sorry for the caution, old habits. Is he still alive?" Cipriano could just make out a body hanging half in and half out of the rear passenger door.

"I tried moving him to the driver's side, but the fucker's to damn heavy. I wanted to get him into the front seat, before torching the car."

"I asked you a question, is he still alive?" asked Cipriano.

"What's it to you?" Lucas knew that for his plan to work Franz had to take the bait. "Now get over here and give me a hand. I want to get the fuck outta here," snapped Lucas.

"It's not that simple. Franz wants him alive. He'll be here soon." Cipriano had rushed from the club, and had driven up to the first intersection before doubt started to creep in. He shouldn't have been meeting Lucas alone, but it was too late to turn back, hence his reluctance to move closer.

"What's Franz got to do with it?" asked Lucas in an agitated state.

"He needs to be sure." replied Cipriano.

"I phoned you, I didn't want anyone else involved. This fuck," he reached into the car and using all his strength dragged a blooded and battered Ethan out into the open. "This fuck, he repeated breathlessly, "destroyed my life, he had my wife killed and me framed for her murder."

Ethan groaned, partly from the bang on the head he received when Lucas roughly yanked him from the car, but partly to let Cipriano know he was still alive.

"I understand," replied Cipriano, "But you need to wait. Kill the piece of shit, but after Franz has questioned him." And still he remained in the shadows.

"I should have told someone, I should've told Salazar," continued Lucas.

"Yeah, you should have!" snarled Cipriano. Ethan lying flat out in the dirt grabbed at Lucas's leg, his intention to distract Cipriano. Lucas swirled around and kicked at Ethan's body.

Cipriano moved forward into the light instinctively. In that split second Chudzik rose from behind the burnt out wreck and let loose the Thompson, strafing Cipriano's body, stitching a line of forty five calibre slugs across his barrel chest. The big man writhed and twisted with the sudden impact before dropped like a stone.

The smell of cordite hung in the air as Chudzik stepped around the burnt out wreck to admire his handiwork before shooting him in the head to make sure.

Ethan struggled to his feet, his face red with anger, "Kick me one more time and I'll eat your liver while you watch me," he snapped.

Lucas was unmoved. He stared briefly at the body of Cipriano, then turned his back.

"Lorenzo, help Aaron," snapped Jake.

The two men heaved Cipriano's body into the car, then Lorenzo started the engine. Sticking it into gear he drove the car into the position Jake was indicating. Then he switched off the engine and manoeuvred Cipriano's hulking frame into the driver's seat, before switching off the headlights.

"Now we wait," said Jake.

Five minutes went by and the silence was deafening. No one spoke, each of them lost in there own thoughts. Then from a distance they saw the headlights of a vehicle coming from the direction of the farmhouse. Everyone tensed as the headlights grew bigger and bigger, before driving passed at forty miles an hour.

"Fuck; was that them, or some unsuspecting motorist!" exclaimed Aaron Chudzik, his trigger finger caressing the guard of the Thompson.

"We'll know in a couple of minutes," answered Jake, trying to hide the tension in his voice. A further two cars passed, then a fourth came into view. This one appeared to be travelling at a much slower speed, as if searching for something. Sweat stung at Lucas's brow, much as it had when he and Cipriano dispatched Ramon Perez. The car pulled to a stop, flashed its lights on and off. Lorenzo flashed the lights of Cipriano's car in response. Immediately the car pulled into the kill zone.

Chapter 34

As Franz's car drew closer Lucas walked into the central light from where the headlights of all three vehicles converged. In front of him with a gun to his head was Ethan, apparently bound and looking worse for wear.

"Das ist gut," cried Franz as he athletically emerged from his vehicle's passenger side.

"He's someone from my past," cried Lucas.

"We'll soon find out," replied Franz as he confidently strutted towards Ethan, but then he suddenly stopped. He sniffed at the cool night air; a trace of cordite invaded his nostrils. Something wasn't right. His instinct was to run as an air of suspicion crept into his tanned granite like features and his face took on a hunted look. And then he knew; the man with the gun pointed at his head was smiling. Before he could act two more forty five calibre Colt Automatics were pointed at his head.

He froze.

Then the world exploded all around him as Lorenzo emerged from the side of Cipriano's car and let fly with the Thompson at Franz's vehicle. A split second later Chudzik opened up with the second Thompson. The distinctive rattle of the Thompson, the thud, thud, thud of pierced metal, the shattering of windshield and glass and the bloodcurdling sound of men dying filled the still night air with a cacophony of death. Franz's looked on without emotion. The limousine took on a life of it's own as it shook with the impact of the heavy duty slugs as they ripped into the bodywork.

The silence was deafening as the sounds of the two Thompson machine guns stopped spitting death. Franz weighed up his options, his men were dead or dying, his own life looked to be in the balance. But then his instinct for survival kicked in. That he was alive spoke volumes. He'd been right after all; these men were here to bring him and Astrid to justice. How foolish some men could be, he thought arrogantly, he almost laughed at their naivety, did they really think they could kill native Argentineans? Did they think that the government would let them go free?

He'd lost two, no three good men as he looked at the dead face of Cipriano staring at him through the windshield. Yet he was still alive. As he looked at the stern face of Lucas he vowed he'd have sport with him before Salazar administered his own brand of justice.

"So Lucas, who is it you work for; the Americans or the Jews?"

"You could say he works for both," said Jake as he approached from the shadows. "My name is Jake Reis, it's only fitting that you know this, as I'm here as judge . . ." Jake squeezed the trigger of his 45 calibre automatic and shot Franz in the left knee. The German collapsed in the dirt, a look of shock and puzzlement followed by realisation etched upon his ashen face. Without changing expression Jake looked down at the injured man, "Jury," then he shot him in the right knee, "and executioner." He pointed the pistol at Franz's head, then stopped himself.

Franz looked up despite the excruciating pain, "I am a German Officer of the Third Reich and I embrace death, not like you cowardly Jew dogs."

"Maybe so," replied Jake, unimpressed, "but before you go my incestuous fucker, I'd like you to take a good look at the man that will end the life of your sweet sister 'the Jackal of Monowitz.'"

For the briefest of moments Franz didn't understand, then the meaning became clear, "Nien, nien, nien!" Jake levelled the gun and shot him between the eyes.

An eerie silence followed the execution as each man began to realise the implications of their actions. If it was too late to back out before, the gates to hell had just closed behind them.

It was Lucas who broke the silence, "Let's go!"

"We should torch the cars," said Lorenzo Calabria.

"Good idea," cried Ethan.

Less than a minute later the two cars were ablaze just as Lucas's Oldsmobile slowly drove away from the scene of carnage.

"Now the shit's really hit the fan," said Aaron Chudzik. "We just committed mass murder in a foreign country!"

The sudden realisation of what they'd done began to hit home.

"I say we get the fuck out of this country. I won't feel safe until we touch ground in the U S of A!" declared Lorenzo.

As the car sped towards the city Jake spoke up. "Boys, you're free to go, I won't try to stop you."

Lucas felt a sudden feeling of relief.

"You've done all I've asked," continued Jake. "I ain't gonna ask for more. The rest I'll do on my own."

Lucas felt his heart sink. He'd hoped that would have been the end of it, but past experience should have warned him. Jake was determined to carry out his promise to Franz.

"What about Erin and the money," snapped Ethan.

"If I get out, you'll get your money," replied Jake, "I'll guarantee it."

"But if you don't," persisted Ethan.

Jake spun round in his seat, "If you hadn't stuck your nose where it wasn't wanted, this would have been a cake-walk. But oh no, you had to go steaming in!" The L.A.mobster was mad, mad as all hell; he knew it could have been so much easier. "You signed up for this deal, you knew what you were getting yourself into and under the circumstances I'd say you were pretty lucky. I'm giving you a get out clause for fuck-sake! It's up to you whether you take it or not!"

"Ain't killing her brother enough," chipped in Lucas.

"No it ain't, it never was," snapped Jake. "I knew you'd go soft on the deal."

"I don't see why you have to go through with it," insisted Lucas

"Hold it, hold it," cried Aaron Chudzik. "No point in arguing amongst ourselves. It's a sure fire way to get us all killed."

"Aaron's right. We just murdered four men, the chance of us getting out alive looks pretty slim. Lorenzo, you done everything I asked. Go with a good heart. The same goes for you Aaron," said Jake, putting a lid on his anger.

"No can do boss!" stated Aaron. "I'm sticking. You ain't the only one that's got a stake in this crusade," he added. "You forget I'm a Polish Jew."

Jake nodded his understanding, a weak smile upon his lips. "As for you Mike Burnett, not meaning to turn up the heat any hotter than it already is, apart from the money, you've that pretty redhead waiting for you. Are you gonna jeopardise your future for a filthy murdering Nazi piece of scum."

"Ain't you forgetting, she's carrying my child!" snapped Ethan.

"Oh yeah, I was forgetting," replied Jake with a hint of sarcasm. "She's not pregnant, she never was!"

"What!" cried Ethan and Lucas in unison?

"You heard. Red wanted you off her back."

The full implication of what Jake was saying hit home to Lucas. There was no baby, there never was. The possibility of a future with Erin was far more than he could hope for, but it was there, a day, maybe a week away, but there all the same. But could he leave Gretchen to the mercy of Jake Reis. It was a question he had to put to the back of his mind.

Ethan was seeing red. He'd lost; no he'd never been in the race. She'd suckered him good; Erin only ever belonged to one man. Why had he been so blind, he asked himself? His hatred intensified, it was close to boiling point, but Aaron Chudzik was right, they were in a bind, they needed to pull together. Erin was dead to him, but the money she'd collect wouldn't be. Once they were free and clear of Argentina, he'd come out the winner, Mike Burnett would be dead, Jake too and Erin could go hang.

"We can worry about what we're gonna do once we're back at the hotel, but first we need to throw gasoline on the flames," said Lucas, his mind working overtime.

The arguing stopped as everyone waited for what he had in mind.

It was a little before ten when Lucas pulled up next to a pay phone. Within a minute he was through to the news desk of the Buenos Aires Tribune and in perfect Spanish he said, "I'd like to report a crime, there's been a shooting just off the Lujan highway near the old derelict gas station."

He waited for the inevitable questions. "Who are you? How did you come by this information?"

"Never mind who I am, do you want this information or not?"

Within minutes Lucas informed them a number of men had been slaughtered as a reprisal for the murder of Ramon Perez. When he was sure he'd got the Tribune's attention he added that approximately twenty minutes west of the derelict gas station on the highway leading to Lujan there's a farmhouse where girls as young as twelve are being forced into prostitution.

"How do you know all this?"

Lucas ignored the question. "Now listen carefully the man behind the killings is Felipe Salazar!"

Lucas slammed down the receiver and climbed back into the Oldsmobile. "That should cause a shit storm!" he said as he re-started the engine.

"Best of luck, see you in L.A.," said Lorenzo Calabria, as he shook hands with everyone. He figured his best course of action was to head to the airport and book himself on the first flight out of Argentina. By morning the whole of Buenos Aires would be waking up to the mayhem they'd caused. Getting out, in his eyes while the going was good, had to be the best course of action.

As he left, Lucas's words of caution sent jitters up and down his spine. "If they catch you, they'll show no mercy. Better to make a fight of it, than risk capture. You're dead either way."

After checking the flights for the morning departures, Lorenzo decided to sit it out. He booked into a cheap hotel and locked the door, before wedging a chair against the handle. It was going to be a long night.

"Why don't we hit the bitch tonight!" remarked Ethan, "then we can all catch the morning flight!"

"Do you think it'll be that simple," stated Jake. "I urged Lorenzo to take a train, any train out of Buenos Aires, lay low for a few days, a week maybe, but I'm betting he'll head for the airport."

"You think they'll have people watching the airport?" asked Ethan.

"I don't know; if Calabria uses his head he should be okay. I'm just glad Burnett gave him the advice that he did. I only wish he'd followed his own advice."

"Yeah, I thought that was dumb, but hey it's his neck!" exclaimed Ethan.

"Heading back to Alvarado's as if nothing had happened seems sheer lunacy to me, but he seemed pretty confident," said Jake.

"Mike Burnett was never much of a gambler when he was on the force, but I agree with you, heading back to Alvarado's does seem like lunacy," remarked Ethan.

"That or pure genius," said Jake.

"What's that supposed to mean," asked Ethan, the tension in his voice unmistakeable. He's filled you in on everything ain't he?"

"He told me all I needed to know. He seemed to have it all figured out, but if that guy from the restaurant spoke to anyone other than the Kraut he's a dead man."

"He spoke to the German, why would he feel the need to tell anyone else," added Chudzik.

"You've got a point, but would the German have spoken to anyone after he received that call," said Ethan.

"He might have, but you saw that arrogant son of a bitch, he wasn't the type to answer to anyone," replied Jake.

Once Lucas dropped them off at the hotel, he raced back to Granero de Alvarado's. Then he walked the five blocks to the back of the Teatro Premier movie house, where he slipped in the side entrance and was in time to watch the closing credits of the latest Bogart movie.

Then he slowly got up and made for the exit. Unhurriedly he made his way back to Alvarado's. He spoke to the doorman, the cigarette girl and a member of the bar staff before letting himself into the back office. As he sat down his hands began to shake, and he had trouble opening the lock to one of his desk drawers. He steadied himself, then reached inside the drawer for a pen and paper. Quickly he wrote a note to Cipriano stating 'if anything important comes up you can reach me at Teatro's'. Since the attempt on his life at the movie palace it had become common knowledge that whenever a Bogey movie was playing he'd find the time to see it. He folded the note before flipping it onto the floor.

Ten minutes later with his nerves under control he walked into the main area of the club and began talking with his customers and bar staff. He casually asked if anyone had seen Cipriano, saying it wasn't like him not to leave a note if he was off somewhere. Thirty minutes later he returned to his office and the shit hit the fan.

Clemente Ramos and Juan Aquilar with faces set like stone, burst into his office.

"What's with the long faces?" laughed Lucas, his feet up on his desk.

Ramos swiped his feet off the desk, "You know why we're here!" said Aquilar.

Lucas laughed inwardly; it was a trick he and Ethan had used many times before when they wanted to catch someone off guard.

"No, and if you try that again you won't be so lucky," he said looking straight at Ramos. "Now can we start again; what are you so riled up about?"

273

"Start by tell us where you were earlier this evening," snapped Aquilar.

"What's this all about?" replied Lucas, now standing toe to toe, with Clemente Ramos. "then maybe I'll tell you where I've been."

"Franz Kauffman, Cipriano and two others were gunned down earlier tonight!" said Ramos.

"You're kidding," exclaimed Lucas as he sat back down in his chair.

"Does he look like he's kidding," snapped Aquilar.

"Earlier tonight I went to the movies, I left Cipriano a note."

"Empty your pockets," snapped Ramos.

"What!"

"You heard, empty your pockets."

Lucas feigning shock and confusion stood up and turned out his pockets obediently. Clemente Ramos sifted through the change, the crushed pack of cigarettes, and picked up a cinema ticket stub. "What movie did you see?"

"Knock on any Door," said Lucas.

"Don't get smart with me," snapped Ramos.

"It's a Bogart movie," said Aquilar. "What's it about?"

"Not one of Bogey's best. He plays a defence lawyer, it's a court room drama," replied Lucas.

"You mind if we keep this," said Ramos.

"Feel free," replied Lucas, "Now will someone fill me in? What the fuck happened?"

"We haven't got all the facts, but it seems Franz and Cipriano along with two of Kauffman's boys got ambushed and shot to death out on the Lujan highway just past the old gas station."

"Yeah, I know it," volunteered Lucas.

"Too well, from what I've heard," hinted Aquilar.

"What's that supposed to mean."

"You know," he sneered.

"But who . . . ."

"That's what we're trying to find out," said Ramos as he bent down and picked up a piece of paper. "Did you write this?" he asked showing it to Lucas.

For a second he feigned puzzlement before answering. "Yeah, sure," he replied.

"Rumour has it, it was revenge for the Ramon Perez killing," spat Aquilar.

Lucas felt himself going suitably red. "That doesn't make any sense."

"Salazar thinks there might be more too it. He thinks the target was Franz," added Ramos.

"Then this could all be tied in with those guys from Saturday. Oh my God, Gretchen, has anyone informed her? I've got to go," cried Lucas.

"You'll go when we say so. "Like hell I will!" She knows, Salazar has placed a guard with her," said Aquilar.

"Good. How did she take the news?"

"She was in a state of shock; I don't think it's sunk in."

"Is this something to do with the war?" Lucas's question was left unanswered.

Putting on his coat he brusquely pushed passed Ramos. "I'm seeing Gretchen now!"

Aquilar nodded for Ramos to let him go. "Lucas," said Aquilar holding up the ticket stub, "if this doesn't check out we'll be seeing you sooner than you think."

Lucas gave the Argentinean a curt look before disappearing out the door. A feeling of immense relief wafted over him. So far, his plan had worked like a dream. He'd bought the ticket earlier in the evening and had watched the tail end of the courtroom drama before slipping out through the side door.

Chapter 35

Lucas knew that once Franz was killed, security around Gretchen would be tight as a drum, that's why he had to take the gamble that Cipriano or Kauffman would not phone anyone else. It was his only way of staying close to Gretchen. He knew his relationship with her was over, but he still couldn't believe she was capable of doing half the things Jake was accusing her of. He reasoned that if Juan Aquilar let him go, then it would be safe to return to the apartment and Gretchen.

There were two of Salazar's men at the entrance to the apartment; he knew one by sight, so it was relatively easy to gain entrance. On their floor level he was greeted by two more guards. They patted him down and removed his Colt Army issue automatic. Lucas felt slightly undressed without it. He knocked on Gretchen's door and was greeted by a fierce looking woman. "I'm Lucas," he announced.

Gretchen came into sight and nodded her conformation. "My gun," he demanded.

"My men will keep it until you leave," said the woman.

"No way, do you think I trust you to protect her. Give me my gun!" demanded Lucas.

"Salazar's orders," replied the stern faced woman.

"Well get him on the fucking phone!" shouted Lucas.

The woman looked like she'd like to have put a bullet in him. But she reached for the phone as Gretchen ran to him. He put his arms around her and tried comforting her.

"They killed Klaus, my big handsome brother. They shot him down like a dog."

"Klaus, you mean Franz!" countered Lucas.

"Franz, Klaus, who fucking cares what you call him, he's dead!"

It was a side to Gretchen he'd never seen before. She was grieving; yes, he understood that, but there were no tears, just pure hatred. In her eyes, her face, the way she moved, it was frightening.

"Gretchen, why were they after Franz? What's with the guards?"

Before Gretchen could answer the stern faced woman handed him back his automatic.

"Gracias," he said unsmiling, as he tucked it into the waistband at the small of his back. The woman sat down on a chair next to the door.

"What's going on?"

"Mercedes is to stay here until morning. By then Salazar hopes to have a clearer picture of what's happening!"

"I'm staying with you," stated Lucas. "Killing Franz, I can understand, but why would someone be out to kill you?"

"Because of Franz's past, remember I told you he was an industrialist during the war."

"Yes I remember, but why would they want to kill him, surely they wanted him for his skills."

"These people, they don't care about that. He worked for the Third Reich, they blame him for things. They're evil men!"

"That doesn't answer my question, why would they want to kill you?"

"Because, I also worked for the Third Reich!" stated Gretchen proudly.

"But the war is over; it's been over for five years!"

"For us the war will never be over," added Gretchen.

"You called him Klaus."

"Ja, Klaus Buchler, my older brother.

"Then Kauffman isn't your real name."

"Nein. You never really believed that was my real name," she scoffed. "My real name is Astrid Buchler. We came to Argentina to start a new life. But that is now over, Klaus is dead."

"What about us," it was easy for Lucas to continue the conversation. There was so much he wanted to learn about what made Gretchen tick.

"There is no us!" she stated firmly. "Once this business is over, I shall have to relocate, Paraguay, Chile or some other God-forsaken country. I will go somewhere where no one knows anything about me."

"What do you mean, there's no us? Why can't I go with you?" he asked.

"Lucas, it's been fun, in time perhaps I could have loved you, but it's over."

The big American slumped into a chair, feigning disbelief. He'd felt for this woman, he'd believed he had a chance to rebuild his life, but it had all been a lie. Sometime tomorrow Jake Reis would be coming for her, to send her spinning all the way to hell. Lucas knew it was over but he couldn't bring himself to believe Gretchen was bad, misguided perhaps but not really bad. In that moment he made a decision, one that Jake Reis wasn't going to like.

Lucas woke with a start; Mercedes was talking rapidly into the phone, far too quickly for him to understand. But from the smug look upon her face something had happened.

"I'll get Gretchen," he volunteered.

Mercedes only nodded.

A minute or two later Gretchen appeared doing up a silk dressing gown.

"Do you have news for me?" she demanded.

"Si senora. I have just spoken with Senor Salazar; he has informed me that a couple of Americans were picked up trying to board a flight back to the United States. They were apprehended by government troops, and at this moment Colonel Ruben Salazar is making arrangement for their transportation to Estancia Salazar for questioning."

"That's it" snapped Gretchen.

"That's all Senor Salazar told me." replied Mercedes apologetically.

Gretchen started strutting about the room, cursing and swearing, words that Lucas had never heard her utter except during extreme lovemaking. "I should be there when they're interrogated."

"Gretchen, believe me it wouldn't be advisable. I've seen what Salazar's capable of inflicting on those he questions."

"Ha! You Americans are so naïve. You think I haven't seen what Salazar can do!"

"What if the guys they've lifted from the airport are innocent?"

"I pray to God they aren't, but if they are, what does it matter."

It was if he was seeing Gretchen in a new light. Her disregard for human life shocked him to the core. How could he have been so blind? Only last night he'd watched over and consoled a frightened young girl, and had vowed that whatever it took he wasn't letting Jake Reis take her. Those feelings died as he looked at the hard line of her mouth and the intense hatred and venom in those once sparkling blue eyes. Despite not wearing an SS uniform, Lucas could picture her in the biting cold of a Polish winter as she snapped out orders and shot prisoners indiscriminately.

If one of the men was Lorenzo, and it was a strong possibility, then it would only be a matter of time before Salazar learned the truth. He cursed himself for being a fool, he'd thought to dissuade Jake from his mission and it had cost them time. He could so easily have gone back to his apartment that night. He could have made the call, but no, he didn't have the stomach for it. Now time was running out. He thought about shooting both the bitches where they stood, but Jake wouldn't have believed him.

He had to get in touch with Reis, but how, without arousing suspicion? Then an idea popped into his head. He excused himself and made for the bathroom. Locking the door he reached into his pocket for his cigarettes, took one out and flushed the remainder.

Then he returned the single cigarette to its pack and put them back in his trouser pocket. Earlier he'd noticed the mounting cigarette butts that littered the ashtrays, full to overflowing. It wouldn't be long before Gretchen wanted another, hopefully she'd be all out.

Gretchen was calmer when he returned, "I'm sorry I got mad, but I've lived in fear for the best part of five years. Do you know what that's like?" She sat down at the breakfast table and placed her head in her hands. Lucas sat opposite and stretched his arm across the table. He squeezed her hand gently.

"Yes Gretchen, I do."

She looked up at him quizzically.

"I've been living in fear since I left America. The police wanted to arrest me but the Los Angeles mob wanted me dead, it amounts to the same thing. I can't go back to America, no more than you can go back to Germany."

"We all have a past; sometimes it is best we forget."

"That's what I've been doing the last few years," he responded.

She smiled almost sympathetically, then out of the blue she asked, "Have you a cigarette!"

"Yeah sure," said Lucas as he reached into his trouser pocket. "Fuck, I'm almost out!" he declared as he offered the solitary cigarette to Gretchen.

She lit up took a deep drag on the cigarette then offered it to him.

"Nah, you keep it. I've a fresh pack in the apartment." He stood up as casually as he could. "I won't be a minute."

Gretchen stared into space and took another pull on her cigarette. Lucas's whole body cried out to run, but he shuffled his way towards the door. "Any chance of ordering up breakfast," he asked Mercedes as nonchalantly as he could.

"I'll see what I can do," she said. "I'll get mine on the way home; my relief should be here by ten thirty."

"Just watch out for her, I won't be long," he said as he opened the door.

Chapter 36

Lorenzo had made it through check in, passport control and was waiting to board. His heart beat had just about returned to normal when he noticed out of the corner of his eye two men in uniform. It was normal, he told himself, yet his heart rate began to climb. He casually looked in the other direction, his heart rate shot through the roof; three more uniforms were looking straight at him. Mike Burnett's words rang loud and clear, "Don't let yourself be taken alive." By Lorenzo's reasoning, this was a different scenario, these weren't hoods, these were government soldiers. He'd bluff it out; he had nothing to hide. Once through check in he'd ditched his gun in the cistern of one of the public restrooms, he'd left nothing to incriminate himself.

"You will come with me please," said the leader.

"What's this all about," he asked indignantly.

"You will come with me." barked the man.

He wanted to make this man eat his words, but these weren't normal circumstances. 'What do they have on me; I tossed the rod after I'd checked in. I'm just an ordinary Joe, here for a few days of fun and relaxation,' but even as he thought it, he knew it wouldn't hold up under scrutiny. He knew better than to talk, he'd clam up. He'd get himself a lawyer, without a confession they had nothing. Comforted by the thought Lorenzo prepared himself for hard time. He'd heard that South American prisons were hell on earth. If the worst happened and he was thrown in the slammer, he'd live with it. It wouldn't be the first time, how bad could it be, he'd done time up at Q when he was little more than a youngster.

"What the hell are you charging me with?" he demanded

The officer slammed a fist into his stomach, then spun him around and slapped on the cuffs. He was pushed and shoved towards a door at the far end of the hall. 'Interrogation,' thought Lorenzo, hoping against hope this was just routine, and that somehow he'd make his flight. Inside the small room, he was made to sit on a chair facing an officer who was scrutinizing his passport and personal papers.

"You are Lorenzo Calabria, from Los Angeles."

Lorenzo nodded.

"What was the purpose of your trip?"

Instinct had kicked in and Lorenzo had thought up a feasible reason for being there. "Business and a little pleasure," he answered glibly.

"What line of business?"

"The movie business, I'm a screen writer, working on a script for a new movie, set in Buenos Aires. I needed inspiration, and wanted to soak up the atmosphere."

"You expect me to believe you?" The officer looked deeply into Lorenzo's eyes, weighing up whether to believe him or not. "Take him away."

He was taken outside into the early morning light, marched along a series of doors then locked in a windowless room and left. An indeterminable time later, the door was unlocked and he was marched out into the morning sunshine. From there he was escorted from the terminal and put into an open topped truck along with two other sorry looking souls, neither of them he knew. He breathed a sigh of relief, 'They must have pulled every American from flights leaving Argentina,' he thought. Two soldiers climbed up and sat opposite each other at the rear of the truck, while another closed the tailgate.

Lorenzo weighed up his situation, there was a driver, the guy that closed the tailgate and two sorry looking clowns guarding them. If he hadn't had his wrists cuffed behind his back he reckoned his chance for escape could have been possible, but instead he'd have to sit it out.

On the journey to the police station Lorenzo learned that both his fellow passengers were leaving Argentina after concluding business ventures.

"Did anyone say what this was all about?" he asked the two Americans.

"No, they came up to me, asked to see my passport, which I handed to the leader. He looked at it for a moment then ordered me to go with them. I protested, but got a smack in the kisser for my trouble."

"Same here," said the other man. Like Lorenzo their passports and personal belongings had been confiscated. Comforted by the similarity of their stories Lorenzo tried his best to relax as the truck bumped and lurched on its journey.

They'd been in the dusty open topped truck for a little over half an hour when Lorenzo realised they were leaving the city behind them.

"Where the fuck are you taking us," cried Lorenzo with alarm.

The guard seated next to him was unresponsive, while the one sitting opposite looked ready to strike him. Things didn't seem right; Lorenzo could feel it in his water. As the minutes ticked by his uneasiness increased. Then suddenly his blood froze in his veins as they passed a familiar sight. The old derelict gas station from the night before came into vivid view. He looked towards the open space where three burnt out cars, two still smouldering, sat surrounded by police cars and a dozen or so police and officials.

"What the fuck happened there?" said John, one of Lorenzo's fellow captives.

Lorenzo was uneasy as he looked at their previous night's handiwork. Instantly his brain started asking questions, the most immediate, 'Why are we being transported away from the city?' An icy chill ran down his spine as he recalled Mike Burnett's words once more. "Don't let yourself be taken alive." If his growing suspicions were correct, then a fate worse than death awaited all three. According to Burnett, Ethan's rash behaviour had alerted the German and his cohorts to find and interrogate him and the two men he was with. With the death of the German, all hell had broken loose. Without much to go on, suspicion as far as the Argentine mob was concerned would have fallen on the three men. It didn't take a mathematician to work out three men, all American, all leaving on the first flights out of the country would be targets. More importantly only someone with a brother high up in the military could have pulled this off so fast.

Lorenzo didn't know where they were heading, but he knew it was a ride that none of them were coming back from. He had to escape or die trying. His only hope was the guards didn't speak a word of English; if they did he was sunk.

"Listen very carefully to what I have to say. And for fuck sake don't panic. If you do you'll end up dead!"

Both men looked shocked, but nodded their understanding.

"We ain't heading to any police headquarters; we're being taken into the country to be interrogated by a gangster. When he's finished with us, it's a bullet in the head if we're lucky."

"You're joking right!" said John.

"Do I look as if I'm joking? Remember that scene we just passed; that was me!" Lorenzo waited for it to sink in.

"But we're innocent," cried the other man, "We've done nothing wrong! We'll tell them it was you, that you confessed all."

"Listen punk, you can tell them all you like, but you ain't getting outta this alive, unless . . ."

John's face had drained of blood, but he understood the predicament they were in. "He's right, they won't let us live, even if they believed us."

"We're dead men, no matter which way you cut it. Those men back there at the burnt out cars, they're police, our only salvation, and the longer we delay, the further away they'll be. I reckon at this moment we're a mile, maybe a mile and a half away from them. If you want to live, they're our only chance."

"But we're hand cuffed," said the frightened man.

"I'm with you," declared John.

"There's a slight incline up ahead, I've noticed when he switches gears the truck almost stalls. That's the moment we jump these two fuckers. When they put the tailgate up they secured it with wire, I suspect it will break loose with a little force."

Lorenzo stole a look at his fellow captives and wondered whether John would have the balls as he braced himself for the leap. The truck was doing no more than fifteen miles an hour when the driver slammed it into low gear. For a second the truck lurched and slowed. Lorenzo shot forward. The suddenness of his action caught the soldier off guard and the force of both bodies sent the tailgate spinning. Lorenzo and the guard fell heavily from the truck. John seizing his chance as the other guard turned his head at the distraction, shoulder charged and then he and the guard also went tumbling onto the dirt road.

A sickening pain shot through Lorenzo as his left arm broke with the fall, the guard with him wasn't so lucky. Although in great pain he struggled to his feet and began running for his life. From the corner of his eye he caught a brief glimpse of John struggling with the guard while the other captive stayed frozen to his seat, transfixed with fear. He heard a shot, but kept running, as he quickened his pace he heard two more. He guessed John didn't make it. Through the pain he laughed at himself, at the irony of his situation, all his life he'd been running from the law, now he was running to it. He could hear the truck turning, hear the gears crunching, he prayed for it to stall. He felt a bullet whiz past his ear. Then in the distance he could just make out the derelict gas station. His lungs were bursting, his legs were turning to jelly, but he could see them, the police, his saviours, they weren't more than four hundred feet away. The sight of them helped to spur him on faster, but then he could hear the engine of the truck as it drew closer and closer. He closed his ears to the noise, he was almost there, a smile spread across his face; he never heard the shot as his chest exploded from the force of the bullet that severed his spine.

Chapter 37

Lucas returned to Gretchen's apartment to find her agitated and elated in equal measures.

"What's up," he said smiling casually as he lit up.

"It appears they arrested three men at the airport not two."

"That's good isn't it?"

"Ja. It would appear so, only on the way to Salazar's ranch, two of them tried to escape."

"What!" Lucas feigned concern.

"They overpowered two guards, killing one in the process. One of the Americans was shot almost immediately, while the one that killed the guard made a run for it. He didn't get very far."

Lucas guessed that someone was Lorenzo, 'He'd heeded my words after all, poor soul'. He forced a smile, "They've got all three!" he exclaimed. You're safe now."

"It would have been better if those fools hadn't let them escape."

"But they killed them," said Lucas.

"That's not the point, apart from finding out how much they know they should have been made to pay for killing my brother. But fortunately one still lives. When Juan arrives, I'll get him to take me to Estancia Salazar, Felipe will indulge me I'm sure."

Panic set in, he hadn't expected Juan Aquilar; *that in itself could be a bonus,* but he'd told Jake the guards surrounding Gretchen were changing at ten thirty. Lucas had advised the L.A. mobster that he shouldn't make his move until after eleven. Now with the panic over if Gretchen had her way they'd be heading out the door by a little after ten thirty. He had to find a way to stall.

At ten thirty on the dot, Juan Aquilar knocked on the door, a satisfied smile upon his face. He gave a curt smile of dismissal at Mercedes, who wasted no time on her way to breakfast.

"Juan I want you to take me to Estancia Salazar. I want to hear the pig squeal."

Lucas grimaced.

Juan grinned, "I think this woman is too much for you gringo!"

"I don't give a fuck what you think. Have you given any thought to the possibility that these men might not be who we think they are!"

It stopped Juan Aquilar in his tracks, "You know Astrid, this guy is smarter than we give him credit for. I will place a call to Senor Salazar and request he doesn't kill the gringo pig until much later."

Gretchen was about to protest.

"Don't worry little one, I'm sure Felipe will allow you the fatal cut."

"You know . . . . you know how Salazar kills people," uttered Lucas.

Gretchen laughed, "Oh Lucas, you're so naïve at times." Now that her identity was known she had dropped the façade completely.

Juan Aquilar smirked, "Just be thankful Felipe Salazar values your contribution to his empire."

"What's that supposed to mean?"

"When the night clubs fail and one day they surely will, it'll be me that comes looking."

Lucas made a lunge, but Juan Aquilar stepped back and pulled out a gun. "Careful now," he mocked. "It wouldn't do for us to fall out. It's not in Senor Salazar's best interest."

"One day Aquilar, you'll get yours," threatened Lucas.

"Make the call," said Gretchen, tiring of all the machismo.

It couldn't have been five minutes after Juan had made the call, when someone knocked upon the apartment door.

"Who is it?" asked Aquilar through the door.

"Carlos. Did anyone here order breakfast?"

Juan Aquilar looked towards Gretchen and Lucas quizzically.

"I asked Mercedes to arrange for breakfast to be brought up," said Lucas.

Juan looked to Gretchen for conformation. She nodded nonchalantly.

Lucas looked at the clock on the wall; it was only ten forty five, too early for Jake, he thought.

Aquilar unbolted the door and stepped back, his gun trained on the door just in case. Lucas inched his hand behind his back, seeking the comfort of the Colt 1911 army automatic.

"It's open," declared Aquilar.

The door flew open and Carlos came crashing in. Aquilar got off one shot, taking Carlos high in the chest. Before he could snap off another Lucas had drawn his piece and shot Aquilar through the back of his knee, tearing his knee cap right off. The sudden impact sent the tall Argentine hurtling across the room, his gun falling harmlessly from his grasp.

Gretchen though shocked by the swiftness of the action still managed to pull a Walther from her skirts. She squeezed off two shots towards her assailants before Lucas could stop her. In desperation he lunged at her and sent her sprawling, knocking the deadly Walther from her hand.

It was over in seconds. Chudnik slumped to the floor, two bullet holes no more than an inch apart, smashed his heart to pulp. He was dead before he hit the floor. As the smoke settled Jake stepped casually into the room. He surveyed the carnage then as Gretchen tried to get up; he backhanded her across the floor. Ethan backed into the room cradling the Thompson as he looking furtively around. He grinned as he turned around and looked down on the sorry state of Juan Aquilar and Gretchen.

"They don't look so tough now," he remarked. His Thompson commanding respect as Aquilar and Gretchen averted their eyes.

It was Gretchen who regained her composure first. They weren't after her, this was a mob hit.

"Lucas, why are you doing this to me, I've done nothing to you. He's the one; he's the one that slit Lola Santo's throat."

Aquilar could barely speak, the shock and pain of having his knee cap destroyed was excruciating, but he managed a feeble protest. "Don't listen to her, she's the one, she ordered it done."

"Go on," said Lucas addressing himself to Aquilar.

"The farmhouse, it was all her idea, she even procured the girls."

"How?" demanded Lucas.

Aquilar's words were becoming fainter; "Through her job at welfare reform. She selected the girls, the pretty, the poor, the desperate and most importantly the ones without any family."

Gretchen started to protest.

"Enough!" snapped Lucas

A deathly silence descended upon the room.

It was left to Ethan to break the silence, "Now isn't this cosy, we've all got what we're after. Jake's got the woman, Mike's got that piece of shit, and I've got the Thompson." He was smiling malevolently and looking straight at Lucas.

Ethan had weighed up the situation the moment he'd walked in. Without Chudzik, Jake wasn't in a position to call the shots. It was a God given opportunity to rid himself of his ex partner.

Lucas smiled, it was as he'd expected. "Before you kill me, ask yourself how you're getting out of this hell-hole alive?"

Ethan looked puzzled, "What do you mean?"

"Without me you ain't got a cat in hell's chance of getting out of this country."

"I'd listen to him if I was you," said Jake, his gun pointing towards Gretchen's head. "I've suspected for a time that our Mike here has a get outta jail card hidden up his sleeve."

Lucas grinned.

Ethan took in Jake's words and slowly pointed the Thompson to the floor, "Another time," he grinned. "Now let's get this done."

Lucas looked down at Aquilar, pointed his gun at the centre of Aquilar's forehead, and said, "This is for Lola Santos!"

Somehow Aquilar managed to find his voice. "No please, I beg you! Don't kill me!"

Lucas looked down at the snivelling wreck of a man and uncocked his automatic.

"Oh for fuck sake!" said Ethan in frustration as he walked over to the prone figure, pointed the Thompson at Juan Aquilar's head and squeezed the trigger. The noise was deafening.

"Lucas, please don't let them kill me," begged Gretchen. She was that poor frightened girl that he'd once fell in love with. "You love me, you can't let them."

"Goodbye Gretchen."

He turned towards Jake, "I'll be waiting outside."

"Don't leave me . . ."

Lucas felt violently sick; he retched as he closed the door behind him.

"He still hasn't the stomach for it," exclaimed Ethan. "Now kill the bitch and let's get the hell outta Dodge."

Gretchen was stricken with fear.

"Not so fast, I've dreamt of this moment. Gag her."

Without question Ethan ripped the small table cloth from the breakfast table and quickly gagged Gretchen. She stared at Jake wide eyed, as if asking why me.

"My name is Jake Reis, it doesn't mean anything to you, but I had two sisters, both died at Auschwitz, to be precise at Auschwitz 3 Monowitz." Jake watched as Gretchen's eyes grew even more saucer like. "You shot one of my sisters like a dog, but the other you strangled to death."

Jake could see it registering, he could tell she remembered. It gave him satisfaction that she recalled the event, an event that until that moment had remained irrelevant, but not anymore.

"You took a piece of rope no more than two feet long with wooden handles attached at both ends, much like this one," he reached into his jacket pocket and showed it her.

Her eyes grew wide with terror as she lunged for the door, Ethan caught her on the side of her head with the butt of the Thompson, knocking her down.

"Lucas help me!" she screamed.

On the other side of the door Lucas felt his heart being torn apart.

Seconds later Jake had the rope twisted around her neck, his head touching hers as he continued with his narration. "While she was held by two guards you slowly twisted the rope until you'd choked the life out of her." Jake twisted the rope slowly. Gretchen's eyes looked as if they might pop out of her head, her face started to turn blue. Even Ethan appeared shocked.

"Get the fuck on with it!" cried Ethan impatient to get away.

Jake twisted the rope around Gretchen's neck once more. "You ain't so pretty now!" Then tiring of what he was doing, he gave it a final twist and waited until there was no resistance and her entire body went limp. The Jackal of Monowitz was dead.

Chapter 38

"It's done," said Jake solemnly as they rejoined Lucas outside the apartment. With Ethan wielding the Thompson no one was inclined to challenge them as they made their way out of the apartment block.

"Get in the car," cried Jake as he pointed to the Packard they'd hot wired earlier.

Fifteen minutes later they pulled up at the kerbside. Lucas got out and went across to the newsstand where he bought a copy of the Buenos Aires Tribune. He walked back to the Packard and climbed back in.

"What the fuck does it say?" asked Ethan.

"You know something; you're an ignorant fuck Ethan. You lived your whole life in Southern California yet you can't read a word of Spanish," spat Lucas. "Just look at the pictures; that should give you a clue."

The headlines read

> *Four men shot to death!* *What looks to be a gangland execution took a macabre turn as police were alerted to a second location, where it was discovered a number of illegal aliens were being kept as virtual sex slaves. It is not known if both these cases are connected but the Buenos Aires police department are looking into it.*

Lucas read through the article, and although it was thorough in its detail, there was no mention of Felipe Salazar.

"Damn, fuck and damn!" exclaimed Lucas. "That slippery fucks not even got a mention."

He reached in his pocket for some change and started to get out of the car.

"Where the fuck are you going now," cried Ethan.

"To make a phone call, anything that can keep Salazar busy has to help us."

"He's going to call the paper," said Jake calmly.

Ten minutes later, Lucas returned to the car. "You took your time," cried Ethan.

"Time well spent, I hope. I just told the Tribune that if they're quick they could get a major scoop at Estancia Salazar; that several Americans were being held and tortured. I then phoned the American Embassy and told them the same. That should keep Salazar tied up for some time."

"I like your line of thinking," said Jake.

"You'll like it a whole lot more if we get out of Argentina alive. Salazar will have his lawyers all over this and the tricky fuck's liable to walk, but it might take his mind off the money side of things for the time being at least, in the meantime head towards the docks."

On the drive to the docks Lucas informed Jake and Ethan that as the military had grabbed three men they thought were responsible for the shooting; the chances were that all entry and exit points to Argentina would now be downgraded and left to the customs and border agencies.

"If that's the case, why not head for the airport," said Ethan.

"There isn't a flight to the States until Friday, unless you want to fly across the Atlantic to Madrid or some other European destination, which would cost a heap of dough and draw attention to yourself."

"So where are we heading?" asked Ethan agitatedly.

"Uruguay" said Lucas. "Make no mistake, once Salazar and his men find the bodies in Gretchen's apartment, they'll be on the hunt. That's why we're taking the ferry to Montevideo."

"Why Montevideo?" asked Jake.

"Partly because it's another country and because I've a friend there that can help."

"How do you know you can trust him?" countered Ethan.

"I don't, it's a gut feeling, the man stands to come into a large sum of money."

"What money?" snapped Ethan.

"Salazar's," replied Lucas.

"He ain't having my share," stated Ethan.

"He can have mine," said Jake. "If we don't get out alive, the money ain't worth a damn."

They threw the Thompson into an irrigation ditch much against Ethan's protestations. "Without it we won't be able to fight our way out if push comes to shove."

"With it we wouldn't get close to the port, dumping it's the only option," stated Jake.

Thirty minutes later they arrived at the Port of Buenos Aires, where they quickly abandoned the Packard, from there they made their way on foot to the ferry terminal.

"We shouldn't board together just in case," warned Lucas. "I'll go first. And remember get a return ticket it's less suspicious."

Ethan looked around furtively; ready to turn tail if Lucas ran into trouble. They watched nervously as he purchased his return ticket. Jake waited until ten more passengers had bought their tickets before he walked up to the ticket counter. He was now committed, there was no way back. Ethan held his breath as he saw Lucas showing his passport, the custom official seemed to take an indeterminate amount of time scrutinising it, before ushering him onto the ferry. Waves of relief wafted over Ethan, as he quickly got in line and purchased his ticket.

Forty minutes later the ferry slowly left the Port of Buenos Aires for its three and a half hour journey across the Rio de la Plate to Montevideo.

"Tonight we dine like kings," said Lucas. "But tomorrow we might be as poor as church mice."

"What's that suppose to mean?" said Ethan.

"How do you think I was able to get out of Los Angeles, evade the police, and keep one step ahead of the mob? I'll tell you; money!"

"I still don't get it!"

"You should, it was you who showed me how. Open an account in the Caymans, you said."

Jake laughed.

"I did just that! Not a large amount but enough to escape my old life. You see money doesn't go far when you're running. There's hardly anything left, but the important thing is, the account is still open. I've managed over the past few months to test the waters so to speak."

Ethan sat silent, letting everything Lucas had just said sink in. "So what you're saying is tomorrow we go to the bank, but . . . ." He eyed Lucas suspiciously. "Correct me if I'm wrong, but you gave us the distinct impression we were heading for Rio."

Jake grinned, "Yeah I must admit, you gave me the same impression. In fact you told me what hotel in Rio that Red would be staying in."

"I did, didn't I," replied Lucas smiling.

"How much money are we talking about?" asked Jake.

"Like I said, tonight we dine like kings. Worry about the money tomorrow."

Chapter 39

A shit storm hit Estancia Salazar around one thirty in the afternoon or to be precise, a contingence of government troops, the police, the press from the Tribune and a couple of officials from the American embassy. Salazar was nowhere to be found. Instead they found the remains of two bodies in the pig enclosure and a further body strung up by his wrists to an overhead beam in the abattoir, from his appearance it looked like he'd been badly beaten before being shot in the head.

Felipe Salazar had been ten minutes into his interrogation of the third American when he received warning of the imminent invasion from his brother. With no time to lose he drew his pistol and shot the American, then with Tito Gomez and Clemente Ramos they fled across the manicured lawns, over hedge rows and fields to a waiting car.

Salazar's first thoughts were to establish his alibi, the mess that the authorities were to find would create an almighty scandal and possibly ruin him socially, but with a good lawyer he'd escape prosecution. Felipe Salazar always planned for such eventualities. How could he be arrested for something that happened at Estancia Salazar when he was staying in La Fonda hotel in Buenos Aires? At worst it would cause him an uncomfortable few days. Once he got word from the Estancia informing him of the subsequent events he would naturally phone the police, establish his alibi and hand himself in at the nearest police precinct. He would as a matter of course instruct his lawyers to be there ten minutes before his arrival.

By three fifteen, Salazar seething with anger at the inconvenience and humiliation at fleeing his beloved Estancia like a common criminal, sipped a large scotch in his suite at the La Fonda hotel. Just as he was settling into his new surroundings the phone rang.

Clemente picked it up on the third ring. "Senor Salazar's suite," he announced. Ramos wasn't given to theatrics but his drawn expression alerted Salazar that something bad had gone down.

Clemente held his hand over the speaker, "There's been a shooting at the German woman's apartment."

Salazar clearly shaken by this new turn of events slowly lowered the glass of scotch to the table and asked, "How many?"

"Four, from what I can tell," said Clemente Ramos.

"Who, damn you, who?" he shouted impatiently, losing his cool for the first time since fleeing the Estancia.

"The woman, Juan, Carlos and Lucas," stuttered Ramos.

"When did this happen . . . ." A sudden realisation exploded inside Salazar's head. He'd spoken to Gretchen and Aquilar only a few short hours ago. "Those men we had brought to the Estancia, they couldn't have been the shooters!"

"Holy fuck," exclaimed Clemente, "I'll get right on it."

"No, that's the last thing we do. We sit tight; we wait until we receive word about the events at the Estancia."

Salazar sat stewing, his mind going over the events of the last few hours. Then he stood up and threw the barely touched glass of scotch across the room.

"It was that fucking Nazi, he caused this!" he shouted, spittle spraying uncontrollably from his mouth. He cursed the day that he first got involved with Franz Kauffman. It was true his business arrangement with the German had been very lucrative; he'd paid extremely well for himself and his sister and had proven to be a worthy ally. But because of their notoriety everything they'd built up together was gone. He didn't mourn the German or the men that died with him, they were of no consequence, but Cipriano was irreplaceable. And now this fresh atrocity, the German bitch dead in her own apartment, that he could take, but the needless deaths of Juan Aquilar and Lucas Garrett, a man that had shown him the future, that was beyond the pale. Granero de Alvarado and its sister at Casa Rosada were intact but without Lucas or Cipriano to guide the ship, that future was now uncertain. What was certain, the three Americans whoever they were would pay, he'd see to that!

An agonising twenty minutes later Salazar as expected received word about the raid on his Estancia. Minutes later he was on the phone to his lawyers; a brief moment later he spoke indignantly to the Chief of Police at the nearest precinct and agreed to appear there at his earliest convenience.

Around five o'clock in the afternoon Felipe Salazar handed himself into the police precinct. He was confident that his alibi would stand up, he'd put it in place three years earlier, it was fool proof. It was just one of Senor Felipe Salazar's contingency plans. It was well known *in circles that counted* that Salazar was a great benefactor of others less fortunate than himself. Earlier reports *instigated by Salazar's brother* indicated that suspicion had fallen on two people with dubious backgrounds that Salazar as patron had employed at the Estancia. Salazar considered it money well spent.

What he hadn't taken into account was the furore the death of foreign nationals at the Estancia would cause. Salazar, along with Tito Gomes and Clemente Ramos were interviewed separately for hours on end. The interviews were cordial, friendly even, but intensive. The American Embassy put immense pressure on Peron's government to get to the bottom of the matter. No stone was to be left unturned. But after hours of questioning and arguments back and forth, Salazar's alibi held. He was told in no uncertain terms that his generosity had caused a major embarrassment to Peron's government.

Salazar seethed with anger. He'd had to sit through several interrogations before his version of events was accepted. That version being whilst in his employment he'd unknowingly allowed the accused men free rein around the Estancia. Because of that they'd abused their positions and murdered for profit, using their employer's workplace to disposes of the bodies. By six in the morning Felipe Salazar, Tito Gomez and Clemente Ramos walked free.

Three and a half hours later Lucas Garrett walked into the National bank in Montevideo and forty five minutes after that crossed the street and entered a coffee house where Jake and Ethan sat nervously waiting.

"It's there," stated Lucas as he sat down.

"When do we get our hands on it," asked Ethan eagerly.

"All in good time," said Lucas.

"How much are we talking about?" asked Jake.

"One million, three," replied Lucas.

"What!" exclaimed Ethan.

"You heard, now keep your voice down."

"Now how the fuck did you manage that. It can't be a wire transfer," argued Jake. "It can't be done, not that amount."

"You're right but you're wrong, it can be done; I'll explain. Over the last year I've gained the confidence of Felipe Salazar, partly to do with the money I've made for him from the two night clubs, but mostly because of the fear he's managed to generate amongst the people under him. No one person in their right mind would even dare to think about crossing him. Because of his greed and confidence he's used me to launder money though the Alvarado night clubs.

"Yeah, I get that," said Jake.

"Over the past few months, with the success of the new club and talk of investing in another I'd managed to persuade Salazar to invest heavily, so laundering more money, a win, win, situation. For my part I was making money for him hand over fist and wanted to invest in the future. So in turn I convinced Salazar to make me a co-signee of cheques, big cheques."

"He trusted you," exclaimed Jake.

"Yeah, he trusted me, why wouldn't he, he made me co-signee and he looked at the books twice, maybe three times a week. You see I'd witnessed first hand what he did to people that tried to screw him."

"On Monday I transferred the largest amount ever from this account to several smaller accounts, from these accounts I did several telegraph wire transfers to accounts I'd opened over here during the last few months."

"You've been a busy boy scout," said Jake suitably impressed.

"That's all fine and dandy, but when do I get my share?" said Ethan.

"All in good time," replied Lucas, "I've already successfully transferred my share to the account in the Caymans."

"You've what!" snapped Ethan, "If you've double crossed me, I'll shoot you where you stand."

"If you think that, go ahead," snapped Lucas. "But you won't see any money."

"Kill each other if you have too, but afterwards," cried Jake.

"Hear me out; I took the biggest risk, the rest you split three ways," said Lucas indignantly.

"Three ways," enquired Jake.

"Yeah three ways; that friend I told you about helped me set up this sting; in fact it was partly his idea. But more importantly he's going to get us out of Uruguay. Make no mistake we've been riding our luck, if we get caught Salazar is likely to keep us alive far longer than we'd wish. He ain't the kind that rolls over."

"Where's the next bank?" asked Jake.

"Next door," said Lucas.

Much to Ethan's annoyance Jake pulled rank. Forty minutes later Jake Reis came out smiling.

"When's this friend going to show?" snapped Ethan.

"He's been with us the whole time."

Ethan looked up at a tall swarthy man leaning against a wall with a rakish smile spread across his face.

"Lucas, my friend; it is good to see you. From what I'm hearing you've been plenty busy. I thought for a while you hadn't made it."

Lucas looked puzzled, then he realised his plan was working better than he expected. "It's good to see you also."

"What the fuck's he done to warrant a share," snapped Ethan.

"More than you'll know; suffice to say you're walking these streets a rich man."

"At the moment I ain't, now let's get a move on."

Chapter 40

By midday Ethan was a reasonably rich man, his temper had cooled, but the furnace inside was raging. Putting aside the fact that his marriage to Erin was nothing but a sham, Mike Burnett's sense of fair play had scuppered any chance of Ethan getting his hands on all the money. True one million three hundred dollars was a lot of moolah, far more than he'd imagined, but the thing that rankled him the most was Burnett's ability to make him look foolish. This above all else caused him the most pain; Ethan Kels was nobody's fool.

Rodrigo was the last to receive his share and for a moment Lucas thought he wasn't going to take it. He alone understood what Rodrigo was going through.

"I fear I'm bringing a shed load of grief down on you," said Lucas. "Once Salazar realises what's happened it won't be long before he traces the money to Montevideo."

Rodrigo looked serious for a moment before cracking a crooked smile, "I do not have the pretentions of Felipe Salazar; I care nothing for great estancias, for power, or to be looked up to as if I was a God. I am a young man, thirty five isn't old. I have my senoritas, but no one special. If I stay here I will die, if not by Salazar's hand, then by someone else. It is the nature of our business."

Lucas looked concerned.

"Do not feel bad for me; you have given me wealth beyond my wildest dreams. It would be foolish to hang around."

"Where are you going to go?" asked Lucas.

"With this kind of money, I might try my hand in Europe, Spain perhaps, or maybe America. To be honest I haven't given it much thought. Tomorrow when you leave, I also will leave," stated Rodrigo. "But tonight, we celebrate. It will be our last night in Montevideo and I promise you Lucas, tonight will be memorable."

Jake had come to South America for retribution, not knowing nor caring what might happen to him. He'd been driven by guilt and a burning desire for vengeance. He felt no remorse for what he'd done, but he felt strangely empty. He was returning to Los Angeles unexpectedly a very rich man. Returning to what, an all out war between Cohen and Dragna, he didn't think so. With the money now safely in the Caymans he began thinking about instructing his lawyers to discreetly put his affairs in order. In the meantime he might consider taking time out in the Bahamas to concentrate on his retirement. It was a plan, not a very well thought out plan, but it was a start.

Lucas's first thoughts were of Erin, of the woman he'd lost not once but twice. When Jake told them Erin wasn't pregnant he'd allowed himself to believe they'd have another chance. What they'd had was unique, but that had been a different time and he'd been a very different person to the man he was right now. All he had were shattered dreams. Throughout his life all he'd wanted was to be an honest cop, but life had conspired against him. He'd sought to escape the life, but Jake Reis had reeled him back in using Erin as bait. And for a time he'd been happy, happier than at anytime in his life, before and after. He'd believed Jake had snatched that life from him and it had changed him. He'd become what he'd always despised. Then life dealt him another hand, this one more lucrative than the last, and again he thought he'd found happiness, but along the way he'd found himself sinking deeper and deeper. An honest cop; that was laughable, he'd cheated, stolen, pimped and even murdered, and his reward was wealth, happiness and a possible future, but then fate played another hand and snatched that away in the cruellest form ever. He'd waited outside while Jake choked the life out of the woman that he'd loved and he'd done nothing. And now after all his scheming and manipulating he'd been rewarded with more money than he could spend in a lifetime. He'd become like Ethan and Jake, a man not fit to walk the earth, and certainly not fit to walk in Erin's shadow. He was glad he'd sent Erin to Rio, he was glad he'd given her enough money to start a fresh life, he was glad he'd made her promise not to look back.

They arranged to meet around nine thirty on the corner of Cuidadela and Soriano in the heart of Cuidad Vieja. Rodrigo had promised them the best steak meal in South America.

"Tonight we party!" he said as he led them to the restaurant.

"Ain't you forgetting our friends from across the river," enquired Jake cautiously.

"Have no fear Senor; I have men watching the ferry terminal and the terminal at Colonia. The last ferries have already docked."

Jake looked towards Lucas. The big American nodded his assurance.

"Now relax, enjoy our last evening in Montevideo," laughed Rodrigo.

"Our last evening in Montevideo, are you coming with us?" enquired Ethan.

"Si senor, how else can I spend my money?"

Lucas smiled to himself; he could see the suspicion as it translated though the eyes of Jake and Ethan. He alone knew the measure of Rodrigo, he'd spent more than a few nights, drinking and eating the night away with the man. It was true, he was a bad man, but no worse than Lucas himself, but until he committed himself with the wire transfer he'd never been one hundred percent sure.

They ate their fill at the restaurant before moving along the street to a cantina that Rodrigo recommended; it was a small but intimate place, filled to over flowing with locals.

Lucas was feeling down, the past twenty four hours had been an exhilarating rush, but now that he was almost home free he felt physically drained. That he'd acquired a vast pile of money meant nothing to him, what he wanted most in the entire world was long gone, "I think we should call it a night," he declared.

"No Lucas, before you leave Montevideo you must try La Uvita, it's unique to this bar, and the tango show is most excellent."

It was the last thing Lucas wanted to do, but he didn't want to appear discourteous to his friend, "Okay, we'll stay for one, but remember we have a long journey tomorrow."

"Relax Lucas; our transport doesn't leave until two in the afternoon. Enjoy the show."

It was just starting to fill up, but Rodrigo's influence bought them a table close to the stage. After tasting the La Uvita and washing it down with a glass or two of Uruguayan beer the party slowly began to relax. In the crowded cantina, with the cacophony of music and conversation it was easy to forget the horrific events of the past few days.

The sounds of the bandoneon and the piano gave way to the haunting strings of violins and the lights dimmed. An embracing couple standing at the back of the stage were lit up from an overhead light. The dramatic lighting, the moodiness of the music and the atmosphere of the small cantina were intense as the couple began to dance, moving as one switching their bodies in a gently swaying motion. The couple twisted and turned around each other to the hypnotic sounds of the bandoneon. To Jake, who had never seen an authentic Argentine tango, it was fascinating. Rodrigo viewed it with nostalgia and a crooked grin upon his face as he waited for Lucas's reaction. But sadly Lucas hardly looked up at the dancers. He was deep in thought remembering the last tango he and Gretchen had danced together. It was left to Ethan to grab the attention of the party.

"Holy fuck, she looks like . . . ."

Rodrigo cut him short, "Lucas, my friend, the dancer!"

Lucas startled by Rodrigo, looked up and couldn't believe his eyes.

"Erin! But that's impossible she's in Rio. She can't be . . ."

"She is a very stubborn and resourceful woman. Believe me I tried, I really tried getting her to take that flight to Rio, but she wouldn't budge. Something you'd said, maybe something you didn't say, I don't know. She didn't buy it about Rio."

Lucas recalled the brief conversation with Erin before she left the hotel. "Go to La Mansion hotel and ask for Rodrigo Vasquez. You'll know him by his crooked smile, he can be trusted. He has a ticket for you to Rio, if I'm not there in three days, go home without me."

"Don't ask me how she knew, but she knew you weren't going to Rio. She insisted that I told her the truth. When I did she demanded I took her with me."

"This charade?" questioned Lucas.

"It was her idea."

As the music finished the dancers were given an appreciative applause from the audience. Erin left the stage and nervously approached their table. She looked straight into Lucas's eyes and he was lost. Then quite suddenly she looked away and addressed herself to Ethan.

"I'll make no apology for deceiving you; quite frankly you don't deserve one. You schemed and you plotted, you had a poor girl murdered just so you could have me. And it worked, until I discovered the extent of your lies. Our marriage like your lies was a sham. I'm not proud of what I've done, but you need to know it's over; it never really started," she emphasised her last words by turning her back on him.

"Can we talk?" she said to the startled Lucas.

Jake in an effort to diffuse the tension ordered another round of drinks, while Rodrigo kept a cautious eye on Ethan. It was on one of their last conversations, before the shit hit the fan that Lucas had confided in Rodrigo about Erin and the part Ethan had played in destroying his relationship. To everyone's surprise he didn't react.

Without any words spoken Lucas took Erin gently by the arm and walked her out of the cantina. Under a starlit night they walked silently towards the shoreline. That he loved her there was no doubt, that he wanted her in the worst possible way spoke volumes, but the void between them had opened, it had become a chasm a mile wide. He could see no way back. There was so much he wanted to say, but words failed him. It was Erin that broke the silence between them.

"I knew you weren't coming back to me, I just need to know the reason why? That's why I insisted on Rodrigo bringing me to this place. I love you Michael, I've never stopped loving you."

Lucas's heart beat a little faster, some how he found the words, "I've changed, I'm not the person I once was. You don't know the half of it. You think Ethan's bad, well take a look, I'm a carbon copy."

"I doubt that! You're nothing like Ethan."

"Erin, I've done things, terrible things, I've seen much worse and it's changed me."

"We've both made mistakes, but we can learn from them. We can start a new life together. A simpler life, no more bright lights, just you, me and a baby of our own, I want us to grow old together; I want us to have six kids, to have grandchildren. I don't want the stars," subconsciously Erin gazed up into the night sky. Then she looked deeply into his eyes. "All I want is you."

He almost melted into those eyes, but there were things between them, things that needed saying, "I said a lot of cruel things to you at New Year, things I wish I hadn't said. I was hurting; you hurt me by telling me the truth, but I can see now that once we were happy."

"We can be again, don't give up on us. I don't care what you've done! In your heart you're a good person."

He wanted to believe her, he wanted to throw his arms around her and tell her how much he loved her, but his self loathing wouldn't let things be.

"How can I be, I left Jake alone to kill Gretchen, the woman that I'd grown to love. What kind of a monster does that make me?"

Erin steeled herself for one last attempt, she was hurting deep inside, she could feel him slipping away, "What kind of a woman does that make me, if you're a monster what am I. Sure I came down here to warn you, to stand in the way of Ethan, but I knew what Jake was planning and why. And maybe I was glad about what he planned to do, maybe I believed with her dead you'd look at me again. You see Michael, I'm no better than you. We belong to each other."

It was Erin's final throw of the dice and as her words faded from her lips she looked into Mike Burnett's eyes, because to her; Lucas Garrett no longer existed.

He took her into his arms, looked deeply into those limpid pools of green and kissed her.

Chapter 41

After hours of interrogation Salazar had returned to the hotel in Buenos Aires, his wife Pilar and son Enrico were there to greet him. He asked what news there was from the estancia and Pilar quietly informed him it was now a crime scene. Tired and angry Salazar went to bed and asked not to be disturbed unless there was something important to report. He awoke around five in the afternoon. His mind alert, his first thoughts were of the bodies found in the pig pen and the guy left hanging in the abattoir.

"Just give me the facts," he snarled at Pilar.

"Those men, the two workers from the estancia have been formally charged with multiple murder," she said nervously.

A self satisfied grin appeared upon Salazar's face. 'At least something went as planned,' was his first thought. "Where is Ramos!" he snapped, "He should be here."

"I'll send for him," cried Pilar nervously.

Within minutes Clemente Ramos was in the room, he looked tired and jaded, he'd had little sleep, he'd gone to his room and crashed for a few hours, but from one in the afternoon he'd been piecing together the events that led to the shooting.

"What happened in Gretchen's apartment? Are we clearer than earlier?"

"Its been confirmed that four bodies were found in the apartment, three received fatal gunshot wounds, but the woman had been strangled to death with a piece of rope," stated Ramos.

"Fucking Nazis, I knew it. A fucking hit squad sent to kill, not capture and we're stuck in the middle!" snapped Salazar.

Nervously Clemente Ramos added, "That's not all; according to the Buenos Aires Tribune there are rumours linking you to the killings. Not directly you understand but some of the people killed were known associates. The butchery at the estancia hasn't helped either."

This disturbed Felipe Salazar far more than the wanton killing of the Germans. It was an attack on his position in the community, and not just the respectable side. Every hood that wanted a piece of the action would soon be circling. Salazar knew he had to shore up his defences. As a dark cloud descended over him, Ramos sought to defuse the situation. "One thing in our favour the rest of today's papers although reporting the shooting, doesn't mention you by name."

"Phone my lawyers and arrange a meeting for first thing tomorrow morning. I need to sew up any loose ends as far as my involvement with Franz and Gretchen Kauffman is concerned. Oh and arrange a meeting with the Tribune. I need to make a statement by noon."

By late morning on Thursday, Felipe Salazar's lawyers had legally closed any involvement in the deaths of the Kauffman's. It wasn't in the best interests of their client and others to announce to the world that the Kauffman's were Nazi war criminals.

Salazar's press release was more of a damage limitation exercise, designed to keep certain people in positions of authority at ease. Only time would tell.

Exhausted by his dealings with his lawyers and the grilling from the press Felipe Salazar slumped into the leather armchair in his suite while Tito Gomez poured him a very large scotch. He'd only just put it to his lips, savouring the aroma that pinged at his nostrils when Clemente Ramos walked back into the room, a perplexed look upon his face.

Without tasting the scotch Salazar slowly laid it upon the table.

"What is it?" he snapped.

"I don't know; it could be something or nothing."

"Spit it out!"

"It's the bodies from Gretchen's apartment, something's not right."

"What's not right," cried Salazar as he shot to his feet, alarm bells ringing.

"It's the identification; Juan had been shot in the face several times. But he was identified eventually by his sister. Carlos there was no problem, but the police could only identify Gretchen and Lucas by the identification on them."

"What are you driving at?" the tension in Salazar's voice was near breaking point.

"I knew you wouldn't be satisfied by that so I arranged for Mercedes to come forward and say she was a friend of Gretchen's."

"And!" the strain in his voice was becoming clearly audible.

"She identified Gretchen straight off, but Lucas she wasn't sure of, as she'd only seen him the one time."

"You're saying it might not be Lucas!"

"I'm not saying that, I'm saying you need to take a look yourself."

Within minutes Clemente Ramos, Tito Gomez and Felipe Salazar were in the lift and making for the underground garage.

Felipe Salazar stared down at the face of Aaron Chudzik and looked shocked but quickly confirmed this was indeed the body of Lucas Garrett. Tito Gomez looked perplexed but a restraining hand from Clemente Ramos caused the big man to say nothing.

It was only as they drove out of the parking lot that Salazar broke the silence. "There can only be two explanations. The man in the morgue could have been killed by Lucas, but that doesn't explain Lucas's wallet found on the dead man. Or Lucas knew the killers, but why the exchange of wallets, unless . . . ." The blood drained from Salazar's face. "Drive to our bank and step on it!"

Ramos obeyed immediately, but was caught in the early rush hour of a big city, and despite the wide avenues the traffic was starting to build. Eventually Clemente screeched to a halt outside the bank. It was ten minutes to four; the bank had closed at three o'clock. Felipe Salazar threw himself out of the car and banged on the ornate double doors. He pounded and pounded until a security guard inside the bank came to the door.

"The bank's closed! Come back in the morning."

"It's important, I must speak to the manager!" demanded Salazar.

"He's gone home for the day, you'll have to wait until tomorrow, there's nothing I can do!"

Felipe Salazar began to rant and rave; he cursed and swore, he threatened the guard.

"Okay if that's the way you want to play it, I'm calling the police," said the bank guard.

"No need for that, we'll come back in the morning," said Clemente Ramos, as he steered Salazar back to the car.

It wasn't until eight o'clock in the evening before Felipe Salazar managed to contact the manager. In as calm a voice as he could muster, Salazar relayed his suspicions to the bank manager.

"I can allay any suspicions of large transactions happening, nothing extraordinary happened today. I can assure you of that!"

"That's good, but what about the day before and the day before that!" spat Salazar, his voice showing signs of exasperation.

"This is highly irregular, I don't have these figures to hand, and without looking at the paperwork I can't be one hundred percent sure. However I can assure you that no transactions on the scale you're talking about have taken place to the best of my knowledge."

"That isn't good enough. I want you to meet me at the bank in the next hour!"

"That's impossible. Besides if any transactions had taken place, there would be nothing I could do about it until the morning."

Frustrated, angry, murderous, Salazar finally calmed down and arranged a meeting for nine thirty on the Friday morning.

Chapter 42

A few hours earlier on a lonely airfield some fifty miles north of Montevideo a Douglas DC 2 trundled along a dirt runway. Five nervous passengers each lost in their own private thoughts felt every bump and divot as the DC2 picked up speed. They braced themselves as a belt of trees grew ever closer, but then suddenly the ground disappeared and they were airborne.

An air of tension was replaced by relief for each of the occupancies of the fourteen seat aircraft as the plane reached its cruising height. Mike and Erin sat to the rear of the plane lost in each others eyes, while on the left side gazing out the window sat Ethan still mesmerised from watching the ground below slowly disappear to be replaced by the shores of the Atlantic Ocean. Up front Jake and Rodrigo were heavily in discussion about women, the merits of American football verses soccer and what they would do with the vast wealth they'd so recently acquired.

To Mike and Erin the previous night's events were still fresh in their collective memory. Their kiss on the shoreline had been magical; more than that—for as long as it lasted the past was obliterated. They were two lovers that had found each other, both knowing that if there was to be a future they could only ever look forward. When their lips eventually parted, they held each other breathlessly. Erin's eyes glazed over as she looked up into Mike's and she took hold of his hand and led him back towards the cantina.

As they approached the entrance she turned left and quickened her pace as she located the door she'd been seeking. She pulled Mike towards her and kissed him passionately whilst at the same time opening the door. Stepping inside, she backed towards the narrow staircase, kissing and holding him as she began to negotiate the stairs. Mike responded forcefully as he scooped her up into his arms and ascended the stairs two at a time. Erin indicated the door and seconds later they were inside the room. He kissed her less passionately but kept the intensity at fever point. His actions had indicated that he intended to take it slow, to savour and to absorb every fibre of her body. She responded as only two lovers that understand each others needs can, and moments later they were at the side of the bed. He lowered her gently on to it, kissing her delicious mouth as he caressed her body lovingly.

There lovemaking was slow, passionate, warm and caring. They wanted it to go on forever, but inevitable they reached the point of no return and surrendered themselves to each other. As they lay in each others arms, Mike kissed her gently upon the lips, "My God, I've missed you," he purred as she responded in kind.

Long after their lovemaking, with Erin sleeping peacefully at his side, Mike lay there thinking. He'd been given yet another chance; it was a chance his troubled mind felt he didn't deserve, but he vowed that nothing was going to come between him and Erin ever again.

In his room three blocks from where Erin and Mike slept, another man was lying awake; brooding. Ethan was still reeling from the home truths Erin had flung at him in the cantina. His thoughts were dark and murderous.

On the drive to the airfield Rodrigo filled them in on their escape route. He informed them they were heading to a remote airfield and that within a few hours they would be airborne.

"I have this friend; he will take us all to Brazil, for a price. It is not cheap, but we are also buying discretion. I think once we are in Brazil we are safe, but it pays to be careful."

"How long's this flight?" asked Jake.

"A little under four hours," replied Rodrigo.

"That ain't so bad."

"No senor, you misunderstand, were heading for a landing strip fifty miles west of the coastal town of Florianopolis, Brazil. Pepe, our pilot has arranged refuelling and an overhaul of the aircraft before our final destination."

"How long before we reach Rio?" cried Ethan bad temperedly, "Sooner we get the fuck outta this god-forsaken country the better!"

"This god-forsaken country, as you call it, has been your salvation. Just remember that!" spat Rodrigo, his eyes burning into Ethan like firebrands. "Rio de Janeiro is but a tantalizing four hours away."

"How long before we take off from this Florianopolis?" asked Jake.

"It could be within the hour, it could be much later; it depends."

"Fuck, then we might not make Rio tonight," cried Ethan.

"That my friend is possible," replied Rodrigo, his crooked smile only betrayed by the hatred in his eyes.

The flight to Florianopolis was uneventful apart from the bumpy landing, where the DC2 seemed to slew from side to side before coming to an abrupt stop.

"Wow, I thought I was about to bite the bullet," said Ethan, relief clearly showing upon his face.

Pepe was the first to de-plane. He disembarked and looked around, but the refuelling truck was nowhere to be seen.

"Where's the truck?" asked Jake, the second one out.

Pepe looked at him quizzically.

"He doesn't speak a word of English, leave Pepe to me," said Rodrigo as he emerged from the plane.

Three minutes of excited Spanish later, Rodrigo addressed the small group. "The truck's late, but that's not unusual. Pepe suggests we walk into the village, it's about two kilometres down that dirt road."

"Why?" asked Ethan.

"Because if the truck's any later than an hour there won't be enough daylight for us to land safely," replied Rodrigo.

"Fuck! I knew it!" snapped Ethan bad temperedly.

"Look it's no fault of anyone, things happen. We've just got to deal with things the best we can," said Mike.

"It is not so bad. I have stayed at this village one time. There is a bar, a place to eat and a small rooming house."

"Let's walk," ordered Jake

Pepe arrived back at the village two hours later. He spoke with Rodrigo and informed him that the plane had been refuelled, he'd done his pre-check and apart from the loss of daylight the Douglas DC2 was ready.

Rodrigo informed everyone of the situation. "I don't know about you, but I'm going to get my head down, back at the plane."

"Yeah, judging by the state of the rooming house, I think I'll join you," said Ethan.

It sounded friendly enough, but Jake knew what Ethan was thinking, 'I don't trust you fuckers not to start that plane and leave us in the middle of nowhere.'

'Great minds,' thought Jake.

Mike and Erin elected to take their chances at the rooming house, which was probably the best course of action as Ethan had been availing himself heavily from the bar in the village. By the time he was back at the plane he was a little inebriated.

"I tell you Jake, that son of a bitch ain't having the last laugh on me. Once we're free and clear of that asshole Salazar I'm gonna take that fucker out," whispered Ethan.

"Yeah sure you are," replied Jake, "now go to sleep."

Rodrigo had heard the exchange; Lucas had filled him in on their history.

"Hot air," replied Mike, when Rodrigo told him of Ethan's threat. "If he was going to do it, he'd have done it on foreign soil. Ethan's a lot of things but he ain't a fool."

"That's the trouble with you Luc.. Mike, you act like a wise guy but in reality you ain't. Ethan's wired differently to you."

"Thanks, I'll bare that in mind," replied Mike. 'His friend was right,' thought Mike, subconsciously he'd already discarded Lucas and all that he stood for and had begun to think and act like the man he once was. "Now let's get aboard, Rio's waiting!" he added with a smile.

"Sugar Loaf Mountain," cried Rodrigo. "To your right," he added.

Mike and Erin gazed out excitedly and caught their first sight of Rio de Janeiro.

"It's magnificent!" exclaimed Erin as she took in the bays, the beaches and the green mountains that seemed so much a part of the city

The plane banked to its left and started its descent. Everyone returned to their seats and fastened their belts. Another open stretch of grassland came into sight as the plane dropped rapidly. Erin looked at Mike and squeezed his hand while mouthing 'I love you.' He returned the squeeze and the sentiment. They watched nervously as the tops of the trees on either side of the landing strip raced by and the ground came up to greet them. Then they felt a hard bump of one wheel, then the other, as the trees flew by at a gut retching speed. Erin squeezed tighter until the DC2 finally came to a halt some fifty yards from the edge of the forest.

For the first time since he'd committed himself with those wire transactions Mike Burnett started to believe they'd pulled it off. Jake smiled and shook Pepe's hand in appreciation; he too seemed to have the same overwhelming feeling of relief.

Technically Felipe Salazar could still find them in Rio, but the odds were incredible small. For a start, he didn't know who he was looking for; the three mysterious Americans had disappeared without trace, and even if they connected Aaron Chudzik to the shootings, the only identification on him was that of Lucas Garrett. They knew nothing of Erin and even if they connected Rodrigo and Mike, where would they look first?

"I guess we should find ourselves a nice hotel, kick back for a day or two and figure out our next move," laughed Jake.

"I'm for that," declared Ethan, "It'll give Mike the chance to check on the other half of our investment!"

"What other half," said Mike defensively.

"I'm brighter than you give me credit for. When we all thought Erin was going to Rio you told her to make a withdrawal, but she chose the long route home instead. I figure there's more money for the taking."

Mike laughed, "I never ever thought you were dumb, you have every other unenviable trait but dumb ain't one of them. Sure there was money there, but Erin was supposed to pick it up sometime Wednesday, today's Friday, Friday afternoon to be precise. We can't get to the bank until Monday morning."

"Then we wait around until Monday!" declared Ethan.

Mike was about to protest, but Jake stepped in. "How much are we talking about?"

"You don't get my point, I instructed Erin to make the withdrawal on Wednesday because there was a good chance Salazar wouldn't have known about it, by Friday the chances are he'd have put a stop on it, now to all intent and purpose by Monday that money's gone!"

"How much money?" insisted Jake.

All eyes turned towards Mike.

"Five hundred thousand give or take a few pesos."

"I rest my case," said Ethan. "Once we hit Rio we should book into the swankiest hotel on Copacabana Beach, grab us a handful of martinis and kick back and watch the world go by while we wait it out."

"I agree," stated Jake.

An hour later they booked into the Olinda hotel on Av. Atlantica 2230 Copacabana. Mike and Erin booked in as husband and wife much to the chagrin of Ethan, while Jake, Rodrigo and the disgruntled Ethan booked separate rooms.

Over drinks in the lobby bar that evening Mike stated that he and Erin were going to dine alone. "It's like this, we're here because of your say so until Monday, I get that, but from now until then I don't want to hang around with you guys."

"What if we don't trust you?" said Jake. "What's to stop you taking the first available flight out and return in six months to collect all the dough?"

"Nothing," declared Mike. "We got here right. Against the odds we got here alive. I ain't risking all that for what might or might not be in that bank on Monday."

"Let them go!" cried Ethan. "You came here for a reason, you got what you wanted in spades and you're a rich man. Me I came along for the ride, lost something along the way, no strike that, I never had it to start with, but I'm going home a very rich man. Erin's the real winner, she came for Mike and she found him. I wish she hadn't but what the hell, you can't win them all."

Erin looked at Ethan and gave him a warm smile.

Mike wasn't so sure, Ethan's apparent changing of heart unsettled him.

"See that, that's worth its weight in gold," continued Ethan as he smiled back.

"How do you feel about it Rodrigo?" asked Mike.

"I am already a very rich man; go."

Through the darkening skies the first raindrops began to fall upon the sands of Ipanema Beach. Mike and Erin gazed from the window of the candlelit restaurant and marvelled at the almost neon light from the sky as thunder gave way to lightning and the raindrops increased in intensity. Soon the only thing they could see was a single rain soaked palm tree illuminated by sheet lightning, followed by complete darkness. The scene repeated itself again and again. Looking back it had been the perfect weekend.

Over dinner on that Friday night they talked and talked about their future. Where to go, what to do, what plans they would make, a family perhaps; it wasn't too late Erin assured him.

The following day they did the usual tourist things and for the first time really felt at peace. As they gazed up at the concrete monolith of Christ the Redeemer and scoured the magnificent horizon towards Sugar Loaf, they realised they were the luckiest people alive.

On Sunday they took the cable car up Sugar Loaf Mountain and looked back across at Christ the Redeemer, Copacabana Beach and beyond to Ipanema.

"There is so much beauty in the world it's easy to forget the ugliness that lies beneath," said Mike as he looked out across the Atlantic Ocean.

"An ugliness that's best forgotten," replied Erin. "One day, if we're blessed we'll teach our kids about the beauty of this world, and shield them from the ugly side."

"Amen," responded Mike.

As they continued to gaze at the torrential rain there was a reluctance to leave. It had been a fitting end to an idyllic weekend, but reality was just a few short hours away.

Decisions had been made in their absence. Jake was going back to L.A, to consolidate his holdings; then when the time was right and everything was in place he intended to disappear without trace. Rodrigo had decided to hang with Jake for the time being, check out Hollywood and maybe settle somewhere along the coast of California. "I've time and money; I understand that's all you need in California."

"You better believe it!" cried Mike when he was told of their plans, "And what about you Ethan?"

Surprisingly Ethan was quite amicable, a fact that unsettled Mike for the second time that weekend. "Me, I'm heading home too. Going to put the house on the market, find me something more to my taste, after that I don't know."

Mike walked into the bank with little expectation, but to his surprise and delight the half million was nestling in his account. An hour later a number of accounts in the Caymans were swelled just that little bit more.

"I suspect, things haven't gone too well for Salazar," said Mike cheerily. He could only assume his plans had worked better than expected.

Chapter 43

It was only after the bank manager had finished going over the books that Salazar discovered the full extent of the damage Lucas Garrett had inflicted upon him.

"I'm ruined!" he started to rant, "I'll cut his fucking heart out, how can he do this to me! I treated him like a son, and how does he repay me, he cleans me out!"

Firstly there was Granero de Alvarado and the new venue near Casa Rosada, Lucas had borrowed heavily on the strength of the business and Salazar's name. The bank now owned all but a fraction of both establishments. But that was the least of Felipe Salazar's problems. Lucas had cleverly manipulated Salazar into mortgaging his beloved Estancia, under the pretext of the third (fictitious) night spot, which if it didn't happen was a perfect way for the land owner to launder money. Other accounts had been opened and Salazar's signature along with Lucas Garrett's was clearly there to be seen. Lucas had passed these off as additional expense accounts for the securing of international artists, another sly way to hide money from the tax man. Garrett had presented these same figures that he was looking at right now only a week ago and passed them off as legitimate, which they were, until he began siphoning off funds from one project to another, that's what rankled Salazar the most. Lucas created a mind blowing tax bill when he eventually transferred the funds to a number of third parties. Two signatories were responsible, Felipe Salazar and his late partner. As Lucas

Garrett was officially dead, it was too late for Salazar to retract his
identification. He was already being linked to enough trouble. So
being the sole signatory it would be left to Salazar and his army of
lawyers to do battle with the revenue agencies alone.

"There must be something you can do?" screamed Salazar. "It's
your bank that's at fault not me!"

The manager squirmed and made all the right noises, saying he
appreciated Salazar's position. But later that morning he informed
his superiors and the tax office of his findings.

He even voiced his opinion on Salazar's position. "I don't know
how he did it, it'll take years of investigating, re-investigation and
could tie Senor Salazar up in litigation for years to come."

The following day, the Buenos Aires Tribune and a handful of
others got wind of the story and ran it along with a re-run of the
shootings of the early part of the week.

"Death Knell. The Fall of the Salazar Empire."

*Over the last week and a half the Tribune has received
anonymous tips regarding nefarious dealings resulting in three
separate murder scenes. On each occasion the information received
proved to be accurate, extremely accurate. Felipe Salazar's name
has been linked to these dreadful incidents, that could be entirely
coincidental, except on the last but one incident the informer left his
name, after reporting the penultimate incident as Lucas Garrett. The
same Lucas Garrett whose name is linked to the financial scandal
that Felipe Salazar is so deeply involved with. Only last Wednesday
Mr Lucas Garrett's body was duly identified by a friend of his late
fiancée Gretchen Kauffman. Whatever the true facts to this case are,
we may never find out*

It was short and to the point and had an immediate effect.
Salazar was on his uppers and everyone knew it. Phones stopped
ringing in the Salazar household and more importantly other
phone-calls were never returned.

During the course of three months the clubs were wound up, the receivers took charge and finally workmen put up signs stating 'CLOSED FOR BUSINESS.'

Salazar's dream, his beloved Estancia was temporarily saved by Colonel Ruben Salazar, but on the 15th September 1949 the receivers took it over.

As for Felipe Salazar, he and his immediate family moved into the suite at the El Presidente hotel. From there a small army of lawyers began his legal defence for tax evasion. Over time that army would dwindle as Salazar's own meagre savings started to dry up.

Felipe Salazar believed things couldn't get any worse; the possibility of prison for tax evasion, the loss of his beloved Estancia, his position in the community, the night clubs closing. But he was wrong. Once the police discovered part of a female pelvis whilst investigating the gruesome remains at the abattoir and pig pen, a thorough search of the surrounding area was instigated. It wasn't long before the police uncovered yet more evidence of body parts.

What friends he had, deserted him, and he became a social pariah. Three months later he was put on trial, found guilty and sentenced to five years on tax evasion charges.

With Felipe Salazar starting his five year jail sentence, witnesses began coming forward implicating him in a sex ring involving rape, torture and murder. The only thing Felipe Salazar could look forward to whilst in prison was the break from prison routine when he was put on trial for murder. The body parts scandal wasn't going away.

Chapter 44

From his vantage point atop the cliffs of Marin County, Mike Burnett stared out at the vastness of the Pacific Ocean. It had been madness to return to California, he knew it now. Back then it had seemed the smart thing to do, the clever, the unexpected. The sheer arrogance of it, it made him sick to the pit of his stomach.

He wiped a tear from his eye, 'we got away clean. We pulled the rug from under them. It shouldn't have come to this . . . .'

It was at the check in desk at Santos Dumont Airport, when Mike dropped his bombshell, "Well Jake it was fun while it lasted," he extended his hand. Jake had seen it coming.

"In your place I guess I'd have done the same." He took Mike's hand and shook it.

"What the fuc . . ." stammered Ethan, realising just what Mike and Erin were planning to do. Acting quickly Jake extended a strong restraining arm, and told Ethan not to be a fool. Rodrigo fixed him with a menacing gaze and indicated the security men that were in close proximity. "Don't fuck up now!" ordered Jake.

Ethan brushed aside Jake's arm, but realising now was not the time to cause a scene managed to contain his anger and frustration.

"I'd like to say it's been nice knowing you, but then you'd know I was lying." Yet despite Mike's words he still extended his hand.

Ethan looked at his hand in disgust and ignored it. Then he gave a sly smirk before coldly adding, "You won this round, but it ain't over, one day, one day when you least expect it, you'll get

325

yours. I guarantee it." He looked at Erin, smiled weakly, "See yah around doll." Then picking up his ticket and passport he walked away.

Rodrigo grinned then extended his hand, "I kinda figured. I'll miss you compadre. Take care."

"Don't get taken in by those California broads," replied Mike as he hugged the man from Montevideo. "I owe you big time."

A few short minutes later Mike and Erin watched from the concourse windows as Rodrigo, Jake and Ethan walked across the tarmac and boarded the Douglas DC3. They stayed watching until the cabin crew closed the door of the aircraft. Mike gently squeezed Erin's shoulder as they stood in silence and waited for the DC3 to taxi towards the airstrip. A few minutes later they saw the plane speed along the runway and slowly climb into the gloriously sunny Brazilian sky.

They were finally alone, they were free. It was a strange sensation. Over the weekend they'd declared their undying love for each other, but that had been in a time of uncertainty. The trip to the bank, the realisation Salazar had far greater troubles than to chase across half a continent, and the outmanoeuvring of Ethan, had suddenly released them from the restraints of living in the now. Their whole life was in front of them, but there were issues to be dealt with before that could truly happen.

Over dinner that night Mike brought up what they'd been pussy footing around with since they watched Ethan's plane take to the skies.

"Erin, there's things about me you don't know, dreadful things. If we're to have any chance at a life together we've got to be honest with each other."

"You're right, I know you're right, but is it wise? Why can't we start from here?" implored Erin.

"We could, but there would always be something between us."

"You want the truth, well here goes," cried Erin seizing the initiative.

Mike listened to Erin's confessions, which in his opinion didn't amount to a hill of beans, until she got to the part where she slept with Jake Reis and the deal they'd struck.

"Basically Jake pimped you out!" he said cruelly and regretted it the moment the words left his mouth. "I'm sorry, that was uncalled for."

"No it wasn't, it needed to be said, it's what you feel," replied Erin, a trace of disappointment clearly in her voice.

"Felt," he corrected her. "I'm older and hopefully wiser; you did what you had to do to survive. I should know I worked the streets I saw the hope, the disappointment and the despair, it was written on most kids that came looking for the Hollywood dream."

"I was on the point of giving up, when I met you. I was going back home. But, strange as it might seem, that first night in that all night café, I knew . . . . I just knew you were the one for me."

Mike leaned across and stroked at her hair.

Erin smiled at the touch, "I'd been sent to seduce you, but believe me it wasn't an act on my part. I think I loved you from the moment you left me at my lodgings that first night."

"We were happy, weren't we?" Mike asked suddenly.

"Of course we were happy, we loved each other and if it hadn't been for Ethan, things . . . ." She let the words trail off.

"Yeah, that son of a bitch certainly did a number on us."

"He frightened me with his talk of Jake Reis and what he was capable of, but I was also grateful to Ethan for saving my life. My first reaction was to run, to leave Los Angeles behind, but the thought that if I did I might never see you again. That thought would have haunted me." She paused as she recalled those wasted years. "Ethan was good to me, he was kind and caring, or so I thought, but not once in that time did I sleep with him, or any man for that matter. And I guess it might have continued that way if I hadn't seen the article in Moviegoer. Things changed for me after that, I did what I had to do to find you."

Mike smiled weakly, he was ashamed he'd put Erin through the ordeal. If only he'd known she was alive, he would never have given his love to another. Erin had nothing to reproach herself for, but he on the other hand had much that needed saying.

"I'm sorry I put you through that, you didn't deserve it. I on the other hand have done terrible things. You need to know the real me. I betrayed my badge of office, I looked the other way, I took bribes."

Erin interrupted, "So did a great many others."

"It went further; we cleaned up after prominent people."

"What do you mean?" she asked.

"It could have been a drug overdose, it could have been murder; we covered it up. One day it went too far, I couldn't take it anymore. I decided to hit back, that's when Ethan put his warped plan into action."

The memory of that night in the desert came back to him in an instant. He felt ashamed, and even now he couldn't bear to tell Erin the sordid details.

"When I thought you were dead, I knew it was because of what I was prepared to do. Your apparent death was my fault, and it changed me."

"How did it change you?"

"It dragged me down into the gutter. I entered a dog eat dog world, and because I'd lost you I cared little for anything and anyone. I became a dangerous man." For the briefest of moments he thought of Lola. "I pimped, cheated, stole, I fought anyone that got in my way. I didn't care how I hurt them. My reputation around La Boca increased, I was feared. It wasn't long after, that I was brought to the attention of Felipe Salazar."

"It's not surprising you changed," said Erin defensively.

"Erin if that was all; we wouldn't be having this conversation. I saw how my life was going and tried to change, but not before I'd witnessed a horrific murder, and taken a life. Even that wasn't all; I planned and prepared the execution of another. I wish I could turn the clock back, but I can't."

"Oh Michael!" cried Erin.

"It was kill or be killed," he added defensively.

Still reeling from his shock confession, Erin reached out. "But you got your life back on track."

"Only after I'd become like the rest of the jackals that stalk the weaker amongst us. Naively I thought I had a chance to become legit, to get married, have kids, and that blew up in my face. I'm bad news Erin. You would be wise to walk away."

Erin looked into Mike's eyes; her hands reached across the table and grabbed his, "It's taken me years to find you, if you think I'm letting you go you've another think coming. I love you Michael Burnett."

The smoky glow of candlelight cast a magical beam illuminating the redness in Erin's hair and he knew he could never leave this woman; she was the love of his life.

"I'll make you a solemn promise, from this day until the end; my past life will remain buried forever."

Two days later they boarded a Braniff Airways flight to Houston, Texas, via Lima, Peru. Tired, hungry and a little jaded from their journey they arrived in the States. Mike booked them into a hotel close to the city centre. He registered under the name of Mr and Mrs Nicholas Kincaid. Erin joked on the way to the elevator that it had a nice ring to it.

For the next few days Mike acclimatised himself to being back in the States. Although he'd never been to Houston he could see and feel the changes that had happened since the end of the war. To him at least everything seemed to be done at a hectic pace, something he knew he'd have to adjust too. Erin laughed at the startled expressions on Mike's face whenever he confronted new innovations. Everyday things like going out to eat, to shop for new clothes; even taking a cab took some getting used too.

It was over dinner one night that Mike broached the subject of where they were going to live.

"We can't stay here for the rest of our lives."

"Where do you suggest?" said Erin, "I'll go where ever you want."

"There are a lot of things to consider. Firstly I'm wanted for your murder. If I went back, how would I explain it? I'd get thrown into jail the moment I walked into the Sheriff's Department. Not to mention Ethan's reaction."

"I could testify on your behalf," said Erin naively.

"Questions would be asked, Where have you been, why didn't you come forward when it happened? Sorry Erin that ain't an option."

"What about Jake?"

Mike looked at her, "Do you really think they'd take the word of a known mobster over an Assistant Commander of the Sheriff's Department? And don't kid yourself, Jake wouldn't come forward anyway."

"So Los Angeles is out."

"Pretty much so," replied Mike. "Look on the bright side; we don't have to decide where to live just yet. We can have fun on the way. What's clear to me is we need to create a new identity for ourselves."

"You mean we cease to exist," cried Erin, "but how?"

"Easier than you'd think. We've access to more money than you could shake a stick at, so getting the right paperwork, new passports, new birth certificates, and social security cards shouldn't be a problem."

Erin looked across the table and giggled, "You mean we start life over."

"That's exactly what I mean," he said with a twinkle in his eye.

That twinkle was explained the following evening. They were dining in a Mexican restaurant some three blocks from their hotel, it was small and intimate, good food, subdued lighting, and Mexican music playing in the background, the perfect place for Mike to get down on one knee and propose.

"I should have done this a long time ago. Erin Albright will you do me the honour of becoming my wife?"

A warm glow crossed Erin's pretty face and she smiled.

"Yes Michael, I'd love to marry you."

There was no mention of her sham marriage to Ethan Kels.

Mike smiled and reached in his pocket and produced a small velvet box, he opened it and presented her with a diamond ring.

"It's beautiful," it was then that she noticed the name of the jewellers; it was Franklins of Los Angeles. "Michael, when did you get this?"

Mike smiled, "You remember the night when Ethan phoned?" How could she forget, it had been from that moment the phone rang that their life began to turn sour. "I was going to ask you to marry me that night."

Tears rolled down Erin's face, "Oh Michael, I love you so much." She leaned down and kissed him while he was in a kneeling position, and it was a few seconds before she realised the restaurant had all stopped eating and were also enjoying the moment. Once they sheepishly released themselves from their embrace the restaurant's customers applauded much to their joint embarrassment.

Three days later they boarded the Texas Chief from Union Station Houston for their northward journey to Chicago. The Texas Chief was one of Atchinson Topeka and Santa Fe's premier routes, knocking half a day off the route from Galveston—Chicago to twenty five hours. They'd booked a roomette for the journey, and made reservations for dinner in the dining car and booked a private table in the club car for after dinner drinks. It was strange as it turned out but their reservation in the dining car unwittingly gave them a glimpse into their 'new' past.

Mike was caught on the hop by a woman sitting across the aisle from them when they were having dinner. She was accompanied by three kids, two boys around seven or eight and an older girl going on twelve. Tired of kids' talk she struck up a conversation with Mike and Erin.

"We're on our way to meet my husband; he works in advertising in Chicago."

Mike nodded politely, hoping one of the kids would distract her and bring her back into their world, but once she'd got her teeth into the conversation she wasn't letting go. "It's an extremely stressful job and it keeps him away from the family for months on end. That's why we're heading to Chicago to spend the weekend with him.

"It's a mighty long way to go for a weekend," said Mike politely, hoping the woman would leave it at that.

"Oh we do it at least three times a year, its fun, isn't it kids."

"Yeah mom," came the bored replies.

"Where you all heading," asked the woman.

Without hesitation Erin stepped in. "We're originally from the mid-west, heading back for a visit."

"That's nice, isn't that nice kids." When she received not a word she continued, "You live in Houston?"

"No, as a matter of fact, we flew into Houston a couple of weeks back. We've been living in Brazil and Argentina for the best part of five years, my husband's in property."

"Real Estate?" enquired the woman.

"You got it. Now you'll have to excuse us, we're late to make up a four at Bridge. It's been nice talking to you."

Minutes later they shuffled into the club car and ordered a glass of dry white wine and a large bourbon and branch water.

"Real Estate!" exclaimed Mike, laughing at Erin's theatrics.

"Why not?" replied Erin.

Within a week Mike and Erin had taken out a year's lease on an apartment in a nice neighbourhood in the suburbs of Chicago. While Erin turned the place into a home Mike enrolled in a realtor's course. He'd thought long and hard about their future and decided Erin's idea could be the perfect cover for their new lives. At the same time he got to work on building a new identity Using his knowledge and knowhow as an ex cop he began frequenting the bars and dives of downtown Chicago making discreet enquires about the chance of obtaining forged documents. Like most things, if you've the money there's always someone that can accommodate your needs. In the space of a month he'd acquired new passports, birth certificates and social security cards, in the names Erin Kirkwood and Michael Spencer.

On the sixteenth of July 1949 they put these documents to the test and were duly married. It was a simple affair with two witnesses brought off the street; Erin Kirkwood became Mrs Erin Spencer. A week later she broke the news to Mike that he was to become a father. He was over the moon at the prospect of fatherhood. Working it back they figured she'd conceived in the small hotel near the landing strip not far from Florianopolis.

During those first few months of married life, Mike studied during the day while Erin busied herself as a homemaker. They could have lived the highlife, but they were smart enough to realise that flashing their money around could attract attention sooner or later. They ate out on an occasion but Erin was happy to cook meals at home. They went to the movies once a week, and once in a while they'd sample the bright lights of Chicago. To an outsider they looked just like any other young couple starting out.

By the time little Daisy appeared on the scene, the Spencer's experienced their first Chicago winter and vowed it would be their last.

"I think its time to move on. We need to establish a permanent home, somewhere warm. I've almost finished my realtor's course, and my experience working part time for Prines real estate office should help me get a job," stated Mike.

"If that's what you want honey, let's go for it. I'm like you I think it's time we branched out. The only problem is where?"

During those cold winter evenings with the snow pelting at their windows the Spencer's huddled around the fire discussing their options. Erin still hankered for sea views and Hawaii cropped up more than once. "It's not even a state, we'd stick out like sore thumbs," said Mike on more than one occasion.

Florida was becoming a clear favourite, but the west side overlooking the Gulf of Mexico was preferable, but then the thought of hurricanes was putting them off. They discounted the Eastern seaboard on account they both wanted a home where they could watch the sunset across the ocean. Washington State and Oregon were considered, but ruled out because of rain. Mike laughed.

"I didn't realise how much of a problem having money has created. Any one of these places would be ideal."

"California!" announced Erin.

"What!" exclaimed Mike, "you can't be serious?"

"Think about it, no one in Los Angeles would be looking for you now. As far as the cops are concerned it was a domestic that got out of control. Sure a woman died, and we're sorry about that, but it wasn't our fault. I doubt anyone has given it much of a thought."

"What about Ethan!"

"Ethan will have moved on," replied Erin, "and think about it, who in their right mind would think we'd return to California."

"You have a point, it's a clever idea. But no way are we heading back to Los Angeles, which only leaves San Diego or San Francisco. In my opinion San Diego's out. It's too close."

"San Francisco it is then," replied Erin excitedly.

Chapter 45

By mid April 1950 they'd found the perfect home in Marin County just a few miles north of the Golden Gate Bridge. The house was small in comparison to others in the community but there was room on the plot to expand. Where it gained was the stunning views across the ocean, something they both fell in love with on their first viewing. By June they'd moved in, and within a short space of time Mike was working for a small real estate firm.

Things moved quickly in Marin County, and it wasn't too long before Erin gave birth to her second child, a baby boy, followed a year later by another girl. With Daisy, Blake and Cindy, the Spencer family was complete, but instead of moving they extended and remodelled the house. Having the children and creating a new life together saw Erin and Mike bloom. They soon became popular in the neighbourhood and were invited to barbeques and parties on frequent occasions. Erin busied herself with the children and got involved with toddler and baby groups, while Mike was making a name for himself in the real estate world. Life for the Spencer's was good and getting better all the time. There was of course subtle reminders of their past, beamed to them though the courtesy of television. Mickey Cohen was being released from prison after spending four years on tax evasion charges; Dragna was fighting deportation to Sicily, but there wasn't a mention of Jake Reis. Mike hoped he'd taken his own advice and retired quietly to the Bahamas.

In the spring of 54 Mike was offered a junior partnership in the real estate firm. He accepted with the proviso that when Fred Singleton retired he'd be given the opportunity to buy the firm. Mike Spencer was on the up. He'd got what he'd always wanted, a beautiful wife, three adorable kids, a fabulous home, good friends and neighbours and a successful business, but most of all he'd got legitimacy.

It was all over the radio and television but it was while reading the Sunday paper that Mike got the jolt of his life.

Rex Blaze in Suicide Mystery.

Rex Blaze, beloved star of countless western movies was found dead yesterday at his bungalow in Laurel Canyon. It is reported he died from a single gunshot wound to the head. Reasons for his suicide are numerous, some reports suggest he was about to declare himself bankrupt, but the fact he signed a contract with a leading television studio to star in a new television western series suggests otherwise.

It was an early edition and Mike guessed there would be countless theories put forward as to what really happened. He was glad the bastard had got what he deserved, but when he switched on the television later that evening other details struck a nerve. He'd been found slumped in an armchair; the gun he'd used to kill himself with was found lying on the floor next to the chair. The gun was later identified as belonging to Mr Blaze and the open glass display gun case confirmed it. From people that knew him it was revealed that the gun in question was a short barrelled Colt 45 Peacemaker which he'd used frequently in his films of the late thirties and early forties.

Mike could feel the cold sensation of ice as it shot up and down his spine. It was a carbon copy of the way he'd planned to kill Rex Blaze.

"It's terrible, the man had everything to live for, he must have been out of his mind to do such a thing," said Erin standing in the doorway.

"Who knows what goes through some peoples minds," replied Mike.

He'd never told Erin the facts of that trip to the desert and he wanted to keep it that way. It was a subliminal message, he was sure of it, but fearful that Erin would pick up on his tensions he dismissed the news bulletin and sat back down to watch 'I Love Lucy.'

As he lay in bed that night it all came flooding back, the night in the desert, his plan to kill Rex Blaze and pass it off as suicide and the subsequent events that followed. He kept telling himself it was a coincidence, but Mike Spencer didn't believe in coincidence. Only one person knew the details of his plan, Ethan!

If it was Ethan then Mike needed to know what he was up against. Ethan might have risen further up the chain of command in the Sheriff's Department or he might have become a victim of the police corruption purges that he'd heard so much about. But how could he find out without attracting attention? Then the idea hit him, it was simple and foolproof, firstly he'd do nothing until the weekend, then he would phone long distance to the Los Angeles County Sheriff's Department. Knowing Ethan, he'd be playing tennis at his club so phoning the department's switchboard should give him the answers he was looking for. He'd ask to speak to Area Commander Ethan Kels.

Under the pretence of showing a young couple a house, he drove into San Francisco early on Saturday morning.

"I should be home for lunch," he'd told Erin.

He hated lying to her, but he needed to know if his suspicions were correct.

He drove out to the airport and stepped inside one of the many phone booths that were dotted around the terminal building. He called the operator and asked for a person to person call to Los

Angeles. He waited on the line for what seemed like hours before she asked him to deposit the correct change into the machine.

"Putting you through now," said the operator.

"Los Angeles County Sheriff's Department, how may I direct your call?"

"Area Commander Ethan Kels."

He waited anxiously while she put him through. The phone rang and rang, then the girl on the switchboard came back on the line. "I'm afraid Commander Kels is unavailable. Is there someone else I can call for you?"

"No thanks."

Mike put down the receiver and found he was sweating buckets. He grabbed a drink at the bar to steady his nerves then left the terminal and drove back to Marin County. What had he discovered? Nothing, a big fat zero, it was business as usual at the Los Angeles County Sheriff's Department.

By the time he arrived home the dark cloud had lifted. He'd gone over it, twenty times, and he still couldn't see how Ethan could ever track him down. His humour returned as his kids ran out to greet him.

Three more weeks passed and so did his paranoia, then while Erin was playing with the kids in the garden the phone suddenly rang. Mike picked it up casually, "Mike Spencer's residence."

"Hello Mike."

"Who is this?" Alarm bells rang inside his head, but his brain refused to believe. "Is this some kind of joke?"

"No one's joking, it's good to hear your voice again," came the self satisfied reply.

Mike looked through the window at Erin and the kids playing happily, blissfully ignorant to the turmoil being created inside Mike's head.

"What do you want? How did you find me?"

"All in good time," replied Ethan, "How did I find you, old fashioned police work. Side stepping us at the airport was pretty smart, but in truth I should have seen it coming."

"What the fuck do you want?" demanded Mike.

Ignoring Mike's question Ethan continued where he'd left off. "I was angry for a week when I got back, but before I knew it I was back in the swing of things, and then it dawned on me, the only way to locate you was through old fashioned police work."

"Yeah you already said," interrupted Mike, now fully recovered from his outburst.

"I asked myself what I would do in your circumstances. There wasn't one of you, there were two. Assuming you returned to the States, you'd need fake ID's, social security cards, passports maybe. Using the team I had around me, I sent out an APB for information concerning known forgers of documents to police departments of all major cities. It was a long shot."

As Mike listened he could detect the self satisfaction in Ethan's voice.

"I dangled my hook in the water and waited for a nice juicy fish; I caught a few minnows, nothing of consequence, but I had time on my side. I knew it wasn't going to be easy, and to be fair you were a slippery son of a bitch. It took three to four years, during which time I caught a number of fish but the one I was after just kept evading me, that was until three months ago, when the fish bit deeply upon my hook."

"I ain't interested it how you found me," snapped Mike as he nervously looked at his family playing.

"But you should, you've got to hear me out, there's a great kicker at the end. I'd asked for all top class forgers that were operating around May, June and July of 49 to be brought to my attention. Imagine my delight when this guy gives me chapter and verse about fake identities, social security cards and passports in the names Michael Spencer and Erin Kirkwood. It was like all my Christmas's rolled into one. But then I hit the wall. Do you know how many Mike Spencer's and Erin Kirkwood's there are in these United States, there are hundreds, thousands for all I know."

"Just get to the point," said Mike agitation clearly showing in his voice.

Ethan laughed, "Now this is the kicker. I needed to grab your attention. You could have been living anywhere, so I needed something news worthy, then Rex Blaze's name popped into my head, perfect I thought."

Mike detected a giggle in his voice.

"I knew you'd sit up and take notice. I then thought what would I do in your situation and then it came to me. You'd ring the department; I assumed you'd do it on a weekend so I instructed all the switchboard operators to contact me immediately if they received a long distance call for me over a weekend. They looked mystified, dumb broads, but they came through. Once I'd pinpointed you to the San Francisco area it was just a matter of time before I found the Mike Spencer I was looking for."

"You come within a mile of my family I'll kill you stone dead," warned Mike.

"You've got me wrong; I don't want to harm you or your family. All I want is the money you took from that Salazar fuck."

"I ain't got it, it's all gone," lied Mike.

"No it hasn't, allowing for inflation I'd say you've got at least a quarter of a million in your Cayman account. That's all I want, payment for my wife. If I don't get it, I'll ruin you, that pretty wife of yours and those brats. You'll go to prison for a very long time, Erin will go to prison for bigamy, and those brats will end up in care. All I need do is turn up at the Marin County Sheriff's Department, tell them the story from start to finish and you won't see those kids until you're ninety nine years old."

"How do I know if I get you the money you won't still turn me in?"

"Let's just say, I've still got a soft spot for that redheaded vixen."

Mike knew then and there that Ethan intended killing him. "It'll take a couple of days to set up."

"You ain't got a couple of days."

"Listen to me, wire transactions are a lot faster than five years ago, but they still need setting up and the bank will need notice to have that much cash in their vault. It's liable to attract a few questions." Mike was trying desperately to buy time.

You've got until Wednesday night to get the money; you know a jazz club called the Yellow Canary in the Fillmore district. Be there nine o'clock!"

"No, but I'll find it." It was obvious to Mike that Ethan had done his homework. "How do I know you won't take the money and kill me?"

Ethan laughed, "That depends on how generous I'm feeling once I've got the money."

"I'll bring the money, but I'll be armed," said Mike.

"I wouldn't expect anything else. Yellow Canary nine o'clock."

Chapter 46

From his vantage point atop the cliffs of Marin County, Mike Burnett stared out at the vastness of the Pacific Ocean. It had been madness to return to California, he knew it now. Back then it had seemed the smart thing to do, the clever, the unexpected. The sheer arrogance of it, it made him sick to the pit of his stomach.

He wiped a tear from his eye, 'we got away clean. We pulled the rug from under them. It shouldn't have come to this . . . .'

He'd told Erin he had a business meeting in the city and would get dinner out as he wouldn't be back until late. How he'd kept it together since Ethan's phone call he didn't rightly know, all he knew was if she found out she'd have called the police, and that couldn't happen. He'd weighed up the odds, and the chances of him coming out of this alive were pretty slim. He'd written her a letter, expressing his love for her and their three children. Then he told her briefly that Ethan had found them, but warned her not to seek retribution as all his efforts to protect his family would have been in vain. He'd sealed the envelope and placed it inside their safe.

It had been heartbreaking saying goodbye to the kids, but somehow he managed to put a brave face on it. He kissed Erin goodbye and jumped into his car and gave them all a cheery wave, then he was gone.

The morning passed slowly, but he whiled away the time by guillotining wads of paper into dollar bill sizes. There was no way he was leaving his family destitute. He'd phoned his local bank first thing Monday morning and arranged for a large withdrawal of twenty thousand dollars. Hopefully the subterfuge would work but if it didn't Erin would still have the bulk of their wealth. He was gambling that if Ethan killed him that would be enough retribution.

He withdrew the twenty thousand and placed it on top of the wads of plain paper. In the darkness of the Fillmore district, he reckoned he'd get away with it.

He glanced at his watch; it was time.

He pulled onto the coast road towards the Golden Gate and drove slowly, admiring the beauty of the landscape. To his right the sun was setting, it was a dark red, the colour of blood, but it was majestic all the same. He felt the urge to stop and watch it in all its glory, up ahead he spotted a vacant viewing point, he pulled in, stopped the car and got out.

He stood there and watched until the last rays of sunlight disappeared below the horizon. He realised just as he was turning away that he'd only been truly happy twice in his life, the war years, and the years that followed his tango sojourn. If it was to end within a few brief hours he could call himself blessed. As he climbed into his car he subconsciously checked the Colt Army automatic that was sitting in the waistband at the small of his back.

He parked the car, walked several blocks then turned down Geary, then made a left into Fillmore before turning first left into O'Farrell. Right at the end he spotted the sign for the Yellow Canary. He stared at his watch and then at the entrance to the club, it was nine o'clock. He started to panic, then the unmistakeable sharp dresser that was Ethan Kels filled the doorway.

"Glad you could make it. Have you brought the goods?"

Mike motioned to the case hanging at the end of his left arm.

"That's a good boy, come inside; we might as well have a drink for old time's sake."

Mike followed him in and sat opposite in a secluded booth.

Ethan ordered a couple of beers.

"Okay open it!" snapped Ethan.

Mike laid the case on the seat next to him, snapped the catch open and swung the case around for Ethan to open.

Ethan peered across and his greedy eyes sparkled. "You know, I never thought you'd pull it off, a quarter of a million; that takes some serious clout to have that sitting opposite me."

He reached across and fingered the green and for a second he was shocked, "You know I never expected you to bring me the whole amount, but then he saw the plain wads of paper, but instead of getting mad, he looked across at Mike. "You don't disappoint after all. For a second you had me fooled. I was starting to feel bad about what I'm going to do."

Ethan's eyes shone like a crazy man. "We're going to walk out of here; you're going to hand me the rod that you've got concealed at your back. Then we're going to take a little walk across some waste ground. It ain't far, then you're going to get down on your knees and beg me to end your life, which as an obliging man I'll do."

Mike smiled. "What makes you think I'll walk out of here with you?"

It was Ethan's turn to grin, "Oh I think you'll do everything I say." He looked at his watch, "About now that pretty wife of yours will be sitting trussed up along with those brats of yours. You see this money and the fun Chuck and Lester will have with Erin is their reward. I only want you dead."

Mike felt like he'd been hit in the guts, "You bastard, I'll kill you!" He lunged across the table, but Ethan had already anticipated his move and dodged clear. Before Mike could recover Ethan pulled his gun and under the concealment of the booth and table pointed it at his head.

"Not much fear of that if you want your kids to have a mother, when she gets out of hospital," he said coolly. This stopped Mike in his tracks. Ethan was firmly in control and was clearly enjoying the situation he'd created. "You see, I showed them Erin's photo and they were up for it. You know the type, drug addled, low life scum. "To hell with the money, that's just a bonus," said Chuck. "Hell, we'd do it for free!" added Lester. They really are the lowest of low life; expendable you might say."

Mike's anger subsided and was quickly replaced with sheer panic, he'd left his wife and kids at the mercy of scum, "Please don't let them harm her! I'll do whatever you want!"

"You'll do it anyway," replied Ethan cruelly.

"Promise me you won't let them hurt her, please. I'm begging you."

"I already promised the boys. I'll tell you what, I'll give you my word they won't kill her. But if you struggle I'll tell the boys to kill her and your damn kids!"

Mike's face took on a mask of terror.

"Now let's go!" Ethan had had his bit of fun, now it was time to get serious.

Mike's legs were like jello as he stood up. This was turning into his worst nightmare.

"If you're thinking about jumping me when we get outside forget about it. If Chuck and Lester haven't heard from me by nine thirty your kids are dead."

Once they were outside Ethan patted Mike down and retrieved the Colt Army Automatic, "You won't need this anymore." He giggled maniacally, he was clearly enjoying himself.

"The time, Ethan! The time!" cried Mike panicking.

"There's a phone booth on Fillmore, if we're quick I should make that in time. Just hope it ain't vandalised."

The clearing came into view, Ethan now pushed Mike forward, "Move it" he urged.

Ethan checked the surrounding area, it was still early and most of the jazz geeks hadn't arrived on the scene. Once he was sure they were obscured from view, he ordered Mike to stop and turn around.

Mike was in the shadows as he slowly turned around.

"Now get down on your knees and beg!" spat Ethan.

Ethan heard the shot a fraction after he felt the shock as his right knee buckled and he went down like a stone, his gun spinning from his grasp. Mike stepped forward from the shadow, a Walther

PPK held firmly in his right hand, the barrel still smoking. Mike's finger tightened on the trigger.

"Where the fuck did that come from," cried Ethan as he looked at the tiny pistol in Mike's hand.

"Oh this, this was a present from Gretchen on the last day of her life."

Suddenly Ethan's mind flashed back to the murders in Gretchen's apartment. He could see Mike retrieve it from the floor as he knelt down and exchanged his documents with Chudzik's body.

"Jesus fuck, think about Erin," he cried as Mike levelled the gun. "We're married for Christ-sake."

"Consider this a divorce." Mike squeezed the trigger. The bullet smacked high into Kels's upper arm, smashing his shoulder bone to pieces but missing vital organs by a whisker. The impact sent Kels spinning into the rumble, where he slumped to the ground. Mike looked down at the man that had caused him such misery. There was no mercy in his eyes as he stared at the broken body of Ethan Kels.

This wasn't how it was supposed to end, thought Kels as he looked up into those merciless eyes. His face grew ashen with shock, the pain of his wounds now forcing themselves into his consciousness.

"What about Erin, the kids," he pleaded. "I can stop it happening!"

"All taken care of," replied Mike coldly.

Ethan knew he was bad hit, but the fact he was still alive must mean something.

"You're not like me, I'm a cold blooded killer; you were just along for the ride! I know you haven't got it in you." he managed to say though a weak smile.

"Like I said, I've changed!"

Ethan's eyes grew big as saucers, "No!"

Mike raised the automatic and shot Ethan between the eyes. Then instinctively he reached down and felt for a pulse, there was none. Ethan's dead eyes stared blindly up at the night sky.

Chapter 47

It was mid afternoon when the doorbell rang. No one was more surprised or shocked than Erin when Rodrigo Vasquez appeared framed in her doorway.

"Oh my God!" she exclaimed.

"Sorry for the surprise, but Mike asked me to call."

Erin looked cagey, this was a man from their past, a past that until that moment she'd thought buried.

She edged back and slowly began to close the door, "I'm sorry but Michael never told me any of this."

Rodrigo smiled that crooked smile of his, "I'm sorry Senora Erin but if you take a look inside your safe, you'll find a letter addressed to you from Mike. Shut the door by all means but take a look at the letter."

Erin apologised but shut and bolted the door. She raced to the bedroom and quickly opened the safe. Sure enough there was a letter with her name on it. She hurriedly ripped it open and began to read.

My dearest Erin,

I love you with all my heart, I love Daisy, Blake and little Cindy, but for a few days now I've been keeping something from you. Don't be shocked I've got it under control. Ethan rang me last Sunday morning, the how why and wherefore aren't relevant at the moment. Suffice to say he asked me to meet with him, he's demanded a large sum of money to keep his mouth shut about our relationship, he's prepared to go to the Marin County Sheriff's Department and tell all. Needless to say, I'd end up in jail, so would you for having the graciousness to marry me, the kids would end up in care and I'd never see you again. Trust me, that isn't his agenda, he aims to kill me and punish you, but that ain't going to happen. If you're reading this then I'd hazard a guess that Rodrigo is on the other side of our front door.

Erin though shocked by the letter's contents stifled a smile.

I want you and the children to go with him; I've booked you a family room at the Sea View Inn, where he will leave you. The rest you don't need to know, just in case things go wrong, which they won't. Trust Rodrigo, do exactly what he says.

I love you all, with all my heart.

She was full of questions when she opened the front door.
"All in good time Senora."
Quickly they packed and got into Rodrigo's station wagon and within minutes were speeding down the hill towards Sausalito. Rodrigo told her about Ethan's phone call and the painstaking work that he'd put into it. Clearly concerned for Mike's welfare it took Rodrigo until they were almost at the Sea View Inn to convince Erin that Mike had it under control.

Though still shocked and traumatised by Rodrigo's revelations Erin realised she needed to remain calm for the sake of the kids. She asked the one question that perplexed her most. "Tell me, how did Michael find you?"

Rodrigo laughed, "Mike listened to Ethan's bragging and saw a way to contact me."

"How?" asked Erin.

"I think it was on the last morning before we went to the airport. I'd told him I was going to hang around with Jake in L.A. at least until I got my sea legs. "Good idea," Mike had said, "but when you grow tired of Jake's company, look up Francisco Garcia, he owns . . ."

"I know Francisco, not the best tango in town, but he's Argentinean. We used to go to him for lessons. He became a very good friend."

"It was a good place until I descended, now thanks to Rodrigo the place is jumping. I usually hang out there once or twice a week. I have my mail delivered there. I had just picked up Monday's mail when Francisco came up to me with a telephone number; he said I was to ring it as soon as possible. Imagine my surprise when I heard Luc . . . , sorry Mike on the phone. The rest I think you already know."

"But Michael, he's in danger."

"Not half as much if I wasn't here."

Five minutes later they checked into the Inn. Rodrigo escorted them to the door and handed her the key. "Stay here, don't move, don't even think about returning home. Mike will contact you."

The way Rodrigo said it, left no doubt in her mind.

An hour later Rodrigo re-entered Mike and Erin's Marin County home. He began to prepare the floor area, he'd bought a roll of tarpaulin, designed to keep dust and dirt of the carpets and furniture, which he lay all over the front room and hallway, then checking his watch he sat down to watch the Roy Rodgers Show. He did so love Roy's fringed outfits and he kinda had a sneaking crush on Dale.

At around eight thirty he heard the door being opened, he tensed himself for action as he sat there watching some game show. He readied his specially silenced Colt Army 1911 automatic. He felt he looked ridiculous in the red wig he'd purchase on Hollywood Boulevard, but he'd been assured it was the best Rita Hayworth wig you could buy. Personally he didn't think it worth a rat's ass.

The television flickered; he'd been warned not to watch it in the dark, but what the hell. His senses pictured where they were in the hall; and allowed them three more steps before he stood up and turned around.

"Hi boys, I've been expecting you. His first silenced slug took Lester out of the game, his second and third caught Chuck in the left eye and shoulder. Rodrigo looked down at his handy work and put another bullet each into Lester and Chuck's forehead.

"Amateurs," he muttered.

He looked at the time, it was a little before eight thirty five. Working quickly he rolled each man separately into a roll. He produced wire and secured both ends of the rolls, before he looked outside. He wasn't surprised but relieved there were no flashing lights.

Walking quickly for several blocks he climbed into the station wagon and drove slowly back to the house before backed up Mike's drive. He checked outside once again and then opened the tail gate. Working as fast as he could he slammed the bodies down like carpets. Securing the tailgate he drove slowly out of the Spencer's driveway. Thirty minutes later he undid the wire and let Lester and Chuck slide gently into the bay, after another twenty minutes in a secluded cove, he set fire to the tarps. At a quiet beach an hour south of San Francisco he torched the station wagon. You couldn't be too through. He'd heard there was a prison up in Marin County where they were free with their gas pellets.

It was around eleven thirty when he pulled up in yet another hot wired car outside O'Mara's tavern. He walked in and sat down next to an anxious Mike.

"It's done."

Mike pushed a Miller down in front of his. Rodrigo looked at the bottle, "We celebrating?"

"You could call it that."

They chinked bottles. "I'll head home after this; I've a very important phone call to make," said Mike, with an air of relief in his voice.

She sensed rather than heard the gentle tapping on the door. Her heart had been in her mouth since Rodrigo had dropped her and the kids off at the hotel. She'd whiled away the hours listening to the radio and playing cards with the kids until they grew too tired to stay awake. That had been the true beginning of her ordeal. Not knowing, that was what tortured her the most. When the phone rang she was hesitant to answer, afraid of what she was going to hear. The relief, the unadulterated relief, she felt as light as a feather and could hardly speak. Mike's words were soft and gentle, warm and caring, she let them wafted over her, caressing her, protecting her, and she realised if he hadn't have come back she'd have died of a broken heart.

"Come to the motel, it doesn't matter what time it is, I need you," said Erin.

It seemed like hours but couldn't have been more than forty minutes when Mike tapped gently upon the door. She was out of bed, swiftly tip toeing to the door, her heart beating rapidly. Mike looked into Erin's eyes and pulled her to him. No words were exchanged as they kissed each other passionately, warmly and in a loving way. Silently while still in their embrace she backed into the room and instinctively found the foot of her bed. In the darkened room he followed and quickly disrobed. Their lovemaking was warm and tender, gentle to the point of ecstasy, not rushed, just the joining together of two bodies that cared so deeply for one another.

Epilogue

"Has the bad man gone away daddy!" asked Daisy the following morning.

Mike knelt down and spoke gently to his oldest child. He stroked her hair, smiled and replied.

"Yes sweetheart, the bad man's gone, he's gone forever."

Mike risked a glance towards Erin and the look confirmed what she already knew.

They drove back to their house later that morning. With trepidation Mike opened the door and before he could stop them the kids rushed in. It was exactly as they'd left it. Mike sighed with relief. Rodrigo had told him how careful he'd been, but knowing what went on in that very room, he was amazed at how clean and tidy it was.

Erin waiting until the kids were in bed that night before broaching the subject of Ethan. Mike had thought to lie, but knew Erin deserved the truth, albeit a little altered.

"He's gone Erin, and he ain't ever coming back. He was a bad man, one of the worst kinds." He spared her the grisly details of Ethan's plans; all he ever said was that Rodrigo took care of it.

While Mike and his family sunned themselves on the beach at Waikiki, with a portion of the twenty thousand he'd withdrawn from the bank, the San Francisco papers were alive with speculation as to why a Los Angeles County Sheriff's Department officer should end up shot too death gangland style on waste ground in the Fillimore District of their city.

Ethan Kels Police Hero or Gangster?

Speculation as to why Area Commander Ethan Kels was gunned down in a gangland style execution had sparked rumours. Most purporting that Kels was corrupt, a bad copper, but we have uncovered facts, that not proven, suggest otherwise. Ballistic reports leaked to the press, state that the gun used in the death of the Commander was undoubtedly a Walther PPK. A weapon favoured by the Nazi's during the war years. Speculation? We don't think so. We have since learned that Kels took a trip to Argentina in 1949. A trip incidentally he took with his young wife, a trip that she never came back from. Kels had stated at the time, that their marriage hadn't worked out and that she'd decided to stay in Argentina. During this brief stay in Buenos Aires, two notorious Nazi war criminals were found executed, one in a similar manner to the execution of Kels. Then it becomes interesting, alongside one of the dead Nazis was the body of a fellow American, identified as a Lucas Garrett. He'd been shot twice, with a Walther PPK. Since the story broke we have an unconfirmed report that Argentine Police ballistics have come up with a match to the 38 calibre slugs taken from Ethan Kels body. This would suggest that if confirmed, the death of Kels was probably brought about by an ex-Nazi seeking revenge.

Hero or villain? It's your call!

Although the Los Angeles County Sheriff's Department didn't believe in speculation, it was better from a public relations point of view that Ethan Kels had died a hero rather than the corrupt cop most knew him to be. He was given full honours by the Sheriff's Department and his name made it onto their list of fallen heroes.

The hot Havana sun filtered though the trees basking the outside tables of the bar in speckled shadows and sunlight. Beneath this canopy shrouded by smoke, and shaded from the sun in his straw panama sat Jake Reis. He chuckled as he read and re-read a bunch of week old American newspapers. Sipping on a Cuba Libre and puffing on a fine Cuban cigar, the retired mobster reflected on the death of Ethan Kels and his fight against the Nazi's of South America. He chuckled again; he'd always believed Kels would meet a sticky end, but an all American hero, that took some swallowing. Jake took another sip of his Cuba Libre, followed by another pull on his fine cigar and laughed loudly.

Life sure was good.

"Here's a full stop!"
created by Evie Harding.
It makes a change from writing The End

3rd February 2013
Michael Kennard ©

Notes

1. Apologies for those purists amongst you, but to enhance and move the story along, I was partly winging it. It is fiction after all.

2. $1,000,000.00 in 1949 equates to $9,646,806.72 in 2013

3. My spelling throughout this text has been in *English-English* rather than *English-American*. My apologies if this has distracted you in any way.

4. This is a work of fiction. Names, characters, places and incidents either are the product of the author's imagination or are used fictitiously and any resemblance to actual persons, living or dead, business establishments, events or locales is entirely coincidental